8/69

FEAR
ITSELF

BARRET SCHUMACHER

A Tom Doherty Associates Book
New York

FEAR

ITSELF

FEAR ITSELF

Copyright © 2002 by Barret Schumacher

This book is printed on acid-free paper.

Book design by Jane Adele Regina

A Forge Book
Published by Tom Doherty Associates, LLC
175 Fifth Avenue
New York, NY 10010

www.tor.com

Forge® is a registered trademark of Tom Doherty Associates, LLC.

ISBN: 0-765-30130-X

First Edition: January 2002

Printed in the United States of America

0 9 8 7 6 5 4 3 2 1

For Ally

ACKNOWLEDGMENTS

Things in the Universe just wouldn't be right if I didn't make mention of a number of people who've been instrumental in helping this first-time novelist see his book from "wild" idea to publication.

Hans Holzer, for his invaluable direction and insight into both the supernatural world and the publishing business;

Stephanie Lane at Forge, for taking on this project and seeing what I did not;

Jean Shaffer, for her command of English usage and some great editing early on in the manuscript's life;

My parents, Mary (a terrific writer in her own right) and Gene Schumacher, for their intelligence and constant encouragement in everything I've ever wanted to do, as well as for some good writing pointers;

Karen Jones, for her tremendous enthusiasm, and invaluable advice;

My agent, Paige Wheeler, for believing in the book, keeping me hopeful, and never letting up;

Robin Dadisman, who's been keeping me laughing since the fifth grade;

Dayton Taylor, lifelong friend, indispensable critic (you never leave me wondering what you really think), and living example of the value of determination;

Edythe Edelstein, for her undying faith, love, and ever-available vegetarian chili;

And my wife, Ally, for your love, for giving me the seeds for this story, and for tolerating my second job for all these years (even with a baby). I really love you.

I'm indebted to you all.

AUTHOR'S NOTE

In researching various medical sciences, and the Human Genome Project, I readily identified the fascinating area of disease-related genetics as the most appropriate field for my purposes. I've made diligent efforts to combine actual methodologies, terminology, and concepts in portraying a hypothetical line of research, and its potential, though fictional, consequences. My intention is purely to provide a "ring of truth" and not to suggest a scenario capable of withstanding close scientific scrutiny, nor anything actually occurring at the University of San Francisco. I assume sole responsibility for any omissions or mistakes in accuracy, and hold those dedicated to the treatment and cure of illness in the highest regard.

Concerning the town of Alamosa, Colorado: I used the name purely for the sake of convenience, and do not intend to portray the actual character of the town nor any of its residents.

And I beheld, and heard an angel flying through the midst of heaven, saying with a loud voice, Woe, woe, woe, to the inhabiters of the earth.

—Revelation 8:13.

Of all the earth's creatures
Whom nature gives rise,
The saddest evolves
To its own demise.

—Anonymous

PART I

The noises coming from downstairs will be wrong. The windows will be relentlessly dark. No one should even be awake. Yet the footfalls, landing somehow too heavily, will near as they ascend the stairs just outside her hollow wooden door. Loud clumsy sounds of unknowable activity will precede the opening of the door. She won't be able to hold on to the sheets, the man will be too strong for her. Her fingers will lose hold and she will fly away from her pillows, ceilingward. Why will he lift her out of bed? She won't know, but she will be able to tell that he's not happy. His voice will be strange, abrasive like raw stone, rough with anger. At first she'll not recognize the voice coming from his lips. What did she do wrong? She'll wonder. She'll have no idea why he's so upset. He'll take her from the room, carrying her under his arm like a bundle of wood, down the hallway, then down the stairs to the living room where the lights will still be on. His arm will be hairy and thick; that will be all she can see other than the gold carpet of the living room floor, then the speckled linoleum of the kitchen. His huge hand will squeeze her elbow so tightly that she won't be able to bend it. A thousand needles will prick at her palms as her fingers lose sensation. It will be hard for her to breathe. She'll want to cry but she won't be able to get enough air. She'll hear the sound of the back door whining open, and watch his feet, one after the other, take her outside. His hand will be hot and moist when it lands on her lips and cheeks. It'll cover half her face, the hair on his knuckles will block her nostrils. She'll begin to suffocate in his jostling grasp. She'll see the cement of the back patio pass beneath her in the darkness, then only raw earth. He'll tighten his hold around her body and over her mouth. She'll close her eyes, and pray.

ONE

The small hands ascended into the air in the usual pattern. The students in the front of the third grade classroom all strained their shoulders to demonstrate their readiness and newly acquired knowledge, while those in the back made a diligent effort at disappearing. It was a tiny forest of arms that appeared to have undergone a heavy clearing operation—strong, tall trunks that reached for the sky, high above the lifeless stumps in between. Summer was only inches out of reach and the Bay Area sun drew eyes and thoughts to the louvered windows.

"Alexander," Devrie Haler asked, slowly, clearly, "can you tell us what country the great pyramids of Giza are in?"

Alexander was at once fearful of, and in love with, his teacher. Mrs. Haler was the most awesome to look at, he thought, but she was also the hardest teacher in the whole school. He discovered this irony early in his third-grade year. Devrie was stunningly beautiful, but she could be a ruthless disciplinarian, and turn from blond angel to Devil's drill sergeant in the beat of your heart. Alexander searched the floor for a fallen pencil that seemed, to the outside observer, perpetually to evade detection.

"Alexander," Devrie voiced again, calmly still, "are you with us today?" Devrie knew that Alexander had not read his homework assignment and that he was now experiencing the distress and guilt of his failing. Devrie didn't possess an ounce of sadism, especially when it came to children, but she did get some measure of satisfaction from putting unprepared students through the "rinse cycle," as she liked to phrase it. Devrie ignored the closer students' earnest pleas.

A fine black cross, where the corners of the green floor tiles met, filled Alexander's world. He wanted to shrink and crawl into those narrow channels in the floor, to explore their depths, away from the torment of the real world.

"Alexander," Devrie's voice now darkened into an oppressive thunder, "look at me . . . NOW!"

Alexander's head bobbed up from his search for the invisible pencil. "Huh?" he answered, his little blue eyes locked in place, his red-mopped head rising only slightly above the level of his desktop. The look of surprise fell on a quite unconvinced audience.

"Did you do the reading assignment last night, like you were supposed to?"

The red mop nodded timidly.

"Answer me, yes or no."

The little squeak of a "yes" was just audible. The rest of the class now had their eyes on Alexander; the warm air in the classroom was thickening.

"Then you should know the answer, shouldn't you?"

Again Alexander nodded.

"Then tell me." Devrie's warm brown eyes now bore down like the twin barrels of a shotgun.

"I forgot," he struggled.

"You forgot?"

More nodding followed.

"I see."

Then: "Can I go to the bathroom?"

As much as Devrie wanted to smile, she maintained her authoritative manner absolutely. "You may go to the bathroom . . . after you tell me the answer to the homework question, and not one moment sooner."

The name "Jeff" and the images of two boys crawling down a concrete tunnel flashed through Devrie's mind, but she wasn't sure exactly why.

Still Alexander said nothing, and started squirming in his seat. Now he focused on the bulletin board behind Mrs. Haler's desk and the collages displayed there, which the class had done for their final art projects. In the center of one collage was a photograph of a high snowy mountain, which was in some faraway country where they ate a lot of cheese and spoke a funny language. He couldn't remember its name. He only wished that he could be on top of that mountain. Even freezing to death on an icy peak seemed better than Mrs. Haler when she had you cornered. The other kids kept him under close observation, those in front still begging to prove themselves, but Devrie was unmoved.

"Alexander, maybe you can tell me something else about the pyramids then. Tell me anything at all from the homework, and then you can go to the bathroom." Again in her mind Devrie saw the tunnel of cement at its opening and the two young boys crawling into it. It was beneath an overpass where a small creek wound its way under the street. She'd seen it before somewhere—somewhere near by.

"They're big," Alexander responded hopefully.

"They're big. That's true, but can you tell me how big?"

"Really big."

"You didn't do your homework, did you, Alexander? And this time I want the truth." Then Devrie remembered where she'd seen the tunnel before; she knew exactly where it was.

Again Alexander nodded his round head.

"Do you want to know what I think? I think that you and your friend Jeff sneaked into that drainage tunnel under Bratton Boulevard yesterday after school."

Alexander's eyes widened in shock.

"You know that you're not supposed to go in there, don't you?"

Alexander sat silently in his chair, his head swirling.

"I'll tell you something. You'll never get to the end. It's a very long tunnel, and it's very dangerous. Or don't you know how to read the sign at the opening that says DO NOT ENTER?"

His friend Jeff and he often sneaked down under the street to explore the subterranean world of the city's water drainage system. They'd never reached the end of the tunnel after two years of trying. It was an ongoing adventure that they shared occasionally in the evenings after school. But absolutely nobody knew about it; it was a pact between them that they conduct their expeditions in total secrecy. Jeff would never have told anyone. They had both sworn not to tell, and no bond was stronger than that. Furthermore, they had always taken great precautions to insure that nobody saw them, and yesterday had been no exception. But Mrs. Haler knew. It was impossible, yet his ears didn't lie.

Devrie saw in the blue of the little boy's astonished eyes that she'd yanked a very sensitive nerve. She pushed a degree further. "The two of you sneaked out of your room while your parents thought you were doing your homework, isn't that right, Alexander?"

"Yeah," he squeaked again. She didn't just know about the tunnel, she seemed to know about everything. "I'm sorry," he said finally, lowering his eyes, terrified that any further eye contact might betray yet more secrets—secrets a lot more embarrassing than a little illicit suburban spelunking.

Devrie hid well the fact that she was almost as surprised at her words as Alexander was. "I'm going to have to give you a zero for the assignment, you know. From now on, are you going to do your homework like I ask you to, and are you going to stay out of that tunnel?"

Cropped orange bangs slapped Alexander's forehead lightly as he nodded emphatically.

"Okay, you may go to the bathroom now, but I want you back in your seat in five minutes, understood?"

Alexander was on his feet, heading for the door before she had finished speaking.

I t was so easy to push the return key, yet so difficult to comprehend the results; Reed Haler pushed it anyway. The sixteen-inch color display on his overburdened desk flashed a colorful schematic representation of a malformed human white blood cell—a lymphocyte—while a rectangular box drew itself from left to right as the software obediently downloaded the most recent data from the research network at San Francisco University. Reed's thirty-five-year-old elbows bracketed the keyboard beneath his stubble-shaded chin as he studied the perplexing information on the screen. His finger held a place on the scarred page of notes at the side of the keyboard while he viewed the *30%* figure at the top of the table— he'd been hoping for seventy percent or better. He entered an additional command, and hit the return key again. After that cycle of calculation, the figure dropped to *28%*.

"So far so bad," he whispered to himself. The springs in the modern desk chair ticked quietly in his home office as Reed's weight gradually eased back into the leathery cushions. The results just weren't there . . . yet, and that fact was like an engine inside him, running on an infinite quantity of fuel. That condition had characterized his career from the beginning, his whole way of looking at the world, at life, at medicine. He had identified a good number of genetic abnormalities in the thousands of leukemic blood cells he'd analyzed over the years. But so far the highest percentage of recurrence of a single abnormality in all the samples was only around fifty-five for acute lymphocytic leukemia or ALL, the most common form of children's leukemia. He was looking for an SNP or "snip," which was a convenient acronym for "single nucleotide polymorphism." Snips formed the ninety-seven percent of the human DNA molecule that was responsible for the uniqueness of each individual. The other three percent was the so-called active part of the human genetic code and generally thought to contain the genes responsible for susceptibility to certain diseases. Reed believed, contrary to a lot of scientific opinion, that much of the genetic cause of certain forms of cancer were to be found among the snips.

Since he'd left his home in Chicago five years before, Reed had been attempting, with a nearly maniacal singularity of purpose, to advance his theory of genetic predisposition to ALL. San Francisco University's Genetic Research arm had been quick to recruit him only a month after publication of his dissertation describing the pioneering work. Reed knew that S.F.U. was the place to be as a genetic researcher. After they approached him, he'd needed no extra inducement to relocate to the pleasant environs of the Bay Area and the wealth of medical expertise and facilities that S.F.U. had to offer. The threefold improvement in his financial condition had been pure icing. If he could prove his hypothesis, and couple his findings with the product of the Human Genome Project, then a bright new world of hope might open to medical science and to thousands of sick kids around the world.

The Human Genome Project was on the verge of mapping the entire human genome, all three billion or so base pairs that make up the human DNA molecule. It would be like finding a treasure map.

Reed's work was instrumental in the newly pending federal grant money, which was now only waiting for the results of the current level of study. But he needed more encouraging results than his team had obtained thus far. Childhood leukemia, being a relatively rare condition, usually received fewer research dollars than more prevalent diseases. But Reed believed his work would eventually lead to far broader application, and that they were now closing in on the elusive variations of nucleotides which would tie it all together. The work had been a slow, painful exercise in trial and error, but the "error" was starting to succumb to a relentless process of elimination.

Reed unlaced his fingers and grabbed the S.F.U. pen at the side of the keyboard. On a note pad he jotted down the specs for the next set of trials, which he'd have his chief associate, Wally Bohrs, begin screening for in the morning. Hovering over all, like a massive storm cloud, was the national symposium. It meant life or death in terms of financing. If everything went well it would be at least another week before Reed's team could complete assays on the entire new series. It was time to face facts. They simply weren't going to have the good news ready in time. The gathering of minds and brain-brokers was only four days away. Reed was scheduled to deliver a speech outlining the progress to date. Grant representatives from the National Institutes of Health were going to be there, evaluating the presentations. A lot of money teetered precariously in the balance, but they just weren't quite ready. They needed that week. One more damn week, he cursed to himself, scratching furiously on the pad as if that would somehow compress the next seven days into seven hours.

He finished his list and tossed the pen back down onto the piles of folders that covered the antique, cherrywood desktop. His eyelids suddenly weighed heavily on the slate blue hemispheres beneath them. He rubbed the rounded back of his wrist into two dark and weary sockets.

A gentle knock at the solid wood door brought his attention back into a hazy focus. The mellow brass *click* of the latch introduced the hazelnut eyes and glowing face of which Reed could never, ever grow tired.

"Hey, Doc," Devrie greeted, stepping into the warmly appointed office. She wore plaid flannel shorts and the long powder blue T-shirt, which she lovingly referred to as her "jammies." If Devrie was ready for bed, that meant it had to be past one A.M.—one thirty-five as it turned out.

"Hey, teach," Reed returned, with the involuntary smile that her presence never failed to inspire. His heart melted at the way she walked, the way she sounded, the way she smelled. She still looked the way she had when they met, and it gave him a growing feeling of inferiority. He was afraid he'd let himself go to the point that he was no longer worthy of her attention. Not that he assigned physical appearance any more value than he gave personality or intelligence, but his wife's diligence in staying healthy and in good physical shape was putting him to shame. He was by no means fat, but he'd definitely developed a gut over the past few years, and had little time or inclination to initiate some kind of regular exercise regimen. And now that the line of his graying brown hair was on the retreat, he'd noticed in himself an increasing resemblance to his father. There was simply nothing appealing about the aging process.

"Get it yet?" She asked, hopefully.

Devrie saw that the smile wasn't one of triumph, but the far more familiar one of resigned determination.

"Oh, sorry," she consoled before he even had a chance to speak.

"It's there somewhere," he said, conjuring faith from depths he had yet to explore. "I can't believe we haven't nailed it yet. It's beginning to worry me." He opened his arms, inviting her to come sit in his lap. She accepted, stepping around the desk and delivering a wet, sensuous kiss as she straddled his legs. His tongue felt the strands of her dusty blond hair, which had gotten caught between their lips. He consumed the scent of her skin and drew energy from her embrace.

When their mouths separated she whispered: "You will."

"We're sthtarting," he lisped, drawing several golden-brown wisps away with his fingers, "to run a little low on pothibilitieth."

"Don't waste your energy worrying. You'll get it. I'm sure of it."

"Not in time for Whitaker and the NIH folks Tuesday night."

"You'll get it."

"What makes you so sure?"

"I'm just sure."

"I love you."

"I know."

"Okay, just checking."

"And you can keep on checking, regularly and frequently."

"Count on it."

This time he kissed her.

"So," he asked, as she tossed her head back, "how were the little people today?"

"I need a vacation," she said flatly. "Why don't we go somewhere when school's out?"

"That bad?"

"Actually, it wasn't that bad. I just feel majorly wiped out lately. But uh . . ."

Reed felt his wife's body stiffen suddenly, her mood change.

"What?"

"Well, it happened again."

"It?"

"You know, like when I knew my parents were coming home that night."

"You mean the night you were deflowered fifteen years ago?"

"Yes, and it was only thirteen years ago."

"Come on, Dev. You were seventeen! It's natural to worry like that—the first time especially. Just because your parents happened to come home early doesn't mean you had some kind of paranormal precognition."

"Reed. I know you hate this stuff. The point is that I didn't just know that they were coming home early, I knew why they were coming home early."

"Dev, I don't hate this stuff. I just hesitate to accept anything that hasn't been adequately substantiated."

"You mean scientifically substantiated."

"You know what I mean."

"Well, today something really strange happened. It wasn't like the usual premonition stuff."

"I promise I'll keep an open mind."

She narrowed her eyes at him. "I don't really care if you believe it or not. I know what I know."

"Just tell me what happened."

"Okay . . ." As Devrie filled her husband in on her handling of Alexander's subterranean adventures and neglected homework, Reed clearly remained unconvinced.

"Look," he reasoned, "kids are getting into stuff like that all the time. You may have seen something similar on one of those real-life tragedy shows on TV, like . . . a kid getting stuck in a storm drain, for example. You might not even have been conscious of it. Then at some point you heard Alexander mention this friend of his, and what kid doesn't blow off doing his homework once in a while?"

"I don't watch real-life tragedy shows on TV," she countered. "Reed, if I had been right about any one of those things by itself, I would say, yeah, it was just a coincidence. But all three? The tunnel, his friend, and the fact that he had to sneak out of his house?"

He shrugged. "I'm not saying that it wasn't a psychic thing, I'm just saying that it's not conclusive."

"Fine. Don't conclude anything then. But honest to God, Reed, it was as if for a few seconds I could read his mind or something. I saw those two kids crawl into that tunnel. It was like I was standing there watching them, right in front of me for a second."

"Okay, tell me what I'm thinking," he challenged, closing his eyes.

"Reed. It's not something I can just do whenever I want. It just happens sometimes."

"That's amazing."

"What?"

"That's exactly what I was thinking."

"Shut up!" she said, slapping his shoulder, a little harder than he'd expected. She removed herself from his lap and walked to the door. "I'm just not going to talk to you about this stuff anymore." She left the room without even a "good night," which she knew he would notice.

"Hey, I'm sorry. I am. Really!" he said to the empty room.

He sat for a few moments in silence, thinking about what Devrie had told him. Finally, shrugging to himself, he switched off the computer, and stuffed his notes away, before he followed his wife up the stairs.

TWO

T he doctor replaced the stethoscope around her neck and folded her arms, clearly perplexed, though she tried not to reveal that fact to her young, uneasy patient. The girl, Emily, an attractive ten-year-old with long, golden-brown hair, sat on the examination table in Dr. Jessica Morraine's office, hunched over, nibbling at her fingernails, and suffering extreme abdominal pain.

"Lie down on your back, and let your arms relax at your sides," Dr. Morraine instructed the fidgety child. Emily obeyed reluctantly with a fearful glance toward the corner of the room where her mother listened and watched attentively everything that Dr. Morraine did. At thirty-four and a mother herself, Jessica had practiced pediatrics for seven years in her hometown of Alamosa, Colorado, and well understood the woman's concerns. What can start out appearing to be nothing serious can turn into a lifetime of anguish. The evening news was full of such tragic stories. Dr. Morraine brushed a rich, tawny curl from her lightly freckled forehead, and pressed gently around the girl's stomach, until she got a reaction. The most tender spot was an inch below the navel. "Right there, eh?"

"Yeah. It hurts."

"Any vomiting?" the doctor asked Emily's mother.

"No. None," the woman answered. "But she's been slightly feverish, and nauseous over the last couple of days."

"A little flulike?"

The woman nodded.

"And her bowel movements—have they been normal and regular, as far as you know?"

"I'm not sure. I haven't really been keeping track."

"Okay." Jessica's voice softened as she turned her attention back to the little girl. With a warm disarming smile and a friendly twinkle in her sea-blue eyes, she asked, "Emily, sweetie, do you remember the last time you had to make a doody?" Emily turned her face away with a blush, not answering the question. Jessica encouraged the girl, placing a reassuring hand on her arm. "It's okay to tell me. I'm the doctor, okay? I've seen lots of doody." Jessica noticed the tiniest hint of a smile, but Emily's face remained turned away, flushing. "Was it yesterday? Day before? Try to remember, honey." Emily shook her head, embarrassed.

"Don't remember," finally came in a frail, little voice.

"That's fine if you don't remember." Jessica continued to examine the little girl, finding no other areas of discomfort, but noting that she did feel warm, as was indicated by her temperature reading.

"All right, sweetie, you can sit up now, and put your shirt back on." Jessica helped the girl up, giving her a pat on the shoulder. It was obvious that the child was in genuine pain. Jessica jotted a few things down on the chart, and then turned to Emily's mother. "Well, I'm ninety-nine percent sure that it's not appendicitis, and I don't think it's an ulcer, though that's not unheard of in a child Emily's age."

"So?" Emily's mother asked.

"My guess is good old-fashioned constipation, and maybe a little bug associated with it."

"Constipation?" the other woman responded, sounding relieved.

"Yep. Very common. Try a little laxative. Something over the counter will probably do the trick. You might try castor oil, if that doesn't work. A big tablespoonful. But make sure she gets a little treat not too long afterward, because that stuff is nasty." Jessica made a face at the little girl, hoping to stir the smile again, but got no such response. Emily had resumed her nail biting, apparently less than thrilled with the diagnosis, and the treatment plan.

"Give me a call in a few days if she's still having problems," Jessica said, as she opened the door, leading the girl and her mother out.

After her patient had left the office, Jessica stopped at the receptionist's desk and handed Emily's chart folder to the record keeper, who filed it among the hundreds of others stored in a tall cabinet that almost reached the ceiling.

"Robert, were you able to get Dr. Canidey on the phone?" Jessica asked the receptionist, who also functioned as Jessica's secretary.

"Sorry. His office says he's out. Getting ready for San Francisco."

"Oh, bullshit!" Jessica said, looking at her watch. "I'm getting sick of this. I'm never going to make this meeting." She was supposed to attend a meeting to discuss financing for a new children's hospital she was fighting to create—had been fighting to create for years without success. "Is he ever in? How the hell does he see his patients?"

"Maybe he doesn't have any," Robert suggested. "It looks like they all came to you." He glanced at the overstuffed cabinet.

"Yeah," she agreed, forcing a smile. "Okay. Obviously he's not going to cover me today like he promised. See if you can reschedule this thing for the weekend, that's the only time I'm going to have for weeks. And tell them I apologize, apologize, apologize."

Robert picked up the phone, and Jessica picked up the next chart, from an ever-growing supply.

T he sun broke through the light, golden curtains which hung in front of the small upstairs window of Lucy Morraine's bedroom. She sat up, eyes wide, and hopped from bed. She adjusted her pajama top which had gotten twisted around her little torso during the night. It was Saturday morning and Bugs Bunny would be coming on in just a few minutes. Hugging her pillow, the seven-year-old ran down the stairs to the living room where the TV waited silently. She found the remote control and soon the zany sounds and animated antics seemed to bring the whole world to life. Lucy was happy to discover that she still had time to get the cereal and milk before Bugs started.

She settled into her spot on the floor in front of the tube and filled her bowl, readying the spoon, the ends of her coppery-brown hair falling in the milk. Bugs joined her after a long series of commercials for dolls, toy cars, laser pistols, and junk food.

Her mother usually came downstairs on Saturday mornings just as Bugs was ending. This morning the "wascally wabbit" came, went, and had been over for nearly two hours before the first sounds of movement reached Lucy's ears. The trouble was that the coughing and hacking noises coming from the upstairs bathroom were those of a man. She immediately knew that Gart had stayed the night—had slept next to her mother. Then came the sound of feet on the stairs.

" 'Morning, kiddo," Jessica called out on her way to the kitchen. She heard no reply and knew that Lucy was displeased about something. It didn't take much to figure out what that something was. After starting a pot of coffee, she wandered out to the living room where Lucy sat on the floor, attention buried in her drawing pad. Jessica sat down next to her daughter. "Hey, there. You want to talk to me?" Lucy didn't look up from her crayon drawing of a forest of pine trees, under which she was in the process of coloring in a blue tent next to a small campfire. "Come on, Luce. I know you're upset about Gart staying over." Her daughter only shrugged silently. "Why don't we talk about it? I'm right here, ready to talk about it. I know you want to tell me what you're thinking."

"What good would that do?" Lucy finally said.

"Well, it might make you feel better."

"It won't."

"How do you know?"

Lucy put the crayon back into its box and closed the pad. "Because you'll still go to the meeting."

That was not what Jessica had expected to hear. "The meeting? What does that have to do with Gart?"

Lucy kept her head down, and fumbled with her crayon box. Jessica put an arm around her shoulder.

"What is it, Luce? What's my meeting have to do with Gart?"

"He got to spend all morning with you, and . . . and those businesspeople get to spend the rest of the day with you."

"Oh, sweetie." Jessica realized that it was past eleven. Her meeting was set for one-thirty, which left time for breakfast, a shower, organizing her papers and . . . well, she now understood her daughter's mood. "I promise that tonight, we'll do something together, just the two of us, and maybe tomorrow we can go to the mountains or something. How's that sound?"

Lucy looked at her mother, and threw her arms around Jessica's neck. "Okay."

"Okay. Now I'm going to get breakfast ready. Want anything special?"

Lucy smiled and nodded. "Pancakes?"

"Pancakes. You got it."

"Did I hear somebody say 'pancakes'?" It was Gart's voice, a voice Lucy had known for the past nine months as her P.E. teacher's. She felt the air suddenly change, her mother's attention shift from her to the man who now seemed to be trying to take her father's place.

THREE

The S.F.U. medical center was conveniently situated a block away from Golden Gate Park—an enormity of indigenous and exotic foliage and footpaths, which extended some five miles from the Haight-Ashbury district to the Pacific Ocean. The mild breezes of late spring had drawn people out in multitudes. The park was alive, not only with spectacular and fragrant greenery, but also with the lovers of sunshine and chlorophyll. Even on an unexceptional Tuesday afternoon, the park bore an overabundance of people, relaxing and taking advantage of their little slice of nature.

"Have you ever predicted something that you couldn't possibly have known about ahead of time?" Reed asked Wally Bohrs, as the two men ambled down the south perimeter of the park on their way back to the hospital after lunch.

Wally noticed an elderly Chinese man who was practicing Tai Chi on the grass. Considering the man's advanced years, his movements were remarkably smooth and graceful—something that seemed as foreign as the planet Mars to Wally. "You mean like some sort of psychic thing?"

"Yeah. Like that."

"No, Reed. I've never predicted anything like that."

Wally was different, an oddball, a quirky, overweight, funny-looking recluse, whom few people were interested in knowing beyond what was professionally necessary. He'd been on the losing end of a disastrous marriage, and lost custody of his two children. But Reed respected and liked him, and had stuck by him over the preceding five years of slow, hard-won progress. Work was just about all Wally had left, and he made the most of it.

"But do you believe in stuff like that?" Reed persisted.

"Sure, why not?"

Reed had come to rely on Wally Bohrs absolutely in carrying out instructions and providing valuable insight. He felt that academically Wally was every bit his equal. Politics and personalities were the only real reasons that Wally held the subordinate post between them. Reed knew that he could trust Wally's abilities implicitly, and somewhat resented the department for its failure to bestow the well-earned recognition where it was due. But as they walked along the grass, Wally wasn't giving him the answer he wanted to hear.

"Why not!" Reed objected. "How 'bout because it's never really been proven . . ." Reed answered.

"Why, did something like that happen to you?"

"No, I was just wondering what you thought about all that stuff."

"I don't really think about it too much. But I guess it happens. I've heard some pretty compelling stories."

"So, you think it's real?"

"How should I know, Reed? What are you getting at?"

"Nothing. I'm just going a little nuts about the symposium, I guess. I'm . . . I'm really worried, Wal. Sixty-five percent isn't even close to good enough for these NIH people."

"It is a new record . . ."

"Exactly."

"So, make a prediction," Wally suggested.

"I predict we're doomed," Reed said resignedly. "But you don't have to be psychic to know that much."

"So, Reed, is the prediction a result of the future event, or is the event a result of the prediction?"

Reed looked away, also noticing the Chinese man who was now standing on one leg, his arms moving in a complex and elegant series of arcing motions. The man's face was set in intense, yet relaxed concentration. Reed thought that the Tai Chi practitioner was probably better suited to answer Wally's question than he was.

"I predict that we're going to find the snip, amazingly at the last moment," Wally said.

Reed passed him a dubious look, as they crossed the street in the direction of the medical center.

"Just in case," Wally came back. "Just in case."

The image of the blast cell schematic loomed on a large screen behind Reed as he spoke before a densely populated banquet hall in the St. Francis Hotel.

"For the great majority of those who currently suffer with this disease, medical science still fails them. Radiation therapy, chemo, even bone marrow transplantation, which has improved matters considerably in the lucky cases, are far from ideal solutions. While placental and cord blood transplantation seem to offer an enticing alternative where BMT isn't possible, there are still too many cases in which these treatments do little to help. To understand these mechanisms, which I've just described and demonstrated," Reed said into the microphone, "is to seize the ability to recognize the disease before it has a chance to torture and kill any more human beings. If we find that key, and use the tools, which recent advances in gene cassette transfer technology have given us, we may be able to permanently cure existing disease, and in a single generation eradicate the scourge of leukemia in human populations. Now that we're closing in on a map of the entire human genome, thanks to those involved with the Human Genome Project, our research will accelerate by unknown factors, opening still more possibilities. Other forms of cancer and illness will certainly come under our control. Right now we're on the fragile edge. We've glimpsed the other side. With a little more time, the right resources, and the political will, we'll be able to step boldly over that edge and find ourselves fully in a world free of this tragic, insidious disease, which attacks mercilessly the most innocent of victims—our children. That moment is fast upon us. On behalf of my colleagues and the many who have stood with us, I thank you for your gracious attention." Reed concluded his speech and returned to his seat. He could see his wife clapping as he neared the table. She looked exquisite in the black velvet evening gown and diamond necklace he'd given her on their fifth anniversary. She cast a slender arm around his shoulders when he took his seat next to her. His heart still hammered at his ribs as the applause around the room settled down. He had never been comfortable speaking in public.

"That was brilliant. I told you you'd find it," she whispered in his ear.

He looked into her clear, amber eyes. "I felt like I was suffocating, and in case you haven't been paying attention," he now whispered, "we haven't found it yet, but thank you."

"You've found it. You just don't realize it."

He took a swallow of his wine, then returned the jubilant smile, which he cut with a touch of skepticism. Reed knew that if he didn't get his mind off his speech immediately, he would spend the remainder of the evening futilely analyzing his own words. Quickly he turned his attention to the tall man at the podium named Dr.

Louis Canidey, a pediatrician who was beginning what sounded like a pitch for funding of a proposed children's hospital.

The music from a live orchestra eased some of the tension in Reed's chest. He exchanged his empty glass for a full one as the floating waiter swept by. He kept Devrie's arm securely locked around his.

"Dr. Haler," Reed heard a familiar voice say. Martin Whitaker, the head of the S.F.U. Genetics Department, was suddenly standing next to Reed and placing a fatherly hand on his shoulder. "I'd like you to meet Dr. Ed Samuel, clinical biologist, and Leslie Shearing, Esquire. Ms. Shearing has represented the interests of the medical community for years. They sit on the NIH grant board."

Reed extended his hand to the tall dark-haired gentleman and the platinum blond lady standing next to him. "Yes, of course. It's a great pleasure. Your reputations precede you both and I trust that you're finding the symposium interesting." Reed hoped that he hadn't sounded too obvious in his praise.

"Very," both replied.

"Nice presentation, Doctor," Dr. Samuel complimented.

"Thank you."

"And this is Dr. Haler's wife, Devrie," Whitaker continued.

Devrie shook hands and exchanged niceties. "I just want to say how much your efforts are appreciated."

"Thank you, Mrs. Haler," Ms. Shearing returned with measured reserve.

"Well," Devrie said, realizing that the two guests probably kept their guards up automatically during these receptions, "I hope you're enjoying your stay here in San Francisco."

"Very much," Dr. Samuel replied.

"Yes, and what field are you in, Mrs. Haler?" Ms. Shearing asked somewhat artificially.

"Oh, I teach the third grade."

"That is excellent," Ms. Shearing warmed slightly. "You know I've always felt that one of the greatest weaknesses in this country is our low regard for the people whom we entrust with the education of our children. You're truly one of the unsung heroes of our nation, and our times, and you're to be congratulated."

"Thank you, thank you very much, but frankly I'd settle for a raise just now." The remark met with only awkward smiles.

"You know," Reed said, hoping to recover the moment, "I know some excellent Thai restaurants right in this neighborhood if you're interested."

"Actually, we'll be flying back to Washington tomorrow afternoon," Ms. Shearing indicated, "but thank you all the same."

"Oh, sure," Reed acknowledged, his tongue firmly clamped between his teeth.

"Well, continue the good work, Dr. Haler," Dr. Samuel spoke again. "We'll be watching your progress with more than just a little interest."

"Thank you," Reed said, offering his hand one more time, "we'll keep at it."

After a few more "nice-to-meet-you's," Dr. Whitaker tactfully directed the financial contingent toward the bar.

"Oops! Hope that raise comment wasn't as bad as I think it was," Devrie confided to her husband when they were alone.

"No no, you were fine. I'm the one who should have kept my mouth shut. Thai restaurants!"

"Here," she offered him her champagne, noticing that his glass was empty."

"Thanks," he said, tossing back the golden bubbles. Now with two empty glasses in his hands and a strangely blissful smile on his face, he gazed at his wife. "You're the greatest human being who ever lived!" It came out as if he'd just realized for the first time how special his wife was to him.

Devrie drove while her husband leaned his head against the window of the smoke-gray Acura. The champagne hadn't worn off yet. Reed watched the enormous rust-red suspension cables fly past as the car entered the mile-long span of the Golden Gate Bridge, which took them north out of San Francisco and into Marin County.

"I think they'll award the grant," Devrie said, feeling compelled to tell Reed of her feelings on the matter. "But not immediately. You need to give them something more first, but you will get it."

"Is that your official, psychic projection?"

"Official projection."

"Ah. So, you don't think my pitch did the trick?"

"I think it helped a lot. But they want more of a sure thing. That's how they feel."

"You're sure?"

"Yeah. But I also think that you're going to have to change your way of looking at things somehow."

"Really?"

"Yeah."

"Like how?"

"I don't know. Just somehow. A different interpretation or something."

"Well, that narrows it down."

"Just giving you gut reactions."

"I'll believe it when the check clears."

"And when it does, I'll be expecting a full apology for all your nay-saying."

"Fine."

When they were beyond the bridge, Devrie maintained the car's speed as she followed the road's tight left-hand curve. Reed's head pressed against the glass.

"It's a girl," she said abruptly, easing out of the turn.

Reed groaned uncomfortably as he placed a cushioning hand between his head and the window.

"A girl?"

"Yes, a girl."

"Who's a girl?"

"Um, Reed?"

"Yes?"

"I guess I should just tell you."

"Tell me what?"

"Well, I'm pretty certain that I'm pregnant."

"Oh, really? And we're having a girl?" The sarcasm was returning to his voice.

"That's right. We're going to have a girl," she let out a single, nervous laugh.

"All right. Hold on one second." Reed was now sitting fully upright. "Didn't you just have your period like last week?"

She counted in her head. "My period was nineteen days ago."

"Whatever. How are you so sure you're pregnant? Have we even had sex since then?"

"Unbelievable! You know—"

"I'm kidding . . . kidding. Ha, ha. It just seems a little early to tell, no?"

"Trust me, I know I'm pregnant, and it's going to be a girl."

"So is this another one of those things that you just magically know?"

"Yeah."

"I see."

"You will see. We're having a girl."

"Let's see if you're really pregnant before we start picking out little dresses, okay?"

"Ha! Are you ever in for a little 'I-told-you-so.' "

"Well, if that's true, then I'll never doubt you again."

"Really?"

He nodded with a slightly nervous smile that wasn't there before. "But you have to be right on both counts. I mean it's not too hard to predict the first part considering, you know . . ." he gave her a sly grin.

"Okay. I'll make you a bet. If I'm not pregnant, or if we have a boy, then you win and I'll concede everything. Fair enough?"

"Deal."

They shook on the wager.

"Would you be happy?" she asked, the hesitation conspicuous.

"If what?"

"If you lost?"

"Which part?"

"Either one."

He gave her a confident smile this time. "It would be the happiest defeat of my entire life."

She leaned over, placing a loud kiss on his cheek.

"Of course, I'd be happy if I won too," he added.

"God! I knew you were going to say that."

"Yeah, sure you did."

She shook her head and signaled for the next exit. Then she felt the comforting weight of his hand on her thigh.

R eed looked from face to face. Martin Whitaker had the whole team in the conference room early the following week. The head of the department was clearly less than satisfied. Reed kept his hands firmly wrapped around a folder of notes.

"So, until we can produce a ninety-five percent match—no chance of a grant. That's the word, and that's final. Reed, what's the best you can give me?"

Reed had to squint from the light coming through the windows behind Whitaker. "I think we're a matter of days away. We're moving into the last series, which should only take a week, two at the most to complete."

"And if we still haven't achieved the goal from this last series . . . ?"

"Uh," Reed scanned the ceiling for a second, "well, then it's back to square one, I guess. New approach. Open for suggestions."

"Well, square one sucks! To put it simply."

"Couldn't agree more."

"It's like this, folks," Whitaker went on. "In spite of Dr. Haler's valiant presentation the other night, we reach ninety-five percent in the next four weeks, or the money's gone for at least another year. If that happens, the administration here will be looking at cutbacks. Big cutbacks!"

The eyes around the room were uniformly pointed at the floor, except for those of Tim Hon. Hon was almost exactly the same age as Reed, but was slightly taller, significantly wider, had curly black hair and a raw, red complexion. Hon had proposed a somewhat different avenue of research at the same time Reed had submitted his ideas to the department heads. Reed's approach had won out, and gained the initial funding. Animosity between the two geneticists had only grown over the five years since. Hon's small, reddish-brown eyes now focused right on Reed, casting over him a great mantle of blame.

"We'll get it," Reed finally cracked the tension, directing the assertion at Hon. "We're in the right area. We have to be."

"Then find it," Whitaker ordered. "Thanks everyone for your attention. Let's get to work."

R eed couldn't disguise his despondency as he and Wally Bohrs clipped—or in Wally's case, lumbered—back to the lab.

"Come on," Wally encouraged, "what you said in there was absolutely right. It's just sitting there, right in front of us."

"Then it must be invisible," Reed answered.

Tim Hon suddenly brushed up by Reed as he walked. "You know as well as I do we're not going to find this thing," the man said just loud enough for Reed to hear.

"Then resign, Tim," Reed said, without pausing in his step and without giving Hon the courtesy of a glance.

"If we don't get that grant," Hon continued, "I may not have to resign to be out of a job. How do you think my wife and kids feel about that?"

"If you're looking for a fight, Tim, you picked one hell of a good time."

"I just hope you realize that when this whole thing falls apart, it was you . . . you, Reed, who took us all down."

Reed stopped and now looked Hon directly in the eye. "Tim, unless you've got any bright ideas that I haven't heard yet, just keep your mouth shut and do your job."

"Should have listened to me five years ago, Reed. Those were the ideas you should have listened to. Not much I can do now."

Tim shook his head with the condescending, disappointed look of a father who's caught his son taking money from his wallet.

Reed had no comeback. He only watched Hon saunter away with the last word. Reed looked over to Wally, who was visibly sneering after Hon.

"He's wrong, Reed. And he knows he's wrong. He's always been wrong and he always will be. That's why he acts like such a prick."

"So what?" Reed said, continuing his way down the corridor, now even less enthusiastically.

"So what? So what? Two dozen jobs is what! Medical history, a terminal disease, just maybe a cure . . . that's *what*!"

"Wally, even if Tim is wrong and we're right, the living cell trials could go on for years. And if they do lead to disease prevention, the government will likely ban it for human use for a long time, and the whole thing might wind up coming to nothing. And that's only if by some miracle we actually do find it, which I'm beginning to seriously doubt."

"You can't know that. And what if it doesn't fail? What's with you? You know, our conversations lately have been totally backwards."

Reed let Wally open the door to the lab.

"I guess . . . I've just never been under this kind of pressure, Wal."

"I know. I do . . . I know."

"I'm just having trouble accepting that after five years of work, we're still a million miles from anything close to a cure. Feels like we're pissing into the wind here."

"Five years ago we were a *hundred* million miles away, Jack Charlie," Wally said, armor-clad optimism glowing from his beady eyes.

Reed thought a moment, then smiled. That's why he liked Wally and wanted him around. "Yeah. You're right, Wal . . . we were."

Devrie shivered a little as her obstetrician, Dr. Erica Sagat, completed the exam. The room was cool and sterile; Devrie was anxious to leave.

"Okay, Dev," Dr. Sagat said, looking at a chart, "blood pressure is good, weight is good. You're having some breast tenderness?"

"A little, I think. Tenderness isn't quite the right word for it, though. They're just more 'there,' or something, you know?"

"Sounds very normal. Any nausea?"

"Not really. Just tired mostly."

"Well. You're healthy and doing great. I'll call you if the urine or blood tests show us anything we're not expecting. You can get dressed."

"So . . . you think?" Devrie asked, hoping for a little advance news.

"Why don't we go talk to your husband."

Devrie put her jeans back on and hurried into Dr. Sagat's office, where Reed sat waiting.

"Hey, Babe," he greeted her with a kiss. "How ya doing?"

"Great I guess," she said, pulling her chair closer to Reed's.

Dr. Sagat, carrying Devrie's file, breezed in and sat down at the desk. She flipped open the manila folder. "Okay. I have the results of your radioimmunoassay." Dr. Sagat looked over the page for another moment. "And guess what? You'd better start thinking of names."

Devrie's eyes instantly overflowed. "I knew it!" she burst out. Suddenly she found Reed's arms around her, and hers around him.

"So, you're saying . . ." Reed wanted to be sure he understood everything correctly.

Dr. Sagat sat nodding and smiling. "Daddyville."

"I don't believe it," he muttered slowly, the news bouncing around in his head like a roulette ball that takes its time finding a slot on the wheel. "I just don't believe it. This is really huge. This is too huge." Reed tightened his embrace around Devrie, who didn't even try to control the tears. The world around them dissolved quickly into a single swirling blizzard of emotions.

"I just knew it," Devrie repeated, so choked with feeling her voice almost couldn't escape.

In spite of all his years of medical training and clinical knowledge of what was happening, Reed couldn't quite grasp the reality of the little miracle that was developing inside his wife's body.

"You see . . ." she said, radiating through the glossy sheen on her cheeks, "I've already won half our bet."

FOUR

When he crossed the finish line at the end of the long grass track, Alexander hadn't even noticed that he was in first place. He wasn't accustomed to winning—in fact, it was the first blue ribbon he'd ever won in his life. Jane Carlyle, Alexander's mother, jumped up and down and cheered. Alexander couldn't believe it when they told him that he'd come in first. He almost started to cry.

"This is the happiest day of his life," Jane said to Devrie as Marc

Seeth, Ellinwood Elementary School's P.E. teacher, pinned the award on Alexander's T-shirt during the little ribbon ceremony.

"I'm glad," Devrie returned. "He deserves it."

"You know," Jane continued, "he really does. I never would have expected this a year ago. He hated everything to do with school."

"Well, kids develop unexpectedly sometimes."

"I guess. But I'll tell you something. Whatever you did in that classroom, it worked."

"I just teach as well as I know how."

"No. Something happened. I don't know what, but he actually seems to like doing his homework now. It's as if he suddenly just . . . got it. You know what I mean?"

Devrie smiled. "Yeah, I sure do."

"I wish he could be in your class every year. Thank you." Jane gave Devrie a hug.

"He'll be fine. He's doing it all by himself now."

Alexander ran over to his mother and Devrie wearing a huge grin. He stared down at his blue ribbon, almost drooling on it.

"Hey, sport," Jane greeted him. "You going to be ready for the Olympics soon?"

"Yeah!"

"Come on," Devrie offered, leading Alexander and his mother over to a picnic bench and a big Igloo cooler. "I'll buy you guys a lemonade."

Devrie laughed slightly as she watched Alexander's drink disappear. It was occurring to her that she really had made a difference in his life. Until that moment she'd always been afraid of her premonitions—the things she felt she had no business knowing. It somehow made her feel responsible for them when they came to pass, that she'd somehow brought them about. So often her visions were of tragedies, involving suffering and death, and she feared them. But, now, maybe she'd tapped into a way of using that special knowledge to bring good to people. Perhaps it had been her duty to learn how to do that all along, and now it was up to her to fulfill that mission. The clear, bright air of the coming summer had never felt as comforting and full of promise.

She had been one of the last of the faculty to leave the park after the conclusion of what had been a very special track and field day for Alexander, and for her. By the time she pulled the beefy Toyota 4Runner into the driveway, Devrie's arms and legs were heavy and her eyelids were sinking fast. The rust-hued peak of the house's shake-shingled roof caught the tail end of the evening's amber glow. It gave Devrie a soothing rush to know that the long warm days were just beginning.

Her shadow cut a dark slash across the secluded front yard, as she walked along the winding footpath toward the door. From the garage it was less than fifty feet, but to Devrie it seemed like half a mile. The yard and garden were growing a little out of control. She looked forward to having the time again to attend to the abundance of flowering plants and tropical shrubs all around the perimeter of the elegantly understated home, which she and Reed had purchased less than two years before. She had instantly loved the house and its surroundings. The upscale neighborhood was safe and quiet, the residence nicely situated. It had seemed the perfect place to raise children, and now they were beginning to carry out that part of their plan. But for the moment, Devrie just wanted to sleep.

She dumped her backpack and purse onto a small burled maple table in the Spanish-tiled foyer, and kicked the door closed. The pile of mail on the table told her that Reed had already come home—a very early day for her husband.

"Hello," she called out. There was no answer.

Forcing her shoes off, and freeing her hair from the tie that held it in a loose ponytail, she went directly to the iron staircase that swept a wide, ascending arc to the second floor. The treads were natural maple, which matched the little table and the rest of the hardwood furnishings.

"Hello," she called again, as she reached the top.

Still nothing—nothing that she could hear anyway. But something felt odd. She turned down the hallway toward the master bedroom. "Reed?" she called out a final time.

No reply.

The complete silence gave the air a strange weight and smell . . . more than a smell . . . the air actually seemed to possess a flavor reminiscent of . . . apricot? Almond? She couldn't quite identify it.

The house was usually quiet when she got home from work, but that was because Reed hardly ever arrived before she did. There should have been some audible indication that he was there—there was none. Yet she knew, without question, that she was not alone in the house—the sour tug in her stomach due half to her pregnancy and half to nerves. It was as if the taste she detected in the air was an errant visitor.

At the end of the hallway, the door to the master bedroom stood partially open; the presence was on the other side, drawing her.

Her mouth went dry. The quiet made no sense. She gathered control of herself and resolutely walked to the door, then pressed gently on its center. The heavy wood panel swung silently into the room.

Devrie's hands went straight to her mouth when she saw what awaited inside. Hanging from the ceiling in huge colorful letters was a sign that said I LOVE YOU. On the far side of the king size bed stood her husband, bearing the largest, self-satisfied grin she'd ever seen. Next to him was a brand-new bassinet, full of lavender and pink roses.

"Hey, mom," he welcomed her.

Her hands still over her mouth, she tiptoed around the bed to the bassinet, and leaned down to smell the roses. She felt ashamed that she'd been so frightened only seconds earlier.

"It wasn't easy getting it in the back seat."

"Oh my God, Reed! So, we're really doing this."

"I know it seems a little hard to believe, but I am so ready."

"A year ago you would have been a total wreck, you know."

"A year ago was a very different time for both of us. I told you I'd be ready when I was ready. And now I'm ready. See? All that fuss for nothing."

She fired a scolding look up at him. "Yeah." She suddenly sprang up and tackled him in her arms, sending them both onto the bed. As their lips came together and locked, their clothing started to land on the floor.

"Hey, wait a second," she stopped him, her bra halfway off.

"What?"

"Is it safe to have sex with . . . with you know who in there?"

"You mean our son?"

"No, I mean our daughter."

"We'll see. Anyway, it's perfectly safe. In fact, Mrs. Haler, speaking as a medical professional, I highly encourage it."

"Is that right, Dr. Haler?"

"Yes. That's right."

Devrie let herself relax completely, enveloped in her husband's arms and surrounded with the scent, not of apricot or almond . . . but of roses.

R eed took the corner slightly too fast. He liked driving the 4Runner, but was more accustomed to the handling in the Acura sedan.

"Slow down. You'll hurt my car," Devrie admonished.

"It loves abuse," Reed protested. "Besides, you can't drive on this road without having a little fun."

"Want me to barf on you?" she threatened.

"Why, you feeling a little rumbly?"

"I wasn't until you started squealing the tires."

"All right, all right."

Devrie loved the touch of darkness that always shadowed Reed's jaw and chin in the evening. It gave him the perfect measure of rugged character to complement his remarkable intellect. When she imagined him in his new role as a father, it was almost more than she could stand. She felt incredibly lucky. She loved her husband, loved her work, and loved her home. For Devrie Haler, life was precariously close to perfect.

"Thanks. Now let's go through it again."

"Okay." Reed cleared his throat. "Mr. and Mrs. Chouinard. Your daughter and I have something we'd like to tell you."

"Mom, Dad," Devrie took over, "we wanted you two to be the first to know."

Then together: "We're going to have a baby!"

Neither said anything for a few moments as Reed continued up the winding road to Devrie's parents' house, situated on a small ranch in the hills of northern Marin County.

"I think that went well," Reed assessed.

"How else are you gonna tell your parents that they're going to be *grand*parents?"

"We could just call them, like I do with my parents every time something significant happens," Reed offered.

"Your parents live thousands of miles away."

"I was kidding."

"You're just nervous, aren't you?"

"Uh . . . yes," Reed admitted, wholeheartedly.

"My God, I could go for some chocolate," Devrie blurted out in a radical change of subject. She knew that Reed found it difficult discussing his parents. Though they had divorced many years before, Reed had never fully accepted their separation. "Not just any chocolate either, but the good stuff. Swiss chocolate. Mmm."

"Swiss, eh? With a touch of cucumber dressing maybe?"

"That might not be bad."

"Oh my God. It's starting," Reed moaned.

"I can pass on the dressing, but I've got to have some chocolate. And soon."

"How about after we get this over with," Reed said as he pulled the car into the gravel driveway.

"They're going to flip out," Devrie predicted, staring through the windshield at the front door.

Reed braked the sturdy four-wheeler to a stop in front of the garage and switched off the ignition.

Dale Chouinard loved to cook dinner. His wife Bettyanne was preparing the side dishes and she usually functioned as the kitchen supervisor. But nobody made venison sausage stew like Dale.

"Unreal," was the way Reed described it. "Everything was absolutely unreal."

One of the great pleasures in Reed's life was dinner at his in-laws'. The log house was small and cozy and adorned with Devrie's mother's paintings and sculptures—the ones she refused to sell. The conversation was always stimulating and the food was always off the charts.

"Please, Reed," Bettyanne interjected, "his ego's already too big."

"Never too big," Dale protested. "I'm just glad there's somebody around to appreciate it," he accepted the compliment. "Now, what's wrong with you, Girlie-whirl?" he directed to Devrie.

"Wrong?" she asked.

"Well, you destroyed your peas and carrots, but what's happening over there?" His eyes gestured to her full bowl of stew.

"Oh, sorry, Dad. It's not your cooking, I promise." She looked over at Reed. "Maybe we should tell them?"

"Oh, uh, yeah. Now is good."

They both stood up, two pairs of curious eyes on them.

"All right," Reed began the rehearsed speech, "well, uh, Devrie and I are . . . have, that is, something to tell you . . . both . . . um."

Devrie kicked Reed's shin under the table. Dale and Bettyanne shifted expectantly.

Reed kicked Devrie back.

"We're pregnant," she busted out.

"Hey, I thought we were going to tell them together," Reed complained.

"Oh, my God!" Bettyanne clamored. She was instantly on her feet and stepping around the table to her daughter where the two women fell into a teary hug.

Dale wandered over to Reed, first shaking his son-in-law's hand, then sharing a hearty embrace.

"Well, congratulations," Dale barked into Reed's ear.

"Thank you," was all Reed could think to say.

"That's just about the best news I've ever heard," Dale went on.

"Yeah. We're pretty excited." Reed agreed.

Then it was time to trade parents.

Dale smothered his daughter with hugs and kisses; Bettyanne nearly lifted Reed off the floor.

"I knew you could do it," she howled at him.

Reed loved his sturdy mother-in-law. "Well, it only took a little extra effort," he confirmed.

"Hang on," Dale then said, gathering up wine glasses from the table. He hesitated when he got to Devrie who'd conspicuously been drinking water all evening.

"Don't worry, Dad, water's fine," she said, aware that she had to be conscious of everything she put into her body.

"Can't be too careful, I guess," Dale acknowledged.

"That's right," she said with a smile, holding up her water glass proudly.

"Anyway. Here's to the two of you on this extraordinary occasion. May yours be the happiest, healthiest child ever born."

"Thank you, Dad," Devrie said, her eyes still puddling.

"Thanks very much," Reed repeated.

"Well, I hope everybody saved room for dessert," Bettyanne sang over her joyous sobs.

As Reed and Dale cleared the table, Devrie put on a pot of coffee and helped her mother put away dishes from the washer, in preparation for the onslaught of dirty ones arriving from the dining room. "So, how long have you known?" Bettyanne asked, taking a stack of saucers from her daughter.

"Well, only a few weeks, Mom."

"Weeks!"

"We just wanted to be sure sure. You know. Before we went around announcing it to everybody," Devrie explained.

"Everybody? Who else knows?"

"Don't worry. Only my doctor and a few nurses."

Bettyanne accepted another pile of dishes from Devrie as Reed walked into the kitchen, carrying a handful of glasses.

"Reed," Bettyanne said, as he settled the glasses into the sink, "you must have told your parents, haven't you?" She ventured cautiously, aware that she was broaching sensitive ground.

"Oh, I will," Reed answered, not taking his hands off the glasses immediately.

"Well, good. I'm sure they'll be very pleased."

"Yes. They will be." Reed let go of the glasses, and placed a hand on his wife's shoulder, delivering a short but sweet kiss on the back of her neck. She loaded the glasses into the dishwasher.

"Why don't we all go into the living room while the coffee is brewing," Bettyanne suggested, diverting the subject. "I've got a homemade peach cobbler in the fridge, and I think Dale picked up some of his favorite Swiss chocolate, if anyone's interested."

Devrie suddenly looked straight at her mother, arresting the older woman in the motion of hoisting the stack of plates into a cupboard.

"What?" Bettyanne asked, wondering what in the world she had said to elicit the probing look in her daughter's eyes.

It was well after midnight when Dale and Bettyanne waved to their daughter and Reed as the younger couple drove away. Devrie had the passenger seat halfway reclined as Reed piloted the 4Runner back down the twisting road.

"No. I'm sorry," Reed objected. "Forget it."

"Reed. What did I say two minutes before we got there?"

"You said you wanted chocolate, like just about every other pregnant woman on earth might."

"No, Reed. I specifically said 'Swiss chocolate' as if I knew I was going to be coming into a quantity of it sometime soon. I'm telling you."

"You can tell me whatever you want. This time it was pure coincidence, and not a very compelling one at that."

"It wasn't coincidence."

"Okay. Whatever you say."

"Reed. I wish you'd respect this a little more."

"I don't disrespect it. Come on. I'm just a natural skeptic, and I wish that you'd respect that a little more."

"Can't you ever accept anything just on faith? Or, better still, on your wife's word?"

"I believe that you do sense things. I just don't know for a fact that it's anything beyond normal, albeit heightened, perception."

"How could I have known about the Gulf War? I knew almost verbatim the *Chronicle*'s headline two years to the day before it happened. I even wrote it down. You've seen it."

"Yes, I've seen a few things in your little book, and most of it doesn't make any sense."

"You just don't understand the sense that it makes. A lot of this stuff is symbolic, or is related to things we just never find out about."

"Well there you go, you could make symbolic meanings out of just about anything if you try. Like that one, what was it? Something about dried fruit and a DC-10? What's that supposed to mean, that there's going to be a plane crash somewhere in the world within the next two years because someone on board was smuggling prunes? Or the time you thought that there was going to be a fire in one of the Embarcadero towers . . ."

"There was a fire, one week after I said it would be."

"That fire was in a house out in the Avenues ten miles away."

"It was still a fire, and it still happened almost exactly when I said it would."

"Okay, I predict that there's going to be a serious car accident on a California highway sometime this summer." Reed didn't hear the irritated comeback that he was expecting. "Dev, you okay?" He looked over to see that his wife had grown noticeably pale. "Hey, what's wrong?"

She looked back at him, a thick gloss developing in her eyes. "I don't feel very well."

"You sick? Upset? I didn't mean to upset you."

"No. You didn't upset me. I just don't feel very well all of a sudden." She held on tightly to the handle above the door. "Can you slow down a little?"

"Yeah, sure." Reed brought the vehicle down to a moderate speed.

"Oh, shit, Reed. Pull over."

"What? What's the matter?" Reed angled onto the narrow shoulder, and let the car stop halfway in a shallow ditch between the road and a dense wall of eucalyptus trees.

Devrie unclipped her seat belt and opened the door. She leaned out and emptied her stomach. Reed searched around himself for some tissues or napkins. Finding none, he popped open the glove box and started digging.

"In the visor," she prompted, her head still hanging out the door.

He tilted his visor down; they landed in his lap. "Here," he offered when Devrie was again upright in the seat.

"Thank you," she said, grabbing the little pack of Kleenex. Reed placed a hand on her shoulder. Devrie wiped around her mouth and dabbed at her eyes. She was shaking.

"That came on fast," he observed.

"Yeah," she said, then looked at him. He didn't recognize the worry in her eyes.

"Dev, it's just morning sickness. You can expect to feel kind of shitty for a while."

"I know. It's just that . . ."

"Dev, relax. You're fine."

She shook her head, the look remaining firm.

"What is it then?"

"I don't know exactly."

"What?" he pried.

"You'll just think I'm full of crap."

"Look. I know you're not feeling great. You're kind of freaked out about this whole thing. I know I am. I'll understand whatever's on your mind. I promise."

"Promise?"

"Promise."

"I'm kind of scared, Reed. You're . . . you're going to think I'm nuts, and I don't want to worry you."

"I'm going to be very worried if you don't tell me what's on your mind."

She tried to take a deep breath, but that seemed only to make her trembling worse. She really didn't know exactly what was troubling her. It was nebulous and slippery, but it was threatening all the same.

"I'm not moving until you tell me what's going on in there," he said, pointing to her head.

She gave him another pleading look. "Reed, I . . . I just had a strange feeling that something was going to happen to the baby . . . something bad."

Reed's face softened, his arm circled her shoulders completely. "Honey, honey, honey," he whispered soothingly. "Every expectant parent thinks that once in a while."

"Reed, there's these red boots."

"Red boots?"

"Or blue rocks or something. I don't know. I just feel scared, that's all. This is very new."

"Blue rocks?"

"I see blue rocks."

"Red boots, blue rocks . . . sounds like you're planning a Fourth of July picnic. Just add a white farmhouse, and some potato salad—"

"Reed! This is not a joke," she snapped.

"Sorry, sorry, sorry, sorry," he rattled off with great speed. "I'm sorry. Dev, listen to me. Whatever those things mean, you have to remember that it's so normal to feel whacked out. Your hormones are going crazy right now, you know? You're liable to have all kinds of bizarre feelings for a little while, and think all kinds of scary things. But when it all levels off, you're going to feel great. I guarantee it."

"Okay," she resigned. "I guess you're right." And perhaps he was right, she thought. Her hormones were surging all over, making her feel any number of unusual, unpleasant things. She convinced herself that she was just feeling normal, prenatal jitters, and tried to let the foggy sense of dread go.

"Of course I'm right. Why don't you let the seat go back all the way and just rest. I'll drive nice and slow. Okay?"

"No. I want to sit up. I want to see the road."

"Whatever makes you comfortable."

Reed checked the traffic and put the car back in gear. "You want to stop and get something?"

Devrie shook her head. "I just want to go home."

"Okay." With his hand on Devrie's leg he drove as smoothly as he could.

After a few miles she seemed to settle down.

"Hey," he said encouragingly, "you still feel like getting away after school's out? Just you and me, a tent, the Sierras, and the stars?"

She looked at him, the distress still apparent, but she nodded. "I'd like that."

"Great. You're looking better already."

She rested her head on his shoulder, and closed her eyes.

Devrie had gone to bed almost immediately when she and Reed had arrived home. It was unlike her to want to go to sleep so early, but then Reed realized, it was unlike her to be pregnant too. He had kissed her lightly and wished her sweet dreams, which made her smile peacefully. He gave her sandy hair a gentle stroke, letting his gaze linger on the delicate line of her cheek, the tender fullness of her lips and slender grace of her nose. He let his imagination transfer his wife's wonderfully balanced features into a new face, a face that was forming inside her. What, he wondered, would his child look like? He almost couldn't stand having to wait.

After switching off the bedroom light, he had gone back downstairs to his office and poured himself a half-inch of scotch. He placed his feet on the desk and stared at the ceiling, while the spirits warmed his senses. The phone felt awkward as he pressed it to his ear. The ringing on the other end of the line was muted and weak.

"Hello," the voice of Jared Haler, Reed's father, answered.

"Hey, Dad. It's Reed." Though it was just past four in the morning in Chicago, Reed knew that his father would be awake. Since retiring he'd become almost pathologically nocturnal.

"Oh, hello, Reed. This is a surprise. What's wrong?"

"Nothing's wrong, Dad. I'm just calling you with some news."

"News? What's up?"

"Well, I just wanted to tell you . . . that Devrie's pregnant."

"Pregnant?" Jared said skeptically, as if his son had just told him that he'd won a free trip to Ohio. "As in, you're-going-to-be-a-father pregnant?"

"Yes! As in I'm-going-to-be-a-father pregnant!" Reed nearly shouted, as if still needing some convincing himself.

"Well, it took you guys a while, but . . . that's . . . wonderful! Really wonderful news. Does your sister know?"

"Not yet."

"Does your mother know?"

"No. I'll call everyone tomorrow. I just knew that you'd be awake right now, so . . ."

"Oh. Yeah. That's . . . well, what can I say? I'm proud of you. Damn proud. Wish I could be there."

"Yeah. Me too. Soon, okay? Maybe you'll get out here . . . before the baby is away at college."

"Planes fly both directions," his father answered.

"Yeah. I know. They do fly both directions. It's just been hard with the job and the house and, you know. Time is always the problem."

"It always is," his father agreed.

"So, what's your excuse?"

"What, you think I'm not busy too?"

"Dad, come on. You know it's more convenient for you to come here than for us to go there."

"Yes, yes, I know."

"Look, don't feel any pressure or anything. I just wanted to tell you the news. We'll talk again soon. Okay? I'll let you know how things are going."

"Yeah. Hey, Reed, congratulations again. I'm really proud of you. And wish Devrie well for me too."

"Thanks, Dad. I will."

"All right. Talk to you soon."

"Okay. 'Bye."

The line clicked. Reed didn't understand why it seemed so difficult to simply talk to his father. As he hung up he felt the sense, as he so often had in recent years, that the man he loved, had once known so well, now seemed more like a casual acquaintance. That's the way they talked to each other. Maybe it was just the distance. Maybe it was the divorce. Perhaps it was simple laziness. Probably some combination of things, he concluded. It was at moments like this that Reed truly envied his wife and the closeness she had to her family. It was something that he had gravitated to and enjoyed throughout his relationship. He only wished that he could share his own family with her in the same way. But with his relations scattered all over the country that was a logistical impossibility. Perhaps, he thought hopefully, as the tug of sleep pulled at his eyes, the birth of their child would somehow make the difference.

Dull peach light from the sodium-vapor lamps that lined the empty, suburban street found its way over the fence, through the broad-leafed trees and into the window of the bedroom. Devrie was lying on her back, facing the softly illuminated ceiling when her eyes opened. Reed's rhythmic breathing continued next to her in the darkness. The sheets were damp under her skin. She was hot, and uncomfortable. Peeling the sheet and blanket off her body, she sat up. Reed remained undisturbed. She reached over the edge of the bed and found the T-shirt she had shed several hours before. Her mind was running at capacity; thoughts and words fluttered around without reason. So far being pregnant sucks, she thought.

She looked at the vague outline of her husband's body under the thin sheet. She felt embarrassed about the way she had behaved on the way back from her parents' house. It wasn't like her. She had always been strong, the one in control.

Quietly she pulled open the drawer in her nightstand and felt for the nine-by-twelve-inch cloth-bound journal she kept inside. Her feet free of the covers, she swung her legs around to the edge of the bed, and stood up, listening for any movement from Reed. He breathed steadily on as she lifted the book from the drawer, and stepped silently out of the room.

She had become dehydrated and the cold water was a great relief. She finished one glass, and then poured another before placing the pitcher back in the fridge. The glass in one hand, her journal in the other, she went into the living room and sat down on the couch, curling her bare legs underneath her. A ballpoint pen kept her place in the thick volume. Since she'd begun keeping the journal some thirteen years before, she'd filled about half the pages with one- or two-line entries. She looked down the most recent page where she'd entered the episode with her student Alexander: *Alexander and Jeff, drainage tunnel under Bratton Boulevard. He didn't do his homework. DO NOT ENTER.* That was the entire entry. Then came: *I'm pregnant with a girl*, which had a big circle around it. Devrie smiled a little shyly to herself as she read the words again. Beyond that were several other entries she'd since noted, but which she didn't understand. Her smile faded quickly as she read on: *Cavalier; "She must be hungry"; red boots; blue rocks—fear.*

They were things that had landed in her head—not just random thoughts, but thoughts or dreams that she had a hard time shaking from her memory. That's what distinguished ordinary thoughts from those she elected to put down in her journal. She had never discovered what most of the things in the long chronicle meant, but sometimes she did, like the Gulf War. Precisely two years before it happened, the knowledge of it had come to her. What others thought was of no concern to her, she knew that every one of her entries bore itself out in the real world somehow, somewhere, and so often with terrible consequences. She just didn't seem to have control over any of it, or know why she received the messages. That's why she had started keeping the journal. Maybe someday, she thought, it would all become clear.

She pulled the pen's cap off with her teeth and began to write:

18(p11; q6); telomere; Five million over five. Then on a fresh page, with particular care she wrote a new line: *Ones with guns are blind in the dark.* Then another: *Where there's a tear there's light.*

With each word a fresh wave of nausea came over her, and with it a hostile chill. It was the same feeling she'd had earlier in the car on the way home from her parents'—the same feeling that had afflicted her the day Reed had brought home the bassinet. She shoved the pen back into the journal.

The antique captain's clock on the mantel began its mellow chime. It was three o'clock. Devrie stood and switched out the light, then stopped at the large picture window. The fence and leafy sycamore trees that surrounded the property couldn't quite hide the faint orange glow from the street. Above, the stars peeked through the high, membranous clouds. Devrie wrapped her arms around her middle. She caught a shiver even though her skin bore a misting of perspiration. The air had the strange flavor again, only now it tasted foul and bitter.

Her head snapped around at the noise.

Was it a breath?

Was it her own breath?

The living room remained dark and still. Only the old mantel clock violated the supreme quiet with its muted, even tick. It must have been her own lungs, she thought, drawing air with spasmodic involuntary contractions.

She turned back to the window. The stars were slightly fainter, becoming sealed behind a thickening cirrus blanket. All beneath lay undisturbed. There wasn't even the trace of a breeze. It was too calm somehow.

Devrie couldn't suppress the sudden urge to cry. The overwhelming sadness that had just flooded her heart, brought with it equally profound terror. As the stars became dimmer, her thoughts inversely grew clearer, as though a weak phone connection had suddenly found strength. She grabbed the glass of water on the coffee table, and guzzled the remains, hoping to quench both her tremendous thirst as well as the courage-sapping grief that had seized her.

Fatigue ate at her legs as she returned the empty glass to the kitchen, and then ascended the stairs. She needed sleep, wanted it badly. She just hoped that her brain would allow it. But first she needed to add one more entry before it drove her down any further.

Sitting on the edge of the bed, her eyes spilled tears, while her mind twirled irrationally in the dark. She didn't want to write down the words, summoned all the denial she had within her, but felt the nearly pathological need to anyway. It was a compulsion, a necessity to write down everything that met her criteria for inclusion in the journal. It had to be honest and complete if she was going to live up to her end of the deal she'd made with herself. But what she had to put down, she couldn't place next in the list, as she normally would have. The entry just didn't seem to belong there—didn't belong anywhere—perhaps because she had fought to ignore it, or perhaps because by taking it out of context, it might lose its power. But she couldn't ignore it any longer, and so she squeezed the handful of words in at the top of the page she'd just started. With the final letter down on paper, she snapped the book closed, and stuffed it back into the drawer without reading the entry. She sat motionless for another few minutes, giving her eyes a chance to dry.

When her head again rested on the pillow, the sound of Reed's breathing came again. It had to be a mistake, she told herself. *It was a mistake. IT WAS A MISTAKE!* She repeated the phrase over and over in her head and eventually the anxiety fully subsided. In another two minutes, she fell asleep.

Wally Bohrs stared half-heartedly at his computer monitor, a wide rubber band stretched between his thumb and index finger. When the *no anomalies found* prompt came on the screen, he launched a Bic pen from the rubber band right at the center of his small desk calendar. The pen's nose left another of many little blue dimples on the paper.

"Fine," he mumbled as he collected the small missile from the floor. He entered a command on the keyboard, which instructed the program to produce a list of results from the latest batch of fluorescent in situ hybridization (or FISH) assays, the process through which they could create a picture of DNA from a drop of blood. The rest of the team had gone home for the day, but had left Wally with another two hours' worth of data from the new samples. "Take that," he said as he reloaded the rubber band.

"After that run I want you to come into my office," Reed ordered from behind him. Wally delayed the next firing, and swiveled around in his chair. "Your office?"

"My office," Reed confirmed, already heading in that direction.

"Okay." Wally turned back to the screen after Reed had left. A minute later *no anomalies found* again flashed on the screen, and he let the Bic fly. This time he left the pen on the floor.

His two knocks were enough to push Reed's office door open. "All right. What?"

"Wal, have a seat, and close the door."

Wally settled into the rigid wooden chair in front of Reed's big gray desk. "Everything okay?" he queried cautiously. Private meetings in Reed's office were a rarity, and usually meant serious news.

"Wally . . ." Reed smiled as he took two cheese glasses and a bottle of champagne from the bottom drawer. "It's still early, but I wanted to tell you before the rest of the department." He popped the cork, and splashed a little of the sparkling wine into each glass. "Here goes." He held one of the glasses up in a toast, and Wally picked up the other, "I'm going to be a father."

Wally's face lit up, his smile stretched to the limit. "Wow! Ho . . . wow! Look out! Well, it's about time. Way to go, Jack Charlie."

The two men *clanked* their glasses together and prepared them for refill in short order.

"Anyway, so let's keep this quiet for a while, you know . . ."

"Zip. Quiet. Totally understand."

"Thanks." Reed took another mouthful, relaxing back into his chair, then: "Tell me something, Wal. How did you and Linda handle it when she was expecting?"

Wally shook his head in thought. "Well, I tried not to think about it, and Linda just cried for the first three months. After that she was fine and I got insomnia, which was actually good practice. After your kid is born, you're going to learn to live on two hours a night right quick. It wrecked me."

"And you went back for more?"

"I never would have done it, but Linda convinced me that Andy shouldn't be raised an only child."

"Ever regret it?"

Wally poured his third glass. "Which part?"

"Having your second kid."

"Reed, having a child changes your whole concept of the world, of life, of people and yourself. You are in for the most challenging, and the most incredible time of your life. And that's a prediction you can count on. I wouldn't trade a second of it for anything. The only thing I regret is letting it get away. I see Andy and Nora once every six months, so I'm damn glad I had both of them. Whatever you do, Reed, don't lose your family. No matter how important the work we're doing here may be, it's not worth that."

Reed contemplated the words of his friend as he refilled his own glass. "Well, to that end, Dev and I are getting away weekend after next. Right after she's done with school."

"Great for you! See, that's the kind of thing that I never did."

"I guess sometimes you just have to say fuck it."

"Yes you do, boss . . . yes you do." Wally knocked his glass into Reed's one more time.

FIVE

On the front lawn of Alamosa Elementary, the odor of freshly cut grass wafted by, as Lucy Morraine sat waiting for her mother to pick her up from school. Only a few swatches of white, and the occasional dark streaks of recently returned barn swallows interrupted the infinitely deep blue sky. The flags drooping from the tall pole in front of the building shifted only intermittently in the mild breeze, which carried the voices of children, thrilled that the school year was at its end. Lucy began a new drawing in her coloring pad while she waited. She made a dense field of squiggly black X's that looked like pairs of worms who were joined in the middle—like Siamese twins. She filled in the area around the worm shapes with red.

The afternoon sun was hot on her face, a sign of the warm temperatures to come. She loved summertime, and this summer would be different than any that had come before. One of the things that she was going to do when her mother arrived was to sign up for the summer gymnastics program.

When she saw the familiar silver Honda CR-V pull into the parking lot, her heart lifted. She closed her drawing pad and put it and her crayons into her small orange and blue knapsack. Lucy ran to the car and met Jessica as she got out.

"Ready, sport?"

"Ready," Lucy answered, handing her knapsack to her mother. Jessica placed the small bag in the backseat, and closed the door.

"Okay, let's go." They walked side by side up to the door of the school gymnasium. Inside, lines had formed at two tables. It seemed that every boy and girl at Alamosa Elementary wanted to take gymnastics. Lucy waited eagerly in line, as she talked with her mother.

"It's going to be a lot of hard work. Are you ready to come every day and do your best?" It was a fairly intensive program, especially for a seven year old, involving both morning and afternoon sessions, five days a week. But to Lucy it sounded like a lot more fun than baby-sitters. She nodded enthusiastically.

"Okay."

"Mom?"

"Yeah?"

"What's a telomere?"

"What?"

"What's a telomere?"

"Where did you hear that word?"

"I don't remember."

"Well, let's see. That's a little hard to explain." The line advanced, giving Jessica a moment to think about an answer to this new, unexpected query. That was one of the things Jessica loved the most about being a parent—the endless surprises that came out of her daughter's mouth. "Uh. Telomeres." Jessica herself was no expert on telomeres, but she was aware of them from her medical education and from reading various articles in the journals. "Well, they're part of what are called chromosomes. We all have chromosomes in every cell of our bodies. They're what make you, *you*, and me, *me*. It's something called genetics."

"Genetics," Lucy repeated.

"Right. You know how you and I have the same color eyes?"

"Yeah."

"Well, that's because I gave you some of my genetic information."

"Do I have some of Daddy's genetics too?"

"Yes, you do. You're made up of half of your daddy's and half of mine. Some parts of you are like him, and other parts are like me. Understand?"

"I think so. But so what are telomeres?"

"Well, they're what make us get old."

"I don't like them."

"You don't? Well, guess what?"

"What?"

"We're stuck with them. Everybody has to get old. But that's okay, because that's the way the world works. Does that make sense?"

"Yeah."

They were up to the table where Jessica gave Lucy's name to the woman who was registering students. As the woman entered the information on the sign-up sheet, Jessica noticed the teacher who was indicated at the top of the page. "Well, Luce. It looks like Gart's going to be your teacher again."

"I know."

"How do you feel about that?"

"It's okay."

"Really?"

"I guess it's just the way the world works."

Jessica kissed her daughter on the cheek, amazed again at her child's ability to comprehend.

SIX

Devrie had always found something sadly pleasant about the quietness of her empty classroom at the end of the school year. The calm after the storm. The anxieties that had plagued her the night she and Reed had gone to her parents' house for dinner seemed to have abated too, and her confidence was returning.

Except for her own desk in front of the blackboard, the room had been cleaned, straightened, and stripped bare for the next three months of disuse. As she held the report card in her hand Devrie thought back with a smile. Alexander had come a long way since his first day in her class. During the last month he had especially improved in social studies. Devrie marked his final grade for the year a "B+," instead of the "D" she had given him midway through. His lowest grade was a "C" in math, a subject Devrie had been sure he would not pass without a lot of extra help. Now he'd learned to help himself.

Methodically she completed the remainder of her grade reports, and bound the stack of brown envelopes with a rubber band. She tidied up her desk and collected the few things that remained: her Magic Eight-ball, a stapler, her Diskman personal stereo, a handful of Post-it pads, and a two-by-two-inch, framed photograph of herself and Reed. From a hook above the blackboard behind her, she pulled down a delicate, ceramic wind chime, and carefully placed it in a small box. She stuffed the items into her bag, and stared out over the vacant desks. Not one failed student. Her job was its own reward, and she never wanted to change it.

I t was a short walk down the hall from her classroom to the main office. Pete Barton, the principal, was there chatting with Marc Seeth, the P.E. teacher, and Megan Wilmore, who taught fifth grade. The small group regarded Devrie as she dropped her stack of envelopes into a large box marked REPORT CARDS at the side of the reception desk.

"That looks like it felt good," Marc said.

"Damn good," Devrie confirmed. She hadn't told any of her co-workers yet about her pregnancy, and was glad that the year was ending before it would become all too obvious.

"I wish just once I could get mine in before the last second," Megan expressed, swirling a cup of black coffee between her long-nailed fingers.

"Hmm, just like filing income tax," Devrie noised, extending a hand to Pete. "It's been another great year."

Pete had been the principal of Ellinwood Elementary for eleven years—five years longer than Devrie had been teaching there. They had grown to like and respect each other a great deal.

"Another great year," Pete agreed. "Hope your summer is too."

"Thanks. Well, *adios*, guys."

They said a few parting words and Devrie stepped out of the office. Her intention was to go straight out the exit, but after a few steps she pulled a quick left toward the faculty women's room. She had only seconds to spare. Again the nausea had come on almost instantaneously. The cold tile was hard against her knees as she leaned over the commode. There was no stopping the upward surge. Her entire abdomen convulsed violently, expelling everything it could in several rounds that ended in a spasmodic series of dry heaves. *Oh, lord, I can't go through with this*, were the only words in her mind. A heavy dew of sweat had broken out across her forehead. She wiped her mouth with a bunched-up handful of tissue, and slowly raised herself from the floor. The episode was subsiding. A few moments later she found the stability in her legs to exit the stall and reach one of the sinks.

The water felt good on her face, but failed to wash the foul taste from her mouth. In the mirror she examined her flushed skin, the slight darkness under her eyes. The color had drained from her usually robust lips, and the hollows in her cheeks seemed too deep. She pressed a paper towel to her face, soaking up the moisture, and tried to ignore the feeling of exhaustion as she walked out of the women's room. She purchased a can of Coke from the vending machine in the teachers' lounge before she finally left the building.

The evening sun hit Devrie's left side as she drove the 4Runner north through Mill Valley. The golden warmth was not enough to settle the chill that had worked its way to her bones since she'd left work. She didn't know if it was just the morning sickness, the caffeine from the Coke, or just nerves, but she couldn't stop shivering.

The nauseous anxiety was again squeezing at her middle, while her eyes were continually drawn to the rearview mirror. She wasn't sure how long the green car had been behind her, but she decided to take the longer route home, and veered onto the exit, which placed her on another northbound thruway. But it was still with her, and steadily gaining. As it gradually neared, she identified it as a Chevrolet from the logo on the grill. It appeared to be an older model from the late eighties—a boxy economy car trying to pass itself off as something more sporty. After another two miles, the next exit came up and she took it as well. At first she thought the Chevrolet had continued on, but before she could let out a breath of relief, there it was again, and coming up on her fast. Ahead the traffic was starting to congest.

She moved into the far-right lane, preparing for the interchange, which would put her back on the road toward her destination. The green Chevy made the lane change as well, now only five or six car lengths behind.

Devrie tried to put a little more distance between herself and the Chevrolet, immediately accelerating and jumping into the far-left lane as soon as she was back on the broad, multilane freeway. Still the Chevrolet stayed on her. Her heart began a tumultuous thumping. She wasn't imagining it: that car was following her. Or was it? It certainly seemed to be.

Nerves?

Her imagination?

The grip on her waist tightened; her pulse intensified. The Chevrolet then started coming up behind her on the right. She tried to discern the car's occupants, but its windshield was too dark, the glare too bright. On the car's side panel, little metallic letters spelled: "Cavalier." Fixed on the rearview, Devrie could see the name glint in the evening light. Then something in front of her stole her attention, as if a bomb had detonated in her lane. She was coming up on the car ahead much too fast. Traffic around her had slowed to a near stop, while she had been studying the green Cavalier, the car's name ricocheting around inside her skull. She hit the brakes hard, screeching the 4Runner's tires. Purely reacting, without conscious thought, she swerved left, nearly smacking into the side of the car in the adjacent lane. She corrected again, but that put her on course with a stopped pickup. She had to steer the 4Runner out of the stagnating traffic through a fast-narrowing path between the other vehicles. In less than a second the available options shrank to nothing; there was nowhere left to go but off the road.

The jolt of the median under the tires traumatized the whole frame of the 4×4; concrete scoured the undercarriage with a resonating metal shriek. Bucking off the raised cement, Devrie suddenly found herself going the wrong direction—on the wrong side of the broad thoroughfare. But stopping at that point meant certain head-on collisions. She frantically wove between the traffic, nearly smashing into an enormous eighteen-wheel tractor trailer, as well as half a dozen cars. Tires screamed; horns blared; cars swerved and veered, and voices yelled as she traversed the five lanes, aiming for openings between the cars. Finally her front wheels popped up onto the sidewalk. Several terrified pedestrians bolted from harm's way. At last she had the opportunity to slam the brakes, and brought the big off-roader to a noisy stop in the parking area of a Shell station. She rocked back into the seat, not quite sure if she had come through the chaotic ride okay or not.

She looked back at the roadway to see if she had left any accidents behind her. To her relief, the flow of cars was quickly normalizing. There was almost no sign of what had just happened except a few more honking horns and loud, profane criticisms of her driving ability and general intelligence.

Her hands were soaking the steering wheel as a service station attendant ran up to her and asked if she was all right.

"Yeah. Yeah, I'm okay. I don't know what happened. I just . . . I'm okay," she assured the young man in the uniform.

"Can I use your restroom?" she asked, still trying to recover her breath.

The young man pointed toward the side of the station. "Sure, ma'am. Get the key inside. You sure you're okay?"

"I'm fine. I just need to, uh . . . use the bathroom."

"Wow! You must really need to go," the attendant observed with a chuckle.

Devrie nodded with a sarcastic little smile as she stepped down from the high seat. The kid in the Shell uniform turned away quickly, his lower lip firmly between his teeth.

Devrie looked again across the breadth of traffic. Some distance away she could see the green Cavalier, still inching along on the other side of the median. The license plate was hidden by other cars, the driver still obscured behind the glass. The chill remained, but she convinced herself that she'd once again simply let herself get swept away with her anxieties. I really do need a vacation, she thought, resolving absolutely to maintain control of her life.

As she walked behind the attendant, she heard a new phrase loudly in her head. She tried to shake it off, but it came again, persistent, louder: *Shbyi'aye from the sky, sees, hears, and smells.*

The first word was just a sound, some foreign term that had no meaning to her, but it rang clearly in her head: *Shbyi'aye*. It was nonsense. Being pregnant, she decided, was jumbling her perceptions, obscuring and distorting them into meaningless gibberish and exaggerated emotions. That notion soothed her nerves, but did nothing to settle her rebellious viscera.

When she had the rest room key in her hand, she had to run— that one can of Coke simply wasn't going to stay down.

SEVEN

The soft reading lamp was the only light on in the room. Sitting on the edge of the bed, Devrie stared at the blackness outside the window as she listened to the ring on the other end of the line. She consciously relaxed her shoulders to keep the phone from pressing too hard against her ear.

Bettyanne picked up on the third ring. "Hello?"

"Hi, Mom. I just wanted to let you know where we're going to be."

"Oh. Okay. Let me get a pen."

Devrie waited until her mother was back on the line, and then described the area where she and Reed were planning to spend the weekend camping. "So, we'll be back Sunday night."

"Call."

"Of course, Mom."

"And no hiking. Not in your condition."

"Mom."

"Well, you've never been pregnant before. You need to be careful, and you're coming right home if you're not feeling well. You tell Reed that."

"Okay. No hiking."

"Good. And, Devrie?"

"Yes?"

"Try to relax. You're wound like a rubber band. I can hear it in your voice."

Devrie realized that she was squeezing the phone too hard again; she forced her shoulders to drop. "It's nerves, Mom."

"Just remember to breathe."

"I'll try. Gotta go now. Say good night to Daddy for me."

"I will. Have a great time."

"Talk to you when we get back."

" 'Bye."

As Devrie hung up the phone, and placed it on her nightstand, she could hear the sound of a car door through the open window. Reed was loading the 4Runner for the trip. The hook that still clawed at her insides wasn't going to ease until she wrote down the words. Reluctantly she opened the drawer next to the bed.

She spread the cloth cover and paged to the most recent entry. Quickly she scribbled the new passages: *Shbyi'aye from the sky, sees, hears, and smells.* Then: *Morning stories fall from mourning glories.* Gradually her clamped stomach relaxed as the words stared back at her. She still had no idea what *"Shbyi'aye"* meant. Then she noticed that she'd unintentionally transposed the spelling of the words "mourning" and "morning" in the last entry. I'd give myself a "D," she thought, feeling foolish, and a little crazy for writing the odd sentences down in the first place. Leaving the spellings as they were, she wrote a third entry, which had since roosted in her mind: *Dry waves lie in the Blood of Christ.* The words rolled around in senseless streams. But like crumbs in the wind, her ill-ease drifted away as she wrote them, until she was again feeling calm, relaxed, and at peace. She wondered why it always happened that way—why writing the words down relieved the anxiety. It was probably simple psychology, she thought, putting the journal back into the drawer. Accepting, if not understanding, these terms, she went downstairs.

The night was still and warm, almost summer hot when Devrie stepped out onto the front patio. The stars were intense, diamond-bright, and winking in smug silence—their secrets safe for another night. She took in a deep breath, full of the scent of tropical flowering plants. In the driveway she saw Reed loading equipment into the back of the big car. Amazingly she hadn't put a scratch on the thing. It would probably need an alignment job, but there was no sign of what she'd put the 4×4 through earlier in the day. She saw no reason to tell Reed about the incident. It would just make him worry unnecessarily.

She walked up to him as he fit sleeping bags and their tent into the back of the spacious vehicle. Sensing her behind him, Reed turned and kissed his wife.

"Hey, take a look here," he said, pulling a map from his back pocket. He spread the California road map out on top of the camping gear. "I was thinking about taking the southern route." He drew his finger from Marin County, across the San Rafael Bridge, and south through the East Bay. "We can follow these local roads all the way across. That'll be a lot more interesting than the interstate." His finger ended up on a mountainous area near the Nevada state line south of Lake Tahoe. "This whole area is really secluded and beautiful."

She threw an arm around his shoulders and kissed him on the ear.

Reed turned and placed his hands on her waist. "How you doin'? 'Cause we don't have to do this. We could—"

"I'm better. Really. I was sick at school, but I'm fine now. Seems like it's once a day and then I'm fine."

"You're sure?"

"Positive. I can't wait to lie back, take in some sun, and read something just for the fun of it again. The weather is supposed to be perfect all weekend."

Smiling, he kissed her again, and refolded the map. "We'll stop in the morning and pick up food and ice and whatever you want: pickles, chocolate, ketchup, and ice cream . . ."

"I love you," she said.

"I love you too," Reed whispered, placing his hand lightly on her abdomen. "And I love our son."

Devrie pulled away with a sly grin. "I can't wait to see the look on your face when you're proven wrong."

"Want to know ahead of time, or do you want to wait?" he asked.

"Hmm. Maybe we should let the suspense build up. It would be a more satisfying victory if we waited. But, on the other hand, it would be nice to start enjoying victory sooner."

She leaned back into his arms.

"I say let's wait," he expressed.

"Chicken."

"That's me." He kissed her deeply this time, and she indulged herself in the warm security of the embrace.

Devrie awoke with a jolt of anxiety and nausea. Two visits to the bathroom allayed the latter problem, but as she pushed her legs into a pair of jeans, recollections of troubling dreams chafed at her. While Reed showered, and she looked out the bedroom window at the new day, she felt compelled to jot down four more phrases:

Slain in train yard;
See that she is the next of life's soldiers;

No moon's glow in the middle of summer;
Forbidden, forever hidden inside the trunk.

Nothing in her journal had ever seemed as cryptic as the last several entries. Reading them back to herself, she realized that the puzzle wasn't going to crack that morning, so she tucked her journal back into the drawer, and finished dressing. Again a general sense of well-being replaced the needling psychological torment that had been an increasingly frequent visitor in recent days. By the time Reed had finished showering, Devrie again anticipated their journey with eager excitement.

By midafternoon the temperature was a perfect eighty degrees. Devrie let the passenger seat recline as the 4Runner powered up the winding highway into the high Sierras. The sky was a flawless dome of cobalt. She squinted as sunlight flickered through the tall firs and majestic blue spruces that lined the road. It was an effortless ride at the bottom of a deep canyon of pine. Devrie turned the stereo up a notch, and settled back as the splendor flew by to the sound of her favorite music.

It was impossible to keep the smile down.

"What?" Reed asked, when he noticed his wife on the verge of laughing.

"Nothing. I'm just happy."

"No nausea?"

"Not at the moment, anyway."

"Good." Reed tried to force himself to relax too. With the way he'd left things at the lab, he was badly preoccupied, but was doing his best not to show it. Gradually he shoved the ramifications from his mind. He and Wally had found only one additional snip, which appeared to be a common factor, but they were still a long way from the required ninety-five percent. He knew that Wally would be at work all weekend trying to find another one. Reed wanted to call to see how things were going, but resolutely blocked the urge.

Still, he imagined that he would give in at some convenient point and call from a gas station.

He maneuvered his thoughts back to his wife and the beautiful scenery around them. Her head was resting back, eyes closed, a peaceful composure radiating on her face. It was contagious. Reed let his foot fall a little more on the accelerator. The big machine shot up the steepening hill until they came to the turn he'd been looking for.

The gravel road deteriorated fast, but the four-wheel-drive handled the irregularities in stride. Reed loved the challenge of a rutty, washed out mountain trail.

"Reed, maybe we should turn around. If you break my car, you're in a lot of trouble." Devrie wasn't so happy about the dry creek bed of a road.

"Your car? I thought it was our car."

"When I'm driving it's ours. When you're driving it's mine."

"I see. Well, you underestimate your car's abilities."

"It's your abilities I'm worried about."

"Stop worrying. Once we get to the top of this hill, it'll smooth out."

"What makes you think so?"

"I've done a lot more driving like this than you have."

When the road leveled off, it did smooth out, just as Reed had predicted, but only for about thirty feet. Beyond that, the rounded tops of massive boulders, sharp rocks, and deep troughs in the dirt served well as the mountains' guardians. The way appeared even less a means of vehicular approach than it had before, but Reed was determined. He gained speed, building momentum for the sharp incline. The knobby tires slipped and grabbed intermittently, shooting rocks and gravel back in a dusty spray. He took periodic glances over at Devrie to see how she was reacting. She betrayed no sign, good or ill; she simply clung to the overhead handle, so Reed pushed the 4×4 a little further.

Then came the loud scrape of rock against the steel underside of the machine. One last surge of power from the roaring engine pulled the 4Runner over the last obstacle and the road was defeated. A wide plateau opened up, revealing a grassy meadow at the base of a daunting snow-patched peak. The road suddenly cleared, offering an unobstructed path over a gentle rise. Reed continued until the trail sloped downhill again into a shallow gully. Before the road again fell into a scarred and pocked mess, Reed wheeled off into a small clearing, traveling between the trees and around a low hill that hid them from view. He pulled the 4Runner to a stop.

"Well. How's this?" he asked.

Devrie gave the area a three-hundred-and-sixty-degree assessment, then opened the door. Without pause, she leaned out over the ground, and lost her breakfast. Reed tipped the visor down, but this time no tissues fell from the perch. He fished wildly between the seats.

"Got them already," she said, holding up the pack for him to see.

"You okay?" he asked, feeling a little responsible.

She pulled herself back into the seat, the color returning to her cheeks. "You had to come the bumpiest way you could find?"

Reed shrugged, and they both got out of the car.

Beyond a stand of aspens, the rocky peak seemed to watch over the two minute people. Devrie immediately heard the quiet, steady whisper of rushing water. Reed swung his door shut and followed her.

There was no sound except that of nature. "A creek," she said as she met her husband at the rear of the vehicle.

"Yeah. There's a creek on the other side of the road."

She wandered around the clearing which appeared relatively level and stone free. "This seems perfect."

"Is this it then? I don't think we're getting much further up the road."

"I think this is it."

"Then this is it."

"Yeah, this is it."

"Great."

"And I need some water," she announced.

Reed opened the back hatch and extracted the cooler, which he had filled with an assortment of sodas, water, fruit juice, and beer. He pulled one of the bottled spring waters from the ice, and then they surveyed the area further, picking the best spot for the tent. Reed cleared some small rocks away and gathered other large ones for the fire pit.

Devrie pulled the compressed tent from the back of the 4Runner. Within a few minutes she had erected the lightweight, high-tech shelter, and soon Reed had formed a deep circle of stones, which would later contain a healthy campfire.

Devrie continued setting up camp, rolling out the sleeping bags inside the blue nylon igloo. She had brought along four pillows and a foam cushion. Why be uncomfortable if you don't have to be? That was always her philosophy of camping.

She backed out of the zippered door when she was satisfied, and closed up the mesh screen. Reed stumbled out of the forest, carrying an armful of wood. He dropped the load next to the fire pit, and looked up to see his approving wife standing next to him.

"There's a great downed tree just a little ways into the forest. Should be plenty of wood for the night."

She put her arms around him, feeling the dampness of his shirt and the strong pulse in his muscles. "You're awesome."

He gave her a kiss and said, "I know. Gotta go. Still lots to do."

He neatened the pile, making it ready for the next several loads.

"While you're doing that, I'm going to go check out the creek."

"Okay. Have fun. See you in a little while." Reed was already hopping back into the trees, which surrounded their campsite.

Devrie smiled to herself. Her contentment was nearly flawless. From the back of the 4Runner she pulled out a large beach towel.

Walking in the direction of the sound, she crossed the clearing into a thick stand of forest. As she made her way through the woods, the rushing sound grew. She tried to stay aware of her path between the trees, soft rust-colored needles quietly crunching beneath her. She knew well how easy it was to become disoriented in the forest. But the sun now provided a good indicator of west as it began its late afternoon dive. Ahead Devrie could see that the trees thinned. Now the sound of the creek was loud, present. After walking only several more feet, she came to the bank of the shallow brook, which was no more than ten feet across. The water ran fast over copper-colored stones. The ground sloped down slightly to a tiny beach of pebbles. She sat down on a wide flat rock, half of which was on the shore, the other half submerged in the clear moving water. There was just enough room on the dry end of the rock for her to lie down on the towel and absorb the soothing rays. She took her shoes and socks off, and let her feet slide into the chilling flow.

Over the sound of the water Devrie could hear the light buzzing of insects around the wildflowers, which dotted the banks of the creek. She opened her eyes to a field of perfect blue. She realized that her isolation was complete, and now the sunlight was becoming a little too warm. She sat up, conducting a quick visual scan of the area to ensure that she was, in fact, quite alone, and lifted her T-shirt over her head. She undid her bra, noticing the tenderness in her breasts. The afternoon light enriched the pale color of their curved, smooth surfaces. The button at the top of her jeans popped open easily, as did the others. She slid the thick denim over her hips and down to her ankles, letting her underwear go along. She gradually scooted herself closer to the water, until she was in up to her knees. Then in one quick move, she plunged herself completely into a deep pool in the stream. The cold was a powerful shock. Almost instantly she was up again, flipping her hair back in an arcing spray of droplets. The feeling was invigorating and splendid, the smooth pebbles soft and slippery under her feet. She plunged herself once more into the icy current, and then backed her way up the rock to the flat, sun-warmed area. Her feet had started to go numb. Drops of water that covered her skin quickly shrank in the dry heat. She sat with her legs crossed for a long time as she touched her midriff, gently placing her hands on the sides of her slightly swollen abdomen. She had started showing, but very slightly. It was difficult for her to believe that there was a person, a human being developing inside of her. It was an overwhelming thought. She had noticed too that her nipples had grown a little darker, thicker somehow. It was all normal, she knew, but still it felt strange, like someone else's body. She'd put on about five pounds already, but her legs and behind were still firm and shapely, and she was determined that she would bounce back after the delivery.

The water had almost completely evaporated off her skin when she suddenly felt very naked. She glanced around again, goose bumps forming over her body. Still, the clean cool air felt good, but as she started to lean back, the rustling came: leaves, branches. Instantly she sat upright, scanning the surrounding foliage. Her hand searched blindly for her T-shirt. Then again. The movement was behind her. She shifted on the rock, fumbling with the soft garment, trying to orient it, to find the correct opening. The noise didn't sound like the motion of an animal. It was too obvious, too deliberate, then too quiet. Too quiet. The shiver had leached into her again. She'd been seen! Someone lay hidden, watching. She was sure. Her vulnerability was total. She continued struggling with the shirt as though the thin cotton might somehow protect her.

"No!" a voice said.

Devrie stopped at the familiar sound, lifting the shirt back up off her head.

"Don't put anything on."

"What are you doing?" she demanded.

Reed stepped through a dense thicket and down to the water's edge. "Sorry," he said with a big smile, his eyes taking in the spectacular image of his wife's unclad body.

She tossed the shirt behind her. "Ever heard of knocking?"

"The door was open."

"Well since you're here, why don't you join me?"

Reed pulled his own shirt off and approached. As he began to sit down on the edge of the rock to take his shoes off, Devrie's foot connected solidly with his extended posterior. His weight carried him directly off the dry shore and into the pool at the end of the rock. The intense chill paralyzed his lungs for a moment until he found purchase in the pebbled creek bed, and lurched back onto the shore, dripping and panting. He crawled back toward Devrie, his pants soaked through. Without pause he climbed onto the rock and seized Devrie in his arms. She let out a shriek as the cold water fell over her bare skin. The shriek degenerated into a fit of helpless laughter as Reed forced his cold wet body against hers. She giggled until the chill had gone, and then she found herself clinging to her husband, pressing her lips against his, and helping him lower his soaked jeans. He fought to free his legs from the heavy Levi's and underwear, not wanting to take his mouth from hers. The universe had become only the two of them, enwrapped within each other, under the virgin summer sky. Devrie kept her eyes open to relish the fact that she was indeed outdoors, experiencing the touch of her husband's skin against the full length of her own. Amid the sound of the creek, the scents of life, and the infinity of nature, she gave herself fully to the moment.

EIGHT

nly the fringes of the lower pine branches caught the orange of the fire light. Reed was settled back against a small boulder, which he'd rolled up to the edge of the fire pit. Two pillows and a blanket softened the granite recliner. Devrie was tucked cozily under his arm, her legs stretched out, warmed by the low crackling blaze. She poked idly at the flames with a long narrow stick, sending up little blizzards of orange. The remnants of a big meal, paper plates, cups, and unfinished food sizzled down to ash on the red coals. Together Reed and Devrie scanned the celestial display above them.

"So, I think we should name her Alana," Devrie said, focusing on the brightest speck of light in the sky.

"Would that mean naming *him* Alan?"

"Moot question."

"Humor me."

"Fine. You can think of any boy name you want, and I'll go along with it."

"Really?"

"Really."

Reed tried to think of the perfect male name, but it turned out to be a lot harder than he'd expected. "I'll get back to you on that," he said, averting his attention to the dazzling canopy of distant suns and planets. "Have you ever looked into this kind of sky," he asked, "and really imagined the universe in three dimensions, instead of just a dome of lights?"

"I've never imagined it as just a dome of lights," Devrie came back.

"Well . . . what the hell is all that stuff?"

She smiled, amused at the unknowable, awed by the eternal wonder. She thought of the earth as a ball, flying through space, just one more of the billions of sparkling white dots that packed the galaxy. She tried to open her mind to the cosmos, to see if it would gratify her with some insight, no matter how slight. It had happened before, she was sure of that. She'd known the feeling of chance glimpses into a great source of knowledge beyond human understanding. Perhaps here, in the mountains, closer to that source, she would receive some answer. The stars just winked back at her. She closed her eyes and emptied her mind, listening, relaxing. Nothing. Nothing but the awareness that she had to pee. She folded back the blanket and sat forward, admitting the coolness of the night.

"Where you going?" he asked.

"Nature call."

"Oh." Reed helped her to her feet with the push of a hand against her rear.

"Thank you. That's fine. I think I can take it from here." She looked back at him with a smile.

Reed took a sip from a glass of wine at his side, then watched as his wife, roll of TP in hand, blended into the black folds of the forest. His eyes fell back to the pulsing embers of the dying fire. "Alana," he said to himself with a smile.

The cracking twig came from the wrong direction. Devrie had gone into the trees in front of him, yet the snapping wood was definitely behind him. Reed made a quick turn of his head. The holes between the trees seemed to suck the light right out of the air, into the impenetrable voids. A muted crunch of pine needles then came from one of the black holes. It couldn't have been Devrie, he was sure of that. It had to be an animal, something moving, watching, *stalking*. The first tightening of his chest had reached his neck and shoulders. His initial impulse had been to dismiss the sound as a product of his overly sensitive eardrums and hyperactive imagination. Then again, the woods were full of animals foraging in the darkness. The forest at night always brought out a sense of heightened vulnerability, he thought. But that was part of the allure of camping, and he relaxed. But it came again, a little closer, a little louder. Somehow it didn't possess the natural rhythm of the forest. Now his pulse rang in his ears. Slowly and as quietly as he could, he reached for the wood pile and took hold of a heavy, gnarled branch. The sounds of compressing earth now came in a continuous flow, growing steadily louder. The squeeze of nerves bloomed into a vibrating surge that ended in a tingling at his fingertips and toes. His mind began to churn with terrible images of some deadly predator. He gazed in the direction Devrie had gone—no sign of her. He reared back on his feet, readying the stick, still not quite believing what he was hearing, yet taking no chances. He could no longer blame his imagination.

The stick had plenty of sharp protrusions, capable of inflicting a great deal of damage. Reed strained to see into the forest, but the light only reached two or three feet before the night devoured the weak luminance. The sound continued to near, now its source could only be a short distance within the concealing shadows. Still Reed could discern no movement. The steps were deliberate, approaching. Wild animals didn't behave like that unless there was something wrong with them, which left a set of equally undesirable possibilities. Something, or someone . . . was certainly coming toward him through the night forest. His hands had gone moist on the wooden club. He backed slightly, ready to strike, prepared to fight for his life and Devrie's life if he had to. His dry throat contracted, swallowing involuntarily; his muscles tightened against the coursing blood in his veins. He felt weak, his own nerves sapping his strength, leaving him little confidence that he could mount a successful defense. The stick felt as if it would slip from his hands at any moment, leaving him utterly helpless.

He squinted harder, summoning all the energy he could out of the depths of his courage. Whatever the thing in the forest was, it was not concerned with remaining undetected. What kind of animal is that bold? Reed scoured his brain. How could he warn Devrie? was his next thought. It was clear that in another few seconds neither question would hold much relevance. The animal, four-legged or two, was not stopping. Reed was most afraid of the latter possibility.

Then the first traces of movement reached his eyes. It was indistinct at first, low to the ground. Someone crawling? It continued its march in a direct line toward Reed. Fighting his own disbelief, he braced for the now imminent confrontation, ready to face the hidden intruder. He considered yelling for Devrie to run for the car, but his voice was frozen, his eyes locked, waiting to see the creature which he was sure by now could clearly see him. It was moving slowly, but very steadily. He focused first on a tuft of tan fur. Then the eyes gleamed in the warm fire glow. A head formed out of the hollow. Reed drew the branch back, his breaths short, quick. The shape became more distinct. There were ears, paws, a tail. Then the sound of a tired pant.

"Well, shit," Reed said, in a great exhale. He lowered the stick, breathed, kneeled, and finally let himself relax, laughing out of pure relief.

The golden Labrador stopped, two feet away, pleading amber eyes turned up, its head nestled between its two front paws.

"What are you doing," Reed asked, the sweat streaking his temples, "trying to put me in the hospital?"

The dog gave a quiet whimper, then inched forward again.

"Well, what are we going to do with you?"

A slightly louder whimper followed another cautious advance. The long strawberry blond tail started wagging; the drooping eyes begged. Reed tossed the knotted stick back onto the woodpile. The dog watched Reed's movements, building trust gradually.

The Labrador didn't appear to be injured, and seemed healthy enough, if somewhat famished. Reed held out a hand, his fingers curled under. The dog relaxed and shuffled forward with greater confidence. When it was close enough, Reed could see that the dog wore no collar, nor ID tag of any kind. There was only short, yellowish fur.

The Lab's eyes suddenly darted up, over Reed's shoulder. The footsteps followed. Reed turned to see Devrie emerging from the forest. She slowed when she saw the dog.

"Where did that . . . come . . . from?"

"Just crawled out of the woods. Must have gotten lost or something. I think it's a female."

"Oh, man! This is just great!" Devrie tossed the toilet paper back in the car and walked slowly over to Reed. Now the dog had found a comfortable spot near the fire. "What are we going to do with her? She looks terrified, poor thing."

"*She* looks terrified?" Reed protested.

Devrie contained a small giggle.

"Hey. That was damn scary hearing something stomping out of the night . . . in the dark," he insisted.

"I'm sure it was," she acknowledged.

"I think I was more scared than she was, but she must be hungry," Reed said.

His comment snagged somewhere in Devrie's mind. *She must be hungry*. Her lungs constricted without warning. The dog made another sorrowful noise. Devrie avoided the desperate eyes. She sat down on one of the rocks next to Reed, her arms closed in tight around herself.

"What's wrong? It's just a dog. So she's scared and hungry."

Devrie stared at the fire, then: "Yeah. You're right. I just . . . don't think it's going to be that easy to get rid of her now. Especially if we feed her anything."

"Well, we can't let her starve. We've got some more veggie dogs in the cooler."

"Reed?" Devrie finally turned to her husband. He saw the worry, the concern.

"What? What's the matter?"

"I . . . I don't know. Nothing I guess." Now Devrie looked over at the helpless animal. "Somebody's probably out looking for you right now," she said, patting the dog on the head. "Well, I guess we can't let you starve, can we?" Devrie seemed to relax slightly as she stood up, and went over to the large cooler. Inside she found a package of leftover veggie hot dogs and some cheddar cheese. She chopped up and mixed the ingredients together with some ketchup. "It's not exactly doggie gourmet, but this should make you feel better." Devrie placed the Tupperware container of food down a few feet away from the fire. The dog sprang to its feet and choked down the meal almost before Devrie had let go of it. "Wow," she said, standing back, as the ravenous creature licked the plastic clean. Devrie then refilled it with some water, which the dog also consumed instantly.

"Yep," Reed confirmed, taking notice, "she's a girl, all right."

Devrie gave her one more helping of water, ran her hands over the dirty but soft coat, and sat down again next to Reed. "We've got a friend for life now, you know."

When the dog had finished her lapping, she again lay down next to the fire, and quickly began to doze.

"I think," Reed recommended, "we should take her to a ranger station in the morning. She's obviously been cared for so I imagine someone's going to report their pet missing very soon, if they haven't already."

"I guess so."

"Of course, so."

"She's very sweet," Devrie observed, trying to keep her renewed ill-ease at bay. The fire had dimmed; the night had somehow closed in a little more. Devrie snuggled again under Reed's arm.

When the last true flame finally died, Reed suggested that they crawl inside their tent. When she didn't respond right away, he realized that Devrie, as well as their new friend, had already fallen asleep.

The urge to pee had been plenty to wake Reed up. He scooted himself from the sleeping bag, and crawled to the mesh screen doorway of the tent. Outside the land lay still and opaque with night. Only the smoldering pink of the last coals in the fire pit indicated that there was anything but the trees and the thick dusting of stars. In the weak light Reed could see the outline of the sleeping dog, still in the same spot, only five or six feet from the tent. Reed stepped lightly across the coarse, short grass to the edge of the woods. A lone owl hooted somewhere in the distance, and the sound of crickets laced the air. Otherwise the forest was unexpectedly quiet. He could hear the light splash of his urine, but could hardly see the ground where it landed. When the supply had exhausted itself, he shook off the last drops with a shiver, and pulled his Fruit of the Looms back up. The lightless air had a deep chill about it, and left the unmistakable impression that the forest at night was not the domain of human beings.

He gave the haze of stars a parting glance with all due awe, and crawled back into the tent. Only when he slid back into the sleeping bag did he realize how cold he'd become. It took several minutes before the shivering subsided. Next to him he felt Devrie adjust fitfully, then sit up.

"Sorry," Reed whispered, "I didn't mean to wake you."

"Listen," was all she whispered back.

"What?"

"Did you hear that?"

"Hear what?" All Reed could hear was his own breathing.

"That," she said again.

Reed couldn't tell if he'd actually heard something or whether the urgency in his wife's voice was just suggesting noises.

"Someone's walking around out there," she said.

"That was me."

"No. Someone else."

Then the soft padding through the grass came to Reed's ears. "Of course something's walking around out there," he agreed, "we're in the wilderness."

"Shh!"

Then a small grunt came from just outside the tent.

"The dog's awake. She heard it too," Devrie pointed out.

"The dog's probably dreaming of more veggie dogs," Reed speculated.

"No. She's tense. There's someone . . ."

"What? You can tell that she's tense? Dev, come on. Lie down and let's go back to sleep."

"Where's the flashlight?"

"I thought you had it."

"I did. But I can't find it now," she said, feeling around blindly at the sides of the tent.

"It's probably under your sleeping bag or something."

"Check your side."

"Dev, I'm going back to sleep. Come on."

"No! List—" Devrie started to say, but was interrupted. The dog's growl lasted only a second before an odd thud cut the sound off.

The blade came through the thin nylon without the slightest resistance. The muted squeal of tearing fabric preceded the black mass by the duration of a breath. Reed could not see what had hit him, he only knew that his face had gone numb and that the floor of the tent was against his back. Devrie's scream, however, came clearly. As if part of the night itself had exploded into the tent, a black form lashed out within the small dome.

Do something! Anything! That was the extent of Reed's ability to reason. He simply reacted, throwing himself, fists hardened, at the faceless evil that had so suddenly intruded upon them. Another blow took him out of reality for an instant. He landed, the smell of goose down and nylon confusing him. As his senses returned, Devrie's voice quickly filled the cavity, not with words but a jagged shrieking. It had her in its grasp, squeezing the breath from her body. Her scream weakened, its source choked off.

Reed commanded his eyes to focus, to see what had taken hold of his wife. Outside the dog barked. In silhouette against the roof of the tent, Reed saw a large head on top of broad shoulders. He could hear a snorting breath between his wife's screams. As the monster lunged, Reed heard a gasp from Devrie's mouth, then his name, cried out in vocal spasms. Reed started to kick madly at the thing, but connected with nothing. It was impossible to tell what was really happening, but Devrie's cries left no doubt it held her tightly. Then a series of further lunges quieted her to a low moan. Each sudden movement was accompanied by another sound, a muffled, sucking noise, like that of a step taken into a wet patch of mud. An arm swept a short, quick arc through the darkness several times over. The moist sound, with each plunging strike, began to make terrible sense. Devrie had stopped struggling, her voice only a thin, broken note. Then an odor, warm and raw began to fill the tent. Reed knew the scent all too well from his one-time rotation through emergency medicine. He thrashed insanely to gain his footing, getting tangled in the folds of the sleeping bags, now slippery with wetness.

The dark body was retreating. It pulled back, out through the rupture it had made in the tent wall, Devrie still securely in its possession. Reed crawled after it, reaching out, grabbing for Devrie's legs, or just a foot, anything he could get hold of. He found her ankle, and gripped hard, but the beast had her halfway out and commanded a great advantage in leverage. Reed held on for life to Devrie's small bones, sliding over the soggy down bags toward the long slice in the nylon wall. Then the pulling stopped. Loud barking echoed through the trees. Reed could see the Labrador growling and bearing its teeth ferociously at the intruder. A large foot at the end of a long, black leg shot from beneath the figure, sending the animal through the air. The dog landed some distance away with a pained squeal. Reed could now see, against the dense field of stars, the size of the man. He was large, at least six feet tall, with a strong, broad back. The powerful arms seized Devrie's body with renewed force. Reed had managed to get himself onto his knees, intending to hurl himself into the man's side, but that effort met only with a solid boot in his sternum. The air wouldn't come. There were only dancing lights in a glittering sky, lungs convulsing for just one breath. He sensed that his legs were folded beneath him. The barking resumed, coming closer, only to be silenced a second more permanent time. Reed managed to roll to his side, getting just enough air to keep from passing out. He saw the Lab helplessly limping around in circles, finally landing in a trembling pile of fur. His own strength was leaving him. Only terror and blistering anger now drove him. He had to fight, to resist. He could see the horrid figure, kneeling over his wife's body, straddling her uselessly flailing legs. The faint orange glint of stale firelight hit Reed's eyes in the shape of a long, curved blade, its face bathed in a rich brick-red. The man held the weapon up, a wide hunting knife, over Devrie's chest; her legs stopped moving.

"*NO!*" exploded from Reed's lips as he dove, reaching for the hand that held the knife. He heard the loud *crack*, saw the world spin beneath him, then he saw nothing but a pair of dark boots, glossed crimson in the scant glow of coals. The heel of one of those red boots suddenly blotted out Reed's entire field of vision. He knew that his head had been knocked back severely, possibly several times; he couldn't tell. When he tried to move again, he found that he was paralyzed. He seemed to have no sense of himself physically, beyond a vague pain—everywhere. Gradually his sight returned, but he was frozen, barely able to breathe, the taste of blood strong in his mouth.

Blood! The *red boots*! Red from blood. He remembered Devrie's words from their drive home from her parents' house. And there the boots were, only a few feet away, now between his wife's bare legs. The man had lowered his own pants, his movements rapid and vulgar. His back arched occasionally, then the thrusting would resume.

Reed tried to form the words: "She's pregnant," but the sound was only a lost breath. As he watched, locked in a world more profoundly hellish than his own death could ever be, Reed saw, through the blur of reddened tears, the man rear back on his haunches, withdrawing himself, still wielding the knife. Reed could now see his wife's blood-soaked thighs, genitals, and midriff. But he also saw her butchered abdomen rise and fall, ever so slightly. She was still alive, still breathing somehow. Maybe the demonic animal would just leave without killing her. Reed begged God to let his wife live, to stop the monster that had defiled her so completely, so unspeakably. He begged for the strength to kill the menace. All went unanswered. The foul creature, his back still to Reed, stood while he lifted his black jeans, darkened with wet stains, over his well-muscled legs. The man fastened the buttons and a thick leather belt. Devrie still breathed, her nude body laid out like a broken doll. The man stepped to the fire and pulled a stick from the ashes. It was the stick Devrie had been using to stoke the fire, its tip still a luminous orange. The man swept the stick through the air several times, drawing arcs of light, the way children sometimes spell their names out in the darkness. The glow intensified with each pass until it burned, brighter, hotter.

The man brought the smoking tip close to his face. Reed could see a black, maniacal eye set back deep into the profile. The face was covered in a wool mask.

In a single, swift move the man again lowered himself to his knees, drawing back the length of knobby wood. He then stuffed the burning end between Devrie's legs, her body scarcely responding to this new, even more hideous violation. Reed could see the man's arm, working the stick in as deeply as it would go, not satisfied with simply inserting it. Then the hand released the searing prod, leaving it in place. The man's body started to tremble. Reed didn't understand why at first, then it became clear that the man was laughing, laughing an insane, silent laugh that represented an eternity of madness. When the man at last stood again, he drew the knife across his thickly haired forearm as if to wipe it clean, and then slid it into a leather holster on his belt. Reed closed his eyes and held his breath—waiting his turn. But all that came was the limitless void.

The moist warmth didn't smell good. At first he could tell little more than that. There was a heavy breath hitting his nose, and wetness against his cheeks. He recognized the panting sound and opened his eyes. It was no longer night. There was a blue light. It was flashing. Then he knew he was looking at the rocks of the fire pit. A blue light kept hitting the rocks in sudden bursts. He could hear the sound of an engine nearby. The nightmare flooded back instantly as he tried to move. Then the dog's nose was in his face again.

"Holy shit!" he heard someone say, followed by an, "Oh, mighty God!" The feet were the first thing he recognized, then the legs, then the stick, then the rest of his wife's body came into terrible, unbearable focus. The nightmare had been real. She had stopped breathing, probably hours earlier. Other feet soon surrounded the utterly motionless body.

He writhed pitifully in an effort to lift himself, the shock of reality consuming him.

"Hey, he's alive," a voice said. Then Reed saw a face. It was a young man's face, boyish with dark hair, wearing a wide-brimmed khaki hat. The man kneeled down to take a look at the survivor.

"Call Flight for Life, right now!" the ranger ordered. "They can set down in that meadow over the hill there, hurry!" He turned back to Reed. "Can you hear me?" he asked, having a hard time concealing his shock. Reed squirmed and wrestled against gravity, making nonsensical grunting noises.

"My wife," he finally managed in a garbled voice.

"You just hang tight here, Mister. Don't try to move. Help is on the way."

Reed began to tire, and sank back onto the hard ground, his eyes fearful, scanning, expecting the next terrible onslaught.

"Can you tell me your name?"

"He killed her," Reed shouted, grabbing the ranger's jacket.

"Okay, okay. Hold on. You're okay, now." The ranger had to physically subdue the panicked man. "Can you tell me your name?"

The question somehow made it through. "Reed Haler, my wife . . ."

"Okay, Reed. I'm a ranger with the Forest Service, my name's Scott Allen. We're going to get you to a hospital, right away. Stay with me, now, okay? Can somebody cover her up, please, and get the state police," Scott instructed someone whom Reed couldn't see.

"This your dog?" The Lab had sat down next to the ranger.

"No," Reed answered.

"Sure acts like it. She led us to you. Looks like she's hurt too."

Reed looked in astonishment at the soft canine eyes, which looked back with inexplicable understanding.

"Can you tell me what happened here?" Scott asked.

Reed swallowed what he could taste was a large clot of blood. "Camping. Last night. A man . . . came. With a knife. Took my wife. She's pregnant. Oh God!" Reed screamed. He sealed his eyes, choking on the horror.

"Okay. That's okay, Reed." Scott did his best to sound comforting. "Take my hand now and give it a squeeze, okay," Scott instructed. "Take it. Come on." Reed gave himself to the support of the ranger and squeezed Scott's hand, as his every sense of peace evaporated. Reed stayed that way until the sound of a helicopter rose up in the distance.

The nearest hospital was in the resort area of South Lake Tahoe, which straddled the border between California and Nevada on the shores of the lake. It was fifty miles from what was quickly established as the "primary crime scene." Reed had suffered a concussion, multiple bruised ribs, a fractured cheekbone, and a sprain in his neck. The doctors wanted to keep him overnight under observation. After the X rays, disinfecting, stitches, and general treatment, Reed was taken to a recovery room.

The sound of the opening door temporarily shook off the effects of the mild sedative and painkillers. Reed fought to sit up in the bed. "What? Who?" he said with difficulty.

A dark-haired woman, wearing blue hospital scrubs and a lab coat, walked quietly into the room along with Scott Allen the ranger. With them were Chuck Everett, a state police homicide detective, and his partner Gerald Jimenez. Everett introduced himself and Jimenez while the doctor, whom Reed only knew as Dr. Deb Thomas, checked Reed's vitals.

"What's happened to my wife?" Reed asked first, his voice scarcely above a whisper.

"Her body is at the morgue, Dr. Haler," the heavyset detective answered.

Reed noticed that Everett was almost bald, probably around fifty years old, and shorter than his partner. Other than that Reed had only stark consciousness that people were standing around him.

"We're going to do everything we can to get whoever did this, so I'm going to need to ask you some questions. Do you think you're up to that right now?"

Instead of answering, Reed asked: "Have her parents been told yet?"

"Not yet. We wanted to talk to you before we do that."

"Oh." Reed seemed on the verge of passing out, his eyes lost, confused, glazed, and swollen.

"We can notify your next of kin as well, if you like."

"No. I'll do that myself."

"All right," Everett said, scratching the light flocking of gray above his ear. "Now, first off, how many people attacked you, Dr. Haler?"

Jimenez readied a ballpoint above a small notepad.

"Only one. A big guy. Strong."

"Are you sure?"

"Yeah."

"Did you get a look at his face?"

"No. He wore a wool mask. But he had dark eyes. Very dark."

"Some idea of what he weighed?"

"Two hundred plus, I suppose." Reed's breath began to grow heavy.

"Besides the mask, could you see what he was wearing?"

The recollection was an obvious struggle, still so fresh and raw. "Black jeans. A dark jacket, or a sweater I think. The sleeves were pushed up. I really don't remember very much. It was . . . it was so dark." Reed took a moment to let his breath normalize. "He wore cowboy boots. Dark tan. Blood went all over them. I remember the blood. And the knife."

"Can you describe the knife for me?"

"Big. About ten inches long. Hunting knife, you know, with a curved blade. He carried it in a leather holder on his belt."

"That's very good. Did you see a vehicle?"

"No. He just came out of nowhere."

"Do you have any idea what time that was?"

"We went to bed around one." Reed's eyes fell to some distant object, in some other world where only pain existed. "I had fallen asleep. It was still dark. I had gotten up to take a leak, and when I got back inside the tent she knew someone was there, outside . . . waiting."

"Your wife knew?"

"Yeah."

"What do you mean, she knew? How did she know?"

"Know?"

"How did she know there was someone outside the tent?"

Reed's memory began to short out from the sedatives. "She . . . uh . . . heard the footsteps."

"I think he should sleep," Dr. Thomas advised.

"All right. I just need you to verify the phone number for me."

Reed managed to focus on the names of his in-laws and the phone number written on Jimenez's notepad.

"That's it," Reed confirmed.

"We'll talk to you more tomorrow."

Reed started to drift into unconsciousness; the doctor showed the group out.

They had been capable of little more than holding on to each other when Dale and Bettyanne met Reed at the hospital the next morning. Devrie's parents had received the call at eight-thirty the night before. By eleven P.M. they had driven from Marin County to the morgue in South Lake Tahoe to identify their daughter's remains, and to hear the police account of what had happened. They had spent the remainder of the night at the hospital, waiting for Reed to wake up, their hearts and souls obliterated and numb.

The doctors kept Reed in bed for another twenty-four hours as his condition improved. Dale and Bettyanne lived in the hospital waiting room, placing long-distance calls to relatives and sleeping when they could. The story of the attack had already attracted the local press.

In spite of the mass of swollen purple that was his face, by the second day Reed had stabilized enough for discharge from the hospital. A car from the police station had come to pick them up. Detective Everett still had some questions and paperwork for the report. He was sorry that no suspects had yet been located.

"I'd like to hold on to your car and camping gear for a while, Dr. Haler," Everett said from behind his desk. "It may give us some useful information as the investigation moves along."

Reed lifted his deadened eyes to the pudgy man's face. "You do whatever you need to do. Anything you need to see, to ask, to search, you do it."

"We're gonna give it our very, very best, Dr. Haler, Mr. and Mrs. Chouinard. I promise you that."

Dale and Bettyanne sat with Reed in the office, balancing precariously on the edge of emotional collapse.

"I'll be in touch with you as soon as we know anything."

"We'd appreciate that," Reed said taking the detective's hand. "Thanks for your help."

"Absolutely."

"Oh, uh . . ." Reed paused. "Where did they take the dog?"

"The gold Lab?" Everett asked.

"Yeah."

"To the pound. Have to wait and see if anyone claims her."

"And if no one does?"

"After a month, they have to destroy the animal."

"Oh. Well. I hope someone takes her. Thanks again."

After leaving the police station, Dale, Bettyanne, and Reed had to return to the Medical Examiner's office to make arrangements for transport of Devrie's body back to the Bay Area following the autopsy.

Reed looked over the preliminary report filed by Richard Glowski, the chief M.E.

The cause of death was believed to be blood loss due to multiple stab wounds to the chest and abdomen. The fetus had been in the way of at least one of the stabbing thrusts, and had been severely burned from the stick. Reed couldn't look at the report for more than a few seconds. The horror played itself over in his head, growing, somehow multiplying like a rampant virus. He handed the page back to Dr. Glowski.

"Uh, listen, Doctor," Reed said. "Can I ask you a favor?"

"Of course." The M.E. offered Reed a seat in his office.

"I, just wanted to ask you if you could let me know the gender of the fetus?"

Glowski ran a hand over his dark beard. "I'll tell the lab to send you a karyotype, if you want."

"Thanks."

Reed met Dale and Bettyanne in the front waiting area to face the logistical problem of how the three were going to get back to Marin County. The simple question rose like a daunting obstacle. Several reporters from area papers and news channels wanted to ask questions. It was all devouring the trio's unstable emotions.

"I'm fine to drive," Dale insisted. "I got us here, I can take us back."

Bettyanne protested, steadying herself on her husband's arm. "We can hire a driver," she said. "None of us is in any condition to drive just now."

"I'm driving," was all Dale said, pushing on the heavy glass doors, and through the newspeople. Such practical matters as expense, and competence to operate a motor vehicle were just about the only distractions from the immense trauma, so Dale actually welcomed the drive. Bettyanne and Reed relented to his stubbornness, and followed him out to the parking lot. Reed satisfied the press with a simple statement about what had happened, with the hope that someone who knew something, might see the report. In three hours, they were home, sitting in the Chouinard's living room, searching for the strength to eat.

Marc Seeth's voice lifted and fell on the whims of the hot dry wind. As Devrie's closest friend at Ellinwood Elementary, Marc had accepted the request to give the eulogy. As he spoke, the small cemetery looked crowded in the bright three o'clock sun. Reed saw the faces around him as if from inside a sealed bubble, as if witnessing the ceremony from inside someone else's battered body. Those who had been close to Devrie held each other's hands, those who hadn't just stood, eyes downcast with just enough solemnity to convey the appropriate degree of respect.

Reed's father Jared, his mother Margot, his stepmother Gail, and his sister Elsie were there, along with Devrie's extended family, encircling the rectangular hole in the ground that would receive the tasteful hardwood casket. Beyond the family were Devrie's friends and coworkers from her school, and only Reed's closest acquaintances.

The reason for the reunion with Reed's own family seemed tragically appropriate to him. It seemed always to take something extreme to get his family together during the fifteen years since he'd moved away from home, and he regretted the distance as he never had before. But standing next to him was the person to whom Reed felt the closest affinity, the person he felt somehow understood best—Wally Bohrs.

"If the flood waters rose up," Marc spoke, "she did not swim for safety, but guided others to the shore. If the Earth shook and crumbled buildings to the ground, she did not run for cover, but led others to the safety of shelter. This was Devrie. This was the person who molded young lives, gave them the power and desire to learn, to use their talents and intellects, as she did—to the utmost, each and every day. This was the person who crusaded against ignorance, while delighting in the adventure of life on this wondrous Earth. It will never be enough to state these or the millions of other truths that only in part describe the person Devrie Chouinard-Haler was. With her passing, Heaven finds itself a richer place indeed."

The service was thus concluded.

Shadows splayed across the verdant grounds as the procession wound its way out of the cemetery, and to Dale and Bettyanne's house.

Reed walked Wally to his car well after night had fallen, and everyone else had gone home.

The two men stood, leaning against the side of the Volvo for several minutes without speaking. Then Wally said, "Seems like it's always the best people who are taken away from us too soon."

"Yeah." Reed sighed.

"Anytime you need to talk, day or night, you call me." Wally placed a hand on each of Reed's shoulders and stared straight at him, past the swollen cheek and discoloration around the eyes, which were as much a result of crying as they were the beating he'd sustained. "You call me."

Reed nodded and embraced his friend. "Oh, God, Wal. Why? Why couldn't it have been me instead?" Reed made no effort to hide his tears, letting Wally hold him for as long as it took.

Then Wally said, "If it had been you, then Devrie would be saying exactly the same thing to me now."

At last Reed fought off the swollen heat of anguish, and nodded. "I wish to God there were something more I could do."

"I know, Wal. Thanks. Thanks so much."

Wally pulled away, his lips pressed together hard. "Oh and take as much time as you need, you know? I'll keep things on track at the lab. That's the last thing you need to worry about, okay?"

Reed nodded again.

"Good. Call me." Wally gave Reed's arm a final pat, then ducked into his car.

Reed stood at the end of the driveway long after the Volvo had disappeared down the hill. He wanted his eyes to dry before he went back inside.

NINE

Dr. Louis Canidey's gray suit jacket hiked up behind his neck whenever he leaned forward, which was most of the time as he spoke about the prospects of receiving money from the National Institutes of Health. The tall doctor twirled a chrome-plated ballpoint pen around on the conference room table as he spoke to the group of other doctors and local businesspeople who had gathered at Alamosa General to talk about money. He cleared his throat often, which disturbed Jessica, who, by the standards of protocol, was seated next to him.

"In answer to the question that everyone, of course, has in mind, is that we just don't know yet. The decision is pending. A lot of people are after those funds. I did my best. All we can do is wait, and pray to the good Lord. See what He says and what they say." Canidey swept a hand across the light coffee-brown skin of his forehead, flattening the swath of black hair that didn't quite hide the deep lines above his eyes.

One of the men sitting on the other side of the table was Mickey Sherman, a longtime owner of a number of highly profitable car dealerships in southern Colorado. He had been elected chairman of the Southern Colorado Benevolence Foundation, or SCBF. He represented the other two gentlemen and three women who were seated around the table.

"As you know," Mickey said in response to Dr. Canidey's report of his trip to the national symposium in San Francisco, "we agreed to a matching deal. So . . ." Mickey put his hands up, raising his peppery eyebrows, ". . . until we have something to match, I don't have an offer."

Jessica bit down on her tongue until it hurt. She knew, through years of fact-gathering, exactly how much money was needed, that the resources were there, and that there was sufficient public support for the project. "If I may," she said. The group turned its attention to Dr. Morraine. "I believe there was some mention, the last time we met, of a contingency plan, in the event the NIH didn't come through. What are the specifics of that?"

The opposing group, the enemy in Jessica's eyes, seemed to bristle collectively. Mickey spoke. "That contingency, as you refer to it, was if and when a final word was delivered from the NIH. Dr. Canidey pointed out that a decision is still pending. And remember one thing—we still have a commitment here to the hospital for an addition—now a year behind schedule."

"Yes, of course," Jessica acknowledged. "I haven't forgotten. Now assume the NIH says 'no,' Mr. Sherman. What do you say?"

Mickey leaned back in his chair and whispered something to one of his colleagues, a strong-looking woman who seemed more resistant than Mickey. The gray-haired man then leaned forward again.

"Let me just say that there's nothing we would like more than to see this hospital built. Sincerely. If I had my way, it would already be built, okay? I have three children of my own and five grand-children. But I can't do this alone. We have to look at our estimates, our other active concerns, the annual projections from various sources, investments, sales analyses . . . you understand."

The evasions were sending Jessica's temper off the chart. She kept herself just under control, like a strained pressure cooker. "Mr. Sherman. Do you have a figure or not?" The question was just short of a demand.

"Not . . . at this moment, Dr. Morraine. I'm sorry. If the news from Washington had been more definite, then . . ."

"When will you know?"

"Let's see what the NIH comes back with."

"Fine." Jessica realized that the meeting had stalled and any more discussion would only damage the tenuous relationship she'd man-aged to establish. "We'll keep you posted. Thanks for coming."

As the meeting adjourned, there was a conspicuous absence of handshakes and smiles. After the room had cleared and Jessica had collected her paperwork into her briefcase, she realized that Cani-dey was still sitting next to her.

"You're not praying hard enough," he said.

Jessica took her seat again, exhausted. "There you're wrong," she contested.

"No," he said with a smile. "You've got to open yourself to faith. Let it guide you. You're not letting it guide you, and it pains me, it really does."

"Louis," she began to protest, "you have your way of looking at things; I have mine. Don't tell me what to believe in, okay?" She got to her feet and headed for the door. Canidey followed right behind, speaking as the two walked down the hallway toward the hospital's elevators.

"I've seen your light, Jess. I've seen it. You've got a special gift. But you're not using it to your fullest advantage."

"Well, you haven't exactly turned in any stellar results yourself. How do you explain that?"

"I don't have your qualities. Ironic, isn't it? I have all the belief, and you have all the light."

Jessica was accustomed to Canidey's lectures about faith and the power of God, but they never failed to push her away more than draw her in. "Well, Louis, we'll just have to work around that, won't we?"

He shrugged. "Whatever happens, it's God's will. Remember that."

"I'll keep it in mind. Say, Louis?"

"Yes?"

"Do you think that God might want you to get back to your patients—back on your rounds? Taking care of the sick?"

"Uh uh uh," Canidey cautioned, wagging a finger in front of Jessica's face. "Never second-guess the Lord. There's work to be done."

"Oh, Jesus!" Jessica moaned just over her breath, as the elevator thankfully arrived.

TEN

The first time Reed set foot again in his own bedroom, his only intention had been to remove the bassinet he'd bought for his child . . . he'd ended up destroying it. Even though he'd been in the house with his immediate family for several days, he hadn't had the strength to go into the bedroom until after his relatives had gone back home. When he finally did enter the room—where he and Devrie had shared their greatest intimacies, had conceived their child, had spent countless languorous Sunday mornings in each other's arms—the gush of pure rage outweighed the hard ache in his bones as the light wooden frame of the bassinet relented and splintered in his hands, under his weight. The physical pain was so much easier to bear than what he endured in his heart. As he twisted and stomped on the broken pieces, mental images of the bassinet's rightful purpose, which it would never fulfill, tortured him beyond what he ever thought he could endure. Eventually there was little left to crush, and the exhaustion of grief overtook him. He dropped to the floor next to the heap of fractured wood and torn fabric that mimicked his own tortured body. A fresh purge of tears broke. He was glad that he'd waited, that his family wasn't around to witness this fit. They had kept Reed company, and he felt they'd all grown a little closer as a family, but their lives, of course, called them back to their homes, and Reed was at the point where he needed some time to himself in order to get Devrie's things sorted out. It was a task he dreaded more than anything he'd ever faced, but he knew that doing it was the first step toward healing. As he picked up two of the bassinet's wheels, which had broken off and rolled over the floor, he doubted that he'd ever really get beyond the emotional effects of his loss. That mountain was just too high, the burden too great. He lifted the pieces of the broken carriage and its amputated parts nonetheless, and carried them outside.

The remains of the bassinet safely bagged and contained in the garbage cans at the side of the house, Reed landed on the living room couch, and answered the ringing phone.

"Reed Haler, please," a husky male voice said.

"Speaking. Who's this?"

"Dr. Haler, this is Dr. Glowski in South Tahoe."

"Of course. How are you?" Reed greeted the medical examiner.

"Fair, to tell you the truth. Uh, I hope I'm not catching you at a bad time, but I wanted to get back to you about the gender of the fetus, if you still wanted to know."

"Oh, yes, certainly."

"Uh . . . it was a girl, Dr. Haler."

"A girl," Reed repeated. "I see." He caught himself in the briefest smile.

"I'll send you the final protocol and all the lab results."

"Thanks. I really appreciate it."

"Not at all. Listen, I wish you well. Call if I can do anything else for you."

"Thanks again. Good-bye." Reed cradled the phone and dug through his wallet for a card. He picked up the phone again and dialed.

"Detective Everett, please," Reed said when the voice answered.

"Everett," came back on the line a moment later.

"Detective, hi. Reed Haler."

"Dr. Haler. How are you doing?"

"Well, shitty actually. Listen, Detective, I'm just calling to see if you have anything new about . . ."

"Ahh," Everett delayed, "not much, I'm afraid. We got some ground impressions from the scene that corroborate the cowboy boots. But other than that, I'm afraid we've come up pretty empty."

"What about semen, hairs, stuff like that?"

"A few hairs we're processing now, but no semen."

"None?"

"Glowski found nonoxynol-nine, but no semen."

"Are you telling me he used a fucking rubber?"

"That's what we think."

"Jesus Christ!"

"We've put out a general description, but that hasn't turned up anything yet. We're right on this, Dr. Haler. It's still very early, you know."

"In other words you don't have shit."

"I don't need to sit here on the phone with you, Dr. Haler. We're doing everything we can, and I don't appreciate your choice of words."

"Yeah. Yeah, okay. I'm sorry."

"I promise I'll let you know as soon as I have anything. I know that this is an extremely hard time."

"Yeah. Thank you, Detective."

"You bet."

Reed clicked the hang-up button and dialed again. An answering machine connected on the other end.

"Hi," he said. "It's Reed. Anybody home?"

"Hello, Reed," Dale answered. "How are you?"

It was then that Reed noticed the red blots accumulating on his pants. He turned his arm to see the long gash which he hadn't even realized was there. "Uh. Not so well. I think I may need some help with this after all."

Bettyanne and Dale arrived about half an hour later. Dale sat in the living room, staring blankly at the television, while Reed and Bettyanne folded Devrie's clothes in the bedroom, and put them into boxes. Reed wore several bandages on his right forearm, having cut himself in a number of places during his fit of rage. He'd explained that he'd slipped in the bathroom.

"I don't know," had been his answer to Bettyanne's question about what he wanted to do with Devrie's things. "You and Dale should take the things that you want. I guess I'll just keep the rest in these boxes, somewhere. I mean what are you supposed to do with stuff like this?"

"I don't know either. I never thought I'd have to think about it."

Reed considered the items on top of Devrie's nightstand—the digital alarm clock, the novel she had been reading, several silver bracelets, and a small framed photograph of her and himself on a trip they'd taken to Europe. He decided to leave the things as they were. Inside the drawer, however, he found the journal and pulled it out.

"That," Bettyanne said, stepping over to her son-in-law, "you must never part with."

Reed sat on the edge of the bed, and turned the cover.

"Devrie kept that journal since she was seventeen years old."

Reed looked at the first few pages and the young girl's handwriting that had nearly faded away. He realized with a flood of guilt that he'd never really read any of it very carefully or seriously. He flipped through to the end.

"Even if you never believe in her premonitions, Reed, keep this close to you. It's a very special part of her. Don't ever lose it."

Reed had never heard the tone in Bettyanne's voice that he heard now. It was an earnestness that she must have been keeping in reserve, he thought as he looked down just catching the words at the bottom of the page: *Five million over five*; he closed the journal. "It will always be safe. I promise you."

Bettyanne placed a hand on Reed's and said, "You're the keeper of her soul on Earth. It's up to you to protect it."

Reed didn't ask her what she meant. It was enough for him to see that behind her tears, she was smiling . . . if only just a little.

H ours later Reed found himself alone once again in the house that was much too big for one person. He sat in his office swirling a glass, but not drinking any of the contents. His in-laws had gone home, and there was nothing left for him to do but sit . . . and think . . . and endure. His computer was off and his desk lamp provided the only light in the entire house. Although it was nearly midnight, sleep would be impossible for a while yet. He found his efforts at distracting himself with television or music simply too much to stand. It was easier just to sit in the quietest place he could find, and wait for never to come. He was about to slam the shot he held in his hand when a faint rustling found his ears. It had come from outside the house, he was sure of that, like an animal negotiating a fallen tree. He strained to hear it again, but the silence returned. He remembered the sound of the blond Lab slinking through the trees toward him. The similarity was unnerving. He carefully rested the glass on his desktop, and leaned forward in his chair. The metallic *tink tink tink* of the chair's springs relaxing registered like gunshots to Reed's heightened senses. It was difficult to tell from which direction the sound had come. He tilted his head in various attitudes to better hear. Then a low, hollow thump and a series of hurried steps confirmed that there was something moving around outside the house. Reed switched off the light on his desk, and crept to the window where he opened the blinds just enough to offer a limited view of the front yard. The space was empty save for the abundant greenery. The slam of a car door tore Reed's attention from the trees and to the street. Through the slats in the fence he saw headlights beam up in front of his residence. The engine started and Reed was running. He had to turn the corner carefully on the smooth tile of the entry vestibule in his stocking feet. He twisted the bolt on the front door and yanked the chain back. The car was moving away from the curb fast before Reed made it to the driveway and around the end of the high fence, which enclosed the lawn. He only detected a flash of color—the streak of a reflection under the orange tint of the street lamps—as the car wheeled around the first corner and away. He hadn't seen the car long enough to know even what the make was. The street was again deserted, the whine of the car's engine fast evanescing into the night.

Pausing on the grass before going back inside, Reed began to wonder if the sounds he'd heard before were even related to the car and its driver's hasty departure. There was the possibility, he thought, that there still could be something, or someone lurking in the dark. Suddenly a strange new form of guilt laced the surge of fear which gripped him. That he even felt fear for himself opened a bastard realm of shame. It meant that he still felt a capacity for happiness, that he might one day transcend the grief, find value in a life without his wife and child. He didn't admit openly that he harbored such feelings, but the fact that a chill of terror raced through him at the thought that an intruder might be threatening him in his home, left him no choice but to admit it to himself.

He saw no movement other than the slight wafting of leaves in the gentle westerly breeze, which brought the smell of the ocean. Cautiously he moved toward the side of the house where the shadows were thickest, but there was no indication now of any presence other than the wind.

An inspection of the perimeter of his property the next morning provided Reed no further information as to the sounds and events of the night before. There was no sign of trespass or vandalism. In the daylight it was a lot easier to attribute everything to overburdened nerves and the aftermath of trauma.

What was real, however, was the envelope which came in the early afternoon by Federal Express. Inside were several photocopied pages which made up the coroner's protocol and a single nine-by-twelve sheet of photographic film with regards from Dr. Richard Glowski, M.E. Reed studied the film—the karyotype, which displayed the forty-six chromosomes of his child. There they were, the two X chromosomes that would have given him a daughter. He examined every one of the little images of genetic material which hid their many secrets so well. He realized that he was beginning to think about work again as he stared at the hereditary DNA structures, half of which belonged to Devrie and half to himself.

"All perfect and normal," he said aloud, unable to take his eyes from the little X-shaped figures. "All perfect and . . . normal."

Reed's first thought as he stepped into his office on his first day back at work was the toast to Devrie's pregnancy he'd shared there with Wally. The cheese glasses, he remembered, were still in the bottom drawer of his desk, unwashed, smelling of stale champagne. He had to chase the memory away before it gained too much momentum, and smothered him. It was a constant battle. The big "welcome back" sign on his door had helped a little.

He dropped his briefcase off and went straight to Wally's workstation, where his associate was already busy looking at sample results from the weekend's tests.

"I wanted to have good news for you, but as you can see . . ." Reed looked over the data. Snip analysis of five hundred leukemic blood samples had still not shown a sufficiently common abnormality to indicate an absolute genetic factor in the disease.

"Wally?"

"Yeah?"

"Any chance we're diggin' in the wrong hole here?"

"What do you mean?"

"Well. We've only been looking for anomalies right?"

"Uh . . . yeah, that is the logical thing to do. You're not letting Tim Hon get to you, I hope."

"No, Wal. I'm not. But what if we started looking at normal, expected variations?"

"Oh . . . kay. Reed, you know if you need a few more days . . ."

"I'm serious, Wal. What if there's a commonality somewhere that we wouldn't normally consider unusual?"

Wally thought through the suggestion for a second, then: "You mean something that's not necessarily causal, but simply present in every case?"

"Yeah. Like a benign signature."

"Or what *appears* to be a benign signature?"

Reed nodded, his gaze intensifying.

"Oh, Whitaker's going to love this."

"Screw Whitaker."

"That's potentially billions of repeat sequences to test, Reed. You know how long it's taken the Human Genome Project to map the molecule. It could take years before we found it, if it's even there. And even if we did find it, where does that leave us as far as some kind of treatment? How would we even know if we found it? There's a lot of common variations out there."

Reed rubbed his chin. "I don't know. I don't know, Wal. But we're about out of options. Unless you've got any better ideas, let's get started."

"Started? What the hell are you talking about? Started on what? Where?"

"Let's try the beginning."

"I think we're going to need more than five million," Wally mumbled.

Reed had started to wander back into his office, but stopped at Wally's words. "What did you say?" he asked turning around.

"What?" Wally heard the suspicious tone in Reed's voice.

"What did you say?" Reed was again standing next to him.

"Nothing."

"Just tell me what you said."

"I said we're going to need more than five million. What's the matter?"

"Five million," Reed repeated to himself, now staring at some vague point in space.

"You know," Wally expanded. "The grant. Five million dollars over five years. That's supposed to be the deal."

"Yeah. Five years, is it?"

"Terms were proposed last week. They're not saying much upstairs, but it's starting to sound like we might get it, even if we come a little short of the ninety-five percent. A million a year isn't bad for a little department like ours."

"Right. Not bad." Reed still didn't meet Wally's prying look.

"You all right?"

"Yeah. I'm fine, Wally. Let's get going. We need that money, right?"

"Yes, we certainly do."

Slowly Reed wandered back into his office, leaving Wally completely baffled as to what he ought to do next.

Reed yanked the drawer open as soon as he landed on the edge of the bed. He found the line from the journal quickly. There it was in her scrawled blue ballpoint handwriting: *Five million over five.*

He'd never told Devrie to his best recollection how much the pending grant was for. Or had he? He couldn't remember, but he was damn sure that he'd never mentioned the time span over which the money was to be paid, because he hadn't even known himself until that morning. *Five million over five.* What else could it mean? Nothing. Nothing that he could guess, at least.

Reed leafed back through the pages and began going through the dozens of entries. He read each one with new interest. The account of Devrie's knowledge that her parents were returning home early from a party the night she lost her virginity now bore unexpected weight. The verbatim citing of the *Chronicle* headline about the Gulf War—fully two years to the day before it was printed—vibrated on the page. The many pages that followed didn't strike anything of particular note in Reed's mind until he came to the words: *I'm pregnant with a girl.* His fingers touched the words lightly, pausing as if to make some connection with that which should have been. Then he turned the page. It looked like a sick joke at first, but he knew it wasn't. What he read constricted his shoulders as if by cables of freezing steel. His stomach clenched into a hard knot; his chest boomed the air from his lungs. He checked the date and shook his head, unable to believe his eyes. There, written only two weeks before their camping trip, at the top of the page, squeezed in above the entries that followed, almost as if it were an afterthought, it said: *My baby is going to die.*

"No." He said fully out loud. "*NO!*" He slammed the book closed, clutching it tightly in his hands, the tears coming freely. A conflagration raged in his head. Why had he doubted her? Why? He beat himself mercilessly with the single word question, as if torturing himself would somehow correct a flawed world. Eventually he found the courage and strength to open the journal again. It both compelled and terrified him.

Scarcely able to breathe, he consumed the page of entries preceding the one about their baby dying:

Cavalier.

"She must be hungry."

Red boots.

Blue rocks.

Fear.

18(p11; q6).

Telomere.

Red boots and *blue rocks* snagged his eyes like barbed wire. The first thing he'd seen when he woke up on the ground after the attack were blue emergency lights streaking across the rocks of the fire pit. His body trembled; the truth was landing hard. Hundreds of questions dashed through his brain. Had she seen the attack in her mind, days before it happened? If she had, he wondered, why would she have gone on the trip and taken such a terrible chance? Perhaps the details of her murder had been mere words with no specific meaning that she could determine, no particular association with the time or place it happened. Or perhaps she had thought going would somehow be safer than staying at home. And *18(p11; q6)* was a form of technical genetic notation, identifying specific locations on the eighteenth chromosome. And *telomere*. Reed knew something about telomeres. They were part of the human chromosomal structure. He had read something about research into a correlation between the length of telomeres and the aging process, but it didn't have much bearing on his own work. What it meant in terms of his wife's journal, he had no idea. At the bottom of the page he found the entry he had seen the day Bettyanne had come over to help him box Devrie's things: *Five million over five.* On the next page, after the entry about her fears of death, came a series of nine additional entries, all written in unusually tidy lines, but which made no sense to him:

> *Ones with guns are blind in the dark.*
> *Where there's a tear, there's light.*
> *Shbyi'aye from the sky, sees, hears and smells.*
> *Morning stories fall from mourning glories.*
> *Dry waves lie in the Blood of Christ.*
> *Slain in train yard.*
> *See that she is the next of life's soldiers.*
> *No moon's glow in the middle of summer.*
> *Forbidden, forever hidden inside the trunk.*

That's where the journal ended. Reed studied the entries for a long time, trying to discern some kind of meaning. He found a pad of paper and a pen, and copied all the entries which were on the final two pages. Taking care to transpose the spellings and word placements exactly as they appeared in the journal, he noticed that "morning" and "mourning" were reversed in the fourth of the final nine entries. He placed question marks beside all those he didn't understand, and put circles around *18(p11; q6)* and *telomere*. Then, reverently, he put the journal back in its drawer, and picked up the phone.

"Wally," he said when the familiar voice answered.

"Reed?"

"Yeah, listen, I want you to do something for me."

"What ya need?"

"If you can hang in there a little longer tonight, I'd like you to run a FISH on the most recent samples. Let's take a look at 18(p11; q6). We're going to have to sequence that entire region. Sorry to ask you to do this right now."

"Oh. That's okay. I guess I don't have anything better to do tonight." The friendly sarcasm rang loud and clear.

"Please, Wal. For me."

"Can I ask why that particular spot?"

"I'm not sure yet. If you don't mind—"

"Sure sure."

"It's just a hunch. Thanks, Wal."

"Okay, you got it, Jack Charlie."

Reed hung up the phone, and looked back at his list. "What the hell is going on here?" he said to himself. Then instinctively he listened. There had been no repeat of the odd nocturnal sounds outside the house since the first episode two nights before. But each day as the light faded from the sky and the wind came up from the sea, he expected it as much as he feared it. This time it failed to come. The thought occurred to him that he'd spent far too many hours lying awake in bed . . . waiting and listening. He pulled the drawer open again and took out the journal. He touched its soft cover lightly, then placed it, carefully and lovingly, inside his briefcase.

R eed was in the lab by seven o'clock the next morning, as was Wally, sipping a cup of strong, hot coffee, and expecting an explanation.

"How we coming?" Reed asked when he stepped through the door.

"Film should be ready in a couple of hours. So, you gonna tell me what this hunch is all about?"

"Eventually."

"Hmm. Reed?"

"Yeah?"

"I don't mean to sound insubordinate, but . . . this new approach of yours is . . . well, frankly it's kinda nutty. This isn't a needle in a haystack, this is a dust particle somewhere in outer space."

"I know, Wal. Just humor me for a few more hours, okay?"

"This I can do." Wally got up from his chair, and walked over to Reed, who was fumbling for his office keys. "But if your hunch doesn't turn up anything today, then I've got to be honest with you . . ."

"Fair enough, Wal. That's fair enough. If we don't find anything significant, I'll drop it." Reed stuffed the key into the doorknob.

"But, Reed . . ."

Reed pushed the door open and turned back to Wally.

". . . if it does turn up something interesting . . . you'd better damn-well tell me where you came up with it."

Reed smiled. "Eventually." He proceeded into his office, and sat down at his desk.

A little after lunch the initial analyses were complete. Wally called Reed in his office and asked him to come out to his work station.

"Well?" Reed asked, when he got there.

Wally was looking over the results of the ten samples he'd used for the FISH assays. He looked up at Reed with a combination of elation and a close cousin of worry.

"Okay. I guess that's one for our side. There are common snips in all ten samples. Across a 10kb range at p11 and at q6, it's on both eighteenth chromosomes in every case."

"Okay. Make probes for both and get everybody on this. We've got a lot of work to do."

"Reed?"

"Yeah?"

"Don't you think you should tell Whitaker before you go launching the team into a brand new direction of research?"

"Oh . . . yeah. Hey, thanks, Wal."

"Sure." Wally made no effort to hide the odd suspicion he now felt. "I hope we're onto something here."

"Me too." Reed gave Wally a little smile, then went back into his office. He closed the door.

The following day Reed let Wally handle starting the preliminaries of the new strategy; his own mind was elsewhere, trapped between the lines of his wife's journal.

As the morning slipped by, Reed thought comparatively little of the promising new development in his research. He placed the great majority of his energies in trying to draw some meaning from Devrie's words. He was satisfied that they meant something significant, that they told of the future. He went on the assumption that there was a purpose to them, a purpose which would either reveal itself, or which he would have to seek.

He only stepped from his office when the need to visit the men's room became more than a nuisance. The rest of the lab staff were making the motions of going to lunch.

"Hey," he heard Wally say, "Let me get you a bite."

"Mmm. You go ahead, I've got some catching up to do," Reed answered.

"You sure? You know, you shouldn't stay cooped up in there for too long at a time."

"I know, Wal. I'm fine. It's just some work, you know."

"Sure. Oh, uh, what did Whitaker say?"

Reed pointed a straight index finger at the ceiling. "One of the things still on my 'to do' list."

"Oh. So, he doesn't know what we've been doing all morning?"

"He will, Wal."

Wally dispatched Reed a woefully troubled look. "What's going on, Reed? I mean, I know you're going through some really rough shit, but . . . I'm getting something more here."

"Wal, that's all it is. It's some really rough shit. I don't expect you to understand it."

Wally made the pretense of accepting the delay tactic and moved toward the door. Reed offered a reassuring smile, and then proceeded down the hallway to the bathroom.

When he heard the sounds of returning personnel through his closed door, Reed snapped out of his mental cocoon and lifted the telephone's handset. "Hello, Marty please. Thanks." Reed tapped a finger rapidly on his desktop while he waited for his boss to pick up the line.

"Whitaker," the familiar voice said.

"Hi, Marty. It's Reed. Listen, I need to talk to you about something kind of important."

"Okay."

"Are you going to be in your office for another half hour?"

"I'll be here. Come up right now if you like."

"Now is good. See ya." Reed collected some notes and took a swift pace out the door.

Martin Whitaker's office was on the tenth floor of the genetics building of the San Francisco University Medical Center. The dull white floor tiles were worn down to dark brown patches on either side of the threshold. In one wall a generous window overlooked Golden Gate Park; the wall opposite was coated with framed degrees. Whitaker sat behind his mammoth oak desk, a hand buttressing his chin, the elbow seated firmly into the cushioned armrest. Surrounding the senior genetics professor was a horseshoe of bookshelves, loaded to capacity with many volumes, a good percentage of which he'd authored himself.

"Grants don't get awarded for hunches, Reed," Whitaker said by way of response, after Reed outlined the latest findings concerning the snip at 18(p11; q6).

"I know that. But I think we can prove that it's more than a hunch. We've already shown commonality in ten random samples, and I'm pretty certain that we may find it in all the samples we have on file."

"Why?"

The question landed like a bag of potatoes.

"I'm not sure yet. But, believe me, it's worth the effort to see if it's true."

"This is precious little to go on, Reed. You're proposing diverting a lot of resources at an extremely critical time. If that grant gets away . . ."

"I understand what's at stake, Marty. You know that very well. I would never go out this far unless I felt damned sure it was worth it."

"Give me one way I can justify it, Reed. What makes you think this particular sequence has anything to do with disease?"

Reed had expected this, but he'd failed to come up with a very good answer, and one wasn't coming now. "If I can show you that two hundred of two hundred samples express the snip by say . . . Wednesday, would that be justification enough?"

"And if you don't get the desired results, I've lost half a week. What do you expect me to say, Reed? Without a sound basis for the investigation in the first place, it's very suspect. Where the hell did you come up with this site, anyway?"

"I . . . I'm not really sure . . . I know it's thin, Marty, but I just can't tell you anything more than that yet."

"The idea had to come from somewhere."

"Call it a happy accident . . . Can I have the time?"

"*Three hundred* of *three hundred new* samples, and you have till Monday lunchtime. Show me that, and we'll talk about it further. And progress continues apace on our real work here. NIH may be coming around. We can't compromise that. Got it?"

"Monday." Reed sighed. "That only gives me the weekend."

"And tomorrow, and whatever's left of today."

Reed stretched out his hand to Whitaker who shook it reluctantly. "Okay. Monday . . . lunch. Thanks."

"And Reed . . ."

"Yeah?"

"If this 'happy accident' turns out to be just an ordinary, *un-*happy accident . . . well, I'll have no choice but to open Tim's proposal for reconsideration."

"Tim's proposal?" It began to dawn on Reed that the NIH's sudden change of heart might have something to do with his rival.

"Give me one reason not to, Reed."

"That's what I'm trying to do." Reed got to his feet as quickly as he could, hoping to escape the office before Whitaker could impose any more conditions.

"Oh, Reed . . ."

His hand had barely reached the doorknob when he had to turn back to his boss.

Whitaker cleared his throat. "I expect a full write-up along with the results. I want an explanation."

"Of course." Reed pulled the knob and started to take a step out when: "Just one other thing, Reed . . ."

Again he had to look back. "Hmm?"

"Glad to see you back." Whitaker passed him a genuine smile.

"Oh. Thanks. Thanks a lot." Reed couldn't quite return the smile. But he nodded, then slipped out the door.

R eed had to divide his staff into two groups, one of which would continue the established line of inquiry. The other would be responsible for probing the two hundred and ninety additional DNA samples for the common sequence on the eighteenth chromosome. In order to meet Whitaker's Monday deadline he'd had to convince his staff to work through the weekend. Tim Hon appointed himself spokesman for dissenting opinion. But with approval from Whitaker, the supplementary work would be carried out despite Hon's protests.

When Reed again dropped into his chair, he called Wally in for a strategy meeting.

"With four people on it, I can run eighty samples a day," Wally reported.

Reed shook his head. "Then you and I will stay after hours to make up the difference." It wasn't so much a suggestion as a simple statement of fact. Reed held Wally's attention with a look of absolute resolve to complete the task.

Wally rubbed his tired eyes. "That's assuming we still come up empty in the areas we're *supposed* to be analyzing?"

"I'd like to see what kind of percentage we get in any event," Reed pressured. He could tell that Wally had serious misgivings, both about his new idea and about spending the weekend at work.

"Look, we only need to do twenty-five or so runs apiece, and we've got three days to do it."

"That's including today."

"Yes, including today."

"Okay, Reed. Whatever. But I hope you work this thing out, whatever it is you're going through . . . and soon."

"Wally," Reed said with a smile, "Dinner, *Chez Panisse*, on me when this is over."

"I'll hold you to it."

After Wally had left, Reed went back to the journal entries. They held no more meaning now than they had before, and it seemed that no amount of reading the words was going to spark any new clues. But he continued to read and reread them . . . in spite of everything.

R eed didn't get home until after midnight. Instead of going to bed, he went into his office and turned on the computer. He'd decided to let Detective Everett know about the journal and so typed a letter:

Dear Detective Everett,
I'm faxing you this letter in the hope that the attached

information might provide some insight into the case of my wife's murder. I myself can discern no usable intelligence from the several notes, but perhaps those of you involved in the investigation can. I will say only that I have reason to believe that my wife had foreknowledge that our child was going to be killed (her own death as a consequence) as you can see from the first entry (please note the date). These—"predictions," if you will—come from a journal my wife had kept for over thirteen years. I am convinced that she had the ability to anticipate future events, and suspect that the nine entries following the one explicitly concerning our daughter's death may have something to do with the event, or the murderer, or both. I could be completely mistaken and I realize, of course, that this is a wild and blind grasp in the dark, which will in all likelihood lead to nothing. I am only sending you this information on the slim chance it will illuminate matters in some respect, no matter how slightly. Thank you for your time and attention.

Sincerely,
Reed Haler

Reed proofread the letter, then typed the journal entries in question. When he was satisfied, he dug through his wallet for Everett's fax number, and transmitted the letter. He didn't expect the police to believe that his wife had made psychic predictions concerning her murder or the perpetrator. But if anything in the journal helped identify the killer, it wouldn't matter what they believed.

When the fax had gone through successfully, Reed switched off the machine. The room fell quiet and very still. The brass door handle reflected the light of the single desk lamp into his eyes. He expected to see the handle turn, and the door open, as it had so many times. Devrie would be standing on the other side. She would then walk into the room and sit down on his lap. Her lips would feel soft against his, her body warm and welcoming. There they would tell each other about their days, sharing the minutiae of their lives. The worries and woes would ease, the burden of responsibility would lighten, and the strength to get through it would return. The brass handle reflected the light. Reed's mind was no longer occupied with worries about strange noises coming from outside. The room was quiet and very still . . . so quiet that one could hear the tears as they landed.

ELEVEN

The first news came at twenty after two Saturday afternoon. Of all the one hundred and five DNA samples probed the previous day, all expressed the desired snip. That brought the total up to one hundred and fifteen. Reed took the news without surprise, a marked contrast to Wally and the rest of the staff's astonishment.

"Let's keep moving as fast as we can," had been Reed's only verbal directive. That night eighty more samples were in the "oven" and Reed and Wally were preparing another fifty. That would leave sixty-five to complete the next day, and the results could be formalized and submitted to Whitaker. Reed was now certain that it was a simple matter of staying on schedule and preparing the paperwork. He chose not to speculate about what would happen after that.

He noted the time on his watch when he and Wally placed the final batch of the day into the hybridization chamber. It was one thirty in the morning. The pouches under Wally's eyes sagged, his shoulders looked too heavy, and he needed a shave in the worst way.

"Get out of here. I'll see you in the morning," Reed said, encouraging his partner to the door.

"What about you?" Wally returned, his expression suspicious.

"I need to get a jump on this paperwork, and do some follow up stuff on the other team. See where they are. But go get some sleep, and thanks a lot for fucking up your weekend for me."

Wally just nodded, clearly unsatisfied, and a little resentful of Reed's secretiveness. He lifted his shoulder bag off the coatrack, and stepped out the door.

Reed did, in fact, have paperwork to start—and finish. He didn't need to see the results of the remainder of the tests to know how they would turn out. Going home again felt like more than he could bear, so he proceeded to complete the formal write-up as Whitaker had insisted. He would keep the report hidden until it was time to submit it, and add the appropriate date then.

By four A.M. it was done, and Reed made himself as comfortable as he could on the small couch in the faculty lounge.

The sounds of the weekend cleaning crew arriving woke Reed at around eight-fifteen. He washed his face in the bathroom, and tried to straighten his clothes as well as he could. Two cups of coffee later he was back in his office, making sure that what he'd written the night before was comprehensible. It all looked good, if somewhat evasive. He knew that Whitaker would try to pin him down about specifics, but those would have to come later, when and if Reed himself knew what they were. For now, all that was left was to verify his predrawn conclusions.

Wally was there by nine-thirty, and the rest of the staff who were loyal to Reed by ten. Immediately Wally set the team to work on the last sixty-five samples, which had arrived by special delivery in their liquid nitrogen-cooled cylinders at nine fifty-five.

The knock on Reed's office door was intentionally loud. Wally didn't wait for Reed to ask him in, he simply closed the door behind him and sat down in front of Reed's desk, direct and determined.

"Why don't you have a seat, Wal," Reed said, revealing a little smirk of sarcasm.

"Christ, Reed . . . you look really terrible."

"Oh. I thought I was hiding it pretty well."

"You're not."

"Thank you. Now was there anything else?"

"Yeah, there is. I'm just about as sure as you are that these last sixty-five samples are going to show positive results. Now I want to know why."

Reed gave him a strained smile. "Yeah. I know, Wal. I wish I had a good answer for you."

"All right, knock off the crap, Reed. How did you know about this?"

Reed had never seen Wally this agitated. "I know I owe you an explanation, Wal. I just . . . You're going to find it a little hard to digest, that's all."

"I have an iron stomach. Come on, Reed. Enough of this mystery shit."

"All right, Wal . . . all right. But it doesn't go beyond this room, and you're the only person I'm going to tell. I can't even let Whitaker know. Not right now anyway. I have to trust you completely. Can I?"

"Reed. It's me, come on. You're starting to spook me."

Reed opened his briefcase and produced the clothbound book. He turned to the page bearing the genetic notation, and handed it to Wally.

"What the hell is this?"

Reed pointed to the operative entry, and explained to Wally what he was looking at. It didn't go over smoothly.

"You're telling me that Devrie knew about this snip?" Wally didn't know what else to ask; his difficulty in accepting the vague explanation was apparent.

"That's just it, Wal. She had no idea what she was writing down. It just came to her, like the rest of the crazy things in there. I don't know what most of them mean, and she didn't either. She just wrote them down. But they do mean something, Wal. Obviously they do."

"Oh, this is good. We just found a major component, maybe even the key to this disease, and who knows how many others, and we can't even say how we knew where it was."

"You think I'm having any easier a time buying this than you are?"

"What the hell are you going to tell Whitaker?"

"Anything but the truth. Got any suggestions?"

"Yeah. Think of something soon."

Reed sat in the car just staring at the house. Somehow it was getting harder, not easier, to be in the home that he had built with Devrie. He'd spent the last two days at the lab, sleeping in the faculty lounge. He'd left the final results and formal report on Whitaker's desk for him to find first thing in the morning. Three hundred of three hundred random DNA samples. He'd beaten the deadline by a whole day, and in so doing had managed to avoid explaining the source of the "hunch" to Whitaker. Sooner or later, though, he'd have to come up with something a little better than a "happy accident."

But for the moment he had the afternoon off, and intended to prolong the weekend for a least a few more days. He squeezed the steering wheel of the Acura, and pulled the key from the ignition. He'd have to go inside sometime, he resolved, cracking the car door to a whoosh of warm air. The afternoon sun was intense, glaring.

The yard was browning; the plants were large but drooping. He'd watered nothing in weeks.

Maybe a little yardwork would be good for him. He let a lead foot drop to the driveway. His whole body felt heavy, as if the earth's gravity had somehow doubled. Pulling himself out of the car, he dragged his briefcase along and nudged the door shut with his foot. He stood, winded, sore. The sun felt good on his shoulders. It was time. He gripped the leather handle of the case, and put up the emotional defenses he would need. Blocking out conscious thoughts, he walked the little stone path to the door, the key clamped in his sweaty hand.

Having the TV on was a necessity, the volume up nice and loud—even through the stupid commercials. On the cut glass coffee table in the living room, his bare feet rested next to a full bottle of Jack Daniels. Next to that was a glass with melting ice in it. The liquor had seemed like a good idea at first, but he associated alcohol with celebrating, and that was now a distant part of the past.

So he sat, staring at the endless car ads that saturated the afternoon advertising market. He tried to watch the news, but every story seemed to be about some terrible disaster or horrible crime, so he switched the channel, landing on a talk show. He forced himself to push the *mute* button on the remote control—it was time to call Everett. The line picked up after several rings. Reed asked for the detective who promptly answered.

"Good afternoon, Detective. I wanted to follow up and ask you if you received the fax I sent." Reed watched the voiceless heads on the TV screen. A heavyset woman with fiery red hair was speaking about something that must have been very serious indeed, judging from the audience reaction shots.

"Yeah, uh, Dr. Haler, I did get the fax and I circulated the information. I have to tell you, though, it doesn't make any more sense to us here than it does to you—"

"Yeah, yeah. I didn't really think it would." The picture on the TV screen was now of a dirt road, which ran through a heavily forested area. Then a police officer walked off the road and into the trees, pointing. A mug shot flashed on the screen. Reed recognized the face from a news broadcast of ten months before. It was of a man named Howard Henny, who'd murdered his wife. The redhead walked at the officer's side, pointing as well.

"If you would, please," Reed continued, "just keep it in mind. I know it seems pretty off the wall . . ."

"Oh no. We'll keep it in mind."

Reed could hear the condescension in Everett's voice. "Detective, please take this seriously."

"Dr. Haler. I know you want this guy caught. Believe-you-me, we do too. You've had a hell of a shock. We're doing all we can, and you've just got to be a little bit patient."

"Thank you. Good-bye." The receiver clapped into place. He didn't know exactly what he'd expected from the phone call, but it left him more despondent than ever. He pushed the *mute* button again as the redhead was describing a location in the woods: ". . . and I knew that she was by a well, or a small brick structure of some kind. Maybe inside it." Then the police officer came back on: "I knew that there had been a mining operation in that area over a hundred years ago, but as far as I knew there was nothing left of the place. I knew roughly where it was, so we started off in that direction."

"As we walked," the redhead continued, "I knew we were heading the right way. I began to see the woman. I felt the terror she'd suffered. She was dead. I knew that too. She was upside-down somehow, in a small space. Again I saw bricks."

"As we got closer, I could tell that Maysie was getting more and more upset," the police officer said. "Then she pointed up a hill and she became very disturbed. I'll never forget what she said: 'The body is in a hole at the top of this hill.' We climbed up the hill and found a hole, only two feet wide, and lined with bricks. From the smell I knew we had found the body. I shined my flashlight down that hole, and I saw two feet sticking up about ten feet down."

Reed took a newly heightened interest in the story. As he watched, he learned that this large, red-haired woman was Maysie Fabrioso. She claimed to be a psychic, and had an impressive track record to prove it. Evidently she had helped police in many criminal investigations over the years, most notable of which was the How-ard Henny murder case. Previously Reed would have switched the channel immediately. Now he absorbed the story like the desert floor under the first autumn rain. He found out that Maysie Fa-brioso lived and operated out of a small town in Tennessee called Cowhollow. Reed wrote the woman's name and the name of the town on a notepad. The journal entries tumbled around in his head. He'd now memorized them, keeping them close in his mind. A possible meaning emerged as he reviewed them: *Ones with guns are blind in the dark.* He thought of his letter to Everett. He'd used the words blind and dark. He wondered if the *ones with guns* were the police. They did have guns, and they were in a sense *blind.* So the police were blind, what else was new? He considered the next entry: *Where there's a tear, there's light.* What tear? What light? He considered again what he knew: The police were blind. That meant that they would be of no help, unless perhaps this *light* could be found. *Where there's a tear* . . . There had been a lot of tears lately, all over the place. His next idea came to him in the most obvious way; he literally had only to turn his head to see it. Maysie Fabrioso—a psychic. Reed bolted up the stairs toward the bedroom to search for the old tattered road atlas that he and Devrie had used on . . . their camping trip! It was still inside the 4Runner—in South Lake Tahoe, he realized. He checked his watch: ten to four. He would make a quick change of clothes, and with a little coffee, he could be in Tahoe by seven.

He opened the door to the bedroom and stopped before he even had one foot inside. What he saw dropped him to his knees. His lungs failed and his heart seized. In a single moment he felt the combustible mixture of raging sorrow and raw terror. Piled in the center of the bed were the remains of the bassinet, its fractured wooden members dumped in a heap. On top, a piece that had been one of the side rails bore a mark. Reed crouched low, as if taking cover from gunfire. He crawled to the side of the bed, resisting the sight of the pile with all his will, but it wouldn't go away. Now he saw what the mark was. Crudely carved into the wood were the letters A-L-A-N-A. He retracted, backing away in an instinctive, involuntary retreat. He could only get to his feet again when he was outside the door. As he stumbled down the stairs, nearly tripping with each step, he glimpsed through the archway to the kitchen, the glistening sparkle of glass fragments. Wind played with the diaphanous sheers that hung over the large rectangular opening above the kitchen sink. Reed stood, nothing between his eyes and the backyard, the crunch of glass splinters under his feet. He whirled around, certain that he would find the attacker behind him, wielding the deadly blade, intent on finishing a job not yet completed. There was no one. Reed spun around again, jumping at noises that existed only in his besieged imagination.

He ran to the front door and out, down the stone path to the driveway. This time there was no car parked by the curb, yet all around was the palpable sensation of eyes upon him.

After he hastily nailed a scrap of plywood over the depaned kitchen window, and swept up the shattered pieces, Reed burst into his office, and scooped up the phone.

"Everett," the detective answered.

"Hello, again, Detective. Reed Haler. Listen, I was wondering if you're still needing to hold on to my car." Reed had to consciously keep his words slow and clear, his breathing steady.

"Oh. Yes, the 4Runner. I suppose not. You need it back?"

"I need something that's inside it, actually."

"I think we've gotten just about all we're going to get from it, so if you need it back, feel free to come get it. But we may need it again at some point if the situation warr—."

"If I got there this evening, between say seven and eight, could I pick it up then?"

"I don't see why not. There's always somebody here."

"Thanks." Reed dropped the handset back in place, and stepped to a cabinet under a wall unit of bookshelves. Inside he found his Polaroid camera. There was still one shot remaining. He ran upstairs to the bedroom. This time he charged in and went straight to the broken jumble of wood. Looking through the camera, he brought the lens in tight on the carved letters that spelled his daughter's name. The flash popped, and the camera spewed the photo out. The image developed slowly, the letters appearing gradually, their colors strengthening by degrees. After another minute, for whatever it was worth, the evidence stood clear and legible in his hand. Then his eyes fixed on the closed closet door. The rush swelled in his chest. He hadn't searched the house since discovering the bassinet, assuming that the intruder had come and gone during the night. He'd noticed nothing missing or anything else out of place. But the closet loomed suddenly as a distinct and obvious hiding place. As Reed approached the closet, he listened intently for any sound that would tell of a presence inside. The quiet was absolute save his own breath. He reached for the knob, which he nearly believed felt oddly warm in his hand. Turning it, he felt the latch click like an electric shock in his palm. He swung the door open, not in a lightning swift motion, but as if he had been seeking a clean shirt. Inside his clothes hung neatly and in order, exactly as he'd left them. The closet was uninhabited.

He didn't bother to search further. He picked up the phone and dialed 911, but when the operator came on the line, he only heard the words of Devrie's journal in his mind: The police were in a sense *blind*, useless, like the police in Tahoe had been. His only instinct at that moment was to get out of the house. If the intruder were still inside, hiding, waiting for the ideal opportunity, Reed imagined himself lying dead on the floor for the officers to find. He looked at the Polaroid again, then at the crushed object on the bed. The operator was asking if anyone was there. Reed held fast to the picture and dropped the phone; his impulse was to run, and so he did, stopping at the bottom of the stairs only to retrieve Devrie's journal from his briefcase. He slid the Polaroid into the book, just inside the back cover.

The tires squeaked as Reed pulled back into the street. Pounding the accelerator, he sped away, making a number of random turns on the possibility that he was still being watched, pursued . . .

PART II

The odor of vinyl will be the first thing she will smell when he releases his grip from her face. It will be the smell of a car seat. She'll know that she's in the back, lying face up, staring at the low ceiling. His enormous hand will press hard on her chest and belly, while the sound of tearing fabric hits her ears. Then his legs will take over for his hands, pinning her under his immovable weight. Something else will cover her mouth ... something strong, like glue—or tape. Yes, it will be tape. He'll wrap the wide strip all the way around her head three times before he will proceed to wrap her wrists, not three but eight times. Then her ankles and feet—ten wraps, then her knees—twelve wraps. Her arms will press hard against her sides as the tape goes around her body . . . fifteen times, perhaps more. She'll be completely trapped in the sticky binding, able to do nothing but breathe in just enough air through her nose to remain conscious. He'll tell her not to struggle, to relax. He'll close the back door gently, then get into the driver's seat. The springs under the cushion will squeak as he settles himself. The car will start with a deep rumble, and she'll feel the bumps under the wheels as he drives. She'll have to pee and won't be able to hold it. The warm flow between her legs will puddle under the small of her back. She'll be terrified that this will make him even more angry.

TWELVE

Reed took the fastest route that he knew onto the highway toward Lake Tahoe. After several miles of traveling well over the speed limit, he finally slowed down. He made continual checks in the rearview mirror. He saw a number of cars that could have been the one he saw speed away from his house, but there was nothing particularly suspicious about any of them.

Once he was fully beyond the scope of the Bay Area and into the rolling, more sparsely populated farmlands of the Central Valley, he made a sudden but deliberate turn off the highway. He drove about thirty yards down a straight gravel road, then U-turned, pulling over to the side once he was facing the state route he'd been on. He rolled forward slowly until his position granted an adequate view. He parked and waited, assessing each car that passed, looking for any hesitation, any notice on the part of the other drivers that he'd left the main road. There he sat and there he waited for the car that would suddenly screech to a halt, reverse back to the turnoff, and continue the hunt. But no such event happened in the twenty minutes Reed idled and watched.

Finally he felt satisfied that he was not being followed, and in just a little over three hours he was riding along the south shore of Lake Tahoe.

The sun had just set and the mountain air had grown cool. He remembered that he had a light jacket in the 4Runner as well. The vehicle, which he hadn't even thought about since his wife's murder, now dealt a foreboding gloom in his mind—so close to the hell he still suffered, so much a symbol of the horror. Just being in the Tahoe area again brought back the place, the night, the stench of the faceless killer—the smell of his own fear.

Everett had gone home for the day when Reed arrived at the station house. A southerly wind whipped the cords against the steel flagpole with a jangling, uneven rhythm. The desk sergeant took Reed's request, and passed it up the line. A few minutes later another officer came down the hall, and reached out a hand to Reed.

"Dr. Haler, I'm Sergeant Colwin. Detective Everett told me you might be coming by. I just need you to sign these release papers, and I need to see some I.D. Then I'll take you over to the lot."

Reed took the release forms and signed. Afterward he followed Colwin to the police impound lot where the Toyota sat with half a dozen other cars. The keys were in the ignition, and the road atlas was in the door pocket on the passenger side.

"Dr. Haler?" Sergeant Colwin said through the driver's side window, with a light tap of his knuckles against the glass. Reed turned to the sergeant, lowering the window.

"Yeah?"

"You come here in another car?"

"Yeah."

"You park it out front?"

"Yeah."

"You with somebody who can drive it back for you?"

"No."

"Were you planning on driving both cars at the same time?"

"Hmm. You know where I can keep it parked for a little while?"

"Uh. Yeah, there's a public lot across the state line a couple miles down the road."

"Good enough."

Reed got directions to the parking lot from Sergeant Colwin, and drove the 4Runner out the gate. He parked it on the street across from the station house, and then drove the Acura to the private lot. The establishment offered hourly, daily, or monthly rates. Reed paid the attendant the two hundred dollars for a month of parking privileges, and started the hike back. As he walked through the small mountain community, past the big hotels and casinos that shot out of the sidewalks at literally the exact point where California became Nevada, he wasn't sure what he was doing there, or even what his plan was. He was just walking.

The creased, limp, food-stained and out-of-date atlas had guided him and Devrie on many road trips over the years. It had taken him across the country and back on more than a few occasions. Its familiarity warmed his emotions as he thought back to some of the best times of his life. Before starting the car, he flipped on the overhead dome light, and tabbed through the pages to the map of Tennessee. The page was torn almost completely in half. He had to piece the two sides together as he searched for Cowhollow. He scanned the right side of the rip, and then the left, finding no such town. He resorted to using the grid index. The coordinates led him to an area near the center of the map . . . right on the tear. In fact, the town's name was almost perfectly bisected. His mind went back to the journal: *Where there's a tear, there's light.* He had noticed the rhyming scheme of the last nine entries, but hadn't given it much thought before. Now it clarified one important thing: *tear* rhymed with *where*. He had been thinking of the tear that rhymes with near. *Where there's a tear . . .* He was suddenly sure he'd found the *tear*—Cowhollow, Tennessee. But would it lead him to the *light*?

He found a vacancy in a small motor inn on the California side of town, only two blocks from the neon-spangled casino strip.

He had picked up a burger and fries for dinner, and ate on the sagging double bed while he watched television. The weather looked like it was going to be hot and dry where he was going. He pounded the "off" button on the remote control when an advertisement for something called the SuperPsychics Hotline came on.

Using the atlas, he planned out his route while he finished off the fries. Then he picked up the phone. He called Devrie's parents to tell them where he was going, and he called Wally to tell him that he was going to be needing a little more time off after all. Wally reminded him that Whitaker was going to want to see him first thing in the morning.

"Keep 'em happy for me, Wal. Just for a few days. Okay? Thanks, buddy."

"Reed. What the hell is going on? What should I tell Whitaker? What are you do—"

"I'll call you when I can." Reed hung up. It wasn't easy for him to be that abrupt with his closest friend—his sole confidant, but he felt he had no choice if he was going to follow through on the plan that was now beginning to emerge.

Traffic outside the small motor inn was loud and carried on all night. Reed slept intermittently in the small, cheaply paneled room, fighting bad dreams and indigestion.

The image of a door at the end of a long hallway possessed his mind as he sat up in the deep valley in the center of the bed. The digital clock on the night stand said four-fifty A.M. Sweat trickled through his hair and down his face. Only then did he realize that he had awoken. He felt as if he'd just run a mile. Outside cars continued to zoom past. The image of his dream became animated as details crept back into his memory. He had needed to reach the door at the end of the hall. He had walked toward it. The walls and door were a gruesome swirl of color, rather like the kinetic iridescence of gasoline on the surface of a polluted lake. Deep beet red pulsed beneath intense blue and green streams and vortices, all cast in a penetrating darkness that infected the viewer. The spectrum was not that of the natural world. Colors that never existed on earth danced before his eyes, under his feet. As he neared the door, it opened. A dark, faceless entity, a figure in colorless powerful strength stepped through the doorway and into the hall. Through the crack in the door Reed could see that there was a flickering light on the other side. He had to get through that door, but the dark figure blocked the way. Reed couldn't identify it as a man, except that it wore the red-stained cowboy boots. He tried to run to the door, to the room, but his muscles seized, locked, froze him where he stood. His eyes lowered, too heavy to stay directed at the narrow gap. The dark figure held him in its power, controlled his ability to move, to see. There was no way to overcome its strength. The colored walls around him faded to a coal gray like the charred brick of a blast furnace, but with the moist sheen of a ghetto street after a midnight rain.

As impossible as it had been to move toward the door, Reed was equally possessed with the dire need to reach it, to enter into some unknown realm, where something lay hidden beyond a flickering light.

That's when he'd found himself sitting up in the bed, the sheets damp, his heart thudding frantically, his eyes swollen and blurred. He clasped his arms around the pillows, which smelled used, musky, and overly laundered.

Slowly he lowered himself back down. There he lay for two more hours, falling in and out of sleep. But the dreams stayed away this time. By seven o'clock he was in the shower, anxious to be out of the claustrophobic little room.

By eight o'clock he had checked out of the motel, and filled the 4Runner's tank. He drove through town, chewing on an Egg McMuffin, trying to remember what Ranger Scott Allen had told him. He made a pair of wrong turns before he found the building. The municipal domestic animal pound was a one-story, modern building near the city limits. The young woman sitting at the reception desk listened attentively as Reed described the golden Labrador that had been brought in several weeks before by the forest ranger. The young brunette, who introduced herself as Karen, knew immediately which dog Reed was talking about.

"I just wanted to know if anyone had claimed her," Reed said.

"Not yet I'm afraid," she informed him.

"Oh. That's too bad."

"It's such a shame," Karen expressed. "She's such a sweet animal. I wish I could take 'em all home."

"How long does she have . . . until . . . they have to . . ."

Karen grimaced, reluctant to answer. "Five more days. I really hope someone takes her. If you know anybody . . ."

"I do," Reed said very plainly.

It was a simple matter of filling out some adoption forms and buying a leash. She'd already been given a full update of shots.

When the handler brought the dog out to Reed, the memory of the terrible night flashed through his head. It was still so fresh, the odors of death, of loss, of blood . . . still so powerful. But the eyes were soft, kind, and sad. Reed clipped the leash to the dog's collar and led her out to his car.

As if the dog didn't really believe it until she was actually out the door, she exploded into an excited run at that precise moment, pulling Reed with all her strength toward the car. She knew immediately which one was his . . . now hers too. Her jubilation was contagious, and Reed found himself smiling as the elated animal circled and panted at his feet. It was almost as if she'd been waiting for him, waiting to start a journey to her new home.

Reed pointed the 4Runner east, and drove straight out of town. He took state highways, first across and then down, intentionally keeping to the Nevada side of the Sierras as he worked his way south, through the high deserts, past the Nevada Test Site and on through Las Vegas. He was now reasonably confident that no one was on his trail.

The dog's lustrous coat shone in the sunlight that pounded through the windshield. He could sense her genuine happiness, if dogs can feel happiness, that is. "So, now we're even," he said, with a smile. She returned a grateful look. "So, what are we going to call you?" She sat obediently in the passenger seat, watching everything they passed with intense interest. She looked at Reed with a slightly confused tilt to her head, brows twitching.

"You just let me know if you hear something you like, okay? Okay. How about Dog? No. Okay try this: Ruff? Bark? Yeller? No, I'd never do that to you."

By the time they crossed the mighty Hoover Dam—seven hundred and twenty-six vertical feet of cement, holding back the ten trillion gallons of water in Lake Mead—the outside temperature had reached one hundred and eight degrees, and they still hadn't decided on a name. Then it came to him. They hooked onto Interstate 40 near the little town of Kingman, Arizona, and kept on going until once again they were ascending into mountain country, and the cooler air of Flagstaff.

That's where Reed and Hoover spent their first night. Reed didn't bother to ask the management if they accepted pets. He just sneaked the Lab in. The motel was called the Bumblebee Lodge. After he had registered, Reed took his credit cards and went shopping. Main Street was busy with tourists, most of whom were on their way either from or to the Grand Canyon farther north. He found a sporting goods and clothing store that was open late, and picked out a new pair of jeans, five T-shirts, and changes of socks and underwear to last him a week. He also needed toothpaste, a toothbrush, razors and shaving cream, and a hairbrush. He'd not even thought about the basic necessities when he'd fled his house the day before. But now he was some nine hundred miles from home, driving to a place he'd never been, to find someone he didn't know, in search of something he wasn't even sure existed.

He also needed dog food and bowls. At a twenty-four hour grocery store he purchased the matching items in bright blue, and provided well for his new dependent.

Sleep at the Bumblebee came much more easily than it had the night before in South Tahoe. The dreams were innocuous, back to their usual meaningless nonsense. Reed woke to find Hoover sleeping next to him.

After a healthy breakfast and a gas fill-up, Interstate 40 took Reed and Hoover across the rest of Arizona, through the painted desert region near Winslow and Holbrook, and into New Mexico.

He absorbed some of the most spectacular natural landscape he'd ever seen, as they crossed the continental divide. Great red-rimmed bluffs towered between deeply forested mountains and valleys. It was simply astonishing scenery. The great diversity of the geography throughout the country continually amazed him, and gradually the high mountains lowered into the plateau regions and tall mesas west of Albuquerque: the Acoma and Laguna Indian reservations. He decided to stop for lunch in a little settlement called *Mal Agua*, which he knew meant "bad water" in Spanish. Looking at the atlas, Reed noticed that there wasn't so much as a pond within a hundred miles. The restaurant, called the *Sky Hawk*, looked possibly a little too traditional. Its simple adobe and timber construction was in acute disrepair. There were two cars parked in front of the little earthen structure, and an OPEN sign hanging crookedly from a chain on the door. The overriding factor, however, was that it appeared to be the only restaurant for miles, and Reed's stomach was on the verge of imploding. He leashed Hoover to a post in the dirt parking area, and opened the screened door. It was no more than four walls and a roof. A long counter divided the room into a dining area and a kitchen. There were about ten empty dinette tables but four men, obviously locals, occupied diner stools at the counter, drinking coffee and eating. They all turned to look at Reed as the door slammed shut behind him. A young girl looked up nervously from behind the cash register. Her hair was pure black, her skin a deep gingerbread.

The five pairs of dark eyes seemed to exert a physical force on Reed's body, stopping him at the door. "Can I . . . get some lunch?" he asked, fighting the hesitation in his voice.

The girl behind the counter, who Reed noticed was wearing a waitress's uniform, seemed to look at the four men sitting at the counter for approval. One of them, an enormous man, not fat or in the least overweight, just big, wearing a black felt cowboy hat with a hawk feather in the rattlesnake band, and clearly a full-blooded member of his native tribe, gave Reed a once over. Reed smiled and stepped with great effort toward one of the tables, trying to shake off the invisible grasp that held him.

"What's your name?" the large man asked.

Reed's feet stuck to the floor again. He reinforced his smile, nervously. "Why?"

The giant Indian rose from the stool, which now looked like a child's toy beside him. He suspiciously regarded Reed once again, then sidled over to the door, too close. The man's eyes were all pupil, like two tunnels leading into the emptiness of deep space. His glossy gray-streaked hair swept back under the hat, and hung down in a long pony tail behind his head. Reed saw that the skin on his face was smooth and perfect—almost the complexion of a child, but the man had to be at least forty years old. He was not smiling.

"You have a smell . . . about you." The big Indian said.

"Sorry. I try to bathe as often as I can," Reed answered, trying to ease the tension.

"Name?" The black eyes moved around the periphery of Reed's body, as if looking at some bubble that surrounded the smaller white man, that only the Indian could see.

"My name's Reed Haler. Doctor Reed Haler." He reached out his hand, which the Indian did not take.

The ruddy nostrils flared as the Indian took in a scent that only he could smell. "You smell of fear, Doctor Reed Haler," he said, particularizing the observation.

"Fear?" Reed asked.

"Mmm." The Indian nodded. "It's on you."

"What's on me?"

"I hope you overcome it, Doctor Haler, but take it away from here."

"Hey, I just stopped in for something to eat, you know?"

The Indian shouted something in Keresan, the native language of the Laguna and Acoma people. Reed had no idea what the man had said, but the young Indian girl behind the counter dashed into the kitchen an instant later. "We will give you food, but you may not stay. Take the fry bread and beans, then go."

After a minute the girl emerged from the kitchen with a brown paper bag. She handed it to Reed, then hurried back behind the counter.

"You're telling me I can't sit down and have lunch? I mean this is a restaurant, isn't it?"

"Take the food and go. You need nourishment."

There was no hostility in the big man's voice, but Reed knew that for whatever reason, he wasn't going to be accepted. "Right. Well, how much do I owe you?" Reed asked, reaching into his pocket for his wallet.

The Indian lifted his hand, palm up as if to feel for a drop of summer rain.

"Nothing. Just go. Eat all the food, but leave none of your fear behind you . . . go now." The last words came out softly, but with the unmistakable tone of an order.

Reed pushed his wallet back into his pocket, and felt behind himself for the door. All eyes were still on him, especially the bottomless pits in the head of the big man. Reed backed out of the restaurant into the punishing heat. Only when his feet hit the brown dirt of the parking lot did he turn around to find Hoover, panting and ready to get back in the car.

He didn't stop in Albuquerque. The Indian's admonishment kept repeating itself in his head. He intended to put as much distance between himself and *Mal Agua* as he could. The eastern part of New Mexico flattened out, and Interstate 40 straightened into a rail of pavement that went to infinity. The speedometer read ninety-five, but they weren't gaining an inch on the car in front of them.

At the next gas station Reed filled the dog's bowl with water, and bought himself several bottles of iced tea. The food from the Sky Hawk—beans and an airy disk of crispy fried bread—was strangely satisfying. It had little flavor, but it seemed to increase his strength with each bite. It had kept him going all the way across the baking Texas panhandle and halfway through Oklahoma. Just beyond Oklahoma City he pulled into a two-story affair called the Seminole Motor Hotel. It was a little past eleven P.M., but it was still eighty-eight degrees outside with humidity around ninety percent. Reed had praised Hoover's good car control, and took her for a much-needed walk around the grounds. One more day of driving, he thought, staring out past the glowing motel sign, over the off-ramp and to the coursing interstate. Hoover tugged on her leash. She was hungry and tired.

They both ate in the room, Reed a club sandwich and Hoover a can of Alpo. The weather was supposed to remain hot and sticky, a chance of scattered showers every day. Reed clicked off the TV, and settled back into the flattened, stale pillows, opening Devrie's journal, which he'd been keeping within arm's reach since he'd set out on this peculiar journey. He studied the writing carefully as Hoover jumped up on the bed, and curled into a ball at his feet. The first two entries: *Ones with guns are blind in the dark,* and *Where there's a tear there's light,* had been borne out. He was reasonably sure of that. As for the rest, he didn't know. He considered the next and third entry in the list of nine. *Shbyi'aye from the sky, sees, hears and smells.*

The last word clung in his mind. What had the big Indian said to him? *"You smell of fear..."* Did he also see the invisible with those black eyes? Hear the silence with his ears? Reed didn't know what *Shbyi'aye* was, but he did know that the restaurant was called the Sky Hawk. Hawk *from the sky*? Did *Shbyi'aye* mean *hawk* in the Indian's native language? It seemed to fit.

Hoover suddenly twitched and grunted in her sleep. Reed turned to the back of the book and looked at the Polaroid. The picture kept the fire in his heart burning, his resolve complete. He let the letters imprint themselves on his eyes, and then closed the journal, tucking it under the pillow. After he'd let his head settle back, he switched off the lamp.

In the wet night air, he could still feel the vibration of the road in his body as he lay on the creaky spring mattress. Over the sound of the straining air conditioner, all he could hear was the rumble of the endless flow of trucks passing along the southern transcontinental route. It was an oddly reassuring sound. The real world was still pumping, commerce still flowing and consumers still consuming. It was all a great machine that could never be turned off. You either kept up with it, or you got run over. That was the real world.

The fingers of sleep worked their way into Reed's brain after only a few minutes, and he was in the prismatic hallway again. The struggle resumed. Again the door at the end of the rectangular tunnel opened, letting the flickering light spill out. Now he could see that the light beyond the door was a deep orange, but again his view was blocked by the dark mass, and again his legs slowed as if he were sinking into a thick, acrid syrup. The dark form seemed to exude itself, in invisible rivulets, catalyzing the resin until no movement at all was possible. Then a voice rose up from behind Reed. He couldn't turn his head, nor lift his eyes to see, but he recognized the voice instantly.

"You smell of fear . . ."

The light coming from the door flashed into something brighter. Reed realized that his eyes were open. He wasn't looking at a door any longer, but the edges of the window shade in the motel room. The sun was up and trying to get through the window. Hoover was no longer on the bed. Reed turned to look at the digital alarm clock on the night stand. It was eight-thirty. He'd slept for almost nine hours, but he didn't feel rested. His body was again soaked, his heart still settling. The night had passed. Thank God! he thought, the night had passed.

He showered quickly, and checked out of the Seminole Motor Hotel. As he pulled out of the parking lot and drove toward the interstate on-ramp, his thoughts returned to the bassinet, the smashed kitchen window, and the car he'd seen in front of his house. He was no longer concerned that someone was chasing him. In fact, he was fairly certain that no one was following him at all. What worried him now was the idea that whoever had committed those trespasses, had no need to follow him, but only to sit and to wait.

THIRTEEN

Smoke swirled up in gray clouds above the sizzle of grilling hamburgers. Gart Hanta, a metal spatula in his powerful hand, checked to see if the meat was ready to be turned. From the back patio of Jessica Morraine's house, he could hear voices coming from the open door, which led directly into the kitchen. The patio was simply a barren slab of concrete, and the backyard a lifeless expanse of raw earth. The house was on the leading edge of a new development that was still under construction. Jessica and Lucy were inside getting things ready to bring out to the new picnic table that Gart had just purchased for them as a gift. Since moving into their new house, Jessica and Lucy had nowhere to eat except the kitchen or the dining room, so what better way to kick off the summer than to have a good old-fashioned cookout, especially since grilling was Gart's culinary forte. Now they could dine under the stars, and the gesture had gone a long way, if not all the way, toward easing Lucy's apprehensions about her mother's boyfriend.

Carrying a plate piled with sliced tomato, Lucy stepped out onto the patio.

"Mmm, that sure looks good," Gart complimented.

Lucy set the plate down while she replied, "Mommy let me cut them myself."

"It looks like you did a great job."

"She did do a great job," came from the doorway as Jessica too came out of the house. She carried a package of buns and an armful of condiments. "We may have a chef on our hands."

Lucy smiled at her mother's vote of confidence.

"No. I think that you're going to be an Olympic gymnast," Gart suggested.

"I'm going to be a doctor, like my mom," Lucy corrected, the terms quite certain, and her mood suddenly becoming defiant.

"Oh, yeah! Of course. But you can be a gymnast too. If you want." Gart wasn't sure how to fix the blunder. "You can do anything you set your mind to," he said as his next effort.

"I know," she replied, as if it were a self-evident fact.

"Okay. Just making sure." He began flipping the burgers, and redirecting the conversation at the same time licks of flame shot up around the patties. "Speaking of doctoring," he continued, "NIH say anything yet?"

Jessica shook her head. "Nope. But they haven't committed anywhere else yet either. So, we're still in the running."

"Who's next on the punch list?"

"Well, Louis is supposed to be going to Texas next week to talk to some oil people there, but . . . who the hell knows?" Despondency began to weigh down Jessica's voice. "Maybe it's a losing battle."

Suddenly Lucy's mood brightened, almost in direct proportion to her mother's faltering spirits. "Yeah!" the little girl said, hope ringing clearly. "It's a losing battle."

"Lucy!" her mother scolded.

The little girl lowered her eyes.

"That's no way to talk to your mother," Gart joined in.

"Gart, I'll handle it. Okay?"

He threw his hands up and went back to the burgers.

Lucy stood up from the table and ran inside, tears fast escaping.

"What brought that on?" Gart asked cautiously.

Jessica couldn't help the huge sigh. She suddenly looked exhausted, like giant weights pulled down relentlessly on her shoulders. "She's tired of the whole thing too. It's only natural. We spend so little time together. I mean, I try to organize things so that we share tasks around the house and all that, but I know she needs more. I . . . this hospital is just so important to me. And if these people would just come through with some capital, everything could be different. I could hand off some responsibility finally. But I've already invested so much time and so much effort. I can't just let it go." She looked straight into Gart's eyes through the wafting smoke. "Can I?"

He tried to ease her tension with a smile. "It's your dream, Jess. It was Dr. Kieran's dream, and she gave that to you. How can you let that die?"

"I can't. But I just need more help."

"I'm here to help. I'll do whatever I can. If you need me to take her to school in the morning, or bring her home in the afternoon. Just say so. I'll watch her until you get home. I want to help, if I can."

"Thanks, Gart. I really appreciate that."

"Just let me know. And . . . I think we're ready to eat." He scooped the cooked burgers up and placed them on a serving platter.

"I'd better go see if hamburgers and ice cream are stronger motivators than I am," Jessica said as she got up. " 'Cause you know . . ."

Gart looked up from setting the platter down on the table.

". . . my kid is my biggest dream of all."

When Jessica knocked on the door of Lucy's bedroom, the girl was sitting on the floor, drawing in her coloring pad. She was working with the black crayon again on the picture of the wormy X's, combining a clump of the shapes in the middle to form an ominous-looking figure that appeared vaguely human. It was evident that several tears had run down the page, and that several more were on the verge of following. At the bottom of the drawing, in the red area, she'd written the word "telomere." At the sound of the knock, Lucy closed the book and looked up. Her mother appeared.

"Hey there. The hamburgers are ready. And for dessert, guess what? Ice cream!"

The tears continued to fall, prompting Jessica to kneel down next to her daughter. "Lucy. Honey. Come on. I know it's hard. But it's not forever. Pretty soon things are gonna change. I promise. I just need you to hang in there a little longer. And then we're gonna have lots more time to spend together." At first Lucy said nothing, as she fought to stop crying. "Luce, you with me?"

"I'm scared," the girl said, now staring up at her mother through moist eyes.

The comment, like so many others voiced by her daughter, took Jessica by surprise. "Sweetie, there's nothing to be scared of."

Lucy started nodding insistently, the tears falling freely again.

"Baby, what's going on? What are you so scared of?"

"I don't want to tell you."

"Tell me what?"

"I'm . . . I'm afraid that . . ." Lucy struggled to speak between her sobs. "If you try to make the hospital, then . . . then . . . the same thing that happened to Dr. Kieran will happen to you."

Jessica's hand suddenly covered her mouth. "Oh, no, sweetie. Is that what you think?"

The nodding resumed.

"Sweetheart, that's never going to happen. Never. We've got lots of people around us who won't ever let that happen to anyone again. Okay? And Gart's a big strong man. He'd never let anything happen to either one of us." Jessica put her arm around Lucy and gave her a big hug.

"I don't want you to die, Mommy."

"Oh, sweetie, nothing's going to happen to me. All right? All right, Luce?" Finally the little girl gave another nod, however reluctantly. Jessica held the child for a few more minutes, until the tears stopped. "Now, there's nothing to be scared of, and I'm getting really hungry. How 'bout you? I bet you'd still like a hamburger."

Lucy nodded again.

"Okay, we'll have to hurry or they're all gonna get cold." Jessica stood up, holding a hand out to her daughter.

Finally, with her mother's help, Lucy stood up too. "I'd like some ice cream."

Jessica smiled, managing to lift the child up. "Then I guess we'd better go get some."

FOURTEEN

They were still a couple hundred miles from the Arkansas state line, but Reed hoped to be rolling into Nashville by the end of the day. From there it was a southeasterly drop of about fifty miles to Cowhollow.

He was getting tired of Egg McMuffins, so he sat down at a truck stop diner and had pancakes. He filled two water jugs in the bathroom, topped off the gas tank, and again he and Hoover were on the road.

The Ozarks of western Arkansas proved slower going than he'd expected, so by five o'clock that evening they were just crossing the great Mississippi into Memphis. They still had half the state of Tennessee to cover, but now that they were getting close, there was a new sense of urgency and purpose. Reed started to consider seriously for the first time exactly what he was going to say when and if he found Maysie Fabrioso. All he knew for sure was that he was going to do everything he could to find her.

They stopped for dinner just outside Nashville. Reed figured it was still about two more hours to his destination. It would be too late by the time they arrived there to make any inquiries, but he planned to find a motel and get an early start in the morning. He folded up the atlas and finished his pork chops and mashed potatoes.

The motel Reed chose in Cowhollow was called the Little Dipper Inn. He pulled into the parking lot a few minutes after midnight. As he stepped out of the car, he drew a deep breath, inhaling the unusually sweet air. It had a restorative effect on his road-weary body. The whole place felt good. It smelled good, it was pleasing to the eye, and somehow it evoked an unexpected sense of well-being.

The Little Dipper was the nicest motel they'd stayed in yet. It had a pleasing outdoor swimming pool, the bed was comfortable, the TV was brand new, and the air conditioner was quiet and effective. Hoover was happy about it too.

The first thing Reed did after taking off his shoes and setting up Hoover's food and water bowls, was to check the local telephone listings. A thin phone book was conveniently provided on the lower shelf of one of the nightstands. As he'd anticipated, there were no Fabriosos listed in Cowhollow. Then he checked the yellow pages. There were no listings under psychics, palm readers, or astrologers that matched the name either. Where to start? he wondered. The beginning's always good, he said to himself. He undressed and switched the bedside light off. His eyes gradually adjusted to the dim green of the room; he scolded himself for feeling reluctant to close them. He dreaded the dream like a child fears the dark. It lurked, a hidden yet ubiquitous threat, somewhere in the folds of sleep where he felt the most vulnerable.

The sound of Hoover's calm steady breath finally lulled him into a drowsy relaxed state, and then he was out.

To Reed's surprise and tremendous relief, the dream had not returned. He felt awake and oddly refreshed the next morning. His nerves, however, remained on high alert, his senses trimmed like a sail cutting a lean tack into the wind. He arranged for another night's stay at the Little Dipper, and asked the woman at the front desk what was the best place in town for breakfast. She directed him to a small restaurant about five blocks down Main Street.

Reed loaded Hoover into the 4Runner, and secured Devrie's journal in the glove box. Since waking up, he'd again noticed the pungent smell that seemed to be everywhere—flowers.

Over scrambled eggs and sausage, Reed asked the waiter if he could tell him where the police station was. He recorded the information on a napkin and paid the bill.

Cowhollow was a quaint village of twenty thousand. There was one main street and the rest appeared to be residential and surprisingly affluent. Evidently Cowhollow was a flower-growing municipality. Everywhere there were signs of a large and prosperous industry in flora. Streets bore names like Gladiola Street, Chrysanthemum Way, Daisy Avenue, and Carnation Place, and the fragrance was inescapable. Cowhollow had to rank among the sweetest smelling places in the country, if not the world.

The police station was right in the center of town. Reed parked and walked up the three steps to the main door of the modern and stylish building.

"Hi," Reed said to the desk sergeant, a young blond woman with a pretty, bright smile. "I'm trying to locate a woman by the name of Maysie Fabrioso. I understand she lives here in Cowhollow."

"The psychic lady?" the sergeant asked with a homegrown twang. Reed noticed her name tag pinned properly to the deep blue of her starchy uniform.

"Yes, the psychic lady, Sergeant . . . Meyhew."

"A lot of people come looking for Maysie. Sorry, I can't give out that information."

"No. Of course not." Reed sighed. "I just drove two thousand miles from San Francisco. I need to talk to her about a personal case. It's something she'd be very interested in."

"I'm sure she would be . . ." the intonation in her voice was that of a question, slightly condescending, ". . . but I still can't give out that information."

"Well maybe you know a public place where I might run into her."

"No, I really don't, sir. I'm sorry."

"Well what do people do who've been victimized and want to hire her?"

"That would probably have to be done through the police department. Are you the victim, sir?"

"My name is Reed Haler. My wife was the victim. She was murdered."

"Oh." Sergeant Meyhew's mouth dropped slightly at that. "I'm really sorry, Mr. Haler. Do you want to file a report with a detective?"

"Yeah. That would be great."

"Okay. Hold on." Sergeant Meyhew picked up a phone behind the desk, and asked for someone named Bill.

"Detective Wirth will be down in a minute to help you, Mr. Haler."

"Thanks."

"You can have a seat right over there."

Reed didn't bother to sit down. Detective Bill Wirth arrived at the desk a few minutes later, and showed Reed into an interrogation room.

Reed outlined his situation, but again got the runaround about Maysie Fabrioso.

"Dr. Haler," the short balding detective said, "you're talking about a crime that took place on the other side of the country. We really can't get involved."

"I know that. I just need to talk to Maysie Fabrioso."

"I'd love to help you, but there's really nothing I can do. Ms. Fabrioso is probably not even in town. She's become very popular since the Howard Henny thing."

"You guys must have used her on occasion."

"We have, of course."

"Recently?"

"Look, Dr. Haler. I appreciate that you've come all this way. I wish I could be more help, but you'll have to excuse me now."

"Okay. Well, thanks anyway, Detective." Reed stood up and went to the door.

"Good luck, Dr. Haler."

"Thank you. You've been very helpful actually."

Reed stepped out of the room, and went back to the front desk.

"Hi, again," he said to Sergeant Meyhew.

"Any luck?"

"Oh, not really. But I was wondering if you could direct me to the public library."

Reed climbed back into the 4Runner, and followed Sergeant Meyhew's directions to the public library, a similar building, all glass and metal, only half a mile away on Crocus Street. The librarian, a studious looking young man of college age, seemed delighted that someone was taking an interest in local history. He showed Reed back issues of the local paper, *The Daily Pistil*, for the past three years.

It took Reed a little over an hour to find a story involving a local investigation in which Maysie Fabrioso was a part. There had been a rape two years before in the back parking lot behind the local movie theater. Maysie had helped to identify a suspect when she called the police with a description she had seen in her mind. She had told the police not only what the perpetrator looked like, but what he had been wearing during the commission of the crime. Garments that exactly matched her description were found in the suspect's apartment. Lab analysis of the clothing placed the suspect at the scene, and that information eventually led to a confession. The man had been an employee at the theater and was sentenced to fifteen years.

Conveniently Maysie's address appeared in the article, as is common practice in local journalism. That edition of *The Pistil* was two years old, and at the time Maysie wasn't yet nationally known. It was quite possible that the address was out of date, but at least Reed now had a solid location to continue his search.

Reed thanked the librarian, and returned the stack of papers to the archive desk.

Hoover seemed to sense Reed's optimism as they drove to 944 Hyacinth Drive.

The houses grew increasingly opulent as the numbers got larger, and the street neared the southern limits of town. The dwelling at 944 was a splendidly preserved, two-story Southern relic with a broad, wraparound porch. Pristine white columns, surmounted by finely crafted ionic capitals, supported a deep, overhanging roof. The house was set back forty or fifty feet from the road, the span of property filled in with a plush carpet of Kentucky bluegrass. A path of white stepping-stones led from the sidewalk to a wide set of stairs, which ascended to the porch. It was impossible to tell precisely how large the house was due to the insurgence of flowering plants, trees, and creeping vines. Reed stopped the vehicle, and looked over at Hoover to gauge the dog's reaction to the place.

Reed leaned over the passenger seat, and popped the glove box. He gripped the soft binding of the journal, pulling it from the compartment. He held the book tightly to his chest, as if it were a living thing. Another glance at the dog: it was a go.

The air outside hung like a steaming wet towel. Reed's clothes clung to him a little too affectionately as he walked along the pathway to the porch steps and up to the green screen door. A bell button glowed shyly behind a leafy cluster of vines, which bore lavender flowers. Reed dug through the camouflage and pressed it. He could hear the faint chime coming from inside. Then came the squeak of a loose floorboard, followed by the turn of the doorknob.

A dark gap, little wider than Reed's smile, opened behind the screen door.

"Who is it?" came a husky female voice.

Reed leaned in a little closer to the opening. "Uh, hi. My name's Reed Haler. I'm trying to find Maysie Fabrioso."

The door pulled back letting just enough light into the house for Reed to see a swirl of red hair through the screen. He hardly recognized the face underneath. His pulse quickened slightly. Maysie looked a lot older and a lot paler than she had on television. She wore what looked like a blue terrycloth robe.

"You're catching me at a bit of an inconvenient moment, Dr. Haler," she said.

Reed couldn't quite tell if he saw a smile on her face or a grimace. He noticed that she didn't speak with any of the local intonation, though her speech was strangely accented as he recalled from the television show—slightly foreign, Spanish, he thought, or Italian maybe.

"I'm sorry if I'm disturbing you. I've just come from San Francisco, and—"

The door opened a little wider. Two bright marine-blue eyes flared in the darkness of the house's interior. She stared at him silently for another moment. "I know you're here with good reason. I'm sorry . . . but I must ask you to come back later. I've got a trip to prepare for just now."

Reed could see that it was a grimace and not a smile. "Sure. Later is okay. But I need to speak with you; it's very important."

"Yes. I know. Can you return at seven o'clock this evening?"

"Seven is fine."

"Come back then."

The door closed, and Reed stepped back down the porch steps. His heart was thudding forcefully as he walked back to the car. He turned to look at the house again, suddenly realizing that the flowering vines which draped the entire front facade were morning glories. He hesitated a moment, letting the fact settle in his mind. He was now hyperconscious of the small book he held in his hand. He also realized that at no point in their brief meeting had he mentioned to Maysie Fabrioso that he was a doctor.

Reed spent the day driving around Cowhollow. He ate lunch at a quaint restaurant in the downtown area, then strolled along the open-air mall that went through the center of town. He recognized the municipal plaza, and felt he'd established a pretty good sense of the layout. There was almost nowhere that you couldn't find flowers, either on display or for sale. He bought a local paper and a white rose from a drugstore, and positioned the flower in the sun visor on the passenger side of the 4Runner. There he could look at it as he drove, making a loop around the edge of town. All along the way were huge fields and greenhouses, engineered for floral cultivation. Apparently there was something about the soil in the area that was particularly good for growing.

He spent the rest of the afternoon trying to relax with a beer, reading the *Pistil* by the pool at the Little Dipper. The management didn't seem to mind if Hoover napped in the shade by the water. Tables with garden umbrellas provided enough relief from the sun. The place reminded Reed of the many similar motels that he and Devrie had stayed in during their half-dozen road trips together. He fought to keep the memories from overwhelming him, taking solace from the sun's warmth. He sat in one of the chaises, his feet dangling just above the water and Hoover asleep nearby. Nothing in the paper could keep his attention and he found himself gazing up at the haze of blue, as if the sky were an illusion of serenity, behind which lurked pernicious black angels.

After a cool shower, Reed dressed, fed Hoover, and then found a quick meal for himself at the diner across the street from the Little Dipper. At ten to seven, he and Hoover were on their way once again to Maysie Fabrioso's house. They arrived at exactly seven o'clock.

"Okay, girl. Stay here. I'll be back in a little while." Hoover settled on the backseat. She knew that this mission wasn't something in which she was to be included.

The air had cooled slightly as the sun reached for the horizon, but now the mosquitoes had come out. Reed pressed the doorbell for the second time, swatting at his neck.

Again he heard the squeak of the floorboard just before the door opened.

"Please come in," Maysie said when she saw Reed.

He pulled back the screen door, and entered the dark house. He looked back to see Hoover, panting and staring at him from the car.

Maysie Fabrioso led Reed to the kitchen where she had a pitcher of cold lemonade waiting. She offered him a glass, which he accepted thankfully.

"I'll be right with you, just getting a few things together," she said, racing around in a systematic pattern. Then he was alone in the small but well-equipped kitchen. The only light was that coming in through the window above the sink and through the sliding glass back door. Behind the house, the plantlife was even thicker than in the front. Reed could see only a few feet from the back door into the jungle of dense growth.

On the refrigerator were a dozen small photographs held up by ladybug magnets. Family photos, Reed presumed. He stepped to the fridge to get a better look. The whole kitchen was cluttered, yet every surface was immaculately clean. The countertops were an inch and a half of solid eggshell Corian, not simply Formica-laminated particle board. The cupboards matched, and all appeared to be recently renovated, but frequently used by someone who took her cooking seriously. Next to the refrigerator a phone hung on the wall. Beneath it on the counter was a half-used message pad. Reed pushed the phone's handset to the side revealing the little display on which the number was printed in typed numerals. He jotted the number down on the message pad, and tore off the sheet of paper. He stuffed the slip into his pocket, and made sure that nothing was out of place before walking back to the table where his lemonade waited. He sat down and took a long drink.

A few minutes later, Maysie reappeared. She was dressed in a flowing fuchsia blouse, tight white stretch pants, and squeaky sandals. She had also applied a layer of foundation, powder, and some eye liner since his morning visit. Now she was much more the person he had seen on the talk show, but still not quite attractive.

"So, Dr. Haler," she said, taking a seat across the table from Reed, "you've come a long way to see me. You're lucky. Tomorrow you wouldn't have found me here. I'm going to Florida. Lost infant. Probably a kidnapping."

"You know where the child is?" Reed ventured.

"Not a clue . . . yet. But now let's get back to you, since you came all this way. I normally don't take drop-ins, but you've got troubles, I can see that."

"Yes. Yes I do. Thanks a lot, I appreciate your time."

"Yes, you do have troubles. You have something to show me?"

"Uh, yes." Reed held out the journal to Maysie. "This is—"

"Your wife's. Yes." Maysie paged through to the end, examining closely the final nine entries, and then the Polaroid, which had slipped out of the back. Reed could see her whispering the words on her lips. Her face washed with concern, a worried furrow pinched the bridge of her powdery nose. "These notations led you to me."

"Uh, yeah, I guess, in part. I saw you on TV." Reed went on to explain the Polaroid.

Maysie listened carefully. Then her attention returned to the journal for another minute. She replaced the Polaroid in the back of the book, and set it down on the table, closing her eyes. She placed her hands on either side of the bound pages. Her head tilted and adjusted slightly as if she were straining to hear some distant sound. Then: "Your wife, of course, suspected that her child, perhaps even that she herself was in danger."

"Yes . . . I'm not sure why, but I think that her journal might somehow have information about—"

"The killer," Maysie finished Reed's statement.

Even though Reed now accepted his wife's visions as legitimate, he was, nevertheless, stunned by this woman's awareness, not only of his plight, but of the avenues which had led him to her, and his purpose for being there. This was all still very new and very un-nerving stuff for him.

Maysie's eyes tightened, bracing against some explosive flash, which existed somewhere that only she could see. Her head shook from side to side in a troubled, negative gesture. She finally leaned back in the chair, her arms falling to her sides. Her eyes slowly opened. The true pallor of her skin shone through the heavy layer of makeup. Her breath came in short bursts. She picked up the journal, holding it tightly.

"What?" Reed implored, reacting to her sudden ill-ease.

"You're very right, Dr. Haler," she finally said, her voice low and dry, without a trace of humor. "These notations do tell some-thing of the man who took your child's and your wife's lives."

"And?" Reed leaned in over the edge of the table.

Now Maysie looked straight at him, those two marine-blue lights connecting somewhere deep in his mind. "You don't know what you're dealing with, Dr. Haler."

"So, tell me."

"This was not a random killing. The man who did it knew where your wife would be and when. He also knew that she was pregnant, and what she wanted to name your daughter. She was a specific target."

"What? Nobody knew where we were or that she was pregnant, except our closest friends, and our parents. That's—"

"Dr. Haler," now Maysie smiled slightly. "If I knew your wife was pregnant, then why is it still so hard for you to believe that someone else might have known it too, as well as where you were going to be that night?"

Reed thought for a moment, his mind spinning in faster more erratic circles by the second. He realized that he was still desper-ately clinging to the world of the rational. "All right," he conceded. "But if that's true, then why on earth—?"

Maysie looked away, as if listening to a radio report from the other room. "If you find this man, he'll know who you are, and he won't hesitate to kill you too if you get in his way. I'm not sure if he can know you're coming, but he can block the channel."

"Block the channel?"

"Yes. You see, your wife was able to receive energy through a very powerful channel. That's why she could know that certain things were going to happen before they actually did."

"Is that how you do it?"

Maysie nodded. "I've been able to access several channels, each of which provides different kinds of information. Sometimes it's about future events, sometimes it's communications from spirits of people who've died. I don't pretend to understand how it all works, I've simply learned how to receive on a number of levels. Your wife probably could have sensitized herself to many channels. She was very receptive. But it bothered her a great deal. She wasn't completely accepting of her gift."

"Yes, I know."

"It was developing in her in spite of her resistance."

"So, why can't everyone tap into these . . . channels?"

"It's conceivable that everyone can. I think that most people simply choose not to out of denial . . . fear . . . any number of reasons. Sometimes perhaps the brain just isn't set up for it. I don't know. But your wife's was, and in a very powerful way."

"So, if it's possible to access these 'channels,' then why don't you psychic types win millions of dollars playing the lottery?"

Maysie smiled and poured Reed more lemonade. "I prefer to call myself a 'medium.' Psychic sounds so fraudulent."

"Okay, 'medium' then," Reed acknowledged.

"Now, about the lottery. This isn't magic, Dr. Haler. You have to understand one basic fact: I can't know anything that doesn't already exist somehow in the universe. The results of a lottery drawing don't exist until the very moment that the drawing is conducted. You see there is no way to know what those numbers will be ahead of time. But when I see a vision of someone who's committed a crime, or that you were coming here to see me, that information already exists in some vast reservoir of consciousness.

It's known as the Akashic Records. Really it's a database of every thought and event that's ever taken place, and you can draw on that knowledge. It's literally having every mind that's ever lived, every shred of human intelligence and experience helping you find answers. That's one hell of a powerful thing, and it's available, if you're able to reach it."

"But you said you weren't sure if the man who killed my wife can know that I'm coming?"

"It's possible that he's unable to receive through that channel, which means that his perceptions might be limited. But it seems he can send, and possibly block. If he thinks he's in danger, or someone's on to him, he might try to send out confusing signals that alter the information or prevent it from being received. The notations in your wife's journal might be confusing or misleading if he's had any influence on them. But I think the information is there, if you interpret it correctly."

"How will I know?"

Maysie smiled slightly, not a friendly smile, but the type used to introduce unwelcome news. "How? Hopefully, you'll just know, Dr. Haler. You'll just have to be patient and very careful, if you want to pursue this man and stay alive."

Reed wiped his forehead. "Oh." He had learned to respect that kind of warning lately. "Can't you see what's going to happen to me, or to him through this channel?"

Maysie shook her head with agitation. "I'm trying. I'm sorry. It's . . . it's very muddy. It must be blocked right now."

"By him?"

"Quite possibly. This is a very dangerous mission you've set yourself. He's killed before . . . he'll kill again unless he's stopped. It's his reason . . ."

"His reason?" Reed asked hesitantly.

"His reason for existing. In twenty years of doing this kind of work, I've come across a few people, Dr. Haler, who inflict suffering and take life as if their minds are programmed to make them do it. They seem to have been placed on Earth for the sole purpose of destroying the good of humanity. Their victims are almost always certain individuals who possess a special benevolence—the killers' own antitheses. There's something inhuman about their homicidal acts, yet they usually harbor a kind of perverse justification in their minds for their savagery. I think that the man you're looking for is one such person."

Reed whispered a "holy shit" to himself with a big breath of air. The words that Wally had said on the night after Devrie's funeral came back to him with new resonance: "Seems it's always the best people who are taken from us too soon." "Why?" Reed asked helplessly, falling prey to his emotions once more. "Why do there have to be such people roaming the world? What possible reason could there be?"

Maysie reached out, and took Reed's hands in hers. "Some people call it the natural order of things. Consider the fact that certain animals are predators, and possess special equipment and skills designed to aid them in killing. The hawk, for example, has highly developed vision, and can easily spot prey from high above the ground, and has specialized talons for catching that prey. But the jackrabbit has light brown fur, which helps camouflage him, as well as extremely powerful leg muscles which help him to escape. All advantage enjoyed by one group is countered by effective defenses possessed by the opposition, such that no single group can ever gain the upper hand over the others."

"But these maniacs who go around savagely murdering people don't kill for their own survival."

"True," Maysie conceded. "But human beings have no natural predators in nature. We've used our intelligence to protect us from every other life form on earth, as well as the diseases which threaten us every day. But there still must be balance, so we've become our own predators."

Reed was settling into a grudging acceptance of Maysie's words, even if he didn't fully understand them.

"What I have to tell you next," she continued, "you must take very seriously, because it is at the heart of what troubles you now."

"Okay," he answered hesitantly, almost like a frightened child.

"Now, you may not have even considered this, but your own

science is approaching a breakthrough that could eventually lead to . . . well, it could eventually lead to an indefinite life span in humans."

Reed's face flushed. He pulled his hands from Maysie's and sat back in his chair, not sure what to think, to feel, or to say.

"You're familiar with the term telomere?"

"Telomere? Yeah. Telomeres are the structures on chromosomes that some scientists believe regulate the number of times a cell can replicate itself. But what does that have to do with me, or my family?"

"More than you know. It's in your wife's journal for some reason, don't you think?"

Reed slipped into deep thought. "Telomeres," he mumbled to himself. "Connection. What's the connection? We're working with cancer cells . . . wait a minute." Reed stopped mumbling, and his eyes locked on the book that sat in the middle of the table. "That might be it. Generally cancer cells are able to replicate themselves many more times than healthy tissue cells, because they produce the telomerase enzyme. That's one reason they have such an advantage when they start replicating in the human body. Cancer cell telomeres shrink much more slowly. If the telomeres' length in healthy tissue cells could be maintained through a gene that activates the same enzyme . . . those cells might replicate indefinitely as well. Jesus! I suppose it's possible."

Maysie spoke softly, but with immense gravity. "Nature won't allow immortality of the individual, Dr. Haler. If we discover a way . . . the earth could never sustain the kind of population that would result. And if disease and old age don't control our population. Ask yourself . . . what will?"

The color leaked from Reed's face as he considered Maysie Fabrioso's question.

"It will lead," she continued, "to imminent human extinction. It would be suffering on a scale unknown to history. Earth would become . . . a literal hell."

It took a moment for Reed to absorb that revelation. He couldn't form more words for a moment, then they rushed out in a sudden burst: "So why kill my family?" he roared. "Why not kill me? I'm the one doing the work." Reed stared at the ceiling as he wailed. "Why not have a maniac blow up my lab, kill my colleagues? But not my wife! Not my daughter!" Reed pressed his fists to his temples and leaned forward. A rush of tears spilled from his eyes. Maysie waited patiently while Reed composed himself. She went to a cupboard above the counter, and pulled out a bottle. She sat again at the table, and poured them both a shot of Jack Daniels. Reed looked up.

"You need this right now. Just one shot," she instructed. Reed took the glass in his shaking hand and threw back the bourbon; the sweet burn ran down his throat. He placed the glass down in front of him. "Thanks," he said, collecting himself. "I'm sorry about that."

"Don't apologize. Your feelings are perfectly natural. I'm afraid I don't know why you were spared while your family wasn't. But there is a logic to it somewhere. From what your wife wrote in her journal, I think that your daughter was the actual target, not her."

"How could my daughter be any threat to anyone, for Christsake!"

"You have no way of knowing what things your daughter might have done, had she lived. What she might have become. She represented a threat of some kind, Dr. Haler. The natural order will always maintain itself."

"Are you saying that I'm fighting God?"

Maysie smiled. "I wouldn't say that. But you may be trying to push the order out of balance, and it will always resist . . . violently if necessary."

"But immortality was never my goal. That's not my intention! And you're saying my daughter had to be killed because of what she *might* have done?"

"Your intentions don't matter. It's the potential results that do. Your daughter would have followed your research. Her brain was forming, and that brain was inheriting your intelligence, your passion for discovery. That much is certain, and therefore the potential existed."

Reed had to take another swallow of lemonade. "So, if I go after this guy, what can I do to protect myself? Aren't there any secret weapons, any tricks?"

"Trust the journal and your own intuition. But if at first the words of the journal don't seem to make sense, that's okay. Be patient. Sometimes a little confusion can actually work in your favor. Rely on your feelings more than your intellect."

"What if I need to call you?"

"I don't take calls when I'm on a case; it muddies the water, so to speak. I'm sorry."

Maysie pressed the journal back into Reed's hands. "This is your journey alone, Dr. Haler, and your wife's words are the best weapon you have."

Reed took the journal. "Well, what do I do now? I mean, can you tell me where to go from here? Anything?"

"Follow the journal." Maysie stood, and led Reed back to the front door.

"Follow the journal?" he asked, incredulous. "Follow it where? I don't have a damn clue what the rest of this stuff means. You've got to be able to give me something better than that. How much do you want?"

"Dr. Haler." Maysie's eyes flared bright in the dim living room. "I've told you all I can. I don't want your money. You've got to go now."

It had grown dark outside, but it was still quite moist and hot.

"I can't tell you which way to go," she added when Reed stepped over the threshold. "Be confident that you will discover that for yourself."

"Pick a direction—any direction?" he asked hopelessly.

"It may be that simple. But pay attention to all of your feelings. Be careful and be scared. Your fear may save your life."

Reed thanked Maysie for her time and advice. The door closed.

Hoover was glad to see Reed when he climbed back into the 4Runner, but she could tell that their spontaneous road trip had taken a serious turn. Reed didn't drive back to the motel immediately, he just drove, letting his meeting with Maysie settle in, and his nerves calm down. Her words were snagged in his mind as he moved through the sticky Tennessee night: *"Your fear may save your life."* They rang with stark meaning. Nothing in the world felt the same as it had before. The whole universe suddenly seemed a little smaller, a little closer, but alive with foul entities, preying on human lives for sport. He'd never felt more vulnerable or helpless, and he couldn't comprehend what he was now forced to accept— that there were, undeniably, forces at work far beyond the grasp of humanity. His anxiety had penetrated so deeply that Reed found himself in a part of town he didn't recognize, and had no recollection of the route he'd taken to get there. Perhaps, he thought, as he began searching out familiar landmarks, it would be best just to go home, heal, and try to move on if that were even possible. Why should he be the one to take on the forces of the universe? Maysie was right, he thought: he didn't know what he was dealing with. But he did know that it was dangerous . . . and probably a lot more powerful than he was.

When he finally got back to the motel, the last thing he felt like doing was going to sleep—the specter of the night terror ever-present. He was hot, sweaty, and ripe with body odor. The illuminated pool at the Little Dipper was an irresistible invitation.

There was no one around, so Reed undressed down to his underwear at the pool's edge, the way he and Devrie might have done—had done a few times—while roaming, carefree, across the land. Hoover sat in one of the chaises watching, while Reed dove head-first into the aqua glow.

Under the water, Devrie's absence was a vacuous aberration that tried to suck Reed's heart down to the bottom, into the earth, forever into grief. He began to think that drowning in that pool, at that very moment, would be glorious relief. He remained submerged, keeping his eyes open. He saw only the blurred dark spot of the drain in the center of the marine hue. All he would have to do would be to open his mouth and try to breathe. Water would fill his lungs. The agony would be terrible but mercifully brief, unlike the agony he was living, which promised to remain with him until he died. After half a minute he felt the tug in his lungs, the desire to inhale. He would let that feeling build until he couldn't stand it any longer, but he would keep his head under the surface.

The explosion of bubbles instantly blinded him. The *sploosh* was so unexpected that Reed jerked his head from the water. He gasped for air without thinking and without knowing what had happened. When his vision cleared he saw Hoover's nose floating only inches from his face. Her head moved through the water like a small motor boat.

"What the hell do you think you're doing?" he asked the swimming dog. She let out a small yelp, then set off in a new direction. As she angled toward the edge of the pool Reed realized that he would have to help her out of the water. He pushed her from below, trying to avoid her thrashing paws. She wasn't a heavy dog, but trying to lift her from the water proved to be a very awkward affair. After he finally managed to hoist her onto the cement, and she shook the water from her coat, they looked at each other for a long moment without saying anything else.

The sun was just peering . . . cautiously . . . over the earth's rim when Reed hit Interstate 24 North, toward Nashville. His only thought upon waking was to get moving, to get out of Cowhollow. The dream had come, as he'd known it would. The details of it were staying longer in his memory, becoming clearer. He had still made it no further toward the door before the dark entity had frozen him in the hallway. Again the Indian from the Sky Hawk was there, behind him. *"You smell of fear,"* the Indian had said again. Reed wanted to be home. He sensed that the dreams would stop once he got there, so he wasted no time.

He didn't stop for breakfast until he was halfway to Memphis. Out of sheer convenience it was back to Egg McMuffins. He ate while he drove, not wanting to delay progress any more than was absolutely necessary. The urge to get home was overpowering, yet he dreaded the prospect that his stalker would resume terrorizing him once he returned. Still, he desperately wanted to see Dale and Bettyanne, and to get back to work—whatever that meant now. He looked forward to seeing Wally even more than he'd expected to.

Even though Devrie was gone, he now felt certain that she existed, in some form, somewhere in an unseen world beyond the physical universe. That knowledge would make it possible for him to resume his life in the face of any adversity.

By lunchtime he was hungry, but he just didn't feel like stopping. He pushed on, not eating until seven-thirty, and by then he was most of the way through Arkansas.

This time he wasn't bothering to notice the geography, he was just driving as quickly as he could. After eating and feeding Hoover, he filled the tank, gave the Lab a run around the gas station parking lot, filled her water bowl, and drove on for another three hours. At around midnight he pulled into a rest stop a couple hundred miles from the Texas Panhandle. He was sick of motels.

After five hours of sleep in the reclined driver's seat, he was on the road and looking for a place to get a cup of coffee. He pulled into a truck stop just the other side of the Oklahoma/Texas line, took a booth by the window, and watched as dozens of huge tractor trailers maneuvered around the enormous expanse of pavement. As the bleached blond waitress arrived, her lips painted and her eyes shadowed a bit too violet for six o'clock in the morning, there was something inordinately American about the whole scene. Reed felt pretty out of place among the deeply tanned left arms, wide-brimmed baseball caps, flannel shirts straining at the middle, and cowboy boots. But the scrambled eggs and bacon smelled good with the hot coffee. Reed buttered his toast and ate. This was life for millions of people, he thought. It was hard and honest, and took its toll. He couldn't help coming away feeling a strange sadness. It all seemed so futile and dull, yet strangely noble if you thought about it in terms of survival. They had a system that worked, unaware that it was all being kept in constant check via some invisible force. Reed wondered if any of them knew of the secrets he now carried with him—of a world beyond their own where seemingly impossible things happened. If any of them did, that morning in the lonely truck stop diner, there was nothing to indicate it, and life droned on.

By noon Reed and Hoover crossed into New Mexico. Thoughts of the big Indian from the Sky Hawk came back with harsh clarity. Reed wanted to get out of that state as quickly as possible. As he neared Albuquerque and the reservations on the other side of the city, he felt his stomach tighten, his hands become slippery on the wheel. Just being near the place was stinging his nerves. He dug around on the backseat with one hand until he found the road atlas. He examined his options.

"This is ridiculous," he said to himself. "What's my fucking problem?" As he drove, he tried to shake off the feeling, telling himself that he was just being paranoid and juvenile. But the anxiety mounted. His eyes traced the double-red line of Interstate 40 on the map. At Albuquerque he noticed the junction with I-25, which would take him north to Santa Fe and eventually into Colorado. He'd just passed a road sign indicating ten miles to Albuquerque. Something on the page snagged the corner of his eye. He found a conveniently wide stretch of shoulder and pulled over, flushed, heart working too hard. He scanned the map rapidly, then read the words, read them and reread them, stuck on the little block letters.

On the map he saw that I-25 ran up New Mexico to the southern tip of the *Sangre de Cristo* mountain range. *"Dry waves lie in the Blood of Christ,"* he repeated to himself. The ridge of mountains extended well into southern Colorado. *"Sangre de Cristo—the blood of Christ!"* Quickly checking his fuel gauge, Reed looked back for oncoming traffic, put the 4Runner in gear, and roared back onto the highway. Ten miles later he took the interchange onto I-25. As he began to move away from Albuquerque and toward Santa Fe, one source of his anxiety had just been replaced by another, even more frightening one.

FIFTEEN

Hanging on a wall was the Lord's Prayer, done on a parchment scroll in original calligraphy. Jessica knew it by heart from her childhood, but she couldn't help reading it anyway, while Canidey finished a conversation on the phone. The iconography wasn't excessive, but it was unmistakably present, adorning Dr. Louis Canidey's office. A tasteful portrait of Christ hung directly above the doctor's chair. On his desk was a free-standing cross, done in bronze, and set in a heavy walnut base. On a side wall, next to a tall window, was an enlarged photograph of the Southern Cross constellation.

Finally he hung up, and smiled from behind his desk. "Well, it's a go," he announced.

"Here or there?" Jessica wanted to know.

"Oh, they're coming here. You and I just have to pick a date. They sounded really anxious to meet you. They knew of Dr. Kieran and her work. They think what we're doing is great and well worth supporting. I don't know how much we can expect, but maybe we can take their offer, and go back to Sherman with it. See if the SCBF will match money from somewhere besides the NIH. I don't know, but it sounds like they're ready to do the Lord's work with us. They're God-fearing people."

"Louis, I think that's great that they're willing to come up here to talk to us. And I'm grateful for all the traveling and work you've been doing for this thing. But, we have to talk. I . . ."

Canidey folded his hands under his chin, and rested his elbows on the edge of his desk. He smiled, oddly amused as Jessica spoke. His direct stare unnerved her a little.

". . . I think that from now on, you should put in more time here. I'm buried. I just can't handle the load alone."

"God never said this was going to be easy."

"And that's another thing. Do you have to bring this religion bit into every single thing you say?"

He stopped just short of chuckling. "Jessica. God is a part of every single thing I say. Everything I do, think, feel. And He's a part of all that for every creature on earth. It doesn't concern me that our beliefs differ. It's not my place to hold you in judgment, God knows. But I would hope that you'd extend me the same courtesy. Deep down you're doing the Lord's work too, and He'll forgive you."

At that moment Jessica's beeper sounded. She checked the number and threw her hands up in resignation. "Okay. Louis. You say whatever makes you feel good. I don't care. Just, please. I'm getting crushed, and I need you to take up the slack a little bit. Deal?"

"Sure. You need to use the phone?"

"If you don't mind."

He lifted the handset and offered it to Jessica. "Your office, I presume?"

Jessica nodded; Canidey hit one of the insta-dial buttons. "It's Dr. Morraine, what's up?" Jessica listened closely. "Mmm hmm. Okay. Schedule her in as soon as possible. I'll be back over in a few minutes. Thanks. 'Bye." She gave the handset back to Canidey.

"Problem?" he asked.

"Ten-year-old girl. Recurring stomachache. Slight fever. Treated her a few weeks ago. Pain's back. You know, real life? Gotta go." Jessica stood up.

"We'll get together on scheduling a meeting later then," Canidey said as Jessica reached the door.

"Call," she replied. "I'll see ya." She left.

It was after ten P.M. before Jessica pushed open her front door. Gart was waiting on the living room sofa watching TV.

"I'm sorry it's so late," she apologized, dropping her briefcase and shoulder bag on the floor.

"Nah. Don't worry." He stood and greeted her with a hug and a light kiss. "Rough day?"

Jessica cringed a little at the question. It looked and sounded for all the world as if Gart were her husband, and that was a little too much for her to cope with at that moment. She realized that he was becoming an integral part of her family, and serious talk about the future was imminent, but not tonight, she thought. She was tired, and just glad that he'd been there to look after Lucy. "Rough. Yeah. So, is she asleep?"

"For about an hour."

"Good. Any problems?"

"No, no. She was great." He attempted to renew his embrace, and deliver a deeper kiss. As much as she was attracted to him, his youthful, slender features, kind eyes and boyish face, she resisted, pushing him back just enough to send the message.

"What's the matter?"

Her head tilted forward. A tired curl of hair drooped at the side of her face. Her normally clear, bright eyes looked heavy, and wanted to close. "I'm sorry, Gart. I just can't tonight, okay?"

He relaxed his hold. "Yeah. Of course. Whatever you need."

She suddenly felt a little guilty. "I just really need some sleep. So, if it's all right with you . . ."

"You'd like to spend the night apart?"

She confirmed with a nod.

His understanding smile relieved her, and he stepped back, making a gradual angle for the door. She followed, encouraging his departure.

"So, you need me to pick up Lucy in the morning?" he asked, opening the door.

"No. I'll be able to drop her off." She threw an arm around his neck and kissed him fully. Then: "Good night, and thanks so much. You're an angel."

"Not really. I'm just glad to be around. You and Lucy are the real angels."

"Get out of here, before I make you stay. Now go on!" He smiled and ambled down the stoop. He waved as he reached his car. Jessica remained at the door waving back until his taillights were out of sight.

The door was open a crack, allowing a slice of light from the hallway into Lucy's bedroom. Jessica pushed the door open just enough for her to pass through. The light spilled across the bed, revealing a child in a profound sleep. Lucy's drawing pad was at the side of the bed, open to a new picture of a large dark bird that appeared to be flying above a beige colored dog, who was running through a forest. Jessica smiled at the rendering, impressed with her daughter's artistic ability. Then a small, distressed noise suddenly hit Jessica's ears. Lucy shifted and fidgeted, as if she were trying to flee. Jessica sat down on the edge of the bed, and placed her arm around the girl.

"Shh," she whispered in Lucy's ear. "It's okay, honey, I'm here. It's okay."

There were a few more spastic motions from under the covers, and then Lucy rolled over. Her eyes opened.

"Mommy?" she voiced thinly, barely audibly.

"Yeah, baby. It's me. I'm here. You're all right."

Lucy, clung to her mother. "I'm scared, Mommy."

"You were having a nightmare, Luce. That's all. Everybody has a nightmare sometimes."

"I'm scared."

"Shh. It's all right now. Nightmares can't hurt you, okay?" Jessica held her daughter, rocking her gently back and forth for several minutes until it seemed like the little girl had calmed down. "Are you gonna be all right now?"

Lucy was still upset. "I'm scared."

"There's nothing to be scared of, sweetie."

The girl nodded defiantly. "I'm scared . . . he's going to . . . hurt you."

"Nobody's going to hurt me, Luce. It was just a dream. Nobody's going to hurt me, or you. Now, come on. Close your eyes, and think happy thoughts. That way you'll have happy dreams when you fall asleep. I promise! Can you think of some happy thoughts? Come on, we'll do it together."

Lucy didn't respond right away. Then: "Can we get a puppy?"

"A puppy?"

"Can we, please?"

"Well, we'll have to see about that. But for now we can think about all the puppies you want. And then you can dream about them. And they'll protect you from all the scary things in your nightmares. They'll be like your very own guardian angels while you're asleep."

"But what about you?"

"Oh, they'll protect me too. So, let's both dream about puppies tonight, and maybe, just maybe, we can get a real one sometime."

"Soon?"

"Shh. We'll talk about it later. Right now you have to close your eyes, and imagine a wonderful world where nothing bad ever happens." Jessica stroked Lucy's soft hair, and whispered a sweet lullaby, until the little girl's breathing came in the steady rhythm of a peaceful sleep.

SIXTEEN

After a brief stop in Santa Fe for food, water, and gasoline, Reed was back on the road with the first glimpse of the *Sangre de Cristos* coming into view. He continued northward, skirting the fringe of the mountains. He'd decided to abandon the interstate in favor of a more direct route on the state highways that ran at the edge of the range's western foothills. The terrain grew increasingly rugged, walls of stone and forest rising on either side of the road. As the 4Runner gained elevation, the path started to wind, and the outside temperature began to fall. To the north a thunderstorm was amassing strength for an early-evening performance. As Reed approached the limits of Taos, mighty *splats* of water landed in noisy bursts on the windshield. The sky had turned a dark plum. Veins of light streaked from the hills high into the dense overhead soup, rupturing the atmosphere. The detonations which followed shook the air and land alike.

All the charm of Taos was lost on Reed and Hoover as they worked their way through the little, extremely congested town. Taos, it seemed, had grown more popular even than Santa Fe, but its size couldn't accommodate the number of visitors that saturated it daily. Traffic was at a standstill for nearly thirty minutes in the center of town, while the storm hammered down its ire.

Moving several feet at a time, they progressed through the village, Reed patting Hoover on the head every so often. She found the thunder upsetting, and whined through all of it.

Then in rapid order the rain subsided, and the thunderhead cleared, giving way to a sunset worthy of Cíbola. As the storm moved on, so too did Reed escape the snarl of Taos. The highway opened up ahead, and soon they were racing straight for Colorado.

Night arrived almost instantly once the sun had ducked completely under the fold of mountains. They had made a jog west in order to stay parallel with the *Sangre de Cristos*, which placed them on course for the town of Alamosa. Fatigue was setting in like the dull pound of a migraine. Then he realized that except for a few stops for food and gas, he'd been driving since the rest stop in Oklahoma—nearly fifteen hours. Suddenly Alamosa seemed like the perfect place to get dinner and some sleep.

There wasn't much more to the place than a main street, some small businesses housed in old brick buildings, and a scattering of single-family dwellings. Apart from that there was the usual filling station, movie house, 7-Eleven, and Subway sandwich shop. There was also a short row of cheap motels. Reed selected the nicest one he saw, and checked into the El Halcón. No swimming pool this time, but the bed was reasonably firm and the bathroom was clean—and they didn't mind Hoover staying inside.

Reed ate dinner at a local tavern called the Ox Cart, and pondered the atlas over meatloaf and mashed potatoes. He decided to continue up the remainder of the *Sangre de Cristo* range, and then turn westward again, if he found nothing that correlated with the journal entries. He reviewed them again:

Dry waves lie in the Blood of Christ.
Slain in train yard.
See that she is the next of life's soldiers.
No moon's glow in the middle of summer;
Forbidden, forever hidden inside the trunk.

From his pocket he pulled the compact day planner, which he usually carried with him, opening it to the full July and August calendars. It was the twenty-fifth of July. Summer had officially started on the twenty-first of June, and would end on the twenty-first of September. He calculated that the middle of summer would fall exactly at midnight between the fifth and the sixth of August. Eleven days away.

He finished his dinner, and went back to the motel where Hoover was more than ready for a walk around the block.

R eed wasn't out of the motel until almost nine o'clock the next morning. The dream had stayed away, and he'd slept in for the first time in weeks, maybe months. He couldn't really remember. What mattered was that he felt rested, and the day was sunny and clear.

The road north out of town cut a perfectly straight crease up the center of a wide valley. The mountains to the right were relatively low and barren. It was in every way an arid desert region. At the base of the string of rocky bluffs was an odd looking rise of strangely smooth, light-colored hills that rose from the valley floor. The atlas indicated that he was looking at the Great Sand Dunes National Monument. The hills were smooth because they were formed completely of sand. From the highway, the dunes looked like an aberration of the topography, like an enormous patch of aged snow that had drifted from the wind. He passed a sign indicating that the turn leading to the dunes was coming up in one mile. As he neared he could see that the patch of sand extended for miles and that the highest dunes were nothing short of small mountains themselves. The features grew increasingly stunning the closer he got, as if a chunk of the Sahara had been dropped in the middle of southern Colorado. Hoover seemed intrigued too, so much so that she began to bark at the mounds.

"Hey!" Reed yelled. "Quiet down." She turned her head back to Reed with a whimper. "What do you want?" he asked her as they drove past the turn-off. She looked again at the sand and let out another sharp yelp. "What?" Reed yelped back. She would not be quieted nor did she take her eyes from the dunes except to cast pleading looks back at Reed. Finally he had no choice but to pull over. The barking settled into a low grumble, but the object of the dog's vocal attentions was obvious.

"Okay," he conceded. "Okay." Reed decided to try to find out what was causing his dog so much distress and to have a closer look himself at the peculiar geographical phenomenon. He made a wide U-turn, and drove back. Almost immediately upon completing the turn it was apparent that he'd made the right decision, at least as far as Hoover was concerned.

The highway had been even farther from the dunes than Reed had thought. When he supposed he should be arriving at the base of the huge formations, he was still miles away, and their true size became apparent. They really were mountains, endlessly shifting and moving with the wind. Reed passed through the visitors' center, and drove to the parking area. Hoover was anxious to get out of the car and run through the warm powder.

Reed was surprised at how fine the sand was as he walked across the broad flat plain that led to the first low rises—mere introductions to the giants that lay beyond.

Their progress up the steep incline was exhausting—gaining only inches with every step as the sand gave way underfoot. After an hour of struggle, Reed finally made it to the top of one of the smallest of the major dunes. Hoover lumbered up the slope behind him, her initial energy and enthusiasm depleted. At the rate they had climbed, Reed realized that it would be at least half a day's hike to reach the highest summit. But from where he stood he could see the rest of the enormous sand bed, stretching out northward along the foot of the mountains.

The layers, lifting and folding, were still and perfect, like a beige sea locked in time. Reed could not ascertain what it was about the place that had excited Hoover so intensely, or what was draining her of energy now, but one more thing did make sense. The questions that Reed still couldn't answer, again swelled in his mind as he stared out over the vast dry waves . . . the *dry waves in the Blood of Christ.*

T he bed had just been remade, the bathroom cleaned, and the floor vacuumed. Five hours after checking out that morning, Reed checked back in to the El Halcón motel in Alamosa. He'd asked for the same room, and the management was more than happy to oblige.

Hoover curled up on the bed as Reed switched on the night-stand lamp, and picked up the phone.

"Wally, it's Reed," he said resting his head against the receiver. "How's it going, pal?"

Reed's work partner was as glad to hear from Reed as he was pissed. "You mind telling me what's going on?"

"I'm in Colorado. How's everything there?"

"You get nothing until you tell me why you're in Colorado, and what the hell you're doing there. Whitaker's asking me every day what's going on. We're in business here. He FedExed the results to Washington. We've got grant money on the way, and we don't know what the hell to do with it. You've got to get back here, man. You should see Hon. He's been as quiet and cooperative as a lab mouse."

Reed fell back onto the bed. "We got the grant?"

"Yes, Reed, we got the grant. But they can take it away if we can't start producing . . . something."

"That's great. That's great. Uh, listen, Wal, I've got to be here for just a little while."

"Why?"

"It's impossible to explain right now. I just have to do something here. I'm not sure how long it's going to take. But you should just keep on testing more samples and put together a proposal to start testing volunteer subjects who show no signs of disease. Start doing family histories. Do something. But keep the ball rolling."

"Reed, I don't mean to be a buttinski, but why don't you come back and talk to somebody about all this? It can't hurt."

"Gotta go, Wal. Hold it together there for us. I have complete confidence in you. I'll call when I've finished what I've got to do."

"At least tell me where I can reach—"

"Wal," Reed cut him off. "Please . . . I've got to go." This time Wally seemed to accept Reed's insistence, at least for the moment. Reed said good-bye, hung up, and immediately called Dale and Bettyanne. He told them where he was and that he would stay in touch with them, offering no more than "some personal business" as an explanation for his prolonged absence. They didn't press about what he was doing, but as he cradled the handset, he sensed that his assurances that everything was all right hadn't been completely convincing.

This was the place to be. He felt he knew that much for certain. His thoughts turned immediately to the journal.

Slain in train yard, was the next entry. He had many more questions than he had answers, but at least he had something tangible from which to continue seeking.

He decided to spend the remainder of the day looking around town. From his motel it was only a four block walk to the "downtown" area. Everywhere there were signs of the town's history, from the old City Hall to the courthouse—structures typical of the nineteenth century flagstone construction that was popular in the area at the time of the town's founding. These buildings were made to last, and last they had. With only a few modernizations since their construction, they were much as they had been for over a hundred years, and solid as ever.

The unsettling contrast lay in the buildings of more recent ilk that lined the majority of the main street. These were unimaginative, wood or concrete structures, sided with aluminum—or worse . . . vinyl. It was in these two and three story affairs that one found the diners, pawnshops, and bars.

The most unattractive building of any size was the hospital. Stained bricks climbing to four stories in utilitarian, purely functional form—a box. Age and weather had maligned the color of the edifice, and the ventilation equipment on the roof gave to thoughts of a wrecking yard. The institution was in dire need of cosmetic surgery. Toward that end, on one side of the decrepit building, was what appeared to be the beginnings of an addition, though progress appeared to have come to a halt some time ago.

As the day began to slip away, Reed stepped into one of Main Street's several drab taverns called The Dunes—a rather pitiful attempt at association with the famous Las Vegas casino—to see if he could pick up any local gossip that might prove helpful.

The little bar was cast in the same mold as countless thousands of other bars that typified the small town American "watering hole": Formica bar top with padded front edge; mirrored wall behind; dollar bills from 1967 taped to the cash register; a large plastic jar beside it filled with beef jerky strips and Slim Jims at a dollar apiece; neon beer signs; calendars picturing large-busted women in provocative poses, and the ubiquitous smell of alcohol mixed with a generous portion of loneliness, all shrouded in a dark amber light that helped keep reality just that much more obscured. Inside these places you could always imagine that it was the middle of the night, even if the rest of town was just starting its lunch hour. But as Reed stepped into the hall of deadened senses, it was just about "cocktail hour," and a light crowd had started to gather. At the far end were the old-timers who'd probably been sitting there, on their favorite stools, since mid-afternoon. Then there was the younger working group who had found a way to make a living from the local economy. These were the talkers. Reed took a vacant stool near the front of the bar. A few seats away, a group of three young men and two women were hanging on to a dying weekend, talking about the latest controversies at their places of employment. They eyed Reed with a little curiosity and a little caution. Strangers in town, though not a rarity, were a source of possible intrigue, or danger, and certainly gossip. The pentad were all in their mid twenties, healthy-looking and attractive. The women, it became clear, were clerks at a grocery store. One of the men looked like an auto mechanic, the other two Reed couldn't tell from the simple jeans and T-shirts. Reed looked away, then ordered a beer from the bartender, a charcoal-haired older woman of slight proportion who spoke with a heavy dry rasp. He heard one of the men call her Agnes. She delivered the beer with a quick "two fifty." Reed passed her a five and told her to keep the change. This brightened her face slightly as she dropped the overpayment into a glass jar next to the register.

"There a train yard in town?" Reed asked.

Agnes leaned a sharp elbow down on the bar a few feet from Reed. "You like trains?"

"Yeah," he answered. "I'm kind of a buff."

"Well, yeah, we got a train yard at the station. Half a mile south. It ain't much to see." Agnes gave a little cough, a smoker's hack. "Not a helluva lot of people take the train anymore."

"No, they don't," Reed agreed, "It's a bit of a shame."

"Yes it is."

Agnes proceeded to go into a story about how her grandfather had once taken her on a train to Philadelphia. "You got to see something of your country that way," she reminisced, "not like taking a plane where you're in one place, and then suddenly in another, like there was nothing in between."

Reed again agreed, and asked for specific instructions on how to get to the train station, which Agnes was happy to supply. She concluded by asking him if he wanted another beer, what his name was, and where he was from.

"Yes," "Reed Haler," and "California," were his respective answers, as Agnes set a fresh bottle down in front of him. Before he could finish his second beer, Reed heard the names of all the people Agnes knew in California and accounts of the three times she'd been to the Golden State.

"So, what brings you to Alamosa, Reed?" she then asked.

"Just driving 'cross country. Back home." Reed finished his beer quickly. "Well, Agnes, you've been very nice and very helpful. But I gotta get going."

"All right. Hope you like the trains, and come on back soon."

Reed promised to return before he left town. A few more Sunday drinkers entered just as Reed was leaving. He had to go back to the motel, feed Hoover, and then take a drive down to the train yard before it got too dark.

Agnes had been quite correct: there was very little to see at the train station and adjoining railyard. *"Slain in train yard,"* Reed repeated to himself. The station comprised little more than a small shelter with a shallow-pitched, shed-type roof overhanging the platform, and an arrival/departure schedule posted on the wall. Several small wooden maintenance buildings stood out beyond the main tracks, padlocked and boarded up against trespass. The station office was housed in a parked trailer at the side of the platform. The transcontinental Amtrak came through a couple times a day, and the Colorado Springs–Alamosa–Denver run passed by three times daily, but that was about it besides the heavy freight traffic. There was a small parking lot and a public telephone sticking out of a weed patch that had sprung up through cracks in the old pavement. A row of bright bluish lamps began to flicker on over the platform. Behind the station, several rows of track supported about a dozen out-of-service rail cars. Some were for passengers, others for freight; most were rusting from disuse. Beyond the service tracks, a good fifty yards farther, sat another building, or rather the ruins of one, at the top of a gentle rise. It had been built from the typical pink flagstone of the area, and appeared to be of the same vintage as the municipal building and courthouse. But this building was without a roof, doors, glass in the windows, or any part that had been constructed of material other than rock. Weeds lurked up the walls on all sides, and graffiti adorned the rough stone exterior. It had been a stunning sight once, Reed could tell—arched windows and doorways, intricately detailed capitals, cornices, and window moldings, and very sharp, almost gothic gables facing each direction. In the center of each gable was the framing for perfectly round windows, which he imagined once held spectacular stained glass. Round bartizans at the building's corners gave the structure the feel of a medieval castle. Otherwise it had all the qualities of a small but graceful cathedral. The building had clearly been the object of years, decades perhaps, of neglect and abuse. It was a stone shell, a relic of a far statelier time. Apart from the points of architectural interest, Reed couldn't discern anything of significance from the place, which by itself, it seemed, was going to betray nothing. Had someone been slain there? That was something he'd have to find out. He made one final look around, let Hoover take care of some personal business, then headed back into town for dinner.

SEVENTEEN

The man was about thirty-five, Reed's own age, but was more muscular and trim. The woman seemed slightly younger, and was apparently the mother of the little girl who sat at her side, laughing quietly, and eating her dinner like a grown-up. The three sat in a booth directly across from Reed in the small dining room of the Ox Cart, where he had dined the night before. It was a rustic place with knotty pine walls, corroded branding irons decorating the ceiling, and a massive ox yoke above the swinging double doors to the kitchen. All the artifacts looked quite genuine, and had probably been found lying out in deserted fields over the years.

The chicken-fried steak had been tasty and filling, the mashed potatoes chunky and homemade, the way Reed liked them. In addition to the trio Reed had noticed, there were two other couples in the dining area and a handful of locals stewing at the bar. Country music droned out of an old jukebox at the back of the barroom behind a small pool table, where two colorless youths were engaged in a game of eight ball.

As Reed sipped his beer, he glimpsed the little girl looking at him curiously. She couldn't have been more than six or seven years old, but had a mature, intelligent face, alert brown eyes, and a sweet curl to her blond, cinnamon-streaked hair, which was just a shade lighter than her mother's. Kernels of conversation reached Reed's ears from which he learned two things: one, the woman worked at the hospital, and two, the man was almost certainly not the girl's father. From the way he refrained from making too much physical contact, and his general body language, Reed speculated that the man probably wasn't the woman's husband either.

Reed listened, feigning interest in his steak, as the woman discussed a nervous young female patient who had been suffering from symptoms of fatigue, flu, and digestive system disorders. The blood work had shown normal white cells, which ruled out leukemia, but antibiotics had been ineffective. She spoke like a stumped doctor, which Reed suspected was the case. The conversation was interrupted when the man got up and headed for the rest room. Reed saw that he was a good six feet tall, had short, light brown hair, was physically strong, and had the kind of face that made instant friends. Now, with a clearer view, the little girl increased her eye contact with Reed, turning away with a blush when Reed returned a coy smile. The girl's mother took instant notice, erecting a defensive wall of suspicion with one glance and a very intentional turn of her body.

"Come on, finish your dinner," she instructed her daughter, in an obvious attempt to direct the girl's attention away from the lone stranger, and back to her green beans.

The woman had the same lightly freckled complexion and nut-brown eyes as her daughter. She was the type Reed would have pursued shamelessly had he been single, and not mourning the death of his wife.

The little girl continued eating, but couldn't resist sneaking peeks in Reed's direction, which he indulged with comical expressions. The girl laughed, to her mother's consternation.

"Don't worry," Reed finally said, "I'm pretty harmless."

The woman forced the briefest smile in Reed's direction, and then turned away again, making a pretense of wiping her daughter's mouth.

"Are you from around here?" Reed ventured.

The woman looked back over at Reed, a trace of annoyance slipping into the soft crease between her brows. "You could say that."

"You've got a great-looking kid there."

"Oh," the woman couldn't help softening a little at the compliment. "Thank you."

"I uh, was wondering, since you're from around here, if you could tell me what the old stone building out by the train station is . . . was?"

"Why?"

"I saw it today, and . . . it just looked like a shame that it was allowed to fall apart like that."

"That was the old train station, from the eighteen hundreds I suppose. It's been like that since I can remember. Probably always will be."

"Oh. Well, it looked interesting . . . architecturally, I mean."

"Yeah, I guess."

"My name's Reed Haler," he introduced himself, "I'm just on my way through."

"Oh." The woman's attention was back on her daughter and a few wayward green beans.

"What's your name? If you don't mind my asking," Reed asserted.

The annoyance slid back into her attitude. "I'm kinda tired, you know? So, if you don't mind, I'm not really in the mood to socialize right now."

"So, he's not your husband then . . ." Reed took a chance.

"What?" Now she turned to glare at him.

"The guy who just went to the bathroom."

"Look," she said, shaking her head, now clearly perturbed, "I don't know you, and my personal life is none of your business."

"You're right. I'm sorry." Reed raised his hands in concession. "I was just curious about the old train station."

"Then you can read about it at the historical archives. Downtown . . . can't miss it."

"Thanks, I'll do that."

Reed went back to his beer when he noticed the man returning from the rest room.

"Well, I should get going," Reed heard the man say to the woman. He hadn't taken his seat again, but instead picked up his faded Levi's jacket from the booth, and gave the woman a light kiss on the cheek, and a pat on her daughter's head.

"Okay, see you tomorrow," the woman said softly, looking up at the man with vaguely sad eyes.

"See ya. And you," he directed to the little girl, "we'll start you on the uneven bars, how 'bout that?"

The little girl nodded with a forced "Okay."

"Okay. 'Bye-'bye." He dragged a lazy finger over the woman's shoulder as he walked toward the door.

Reed looked on furtively from behind his beer bottle. Immediately the little girl resumed smiling at him. Reed couldn't help responding in kind. Then his heart seized with thoughts of his own daughter, who'd never even had a chance at life.

A moment later the woman was again cognizant of the goings-on between her daughter and Reed, realizing this time, however, that it was her daughter, and not Reed, who'd initiated the silent exchange. Her expression relaxed almost to the point of a reluctant smile.

"Did you culture for histoplasmosis?" Reed asked, sensing a renewed opportunity.

"What?" came back, the woman's voice again timbred with irritation and now confusion.

"Forgive me, but I overheard you mention a patient earlier. I was just wondering if you'd cultured for histoplasmosis?"

She gave Reed a sharp squint. "If you're a doctor, I can handle my own patients, thank you."

"If the histoplasmosis came back negative, you might take a stomach X ray," Reed persisted.

"Her condition hasn't warranted an X ray. If I want a second opinion, I'll ask for it."

"You said she was a nervous girl. Does she have long hair?"

"I said I can handle my own patients. What is your problem?"

"It could be a hair ball."

"A what?"

"A hair ball."

"She's a little girl, not a cat."

"Next time you see her, watch if she nibbles on the ends of her hair. The symptoms sound consistent with a case a friend of mine had once."

"A hair ball."

"Just a thought." Reed freshly regarded his beer, noting that he only had a few sips left with which to sustain his excuse for remaining.

The little girl was stealing shy looks again.

"So, are you a doctor?" her mother then asked. "I thought you were interested in architecture." Reed's suggestion had apparently taken a chip out of the wall.

"Yeah, I'm a doctor. And you are . . . ?"

"Okay . . . okay." she relented. "I'm Jessica, and this is Lucy, but I see you've already met."

Reed set his beer down next to his plate. "It's very nice meeting you, Jessica, and you, Lucy."

Lucy giggled, her cheeks flushing a light pink.

"Well, I suppose it's nice to meet you too. What did you say your name was?"

"Reed Haler."

"Reed," Jessica repeated, "I like that name."

"Thanks. Jessica's nice too."

"It's common and dull."

"Not so."

"Well, thanks. I'm sorry I wasn't the friendliest before. I'm just really tired, and I hope I didn't give you the impression that people from Alamosa are rude separatists or something. We're not as closed off as that."

"Oh no," Reed assured, "not at all."

"So, what kind of medicine do you practice, Dr. Haler?"

Reed explained his line of research, which seemed to intrigue Jessica more than he had expected.

"So, I'm pretty anxious to get back," he concluded.

"What are you doing here, anyway, with all the advances you're in the middle of?"

Reed hadn't even bothered to consider a response to that question. "I'm . . . uh . . . just driving 'cross country. Vacation. Had to take it now or I'd lose it, you know."

"Vacation. Ha! I've heard of it."

"You sound busy."

" 'Busy' doesn't even describe it."

"Pediatrics?"

"Yeah. I'm basically the department. So, I'm running that *and* trying to start a children's hospital."

"And raising a daughter."

"Yeah."

Lucy smiled self-consciously.

"A children's hospital. What prompted you to take on a project like that?"

"I'm actually continuing an existing project that was started a long time ago. Carrying the torch, I guess you'd say."

"Oh. I see. That's a hell of a load to take on at one time."

"We get by. I've got good friends."

"And a work partner, I assume . . ."

"Yeah. Sort of. He's away a lot. Conferences, fund-raising for the hospital. He does the traveling and I hold down the fort. Not exactly a fair deal, but . . ." she lowered her voice, ". . . frankly I'm better with the patients, but don't tell anyone I said that."

"Shh, promise," Reed said, holding a finger up to his lips. "Any family around?" he continued.

"My parents live in Colorado Springs. They're old and can't travel much. I don't see them very often."

"I know how you feel. I really should make more of an effort to see my parents. You get all wrapped up in your own world, and your career, and you think that you'll always have the chance to catch up at some more convenient time in the future. But that time never seems to come. And then you realize after years of waiting that it never will."

"True . . . and sad," she agreed.

"Brothers and sisters?" he asked.

"Two brothers, one older, one younger. One's in Oregon, the other's in Nevada somewhere, last anyone heard."

"What about Lucy's father?" The air suddenly chilled; Lucy's blush drained away along with her smile. "Uh . . . if I'm not getting too personal, that is."

"He left us when Lucy was three."

"Oh. I'm really sorry to hear that. So, who was . . . ?" Reed gestured to the vacant seat across from Jessica, where the tall muscular man had been sitting.

"That was Gart. He's Lucy's gymnastics coach, and yeah, you're getting a little too personal."

"Sorry."

"Well, kid," Jessica said, turning to Lucy, "it's about time we got going. We've got a big week ahead."

"Okay," the little girl said, in the tiniest voice Reed had ever heard. She didn't seem upset, but her smile had still not returned.

As Jessica and her daughter slid out of the booth and to their feet, Reed scrunched up his nose into a goofy expression, hoping to provoke one more giggle from the little girl before she left. He then flashed her a big grin. She only looked back with a half-hearted effort at cheer.

" 'Bye. It was nice meeting you," he said to both of them.

"It was nice meeting you too. Enjoy your stay and the train station, and good luck with your research. I'll check the journals for your progress."

"Thanks, I'll do the same for yours."

Several minutes later Reed paid his check and left too. He drove several miles until he was well outside the town limits. Traveling east he found a road that ascended into the desolate hills just south of the Great Dunes, where he pulled over at a vacant turnout overlooking the valley and the small town below. It was a clear cool night; the small cluster of lights which were Alamosa twinkled within the lightless surroundings much like stars reflecting off the moonless mirror of a midnight lake. On the surface, nothing seemed out of kilter. But this was the place Devrie's journal had led him. He rolled down the window of the 4×4, and switched off the engine. He listened to the night, listened for more clues, any meaning in the chirp of thousands of crickets and the silent vibration of the universe. Off to the right he could make out the markedly lighter hues of the enormous dune formations nestled at the base of the mountains. The call of a distant coyote only bolstered the sense of normalcy and nature as it was supposed to be. But what about *super*nature? When would its influence throw this little corner of earth into chaos? Would it even have an influence? Or was it all some huge delusion that in his grief Reed had fabricated out of nothing? Then he remembered Maysie Fabrioso. Hadn't she confirmed his beliefs? Maybe he only thought she had. It seemed hard to imagine the serene community below the site of any wicked encounters with messengers of evil. But then the Sierras had seemed equally tranquil, he remembered.

Had Reed been a smoker he would have taken a last pull on a strong cigarette, and flicked the butt out the window, the orange tip spiraling through the air until it landed in a burst of sparks on the ground. As it was, he simply turned the ignition and rolled back onto the road.

When he was again on level ground and winding his way back, his mind returned to Jessica and her daughter, Lucy. He wondered what kind of man would leave such an attractive pair, and why. He boiled inside when he considered the way in which his own wife and child had been taken from him so cruelly, while someone could willingly abandon a woman as lovely as Jessica and a daughter as charming as Lucy. As he rolled these thoughts and ill feelings around in his mind, he passed something on the road that propelled his foot to the brake pedal. He pulled over and swung a wide U-turn on the empty road. He drove back to a sparsely lit wooden building. There were several cars and trucks in the parking lot, and a small sign which he'd almost missed. The little establishment was yet another of the many bars to be found in those parts. The hand-painted sign by the road bore the name proudly: The New Moon Saloon. It had tripped a circuit in his brain. He realized that he had hyper-sensitized himself to anything that might bear some relevance to his purpose. *No moon's glow...* He recalled the words. *No moon's glow in the middle of summer.* He considered the possibility of a connection, and drove into the parking lot. There was nothing outstanding about the place that he could see. He studied the cars in the lot, nothing struck him. He decided to go inside and check things out; he needed to use the rest room anyway.

The New Moon Saloon was about as colorful as the bar he'd been in earlier—same mold. There were four men, all around fifty, at the bar drinking Miller Lite and watching a baseball game on the TV. A younger man played pool with a mildly overweight brunette, apparently his girlfriend. Reed used the men's room, and then took a stool at the bar, casually assessing each man and the bartender: a buxom redhead with a loud cackle and a dingy smoker's grin. In an effort to conform, Reed ordered a Miller Lite too, and watched a few minutes of the game, feeling not the slightest a part of the moment. The conversation was about fertilizer, farming equipment repair, the bullshit the government was trying to put over on its honest hard-working citizenry, and the general deterioration of society, with an equal mix of pitching arms, RBI's, and corrupt umpires. It was the same conversation that was going on in thousands of similar bars across the country.

He'd only finished about half his beer when Reed conceded that the New Moon Saloon wasn't going to relinquish any secrets, not at that point anyway. So he slid a soggy dollar bill to the back of the bar and left.

Hoover was impatiently waiting for her dinner and a walk by the time Reed arrived back at the motel. After completing those tasks, he settled into bed, and freshly considered the remaining messages:

Slain in train yard;
See that she is the next of life's soldiers;
No moon's glow in the middle of summer;
Forbidden, forever hidden inside the trunk.

They hadn't become any clearer since his arrival in Alamosa. He knew that "new moon" meant the same thing as "no moon," but he didn't see the significance of the "New Moon Saloon." Maybe he would by the middle of summer—now ten days away. But maybe this wasn't the right place after all, he conjectured. Maybe he'd made a mistake. Then he remembered how certain he'd felt at the first sight of the Sand Dunes Monument, and his confidence gradually strengthened. The train yard was the place, he decided, to resume his search in the morning. Then he caught some local news and an old black-and-white movie on TV. Reluctantly, he let his eyes slip closed.

The chromatic walls were now bleeding from the ceiling to the floor; the underlying surfaces had taken on the character of raw meat. At the end of the hall, the glow cut to a sharp point from a fine crack in the door. The glow brightened, widened as the door opened further, an orange gush falling over Reed's face. Then black. A silhouette chopped through the beam of fluttering light. The menace rose up, obscured the glow, cast its shadow of invisible resin as Reed tried to move down the incarnadine passage. This time he got closer, a good deal closer than before. He felt the presence of the Indian behind him again, heard his deep nasal breathing. Then the voice came: *"You smell of fear."* The Indian was close, somehow helping him to move more freely through the thickening air that wasn't really air, but more a vapor of blood. The dark figure stepped into the corridor, now revealing more of the world beyond. The floor on the other side of the door was of earth, and the undulating light came from a fire in a pit on the ground. Reed was able to keep his eyes up and open long enough to see the crackling flames. The black figure then made a turning movement, darkening its shadow, locking Reed's muscles. Now the figure was turned away from Reed and appeared slightly hunched over, its hands fiddling with something in front of it. Reed recognized the stance, the posture of a man urinating. Reed could see a fresh stream, not of urine, but of a Mars black liquid, which ran down the wall between the figure's legs. The sound of the liquid flow was distinct. The figure was relieving itself against the wall next to the door that led to the fire. The narrow stream meandered its way closer to Reed's feet, and as it neared, his muscles froze harder, locking him into full paralysis again. But this time Reed was able to keep his eyes open, his head up, and could see that the figure was shaking. He recognized the man's suppressed laughter—a silent, acutely vile mirth. Reed's breathing came harder. The paralysis was extending to his lungs, as if he were about to suffocate on the odor of raw flesh. The obscure hulking man continued to urinate and tremble with glee. The Indian's voice was inches from Reed's ear: *"You smell of fear."*

The flickering light was no longer a fire but a TV, flashing in Reed's eyes. His whole body jerked as he regained control of his muscles; his chest heaved for air. Hoover grunted at his feet as Reed kicked and thrashed under the covers. The only light was that of an infomercial about some get-rich-quick scheme, but the TV was silent apart from a low, electrical buzz coming from its one small speaker. The darkness behind the windows told that the sun was still hidden somewhere below the horizon. Reed didn't remember having turned the volume down, but the lips on the screen moved without voices. Reed sat up, grabbing the remote control next to the telephone on the nightstand. He found the volume control button on the keypad and pressed it, but to no avail. He tried advancing the channel, which instantly restored the sound with a blaring audio explosion. Hoover reared up, howling at the blasting TV. Reed frantically pressed buttons on the remote, trying madly to subdue the roaring music video that threatened to awaken the entire motel. Only by chance did he manage to hit the power button and the room was, in the next instant, plunged back into silence and darkness. He felt his pulse register in every extremity, and heard a ring in his ears. His body was damp with perspiration and his chest pumped fast. Surely the last thing on his mind was sex, but he realized, as his heart slowly returned to normal, and he settled back into the pillows, that since he'd awoken from the nightmare . . . he'd had an extremely hard and uncomfortable erection.

When sleep returned, it was relatively uneventful. He didn't wake up again until ten o'clock. Breakfast was a cup of coffee and a strawberry Danish. Lingering effects of the dream had taken some of his appetite.

The late morning sun was already cooking the earth by the time he arrived once again at the train station. In the bright daylight the station seemed an entirely different place than the deserted expanse of track and rusting rail cars he'd visited the night before. Hoover roamed happily around the parking lot and onto the platform, exploring this new uncharted territory. The hollow stone relic of the old station building stood watch, its round window eyes staring down in impotent judgment upon its unworthy successor. The dirty pink beige of the original building, or rather the remains thereof, was deadened to a ruddy gray in the shadow of a small mountain to the southeast.

Reed noticed a rail worker out on the tracks, perambulating, making some kind of inspection, and another worker in uniform on the platform near the station house, a bundle of keys dangling from a large ring in his hand. Reed presumed that this was the station manager. As the tall bearded man twirled the keys on his way to the trailer/office, he took notice of Hoover galloping up and down the platform.

"Come here, girl," Reed called to the Labrador. She obeyed reluctantly, joining Reed as he approached the shelter on which the train schedule was posted. The manager looked back to make sure that Reed had gained control of his dog, and disappeared inside the trailer, which rested on stacks of cinder blocks at each corner. The yard worker had moved down in the direction of one of the service buildings, his bright orange vest vibrating in the sun. Hoover looked up as if to ask, "What now?"

Reed scanned the area, looking for what, he didn't know. The tracks were deserted again except for the worker, who was now at least forty yards away, and still moving. The rusting cars stood as still and silent as the rock of the old station building—or so Reed at first thought. On second glance, he noticed the shape of a person standing under the main archway in the center of the building's front facade. He peered left and right to see if anyone else was around. The station manager was tucked away in his trailer, and the yard worker was now out of sight too. Reed looked back up at the weathered shell that symbolized a lost sense of elegance. The person (a woman, Reed could see) remained where she stood in the black archway. It seemed to Reed, from that distance, that the woman was looking directly at him. Her brown hair was tied behind her head and Reed could see that she wore a dark green blouse and a black skirt. He couldn't be sure of her age, but she didn't appear old or particularly young. Her apparent gaze induced a sudden self-consciousness in him, a vaguely disturbing chill. He looked away. Hoover sneezed, drawing Reed's attention, and then began prancing in small circles on the cement platform. The woman in the archway was still there, still staring down. The chill rose. Hoover looked ready to go somewhere, and at Reed's slightest movement she bounded off the platform and across the tracks in the direction of the old station building.

"Hey, where do you think you're going?" Reed called after the dog, scanning left and right for any sign of a coming train. The dog ignored him completely, and continued toward the rotting boxcars.

"Get back here!" he yelled, without effect. He had no choice but to follow.

Hoover was sitting just beyond the last stretch of track by the time Reed caught up with her. He gave her soft head an affectionate pat.

"What's with you? Where you going, girl?"

She sneezed again, with a violent shake of her head, then moved off in the direction of the crumbling building; still the woman remained, unmoved. Now closer, Reed could see more clearly. She stood in the center of the high, circular archway, hands folded in front, her feet together. Reed stumbled after Hoover, who seemed to be taking a direct path for the archway. Reed was certain that the woman gazed directly upon him. As he meandered between the thick tufts of grass and weeds, he was forced to keep half his attention on the spiny obstacles in front of him, the other half on Hoover and the watcher. He managed his way through the ground cover, gathering a painful collection of burrs and stickers on his socks and on the length of his jeans. His legs itched and stung from thigh to ankle. Hoover, unbothered by the grasses, had stopped at the foot of the hill on which the gutted edifice reposed. A handsome magpie churred from the peak of the central gable, fluffing its black and white feathers. The sun hung at its midday apex, broiling the earth. It felt to Reed as if the celestial heat, combined with the stare of the woman, actually brought physical weight to bear on his shoulders. Yet inside he felt the strange coolness he'd noticed since first seeing the stranger. Hoover seemed unconcerned with the temperature, and launched herself up the hill.

The slope was not steep, but there remained another daunting barricade of sharp thistles, cacti, and a type of long grass which dispatched needle sharp pricklers into whatever touched it. Reed stumbled his way up the hill, now less than fifty feet from the face of the structure. As he arrived at the top, he found Hoover sitting, patiently waiting. Reed kept an eye on the woman as he got closer. He could now make out the gold of her eyes, the fine lines of gray within her dark brown hair. She was about ten years older than he, and while not unattractive, she had a motherly aspect in the contours of her face. But there was something else about her which bothered him. It was a feeling hinged on the fact that she'd blatantly, purposefully watched him walk all the way from the station platform, through the thistles and briars and up the hill. In a few moments he would have the chance to ask her why, face to face. But that opportunity filled him with an ill-defined yet palpable dread.

EIGHTEEN

As Reed approached, he didn't notice that Hoover lagged behind. When he glanced down to find that the dog wasn't at his heels, he stopped to look back. The Lab sat, gave a quiet little whine, but refused to come any closer.

"Now what's the matter?"

She lightly padded the ground with her front paws, and bobbed her head slightly, but her rump remained firmly seated.

"Come on, you big sissy. You wanted to come up here."

Reed turned back toward the building, expecting to find some menacing entity sufficiently disturbing to arrest the animal where she sat. Instead he saw the woman turn and walk into the darkness of the cavernous structure, the vacant, slightly sad expression on her face remaining unchanged. Within seconds she had disappeared completely, and Hoover was again next to Reed, panting and nuzzling up against his knees.

"Hey, wait!" Reed called out to the void. "Hold on a second."

Together Reed and Hoover stepped closer to the front of what was truly a magnificent ruin. It appeared that a road, now thoroughly overgrown from lack of use, wound in a circuitous route from some remote point at the edge of town to the old station. Reed wondered if he could have actually driven right up to the place, and avoided the thrashing his legs had received. Probably, he speculated . . . probably.

He turned his attention to the wide marble path which led from what had formerly been a parking area to the main entrance. Terraced gardens had flanked either side of the walkway. Now those gardens were stepped weed planters of intricate stonework that matched the building's walls and polished granite-capped parapets. At the corners of the thick planter walls were the remains of polished granite pedestals, which once supported statuary long since destroyed or stolen. The entrance had a great formality to it, rather like the mansions of the industrial barons who owned the early railroads. Etched into the granite entablature above the entrance were the words: BY LAW, LAND AND RAIL SHALL WE SURVIVE AND PROSPER. Posted on the side of the entrance was a sign in bold Day-Glo–red letters expressly prohibiting trespass. Reed violated the warning without hesitation, stepping over a pile of rotting boards that looked like the remains of what had been a barricade, broken down and never replaced.

Inside, the air was cool and rife with the must of age. The floor was smooth rock, slate perhaps, possibly marble—a thick coating of dust made it impossible to tell. It took Reed's eyes a minute to adjust. Above, splinters of light found their way through gaps in the upper floors, but not enough filtered down to provide adequate illumination.

"Hello." Reed called out. As he stepped farther into the black hollow, he listened for a response. There was none . . . no sound of footsteps, of breathing, or any other sign that another person inhabited the space within. He wished that he'd brought a flashlight, but gradually he was able to make out the surrounding walls. There was nothing left of what had been the interior treatment—only raw flagstone and mortar. At the far end of the main room, a block of light angled down from a hole in the ceiling where, Reed supposed, a stairway had communicated to the second floor. The area around the rectangular opening was cast in the bluish glow of the sky. The station was reduced to its structural elements, only standing because the solid walls and supports had been built to endure centuries. At the opposite end of the great hall were the ticket booths, their windows only square openings with a few rusty iron rods clinging to powdering masonry. The ceiling was supported by great columns of rounded flagstone. Wide joists, nearly rotted through, held up the planks which formed the floor of the second level. This was the only wood that remained, as far as Reed could tell, and that was fast disintegrating. It would only be a matter of time before the ceiling fell in, and he realized that he didn't want to be standing inside the place when it happened.

Arched openings in the back wall had been bricked up. These, Reed presumed, had let onto the platform, which was surely buried in overgrowth like the rest of the grounds. Other than the three front doorways, there was no apparent means of exit from the giant monument to a bygone era. Somehow the woman was gone. Reed was certain that he would have seen her had she left through one of the other doorways. The air seemed to frost the perspiration on his face, cooling him from within. Then he noticed the path of footprints he'd made in the dust on the floor, leading from the building's entrance to where he now stood. There was nothing unusual about them, except that his were the only ones.

He hurried back outside and scanned the area. He found no one . . . except Hoover, who'd been waiting just outside the station, now joining him as he rounded one of the outside corners of the edifice.

Nothing but weeds.

He continued to the back where, as he expected, the old platform had been. It was apparent where the track had once paralleled the rear wall of the station. Stone supports rose up at fifteen foot intervals where a roof had protected waiting passengers from inclement weather. Still, there was no sign of the woman.

On the other side of the rail bed, the edge of the forest patiently, persistently encroached, gradually reclaiming its right. An enormous black-charred cottonwood trunk, easily three feet in diameter and apparently the victim of lightning, appeared to lead the assault; little saplings advanced the cause, inspired by their martyr.

Stepping as swiftly as he could, Reed continued through the brush, around the rest of the station, collecting still more burrs in his pants and socks. When he had completed his search of the perimeter, it was clear that the woman was no longer there. Reed looked at Hoover as if to ask whether she had any ideas. The dog gave only an inquisitive head tilt; she seemed as perplexed as he.

Reed once again scrutinized the darkness of the interior for any indication that the woman was still there. Only the NO TRESPASSING sign answered his query. His sense that something was very out of balance came on stronger than ever, but the woman's inexplicable disappearance now seemed, at least, consistent.

Reed's legs and ankles were red and swollen from the attack of the prickly grass and thistles. He had returned to the motel after trudging his way back through the railyard, his jeans loaded with the jabbing little needles, his skin burning with hundreds of tiny stab wounds. It looked like a severe rash that was devouring his flesh. After a cool shower, he swabbed his skin with peroxide, which only intensified the hot itch.

The room was stifling, so he switched on the air conditioner and lay down under the cool draft. The peculiar encounter, or near encounter, at the train yard had taken more out of him than he'd expected. Hoover, too, seemed to require a nap. Reed had learned to fear sleep in recent days, but was fatigued to the point that he couldn't help slipping into a spontaneous doze.

The air-conditioning had chilled the room thoroughly and the sun had moved on when Reed awoke. Hoover welcomed him back to consciousness with a long wet tongue on his cheek. He shoved her snout out of his face with one hand, while straining to a sitting position. Though his legs were still tender, the red dots had settled down and the itching had largely passed.

Having gained two hours of relatively peaceful sleep, he felt sufficiently restored to continue his exploration of the vicinity.

With Hoover loaded into the 4Runner, he drove down Main Street to the other side of town, and found the hospital. There was ample parking in the visitors' and patients' lot so he pulled in, selecting a space that offered a clear view of the main entrance. Between him and the building's automatic doors was a primly kept lawn, bordered by a wide arcing drive that allowed for drop-off and pickup at the door. A sidewalk lined with short grass, sturdy maples, and densely planted hedges of forsythia and azalea connected the parking lot to the entrance portico. The building's relative disrepair presented an odd contrast to the well-kept grounds. Reed checked his watch: ten to five. It appeared that many of the staff were already getting off duty, and heading for their cars in the employee lot on the opposite side of the entrance drive. He scrutinized the faces as they emerged, but over a fifteen minute period, no Jessica. The flow of departing health care workers dwindled quickly. Hoover scuttled between the front seats and into the back where she made herself comfortable, as if in anticipation of again being left to wait while her benefactor went off to continue his quest. Reed looked back with a big smile at the panting dog.

"Good girl. I won't be long."

She settled her nose in between her front paws.

He entered the building through the central revolving doors, assessing each face he saw. No Jessica. Pediatrics, he remembered. He went to the information desk in the center of the entry vestibule and inquired.

The information clerk behind the desk said, "Third floor, east wing."

"Third floor, east wing," Reed repeated for confirmation. "Thank you very much."

The information clerk smiled and went back to her book.

Reed found his bearings, and headed down the hallway to the right of the information desk. A small group of doctors, nurses, and administrators waited at a bank of three elevators for the next car to arrive. No Jessica. Suddenly a tremendous rush of guilt circulated through his arteries to every extremity and back through his heart for a fresh dose. With stark surprise, he realized what he was doing. He imagined Devrie, watching him as he wandered around the hospital like a love-struck kid surreptitiously visiting the workplace of his obsession. He didn't know, himself, his true purpose for being there; he had just felt that visiting the hospital was the next tangible thing to do. As the elevator arrived, he admitted to himself that he had been very attracted to Jessica, but he had no intention of trying to develop any kind of romance with her, or with any other woman for that matter. His conscience eased considerably when the horrific memories of what was behind his mission crowded back in. He was there to get information, nothing more, and Jessica seemed like someone who might be willing to give him some. By the time he stepped off the elevator, Reed had fully justified his present course of action. He followed the large green arrow posted on the wall opposite the elevators, directing him to the nurses' station. He stopped at the counter, and inquired of the balding young man on the other side about a physician's roster. Reed presented his own medical credentials to validate the request, which seemed to satisfy the nurse. The man gave Reed the names of the two pediatricians on staff with the hospital: Jessica Morraine and Louis Canidey.

Morraine. Reed repeated the name to himself, deep into his permanent memory. "Is Dr. Morraine on duty at the moment?"

"I believe she's in a meeting right now," the young man answered. "I can find out for you."

"No, thanks, that's not necessary."

"I can leave a message in her mailbox if you like," he offered helpfully.

"No, I'll uh . . . try to reach her later."

Reed ducked into the next elevator, and descended, bearing at least one more piece of information.

That evening Reed returned to the Ox Cart bar and grill. Still no Jessica. As he chewed through his breaded chicken cutlet, he felt the surge of guilt again. A part of him did long to run into her, there was no denying it. He was secure, though, in the thought that his devotion to his deceased wife was total, unbreakable. He was lonely, and had every right to be, he reassured himself. If there was any comfort to be drawn from contact with others, why shouldn't it be from someone like Jessica? But, he reminded himself, he was getting quite ahead of reality. He'd only met her the night before, and then it had been for all of ten minutes. She might think him an intrusive oddball. What was the use of thinking about it? About her?

Reed finished his dinner and paid his bill. As he walked back to the 4Runner, he recalled what she had told him when he'd mentioned the old train station: "Read about it at the historical archives." Whether thinking about her was any use or not, Reed couldn't seem to shake Jessica Morraine from his mind.

The following morning Reed had little difficulty finding the public archives, located in a facility especially dedicated to the Colorado Historical Society in downtown Alamosa. The building itself, while of relatively recent vintage, was constructed in the same pioneer-era style as the rest of the public buildings in town. As he opened the swinging glass door, Reed counted himself lucky that he'd made it through another night in peace.

The receptionist focused through thick spectacles from where he sat behind the information counter, and greeted Reed with a cordial smile.

"Good morning," Reed extended.

" 'Morning. What can I help you with?"

The interior was very utilitarian, with a plain tile floor and heavy Venetian blinds, masking the few small windows in the foyer. Old black-and-white photographs adorned the paneling, each depicting a period of interest in Colorado's colorful history.

Reed conveyed his interest in the old train station, inventing some research project in railroad history as the basis for his inquiry.

The receptionist was happy to direct Reed down a short hallway to the archives section.

Reed thanked him, and proceeded through a glass-windowed door marked PUBLIC ARCHIVES. The room was divided into two areas: one with several long tables for researchers, the other for records storage. A massive wood-paneled counter ran the length of the large room, separating the two areas. The space was devoid of life except the sounds of someone shuffling around through the narrow aisles between the bound stacks of historical data that had been itemized, categorized, chronologized, indexed, and shelved on many levels, in many rows. Behind the thick wooden barrier, a burly, frost-haired woman of fifty emerged from the towers of densely packed information, cat-eye glasses hanging around her neck.

"Ooh! Thought I heard someone come in," she said, casting a happy grin at Reed.

"Good morning," he introduced. "I'm Reed Haler. How do you do?"

"Good morning. Bren Callum," she said, shooting her beefy hand over the countertop. "Nice knowing you."

Her handshake was firm and to the point. "Now, what is it I can do for you this morning?"

Reed was instantly impressed with her ebullience, and got the feeling that Bren Callum was going to be a big help in his researches. "Interested in whatever you've got on the old train station south of town."

"The old train station south of town!" she repeated as if he'd just asked her for the secret recipe for Coca-Cola.

"Yeah."

"How long you planning on spending in here?" was her smiling answer.

"Why?" Reed gave a small chuckle. "Is it a lot of material?"

"Ha! Mister, I'm not sure what you're after, but I got enough stuff on that old station house to fill ten volumes."

"Oh, really?"

"Really. Now, any idea of the time frame you'd like to start with? That might help narrow things down. It was built in 1882. Burned down after two years. Had to be restored, etc., etc."

"Well, I'm not sure exactly. Has anyone ever been . . . killed there?"

Bren Callum's left eyebrow pricked up like a toothpick had stuck it through the center; her smile vanished. "Anyone killed? Quite a few. Again you've got a broad timespan. Several workers died building the thing. Thirty people died in the fire. Four or five people got run over by trains during its active years."

"Has anyone ever been murdered there?"

"What's your interest in all this, Mr. Haler?" Bren Callum's voice suddenly ran out of its earlier levity.

He gave her his line about a railroad history project, which she didn't buy for a second.

"There's a lot more to that station than who died there."

"I'm sure there is. Look, I need to know about the murder. I've got personal reasons."

"Personal? You're not from around here—"

"True. Now, may I see the information, please?"

The honest approach seemed to work a lot better, and in a few minutes Bren had returned with twelve rolls of microfilm.

"These are back issues of our local paper from five years ago." Her voice had lost its color. She was now just going through the motions. "They cover the time period when the murder took place. It was the worst crime ever committed around here. This is the best I can do for you. You can use number two over there," she said, indicating one of the microfilm viewers. "Just bring the films back up to the desk when you're done."

Reed took the twelve rolls. "Was there only the one murder committed there?"

"Only one," Bren Callum confirmed.

"Thank you very, very much."

She disappeared again into the stacks.

The film started with the January first edition of the paper. Nothing.

For the next hour he went through every day until he reached the July twelfth edition. When the front page came up on the viewing screen Reed didn't know which registered in his mind first, the photograph or the headline. A metallic flavor wrapped around his tongue; his fingers went moist on the control of the machine. He could only stare, unable to swallow. The headline read: DOCTOR FOUND SLAIN IN TRAIN YARD! RESIDENTS IN SHOCK. The photograph of the victim was unmistakable. Instantly Reed understood how the woman he'd seen standing in the archway of the station could have vanished as she had. Then he saw something equally troubling: the name. His whole body shaking, he read:

> The entire community is stunned today upon learning of the murder of Dr. Alana Kieran, 41, of Alamosa. Dr. Kieran's body was found late yesterday afternoon when two youths walking near the train station noticed a woman lying face up on the ground near the old station building. The youths immediately called 911 and police and medical personnel were dispatched. Dr. Kieran was pronounced dead at the scene, the victim of multiple stab wounds to the abdomen, chest, neck and genitals. Early reports indicate the possibility of sexual assault. Chief medical examiner Dr. Sean Aumenta said that an autopsy should reveal whether Dr. Kieran was the victim of rape.
>
> Dr. Kieran was last seen leaving her office at six P.M. on Friday, two days before her body was discovered. According to Dr. Kieran's secretary, it had been a perfectly routine day at the office, and Dr. Kieran was in good

spirits. "Looking forward to a relaxing weekend," the secretary said.

Dr. Kieran was widely known and admired for her work. Her untiring efforts to found a children's hospital here were heralded last month at a benefit dinner, which Colorado Springs Mayor Anthony Delvado attended in support of the project. Dr. Kieran, originally from Pueblo, moved to Alamosa fifteen years ago with the hope of building the hospital, especially for the treatment of children's diseases. Dr. Kieran is survived by her parents Tom and Charlotte, and her brother Craig.

Alana. Reed stared at the letters, willing them to be different. He knew that the coincidence was much more than that, but still he resisted belief. He learned as he read on that in the days following the slaying, more articles appeared containing updated information concerning the cause of death, Dr. Kieran's background as a pediatrician, and her goal of the children's hospital. The single most recurring theme throughout each story, however, was the fact that the police were confounded. A month after the body had been discovered, no suspects were in custody, and there appeared to be no solid leads. The evidence discovered at the scene was sparse and inconclusive. There had been an indication of a brutal sexual assault, yet no semen had been found. The mutilation had been extensive, but only the victim's blood had been recovered. Shoe impressions were taken but that only indicated that one of several million people may have committed the act.

It was late afternoon by the time Reed had gone through all twelve rolls of microfilm. The most recent article had been from the paper of only one year before. The murder remained unsolved, and the hospital project had fallen into disarray, except for the efforts of Alamosa doctors Jessica Morraine and Louis Canidey. Dr. Morraine, the paper said, had dedicated herself to resurrecting the project in the name of her most respected role model.

Reed rewound the last roll, and took the microfilms back to the desk. Bren Callum was getting ready to close up for the day when Reed handed the rolls back to her.

"After all that I sure hope you found what you were looking for," she said, her mood still the color of rain.

"I think so. Have there been any more leads in the case since last year?" he probed.

"Nope. No one has a clue, and people around here don't much like talking about it."

"I can appreciate that. Well, thanks very much for your help."

"Good luck," she said as Reed was halfway out the door.

His feet tingled as he walked down the sidewalk to where the car was parked. The air smelled fresh and mild, that perfect Colorado afternoon. He'd spent over five hours sitting in front of the microfilm viewer, and the blood was taking its time getting back up to speed. That's what he told himself. The reality was that the tingling didn't stop at his feet. He felt it all the way up his legs, through his back, and around his neck. He fought the belief with all his rational will, but the facts defied him—he had seen the murdered woman, standing, watching him, by all appearances alive and well. He had seen Alana Kieran, or some vestige of her, anyway. Either that, he told himself, or she had an identical twin who was playing some absurdly elaborate joke. Inside he knew it was no joke. He'd been getting used to accepting some pretty odd things recently, but this development took circumstances to an all-new level.

The tingling didn't go away when Reed climbed into the 4Runner. His thoughts turned momentarily to Hoover, waiting back in the air-conditioned room for her dinner and a walk. He drove, mentally fidgeting with what he knew. Jessica Morraine was continuing the work of the one *slain in train yard*. He weighed this thought against the standard of his intuition. It fit. That being the case, how did it illuminate any of the remaining entries in Devrie's journal?

See that she is the next of life's soldiers;
No moon's glow in the middle of summer;
Forbidden, forever hidden inside the trunk.

It was now only eight days to the middle of summer, but Reed was beginning to see glimpses beyond the words.

NINETEEN

After her walk and dinner, Hoover seemed ready to go for another ride in the car. But first Reed did a little research in the local phone directory. There was only one Jessica Morraine listed. He wrote down the address and phone number on a Post-it, and secured the information in his wallet. He didn't have a detailed map of Alamosa, so he began by simply driving around, looking at street signs. She lived, according to the phone book, on Westmore Drive. He'd been wandering around for a half hour without success, when he decided to try some of the more outlying residential areas. The houses became more widely separated as one reached the outskirts. Eventually there was nothing but fields, forest, and mountains. He was completing a large sweep of the northwestern edge of town when he drove past a little sign that said WESTMORE DR. He made the right turn, and began to scan for numbers. There were few houses on Westmore, but the area was undergoing the beginnings of a new development surge. Jessica's split-level modern home was modest, but appeared comfortable and unencumbered by homes on either adjacent lot or behind. The property was clear from the back of the house all the way to the next street, which still remained unpaved.

Reed stopped the 4Runner across the street from the house. No vehicle was parked in front or in the driveway, so he assumed that Jessica was not at home, though he couldn't see inside the garage. He studied the house for another few minutes. It was of moderate size, probably two or three bedrooms. The plan described the shape of a bottom-heavy L. It had a low-pitched roof, and was mainly constructed of tan brick. Dark-stained wood siding protruded from the brickwork at the midway point up the outer walls, creating a shallow overhang around the house. In the newly planted front yard stood a small maple, and a rose garden struggled to take hold at the side of the concrete driveway. Now he knew where she lived, for whatever it was worth. The sight of the house gave him an odd sense of comfort and loneliness at the same time. He almost felt that if he walked right in the front door he would be welcomed, and that he would feel at home. He reminded himself that this was a stranger's house, not his, and a stranger's life—a stranger's child.

Suddenly he felt twinges of hunger in his stomach and decided to eat yet again at the Ox Cart. He gave the house a final look, and shifted the car into gear.

There was a thicker crowd than on the three previous nights that he'd eaten there, but still . . . no Jessica. It was early, and Reed delayed by having a pair of beers at the bar before taking a seat that commanded a clear view of the door. A large cowbell hanging from the knob announced all entrances and exits. Reed's head jerked up every time the sound jangled through the small establishment. Still no Jessica.

He looked down again at the menu. He knew he was hungry, but nothing sounded like anything he wanted to eat.

"Figured out what you want yet?" The question startled Reed; he hadn't noticed the waitress sidle up to his table.

"Uh . . . I think," he started to say as he looked up, then the words stopped. The "waitress" was Jessica, standing over him with a devious smile.

"What are . . . how?" he said, pointing to the door.

"What? You look confused."

"How did you get in here?" He finally managed to ask.

"Uh . . . The front door?"

Reed glanced between Jessica and the door a couple of times. "But I . . ."

"Lucy and I are sitting right over there." She pointed to one of the booths near the back of the dining area.

Reed couldn't see any sign of Lucy because the booth was taller than she was. "But I looked . . ." He stopped himself. "Never mind. It's great to see you again."

"I was probably in the bathroom, or something," she suggested.

"Oh. I see."

"Why don't you join us. We're still waiting for our food. Come on."

Reed folded his menu, and followed Jessica over to the booth. He sat down across from Lucy, who gave him a huge but shy smile.

"Hello again, Lucy," he said.

"Hello," she squeaked back.

"I think you've got a fan," Jessica imparted, sliding in next to her daughter.

"Well, I know she does. How'ya doin'?"

"I'm fine."

"Good."

"So, I have a small confession to make," Jessica stated.

"Oh, really?"

"First, though, I'd like to thank you."

"Thank me?"

"The hair ball."

"Oh, the hair ball."

"That's exactly what it was. I . . . I have to say . . . you saved me a lot of time and trouble. I've never seen anything like it. I wouldn't have—"

"Hey. Glad to be of service. Now, what's this confession?"

"Well, we came in here tonight sort of hoping to find you again. I wanted to let you know that you were right, and to say thanks."

"No thanks necessary. But you're more than welcome."

"Lucy was hoping to see you again too."

"Well, Lucy, I'm glad I decided to come back here."

At that moment the real waitress arrived with two plates of food. Reed ordered the grilled chicken, and picked at a basket of rolls, while Jessica and Lucy ate. "I have to confess something myself," Reed conveyed, a little hesitantly.

"Oh?"

"I was hoping to run into you again too."

"Hey, sometimes it works."

"Yeah. Sometimes. I was hoping to have a chance to ask you a little more about the hospital you're trying to start up."

"Oh, God! The hospital."

"Sounds like a sore spot."

"It's people and their damned false promises."

"Oh, them."

"Yeah. It's been a tough week . . . month . . . year . . ."

"So, you knew Dr. Kieran?"

As Reed expected it would, the mention of Dr. Kieran stopped Jessica in mid-bite. She swallowed and took a sip of water.

"Of course I knew Dr. Kieran. Everybody around here knew her. She was my greatest role model. And she was my mentor for years. I wanted to do what she did. And I still do." Jessica was lost in recollection. "She had an incredible way of . . . giving people, especially children, the ability to laugh even though they were in great pain, and knew that they were dying. Her patients lived longer and survived almost fifty percent more often than the national average. It was the best medicine I've ever seen. It really was like magic. Is that why you were interested in the old train station?"

"Well let's say the old train station is why I'm now interested in Dr. Kieran."

"Fair enough."

"I went to the historical archives, like you suggested."

"Oh. Hope it answered your questions."

"Not all of them, but . . . never mind."

"What?" she asked, sensing that he was protecting something too sensitive for dinner conversation.

Reed could feel himself letting things go further than he'd wanted to at that point. The bar and grill was no place to try to tell her what he really knew, what he'd seen.

"No. Nothing. I just hadn't been expecting to read about such a terrible story. I guess it just upset me and . . ."

"So you know they never caught the guy who did it."

"Yeah." Reed saw that Lucy's smile had again washed away.

"Oh, don't worry. Lucy knows the whole story."

"Too bad there's such a story to be known."

"Yeah, but I've always felt it's best to be as honest as possible, especially with your children. They understand so much more than you'd think. Do you have any?"

"Uh, no. I . . . don't."

"Married? If I'm not getting too personal, of course."

Reed relaxed the tension with a broad smile. "No, you're not getting too personal, and I believe that it's best to be honest too. So, yes, I am married, but my wife was killed."

"Oh, my God! I'm so sorry."

"No, please. I'm dealing with it. That's one of the reasons, actually, that I'm on this trip. Sort of a soul searching mission . . . so to speak."

"Those can be very helpful. But don't lose contact with the others you love, and the real world. That's just as important."

"I know. I haven't. Thanks."

"So, was this recent then?"

"Last month."

"Oh, wow! I . . . I'm so sorry. I . . ."

"Don't. I'm okay. I know this isn't exactly the kind of thing you were expecting to talk about this evening, and I really don't want it to be a big downer. So let's talk about you instead."

"Fine. What do you want to know?"

"How well do you know that Gart guy?"

"Oh, Gart. I've known him for about eight months."

"Are you going out?"

"If you mean are we dating, I guess you could say we are, sort of."

"So it's not serious."

"Not extremely serious. Though I think he'd like it to be."

"What would you like it to be?"

"I don't know. I'm so busy with the hospital project, and trying to do the rest of my job practically single-handed, and raise a daughter. It leaves about zero time for a relationship. At the same time he helps me a lot with Lucy. I really don't know what I'd do without him. He's a sweet guy."

"And he's Lucy's gymnastics coach?"

"Yeah. He teaches P.E. and the summer gym program at the elementary school. He just started last year. He's doing a great job. Everybody likes him."

"I don't," Lucy interjected.

"Luce, what kind of thing is that to say? Gart's a very nice man, and he thinks that you've got lots of talent."

"I don't care," Lucy said in her hair-thin voice.

"She's not too thrilled about her mom going out with her coach. The other kids tease her, I think."

"Sounds pretty normal," Reed suggested.

"Excruciatingly normal."

"So, do you want to be in the Olympics some day, Lucy?" Reed asked the little girl.

She shook her head with an emphatic "No!" A lock of her rusty hair landed right over her left eye.

"No? Well, what do you want to be when you grow up?" Reed furthered.

"A doctor, like my mom," she said, now quite seriously, in a frail yet unexpectedly mature tone.

"A doctor, huh? Well, that's a fine thing to become."

"I know."

"Well, good." Reed shared a look with Jessica, which told him that she was quite aware that her daughter could behave well beyond her years when she wanted to.

"So, why did you go into medicine?" Jessica asked, tossing the questioning back in Reed's direction.

Reed swallowed his bite of food. Then: "Because I didn't want to be an engineer, like my father."

"You didn't get along?"

"We didn't *not* get along. We just look at the world differently. His main interest in work was the mental challenge of it. Solving tough problems, regardless of what those solutions would ultimately be used for. See, that part didn't matter to him—who was going to benefit from his work, or even if anyone was going to benefit at all. I wanted the things that I did to really matter to somebody, to directly help people who needed it the most. People who were suffering. What better work could there be than that?"

"And it led you to genetics?"

"Well, I chose medicine, but I was no good at surgery. I still get queasy at the sight of blood, and I don't have the best bedside manner. I just didn't love the idea of running a general practice. So I guess you could say that genetics chose me."

"I think that's how it happens for a lot of doctors," Jessica mused.

"You?"

"Oh, yeah. I didn't have a choice. It was pretty clear even in high school what I wanted to do."

"I guess that makes us pretty lucky. Some people never really find their direction."

"And some people never really get the chance."

"True." Reed took another bite, digesting Jessica's comments. Then he turned the questioning back on her. "So, what about Lucy's father? Why did he leave?"

"I suppose he just couldn't handle it." Jessica's guard had now dropped completely, as if she'd been needing, for a long time, to get her thoughts out, even if to a relative stranger. "I was doing my residency, working eighty hours a week. He'd wanted to be an architect, but ended up working in construction before he could finish school. He'd planned to go back to get his degree, but somehow the money, and the time . . . it was just easier to keep putting it off, you know. He had a drinking problem. There's no other way to put it. But he was stubborn and refused to admit that he was out of control. Finally he got fired for drinking on the job. Injured one of his coworkers. That hit him hard. The accident could easily have happened whether he'd been drinking or not, but the fact was he had alcohol in his system. So with me working, and him out of a job, it just made sense for him to stay home and take care of Lucy after she was born, but . . . he just couldn't deal with that idea, or something. I don't mean to make him sound like a jerk. He was a wonderful man in many ways. We'd talk about our plans after we both got established. And he adored Lucy. He really did. Maybe a little too much, but we had a lot of great times. His biggest problem was his disappointment in himself, I think. He set out with these great big plans, and as he watched his life falling short of those ambitions, he must have just dropped through the cracks somewhere. He simply refused to accept less of himself than this image he'd created, but he must have felt equally powerless to do anything about it—two ideas that can't coexist in one mind for very long, I guess. Shortly after Lucy turned three, he just disappeared."

"Did you try to find him?"

"Oh sure. For two years I went nuts."

"His parents have any idea where he was?"

"I think so. But they weren't saying anything. Not to me anyway. I think he ran away out of shame."

Reed let a wordless moment pass while Jessica worked through the memories.

"So," he asked when she again looked up, "are you divorced?"

"I am now."

"Wow. That's rough."

"Actually it's okay . . . relatively. I've left it behind. All except the name. I still go by Morraine for Lucy's sake. It just seems right that we should have the same last name, you know?"

"That's very good of you."

"Want to know anything else?"

"Yeah. What's your daughter's favorite flavor of ice cream?"

At that Lucy's eyes opened wide as she chewed a big mouthful of spinach. "Ftrawberry," she mumbled through the dripping green slime that she was trying to swallow.

Jessica laughed. "You," she said, casting a scolding stare at Reed, "are taking liberties you haven't quite earned yet."

"Well, with any luck . . ."

Jessica looked as though she were about to add a comment when Reed's dinner arrived.

"Can I get you anything else?" the waitress inquired.

"Have you got strawberry ice cream?" Reed asked.

"Sure have."

"Well, I know we'll have at least one," he ordered.

"Make it two, and a cup of coffee," Jessica added.

"Two strawberry ice creams and a coffee. That it?"

"That's more than enough," Jessica assured.

"Be right back," the waitress said, and charged off.

Reed ate his chicken while Jessica and Lucy waited for their dessert.

"You're a bad influence, I can tell," Jessica said.

"Me?"

"I think he's a good influence," Lucy opined.

"Oh you do?" Jessica asked rhetorically.

"Yes."

"Well, thank you very much," Reed acknowledged.

Ironically Reed had parked right next to Jessica's Honda CR-V without knowing it. He had intended to walk her and Lucy to their car when they left the restaurant, but discovered that he needed to go no further than one space away from the 4Runner.

"Well, thank you for dessert," Jessica said as she hooked her keys with a curled index finger.

"My pleasure. I enjoyed talking with you."

"Likewise."

"And I had a great time with you," he said, kneeling down to shake Lucy's hand, which she took politely.

"Thank you for the ice cream," she said.

"Maybe we'll have the chance to have more again sometime soon."

"Don't press your luck," Jessica warned, unlocking her door.

Lucy ran around to the passenger side of the Honda, and jumped in.

"Seriously, though, I would like to talk to you some more. If it wouldn't bother you," he said.

She looked down at the ground between the open door and the front seat. "Yeah, that would be fine. I'd like that too." She brought her eyes up to his. "If you're sure it wouldn't bother *you*."

"I'm not looking to replace my wife, if that's what you're thinking."

"I'm not thinking anything. I just . . . I just met you, is what I'm thinking. This is a small town, you know? You don't really meet a lot of new people . . . and . . . I've got to go. Thanks again."

She touched his arm lightly, and swept into the seat. Reed stepped back, and gave the door a gentle shove.

"Good night."

"Good night."

She backed the car out and drove away, a small hand waving from the passenger seat. Reed waved back with a smile that reflected a volatile combination of affection, sorrow, mystification, and fear.

He watched until the Honda was out of sight before he fished his own keys from his front pocket.

Y*ou smell of fear.*" The Indian's words came again, so close it was as if they emanated from inside Reed's own head. But they gave him the ability to move. The walls bled. The air stank. Again Reed saw the door at the end of the violent crimson hallway open to reveal the flickering firelight, the earth floor, and the black apparition. Its shadow only slowed him this time, allowing Reed to approach, close. But the face of the looming figure was still obscured, shrouded. It turned to the wall, and again began its urination ritual. The dark liquid, like blood under fluorescent light, trickled down the wall, but this didn't stop Reed either, as it had before; he felt the Indian with him, and was able to continue toward the dancing light. The feverish trembling began in the dark figure, the sick, silent laughter. Reed soon perched on the threshold of the doorway, a full view of the fire in the pit before him. It was a campfire. *His* campfire. On the other side of the flames he saw a dome of blue. Reed heard the splash of black urine stop. The figure shook more violently, then slowly began to turn. Reed was right next to it, but his eyes were frozen on the blue dome . . . a tent . . . *his* tent in the Sierras. Through the flames there was something else, something on the ground, but it was hidden in the bright orange licks. A rush of hot air roiled over his skin as the black figure turned to him. The air smelled moist and decayed like rotting meat. Totally frozen in place again, he couldn't turn his head. The heat, the gangrenous odor intensified, but the flames in the pit lowered as if the dark form were drawing its energy directly from the burning logs. As the fire shrank, shapes appeared on the ground beyond it. Reed could now see what it was: a pair of legs, splattered red, and splayed to the sides. Between the legs was a slender, gnarled length of tree branch, the end of which disappeared into a complex of folds the same color as the walls of the hallway. Reed forced his eyes to close.

TWENTY

His face was buried in a soggy pillow, his eyes clenched shut so tightly his head ached. Reed pushed himself up, off the pillow. The room was light, he'd survived another night . . . sort of. He rolled onto his back; the sheets stuck to his body and legs. Hoover stood by the door, staring at him with big, pleading eyes. Reed checked his watch on the nightstand. Eleven o'clock. He sat up, realizing that again his penis was erect, swollen, vaguely painful. He fell back against the headboard.

"Oh God!" he said aloud.

Hoover whimpered.

"Okay, girl. Just a minute." Thoughts of the night before seeped into his head. Jessica. His chest tightened. The journal was still on the nightstand next to his watch. He'd gone over it again before falling into his hellish sleep. One entry kept gnawing at him: *See that she is the next of life's soldiers. The next!* That implied that another, or others had come before, had died before. *Life's soldiers.* Doctors! It was conceivable. The middle of summer was now seven days away.

Reed crawled out of bed and into the bathroom. It was another two minutes before he was able to relieve himself. He looked down at the toilet bowl and noticed his legs. Tiny red dots, pinhead size scabs, crusted the skin. The itching had started. The urge to scratch them raw was psychotic. He thought about buying a pair of shorts, but felt self-conscious about his pocked, untanned legs.

For the time being, he showered, and put on the loosest-fitting pants he had. After taking care of the dog and promising her he'd be back soon, he drove to the hospital, went straight to the third floor, and asked the nurse if Dr. Morraine was in.

"Do you have an appointment to see her?"

"No," Reed said, "I just need to speak with her for a minute."

"Well, I think she's on rounds right now, but most people take lunch around one. You might run into her in the cafeteria."

"Thanks," Reed said, and went back down to the first floor.

Well-posted signs led him to the cafeteria at the rear of the ground level. One wall, made entirely of glass, afforded a panoramic view of the rocky hills to the west, as well as the remains of the aborted addition project. A door in the glass wall led to an outside eating terrace, with umbrella-shaded tables. Several of the staff were enjoying early lunches in the summer breeze. Reed got coffee and a strawberry Danish, and took one of the vacant outdoor seats.

The air was dry and starkly clear, but wholly comfortable. Reed assessed the others on the terrace. Their faces looked normal enough. The closest was a young man with short, dark hair and a clean-shaven face, an orderly perhaps. At the next table was a dark-complexioned woman, of Mediterranean heritage possibly, wearing full scrubs. Next to her were two men, both overweight, tired and graying, beyond their prime—doctors who'd been in the same job, lived in the same place, for too long. Finally there was a group of four women in hospital attire, all young, perhaps some were married, maybe even with children. They seemed genuinely happy, laughter punctuating their lively conversation. Reed listened with envy as he sipped his coffee and looked through the glass to the inside of the cafeteria. No Jessica. One o'clock was still a half hour away, so he left in search of a newspaper.

When he got back, paper in hand, his table was still vacant, but a new group of lunch-goers had taken over.

Reed focused on anything in the paper that might have relevance to his cause. Other crises in the world seemed infinitely secondary. He found nothing except a story about the general economic crunch that was putting a lot of projects on hold, not just the proposed children's hospital. *The next of life's soldiers. The middle of summer. No moon.* The words wouldn't leave him.

At ten after one, the familiar face appeared on the other side of the glass. Reed sprang to his feet, a little too quickly, nearly knocking his chair over, and drawing the notice of those around him. He didn't care, catching up to Jessica just as she stepped into the line for hot food.

"Hey there," he said behind her.

"What?" She turned around. "Oh . . . Reed. Hi. Well, I wasn't expecting to run into you here . . . so soon."

"Well, here I am."

"Here you are."

Reed noticed that the tall man in front of Jessica had turned around also, and was looking at him.

"Reed, this is Dr. Louis Canidey, my sole colleague in the wonderful world of prepubescent colds and constipation."

Reed took the soft hand.

"Louis," Jessica continued the introduction, "this is Dr. Reed . . . uh . . ."

"Haler," Reed prompted.

". . . Haler. Right. I'm sorry."

"Dr. Haler," Canidey voiced the name cordially. "Nice meeting you."

As they shook hands, Reed noticed the man's coffee-colored skin, thick brows, and oddly bright eyes—the amber of a malty ale. There was something quite relaxed and soothing in the man's demeanor, certainly a plus for a pediatrician, Reed thought.

"Uh . . . listen, please excuse me but . . ." Reed turned his attention back to Jessica. "I need to talk to you. It's kind of important."

"Well, Reed," she said, now a little self-conscious in front of Canidey. "Can't it wait until later? I'm kind of on my lunch break, which doesn't happen very often."

Canidey politely turned away, as if averting his attention from a domestic quarrel.

"Yeah, it can wait, but not very long. When will you be off?"

"I don't know, Reed. Later, sometime. I've got meetings and calls to make. I could be close to getting a big donation for the hospital, and I've got to stay on it. Why don't you give me a number where I can reach you. I'll call you."

The food line advanced as two more staff members arrived behind Reed. They greeted Jessica who returned the "hello," but this time she failed to introduce Reed.

"Okay." He dug a business card from his wallet and jotted the name and phone number of the El Halcón motel and his room number on the back. He said in a low tone, "Please call me as soon as you can. It really is very important."

"What's the matter with you?" Her voice lowered. "Did something happen?"

Reed nodded. "We need to talk privately."

"Okay. I'll call you. I promise."

"Today."

"Today." She was getting uncomfortable with his persistence and sudden anxiety. Finally he backed his way out of the line and out of the cafeteria.

H is mind was on double time as Reed drove back to the motel, and picked up Hoover. He needed to learn more, to find some clue as to what might be coming. He firmly believed that Alana Kieran's appearance bore directly on his wife's murder and on the implication of Jessica as the next victim. Despite the vagueness of these assumptions, Reed's intuition told him that he had no time to waste.

As much as it scared him, Reed sought out the road that led up to the old station. Through some semblance of logical deduction, he found its forgotten beginning behind a single-story row of small businesses—a donut shop, dry cleaners, shoe store, and video rental. The road was actually no more than two parallel troughs in which the weeds weren't quite as tall as their gangly neighbors. A barbed-wire fence ran the periphery of the asphalt rear parking lot of the little shopping complex, restricting vehicular access to the long-expired drive. A narrow opening in the fence offered the sole means of approach.

Moving only fast enough to keep the big 4×4 rolling forward, Reed squeezed the 4Runner through the break in the fence.

The powerful car handled the terrain easily as the path arced out a wide, gradual curve that eventually ascended to the station. It was about half a mile from start to finish. Reed brought the 4Runner to a stop on the barren plateau of the parking area, and opened the door. Hoover piled out over Reed before he himself had a chance to step down. The dog completed a few laps around the front grounds, then found a comfortable spot to lie down in the building's gothic shadow.

Today the site was free of inhabitants, ghostly or otherwise. Even the magpie had abandoned its high lookout. But a blossoming swell of cumulus formations was fast condensing into a black thunderhead to the west.

Reed stood by the entrance of the building, peering into its raw cavity, both hoping for and dreading a sign of Alana Kieran, if, in fact, that was truly what he had previously observed there. The part of his mind he relied upon for reason and logic struggled desperately for an argument that would convince him he was projecting a fanciful belief in some spirit world, born from his loss and the recent string of unusual experiences. It was a losing struggle.

Picking his way around the outside of the building, he attempted to flatten the pesky grasses. The stone paving under his feet was scarcely visible beneath the thicket. Only the muted buzz of a nectar-hungry bee disquieted the platform area at the rear of the structure. There he waited, the lone passenger, for a train that would only come in the realm of spirits. He half expected to see a massive black locomotive chugging noisily around the last curve.

The sound came. His pretend expectation burst into untenable reality. His head turned with a snap. From behind the march of ponderosa pine and spruce, the burned-out cottonwood leading the advance, the coal-devouring engine, the iron horse, boomed its arrival. Then, as quickly as the overture had come, the sound evanesced. The track bed lay unrattled; the bee buzzed. A winding vein of lightning popped in the sky, imprinting itself on Reed's watchful eye. Thunder rolled again, more quietly this time, from the encroaching ceiling of scorched clouds.

The stand of trees, halted on the brink, seemed to debate the fate of their captive. Reed stared into the front lines, outnumbered on every side, his back literally to the wall. The charred, fire-hollowed cottonwood, electing to show mercy, refrained from issuing the command of attack. Clouds laid claim to the sun, and Reed resumed his way, thrashing through the grass, down the platform, and back around to the front of the station. He called to the dog as he ran to the side of the car. She was no longer lounging in front of the building. He called out again. Heavy drops slapped the stone surfaces. The sky bellowed thunder, then hemorrhaged completely, the bloated clouds releasing their payload. Reed shouted the dog's name through the crushing fall of water. Then a head and legs appeared from the darkness of the station's main archway. Hoover leapt over the remains of the wooden barrier, and ran to Reed's side. He opened the door for the bounding Labrador. But even in their haste, they were not fast enough to beat the rain.

R eed had dropped Hoover off at the motel so her coat could dry there and not all over the inside of the 4Runner. He was waiting in front of the hospital's employee exit when Jessica emerged.

"Have you been standing out here all day?" she said when she saw him, his hair and clothes still damp from the thunderstorm, now passed.

He followed her as she walked toward her car. "No, I just came back a few minutes ago. I didn't want to miss you."

"Well, what is so damned important? I told you I'd call," she said without stopping.

"I know, and I'm sorry. Is there somewhere we could go to talk? I've got to tell you some things."

She stopped at her car. "Not right now. I've got to pick up Lucy, and get dinner ready, and a million other things. I'm late as it is."

She didn't hesitate to open the door, forcing Reed out of the way.

"There may not be much time left."

"Time for what? You're not making much sense."

"I can't say what I have to say standing here in the parking lot. Can't we just go someplace for a few minutes to sit down and talk? I'll buy you a coffee."

She got in the car and started the engine.

Reed held the door open. "You could be in serious danger."

"I really don't have time for this right now. I told you I'd call. Now please. Let go of the door."

Reed released his grip; the door slammed.

"You don't understand what's going on," he yelled through the glass. "Just give me a few minutes. This is very important."

The window rolled down about two inches. "Reed. I don't enjoy saying this, but you're beginning to bother me, okay? I said I would call you and I will. But please get out of my way. I need to go. Respect that." Jessica backed out of the space and drove away.

L ucy was the first to recognize the Toyota as her mother steered the Honda onto Westmore Drive and into their driveway. Jessica brought the car to a stop, afraid to look in the direction her daughter was excitedly pointing and saying, "Look, look. It's Reed!"

"Oh no," she whispered to herself, switching off the engine and glancing to her left. It was Reed, parked right across the street.

"What the hell is he doing *here*?" she mouthed under her breath.

He was already on the sidewalk and fast walking toward her driveway.

"Jessica. Hi again," he called out.

Now Jessica did hesitate to open the door. She grabbed a grocery bag from the backseat and handed it to Lucy.

"Take this inside and put it all away. I'll be in in a second," she instructed.

"Is Reed here for dinner?" Lucy asked hopefully.

"No, honey. He's not here for dinner. Now go." Jessica got out at the same moment her daughter did, and stood between the approaching man and the path to the front door.

"Hi, Lucy," Reed said, waving to the little girl.

Lucy turned around and waved back at Reed, her smile reflecting his.

"Get inside, Lucy!" her mother ordered.

Lucy continued to the door, and began unlocking it, confused as to the reason for the urgency in her mother's voice.

Reed stopped a respectful distance from Jessica, who stood her ground in the driveway next to the Honda. Both adults remained in silence until Lucy was fully inside the house.

"Well, well. I see you found the place."

"Yes. I know it must seem a little forward."

"Yeah. It does, actually."

"I'm sorry. And I'm sorry if I scared you back at the hospital," he said in the friendliest voice he could summon.

"You're scaring me right now, quite honestly."

"Jessica, come on. It's me. Remember? Ice cream? I just really need to talk to you."

"All right, Reed. What the hell is so important? You've got one minute."

"Okay. Good . . . thanks. All right. First, look at this." He handed her the journal.

"What is it?" she asked, taking the bound pages.

Reed explained the journal, the Polaroid in the back, and his wife's history of psychic premonitions, leading up to her murder.

Jessica listened to Reed's account, and studied the scrawled messages. As she looked at the Polaroid, she spoke the name quietly, a disturbed look growing on her face. She stuffed the Polaroid back inside, then handed the journal to Reed. "I don't know what you think any of this has to do with me, but—"

"Wait, Jessica. Don't you get it? I'm here because these messages brought me here. I'm not making any of this up. I'm a scientist, for God's sake! A doctor. Why would I invent such a ridiculous story?"

"I don't have the slightest idea."

"Jessica, the point is that I think you're the next of life's soldiers. You took over the hospital project after Alana Kieran. Her murder was almost identical to my wife's. I don't think it's a coincidence. In fact, I'm certain that it's not. My wife wanted to name our daughter after her without even realizing it."

"And you think that I'm supposed to be the next in line or something?" Jessica almost started laughing.

"Yes. I do." Reed was anything but laughing.

"That murder was over five years ago; the world is full of sick bastards. I'm really sorry about your wife, but if you'll please excuse me now . . ." She started to back away.

"Listen to me," he nearly shouted. "I think this is going to happen next week. I'm just trying to tell you to go away from here. Take a trip. Stay with your parents. Something! But don't stay anywhere near here next week. Something's going to happen!"

"Do you really think I'm going to disrupt my entire life for a week because a total stranger, spouting some absurd, upsetting story, thinks something bad is going to happen to me?"

"I know it's a strange thing to tell you, but I don't know what else to do."

"I've got to go now, Reed. Good-bye. Please leave now. Have a safe trip home. Okay?" She hurried toward the front door. Reed knew that it was useless to try to follow. Jessica gave him a last troubled look before she closed the door.

Lucy looked at herself in the plate, examining her frown in the distorted reflection before wiping the excess water from the surface. Her mother was washing them faster than Lucy could dry, but then, it wasn't a race. The little girl placed the dish on the finished stack, and moved on to the glasses next to the sink where her mother was rinsing a pan.

"Missed a spot," Lucy said, handing a glass back. Jessica took the glass and rewashed it. It was a system they had worked out over the years. Jessica washed, Lucy dried and performed quality control. Jessica would then put the dishes away, double checking Lucy's drying job. Each always found at least one infraction on the part of the other, even if there really wasn't one. It was more of a private, ritualized joke that they simply continued because neither wanted to be the first to stop. Jessica had planned to get a dishwasher after moving into the new house, but the truth was that she enjoyed the few minutes the washing/drying routine gave her with her daughter. It seemed that Lucy too was in no hurry to change the system.

"I had a question," Lucy then said, inspecting the glass again, satisfied this time.

"Question? Shoot."

"Why didn't you want Reed to have dinner with us tonight?"

Jessica paused in her scrubbing. "Well, he . . . he's still a stranger, and you don't just go inviting strangers over to dinner."

"But he's a really nice stranger."

"He seems like a nice stranger, but he's still a stranger, and he might not really be as nice as he seems. You know?"

"I guess. But I know he's nice. And he has a nice dog."

"A dog?" Jessica said, surprised.

Lucy nodded with a smile.

"How do you know he has a dog? I don't remember him with a dog."

"I saw her."

"When?"

"I don't know. I just saw her."

"Are you sure?"

"Mmm hmm."

"How do you know it was his dog?"

"I just know."

"Where did you see the dog, Luce?" Jessica could see the genuine effort to remember in her daughter's expression. Eventually the little girl shook her head, now slightly agitated. "I don't remember."

"Will you think about it for me, and let me know if you remember?"

"Okay."

The stress suddenly left Lucy's face as Jessica placed the pan on the drying rack, and began putting away the dishes.

"We just need to get to know people a little better before we invite them over. Do you understand?" Jessica now asked, still not satisfied with the answers she'd gotten about the dog.

Lucy wiped the last glass. "I guess. Are you afraid he might leave?"

"What?" Jessica waited before picking up the next dish. "Lucy, what do you mean?"

"I mean if Reed came over, and you really liked him, then maybe you're scared that he'll leave. Like Daddy did."

"Lucy . . . I . . . no, that's not what I'm afraid of. Okay? I'm just . . . being careful. I just think it takes a little more time before you can start trusting people you just met. And that's all there is to it."

Jessica resumed placing the dishes in the cupboard. "Missed a spot," she announced, handing one of the plates down to her daughter, thankful for the opportunity to change the subject. Lucy smiled and rewiped the plate, then gave her mother a hug around the waist.

TWENTY-ONE

Reed took a seat in front of an old gray desk, a lot like his own back at S.F.U. It reminded him that it was about time he checked in with Wally again. He studied the several WANTED posters tacked to a crowded bulletin board hanging near the desk. Any of the fugitives in those pictures could be the one, he speculated.

After a few minutes, a stout man with a membrane-thin layer of mud-colored hair entered the office, and sat down. The man picked up the clothbound book in the middle of his desk blotter. "I'm

Sheriff Clark Denton," he introduced himself, with a strong grip of Reed's hand.

"Dr. Reed Haler. Glad to meet you, Sheriff."

"Now, what's this?" the lawman asked.

"The future," Reed answered, settling back onto the cracked vinyl of the seat cushion.

The sheriff paged through the journal, his gray-blue eyes forming skeptical slits.

"It looks like nonsense, I know," Reed confessed. "But it's not."

Denton dispatched a doubtful gaze across the tidy desk, but took down Reed's name, a phone number, and an address where he could be reached.

Reed proceeded to give the sheriff a somewhat abbreviated account leading up to his presence in Alamosa, sensing the man's growing doubt as he unfolded the dubious history. Sheriff Denton recorded the information on a report sheet, which Reed suspected would end up in the back of a filing cabinet as soon as he left the sheriff's office. Reed felt himself hesitate, realizing how the words must have been coming across. "I know this is very difficult to accept. But I'm convinced there's going to be another murder. Look at the dates of these entries. My wife had never been here. There are things in there that you must see she couldn't have known about." Reed pointed out the final nine entries and the Polaroid, as reasons for his belief that a disaster was imminent, and his suspicions as to when and where it was likely to happen. The aura of doubt glowed even brighter from behind the desk.

"Sheriff, I'm not a crackpot looking to stir up some sensational publicity to get attention. I'm trying to save somebody's life."

"Jessica Morraine's?"

"Jessica Morraine's."

"You think Dr. Morraine's life is in danger, and that your wife wrote this stuff down so you'd drive all the way across the country and stop here to save her from some unknown murderer?"

"Yes!"

The sheriff allowed himself a restrained chuckle, a condescending smile fluffing his gray mustache. He drew a hand across his thin hair, smoothing it even flatter. "Who would want to kill her? And why?"

"Her ex-husband, maybe."

"So, you've talked to her about that, have you?"

"She's told me some things. This ex sounds like he could be a volatile character."

"Jimmy? He was a drunk and a troubled, confused man, but deep down he was a decent sort, and he's sure no murderer, I can tell you that."

"And I'm telling you that either he or somebody else intends to kill Jessica Morraine, for whatever reason." Reed had elected to keep Maysie Fabrioso's theory about the "natural order of things" out of his recitation to the sheriff for the time being.

"Dr. Haler, your story sounds very interesting. It does. But I've got to be real honest with you. We're generally a very quiet community. We don't get a lot of violent crime around here, and this just isn't enough to raise my suspicions a whole lot."

"But you do have some violence, don't you, Sheriff? Like the murder of Alana Kieran."

"You have learned quite a bit about our little town, haven't you?"

"I've learned some."

"That happened five years ago. Not one homicide here since."

"And still unsolved?"

Denton had to nod.

"I'm telling you there's going to be another one. My wife's murder had a nearly identical M.O. as Dr. Kieran's. Check the national case databases. Devrie Haler was my wife. You'll see—sexual assault, same type of wounds, no good evidence found—no blood except the victim's. Perp used a condom. Only some footprints. Case unsolved. They don't even have any suspects." Reed took out a pen, and wrote Devrie's name on a piece of paper for the sheriff. "Check it," Reed said again. The comparison of the two cases seemed to pique the sheriff's interest at least enough to quell the belittling smirk. "Look at her journal. She knew our unborn child was going to die. She knew about the Gulf War two years to the day before it happened. And she knew that *the next of life's sol-diers . . .* is going to be this guy's next victim. I believe that Jessica Morraine is the target, and that it's going to happen here in the middle of summer. That's exactly six days from now."

"In six days. And where did you say this is supposed to take place?"

"You see the entry about *No moon's glow*?"

"Yes."

"The bar right off Route 160 east of town called the New Moon Saloon. I think that's where."

The sheriff read the last page of the journal again, still unconvinced.

"The reference to *no moon*," Reed repeated. "You know . . . 'no moon' means the same thing as 'new moon.' Look, I know this seems like pretty shaky lead material, but I've learned a little something over the last week about interpreting these things."

"Dr. Haler," the sheriff said, now pressing to his feet. "I've got some things to do. I'd suggest you try to enjoy the rest of your stay. Relax and then go home. Leave the law enforcement to us. If we notice anything out of the ordinary, we'll follow up on it, okay?"

"Sheriff, I'm not trying to tell you how to do your job. I'm just trying to prevent a murder."

"And I appreciate that."

"Look. Just keep an eye on that place from the fifth to the sixth of August. That's all I'm asking. This guy, whoever he is, is going to try to murder someone, and I'm pretty sure it's Jessica Morraine. Please, Sheriff."

Denton finished filling in the report and held the journal out to Reed. "I'll keep what you've told me in mind. All right? That's all I can do."

"Check that M.O., Sheriff. Check it. I'm not some nut. Please."

The sheriff couldn't help noting the earnestness in Reed's voice, the intensity in his eyes.

Reed took the journal, but for another moment would not release the sheriff from the gravity of his stare. With no further words, he shook the sheriff's hand, and left the office.

Denton lowered himself back into his chair. The little smile, the confident smirk, drifted away.

J essica's arsenal of cost-versus-earnings analyses, public petitions, benefit projections, medical advance potential, and industry endorsements had far outgrown her briefcase during her years of pushing for the children's hospital. But her presentation's persuasive influence didn't seem to be increasing along with its bulk. She left the latest meeting on the brink of admitting defeat, having learned that the NIH money had been awarded elsewhere, and not knowing why her potential backers always ended up declining, sometimes just when it seemed they were on the verge of signing off on a deal. Now, on top of that, the institution of her own affiliation, Alamosa General, was grabbing for more funds. She nearly screamed when she thought about the work she and Canidey had done to draw potential investors, only to have the administration stick its nose into the deal and try to scoop up the money that she, on her own time, had attracted to the cause.

As she walked through the dark hospital parking lot, she finally took Canidey's advice and said a little prayer, that somehow things would, just once, come up on her side. And then she thought of her daughter. Whenever she hoped for something for herself, her thoughts always turned to the one thing that made everything else seem unimportant. She smiled wearily and opened the door of the Honda, tossing her two overloaded cases onto the passenger seat. As she started the engine, a light rain began to sprinkle on the windshield and gloss the pavement. She recalled Reed's unexpected appearance in the cafeteria, then later right there in the parking lot, and then again outside her home. A shiver grazed her skin when she thought about what he'd said, the way he kept popping up all over the place. He'd opened the scars, brought back the horror of Alana Kieran's murder. It wasn't a taboo subject; it had been dealt with in the healthiest possible way, she thought. The community had recovered as much as it could, considering that the case remained unsolved. For the most part, the memory had been put to rest in people's minds. But Reed was a stranger, and that made it different . . . worse somehow. The chill on her bare flesh heated into a form of anger within. What right did he have to tread on that ground? He spoke about Alana's death as if he had some type of kinship with her, as if his wife's murder were related. Now something more than a shiver jabbed at her. She realized that she was driving about twenty miles an hour over the speed limit, and let up on the accelerator. Why would he come here? Why make an association with Alana's death? Was he on some deluded vengeance quest, seeking out any past tragedies that resembled the fate his wife had suffered? But what if his words were true? she asked herself, seriously for a moment. It could mean any number of things. Too many questions remained for her to settle her feelings. She didn't want to distrust him; it went against her nature. He'd seemed so friendly and unassuming at first. He'd proven himself to her as a healer, a medical professional, as someone with compassion. The fact that Lucy liked him as well complicated the matter further. She wanted to believe him, felt compelled to trust him. Yet part of her wouldn't allow it.

Jessica was about to make the turn homeward, but stayed on the main road into town. The El Halcón was only a few minutes away, and she had his room number on the business card he'd given her. Across the street from the motel she eased the Honda to the curb and stopped. The digital display on the dashboard read eight forty-six. Reed's Toyota was parked about halfway down the row of rooms. His light was on. She stepped out of her car, and crossed the street. Nearing the 4Runner, she thought about the conversation she'd had with Lucy. The curtains were drawn, but she could see the flicker of light from a TV through the crack between the draperies. A muffled bark came from the room.

"What is it, girl?" Reed's voice came through the glass window.

Jessica turned and started to walk quickly back toward the street, blood throbbing through her body. She'd only covered a few feet when behind her Reed's door opened. He would see her retreating, she realized; there was no convenient corner to duck into. "Shit," she whispered to herself, feeling unprepared for a confrontation.

"Hey," she heard Reed say. "Jessica?"

Stopping to turn around, her maternal instincts suddenly steam rolled over her initial trepidation. She walked back to within a few feet of Reed. He was in a T-shirt, jeans, and bare feet, striking the most unthreatening posture she could have imagined. She saw the dog in the doorway just behind him, eyeing her suspiciously.

"Where are you going? And what are you doing here?" he asked, a little suspicious himself.

"I just have one thing to say to you," she stated firmly, clinging resolutely to her intent.

"Say anything you like. Would you care to come inside first?" he offered, opening the door wider.

"No." She saw the dog's eyes sharpen their focus on her, as if the young Labrador were evaluating a potential adversary. "Just stay away from my daughter. You got that? You stay away."

"What?" Reed couldn't prevent a deep frown, Jessica's demand a baffling, pernicious mystery.

"I know you've seen her behind my back somehow. I don't know why, or what you have in mind, but I know. Okay. So, just stay away from us, or I'll call the police."

"Jessica. What the hell are you talking about? I don't know why you think I've visited Lucy without your knowledge, but you're very wrong."

"Reed. Don't even try. You're a bad liar." Jessica started to move away again. "Just go away."

"Hold it a minute! Jessica. Come back here. You're making a terrible mistake!"

Jessica ignored the pleas and started running toward the Honda. She heard the dog bark again as she fumbled with her keys.

Reed stuffed Hoover back into the room and started to go after the fleeing woman. He shouted her name, but she was already feet from her car. "Just tell me what makes you think I've done this."

Jessica slipped inside the Honda. A second later its engine started, headlights coming on. Reed had to jump out of the way to avoid being run over as the CR-V swung a fast U-turn. He watched as the taillights flew down the street, around the next corner, and disappeared.

He stood at the side of the street for another minute trying to figure out what had just happened, what could possibly have led Jessica to this unexpected accusation. He concluded that someone had to be actively attempting to sabotage him. That, he decided as he walked back across the parking lot, reaffirmed his belief that he was definitely doing something right.

PART III

The car will make many turns and stops. Lights will flash and streak across the surfaces of the ceiling, the seats, the windows. Then the car will slow; the road will become uneven, bumpy, gradually grow-ing rougher, the way steeper. Rocks will strike the undercarriage in resonating bangs and clunks, a hungry beast clawing, trying to tear its way through the steel from beneath. It will seem as though the car is no longer on a road, but lumbering over the angry countryside. She'll see the side of his face in the green light of the dashboard, his hair occasionally, the tip of his nose, an eyelash, a row of fingers wrapped tightly around the steering wheel. All else will be dark—much too dark. No longer will lights from the street flit through the interior. He'll take her to a place where there is no light. The bucking ride will calm slightly as the incline steepens. She'll feel herself press harder against the seat back as the tires pull their way uphill. There will be a strange whoosh as something brushes past the car's metal shell. Finally the hill will ease, the car will slow to a stop, the whooshing will cease, and the engine will die. The door will open, and the man will spring from the driver's seat. Through a small crack between the front seat and the open door, she'll see that tall yellow grass was making the whooshing sound as it swept against the car. The only light will be from the dome in the center of the ceiling. But it will stay on for only a second before the man switches it off with a curse. Then the back door will open, and his hands will surround her body, jerking her out of the car.

"Goddammit! You did this on purpose didn't you? You little whore!" he'll say when he feels the wetness of her nightgown. His hands will purposely touch areas of her body that seem to give him particular delight.

The black air will smell fresh, and feel cool on her skin, especially around the moist areas as she endures the crude, hard groping, the violations of her body.

Then she'll feel herself fly over the ground, the grass occasionally tickling her bare legs and arms between the wraps of tape. He'll carry her for what seems like miles, up and down small hills to what location she can't imagine. Wrapped in his arm, she'll feel him stepping up onto something, climbing some tall black column. She'll see nothing until he lifts her high over his head, and then only the stars will fill her vision. She'll beg the stars to stop the man, to save her, but they will seem not to notice what's happening.

TWENTY-TWO

Lucy looked up from her drawing pad when she heard the front door open downstairs. Her mother was home. The voices came as muted sounds conducted through the floor of her bedroom, Gart's much deeper and louder than her mother's. Even though Lucy couldn't understand the words as they filtered up, she could tell from the intonation that Gart was going to go home for the night. It came as a relief when she again heard the front door opening and closing, and the voices stop. A moment later the sound of a car starting confirmed that she and her mother were again alone. Lucy smiled to herself, and went back to her coloring book, which rested against her knees as she sat in bed. After a few more minutes, the great comforting sound of feet on the stairs brought Lucy's eyes up again from the page. She looked at her bedroom door and waited for it to open.

There was a gentle knock first.

"Come in," Lucy said.

The doorknob clicked, and Jessica stepped quietly into the room, warm smiles washing over both of their faces.

"Mommy," Lucy said, throwing her arms out to her mother. Jessica sat down on the side of the bed, giving her daughter a hug.

"How ya doing?" Jessica asked.

"Good."

"Did you have a nice evening with Gart?"

"No."

Jessica let out a small sigh. "Oh. Well, he said he had a good time with you, and asked me to say good night for him. He thought you might already be asleep."

Lucy didn't say anything back.

"Well. I think you'll get to like him one of these days."

Still Lucy didn't respond.

"Okay. I guess we'll just have to wait for that."

Lucy's eyes dropped back to her drawing.

"Hey," Jessica then said, a more serious tone coloring her voice. Lucy looked up again, sensing the change in her mother's mood. "I want to ask you something, and I need you to think for a second before you answer, okay?"

Lucy's eyes opened wide, reflecting a trace of worry.

"Remember yesterday when you said that Reed had a dog?"

"Yeah."

"Do you remember yet where you saw it? Try hard now." A frown creased Lucy's forehead. "I'm not mad or anything, Luce. I just need to know . . . how you knew that. Hmm?" Jessica smiled lightly.

Finally the furrow smoothed. "I just saw her."

"I know you saw her. But where? When? I don't remember us ever seeing Reed with a dog."

Lucy shrugged. "I don't know."

"Was it at school? Or was it here? Did Reed come to see you when I wasn't around?"

"No. I just thought it. Like this." Lucy turned a few pages back in her drawing pad, and showed her mother the drawing of the tan-colored dog running beneath the large, dark bird. Jessica recognized the crayon rendering that was every bit a child's representation of a golden-haired Labrador.

"That's really good, Luce. Are you sure Reed didn't come by when I wasn't home . . . to show you his dog? It's okay if he did. I just need to know."

Lucy shook her head. "I've never met her. But her name is Hoover."

Jessica fathomed the possible ways in which Lucy might have seen Reed with the dog, and learned its name.

"That's kind of a funny name for a dog, isn't it?"

Lucy giggled slightly. "Yeah."

"How did you know it, Luce? Please tell me the truth, now. It's really important."

The giggling stopped. Again Lucy's face locked in concentration. Then: "I don't know how I know."

Jessica's smile drifted away. "Okay. Okay. Maybe you'll remember tomorrow. You think?"

Lucy shook her head. "I didn't forget. I just don't know."

"You must know somehow."

Lucy shrugged her shoulders.

"I don't want to play games tonight, Lucy. If Reed tried to see you when I wasn't around, I have to know about it. I'm not trying to make him go away, or get him in trouble, or anything like that. Okay? But you've got to tell me how you knew he had a dog, or I am going to get mad."

Lucy's eyes began to gloss over.

"Tell me the truth," Jessica demanded.

"Mommy, I told you the truth!"

Jessica looked her daughter in the eye for a long silent moment until a tear spilled down the little girl's cheek. Then: "Okay. That's okay, Luce. I didn't mean to scare you." Jessica pulled her daughter close, whispering in her ear. "It's okay. Everything's okay." Finally Jessica settled Lucy down into the pillows and kissed her on the nose. "Can you do one thing for me?" she asked, wiping the last tear away.

Lucy nodded.

"Try to think about it some more. And if you remember anything else, will you promise to tell me?"

Lucy nodded again.

"Okay."

Jessica took the drawing pad from Lucy's hands and placed it on the nightstand next to the bed. Then she leaned forward and kissed her daughter again. "Good night, sweetheart. Sweet dreams."

Lucy wrapped her arms around her mother's neck. "Good night, Mommy."

When Jessica stepped out of Lucy's room and pulled the door closed, she didn't have the facts that she'd hoped to come away with. In fact, as she undressed, brushed her teeth, and looked at herself in the bathroom mirror, she felt further from knowing the whole truth than ever. As she dropped her toothbrush into the holder above the sink, the phone rang. She didn't feel like talking to anyone, so she let the answering machine pick it up. Reed's message followed: *"Hi, Jessica, it's Reed. Hi to you, too, Lucy. Sorry for calling so late. Jessica, I really hope that you'll call me back. I'm sorry if I worried you earlier. Really . . . I . . . there's been some kind of misunderstanding that we have to clear up. Please accept my apologies, and give me a ring as soon as you can."* Reed left his phone number again, and hung up. Jessica turned out the lights and went to bed.

T he single-story brick building stretched out in two wings, which sprouted from a larger central structure, forming a big horseshoe. Inside the horseshoe was a courtyard and the building's main entrance. On the outside of the horseshoe was a playground and a parking lot. Reed waited inside his car across the street from the elementary school. The blue double doors at the side of the building's large central section—the gymnasium—remained closed. Reed had patiently watched them for nearly an hour.

Gradually cars began to arrive. Reed stepped out of the 4Runner, and leaned against the hood.

He stood and watched.

At five minutes to five he saw the silver Honda CR-V turn in. He hurried across the street, and approached the car from the rear on the passenger side, thinking this would appear less threatening.

Jessica didn't see Reed when she stepped down from the driver's seat, but turned to find him standing, looking back at her from across the hood.

"Oh, Jesus!" she exclaimed, jumping at the initial jolt of surprise. "Now what? Why are you here, Reed?"

"You didn't call back. I have to ask you a question so . . . I figured you'd be here eventually."

She remained on her side of the car, unsure whether to talk to him, stomp right past him, or get back in the car and go to the police. "I didn't call back because I thought you'd said what you had to say. I don't know what you're trying to do, but you're making me really nervous."

"Jessica, I just need you to trust me . . . a little bit. And I'd like to know why you think I've been to see Lucy, because I haven't."

"I don't care what you say, Reed. I know what I know."

"Jessica, someone's trying to set me up or something. Because *I* know what *I* know. And I haven't done what you're accusing me of."

Jessica looked away, distressed. She checked her watch, fidgeted where she stood, willing Reed to go away.

"Look, I can't make you believe me," he said. "But please stay away from here next week. Don't even tell me where you go. Just go. Now how can there be any danger in that? I'm only trying to protect you."

"From what? You're the only thing I seem to need protection from."

"Promise me that you'll leave town next week. There's someone out there who wants to kill you. He's already trying to make you distrust me. Don't you see what's going on?"

"Nobody wants to kill me. Why would they?"

"Because you're the next of life's soldiers. You're continuing Alana Kieran's work. It's nature's way of leveling the playing field. Please believe me! Or, if you won't believe me, then grant me the benefit of the doubt. I'm not trying to scare you, and I'm not making this up. If I'm wrong, then what harm's done? I'll look like a fool. I'll take that chance a hundred times over."

"In the first place I can't afford to just pick up and leave for a week. I've got patients, an absent partner, and a hospital to found. In the second place, if someone were trying to kill me, wouldn't they just wait until I came back?"

"I have no idea," Reed confessed. "All I know is that next week is when this thing, whatever it is, is supposed to take place. What happens after that is anyone's guess, but if you manage to get through next week safely, then that might be enough to prevent a tragedy. That's all I know."

"I have no reason to believe any of this. You're babbling nonsense," she continued protesting. "I don't know you and you don't know me."

They stood in a silent stalemate for another moment until Jessica asked: "What's your dog's name?"

"What?"

"What's her name?"

"Why?"

"Just tell me!"

"Hoover. Her name is Hoover. What does that have to do with anything?"

Jessica's eyes slanted with agitation. Then the gymnasium's blue double doors opened behind Reed, and a steady stream of children began to flood toward the parking lot. Along with many of the children, proud parents moved along a broad cement walkway, past a row of bicycle racks, the flagpole, and a big sign that said ALAMOSA ELEMENTARY.

Reed instantly recognized Gart who was surrounded by the group of children. He saw Lucy step from behind the gymnastics teacher, her head of light curls barely coming past her coach's knees. She ran toward her mother.

Jessica waved to her daughter and Gart, who seeing Reed, eyed him with suspicion. Reed noticed that Lucy was not smiling, and wondered what Jessica might have told her about him.

"Come over here, Lucy," Jessica instructed, beckoning the child to get in on the driver's side. Reed took a deferential step back. Gart stopped when he was between Reed and Jessica.

"You okay?" he asked, seeing the tension in Jessica's face.

"Yeah, I'm fine. Thanks, Gart," Jessica said, taking the opportunity to help Lucy into the car.

"Who's he?" Gart asked, flipping his thumb toward Reed.

"Reed, this is Gart, Gart . . . Reed," she reluctantly introduced the two men, who only nodded curtly at each other.

"And he's . . . a friend?"

"No," she answered.

"So, who are you?" Gart asked, turning to Reed.

Reed put both hands up innocently. "I'm a doctor who's just trying to help."

"What's he talking about?" Gart asked. Jessica shook her tired head without further explanation.

Gart looked back at Reed. "What's your problem, pal?" It was more a threat than a question.

"My problem is that no one will listen to me."

"Doesn't seem like anyone is particularly interested in what you have to say."

"Listen, Gart, I don't mean to upset anyone. That's—"

"Then why don't you just make yourself scarce?"

Jessica climbed into the CR-V. "Thanks again, Gart. I'll call you later," she said, now purposely avoiding eye contact with Reed.

"Will you please just let me explain," Reed demanded, allowing more urgency into his voice than he'd wanted.

The Honda's engine revved. Reed looked through the windshield to see Lucy staring back at him, not with fear in her eyes, but sadness. The Honda pulled back, and Jessica piloted the car out of the lot.

Reed stood facing the muscular coach, now with no car in between.

"Gart," Reed said, making every effort to soften his tone, "if you can, make sure that she gets out of town next week. Especially over the fifth and sixth. Tell her to go to her parents' or something. Anywhere but here."

"Pal, I'll thank you to mind your own business. She obviously doesn't need or want your help. Okay? Whatever shit you're doing, take it with you, and get out of here, now. Or I'll throw you out myself. You got it?"

Reed backed away. "Get her away from here, Gart. If you want to save her life."

"I'll give you the same advice, if you want to save yours."

Reed was left with no choice but to turn and walk away.

Reed sat in his motel room the rest of the evening trying to figure out what else he could do to reach Jessica. He damned himself for coming on too strong, too soon, especially after such a successful introduction. He had told her some pretty disturbing things, he realized, and his demeanor hadn't been exactly disarming since their first meeting at the Ox Cart. But he didn't have a lot of time to build confidences, and now he had lost valuable ground. The controversy about Hoover nagged at him ferociously. Recalling that Jessica had wanted to confirm the name, he reasoned that someone might have planted the information with Lucy. He struggled to think of all the people who could even have known what his dog's name was. His phone rang. It was Sheriff Denton.

"Hello, Sheriff."

"Listen, Dr. Haler, I just wanted to get back to you about the M.O. on your wife's case."

"Yes?"

"First, I'm awfully sorry about your loss."

"Thank you."

"Uh . . . second, you were quite right. There is a striking similarity between the two cases."

"Yeah. So . . . ?"

"So . . . I'll go ahead and have a unit keep an eye on the place you seem to think is going to be the scene of this guy's next attack."

"A unit? You mean one guy in a car?"

"Dr. Haler, we're a limited force here."

"Sheriff, we're talking about premeditated, cruel murder, with sexual assault, depraved indifference . . . etc. This guy is serious business, and you're sending one guy in a car to keep an eye on the place?"

"Dr. Haler, my better judgment tells me not even to do that much. But since it does seem that there may be something to your story, I'll put a man on it. And you're lucky I'll give you that much credit, which brings me to the other reason I'm calling."

"What's that?"

"Got a complaint about you today from a Gart Hanta. Says you've been harassing Jessica Morraine the last couple of days."

"Oh no," Reed whispered.

"I'm going to ask you to stay away from her. If you don't, she could get a restraining order against you."

"A restraining order! All I did was try to warn her."

"Well, it sounds like you've been following her and her daughter around, and making some strange threats."

"Threats! I haven't threatened her, or anybody! She doesn't understand how much danger she might be in, and neither does Gart."

"Well, if you told her the same story you told me, I can understand why she might be a little worried because of you. Just stay away from her and her daughter, and let the department handle things. In fact, it might be best if you just went on home."

"Are you telling me to leave town?"

"I'm suggesting that you go home, and get some rest."

"I'll leave gladly after the sixth, but no sooner. And you're going to need more than one guy on this."

"Good night, Dr. Haler."

Reed placed the handset down on its base, and pulled his wallet from his pants pocket. He dug through the collection of cards inside until he found the slip of paper he'd taken from Maysie Fabrioso's kitchen, studied the number, and picked up the phone again. He dialed and waited. An answering machine instructed him to leave a message.

"Hello, Maysie, this is Reed Haler. I apologize for calling you like this. I took your number down while I was there. Sorry. I know you said you didn't take calls when you were on assignments, but I thought I'd take the chance that you were home again. I guess you're not there. Uh . . . I'd really like . . . or actually I need to talk to you if you get this message." Reed left his number at the El Halcón and hung up. He sat on the bed for a few more minutes, thinking in circles. Eventually he got up and took Hoover out for a walk—anything to defer having to go to sleep. Of course eventually, he'd have no choice. Six days to go.

It had come fast. He'd closed his eyes only to meet the molten scarlet walls with no sense of dreaming, only that he'd been transported into a corridor of Hades. The tactile reality around him was beyond question, the olfactory and visual input as certain as and more vivid than any perception he'd ever experienced.

Only one step separated him from the dirt floor beyond the threshold of the doorway. In a corner of the hallway the dark figure hunched, giggled, trembled, and urinated. Reed passed through the opening, sensing for the first time the ability to move about freely. He gazed through the flames. The scene was the same as it had been before. The blue tent domed up in the ebbing light of the campfire. He realized that he wasn't in a room . . . he was in the forest, high in the Sierra Nevadas. As he stepped cautiously, he could feel the presence behind him, the heat of the breath, the stench. The thing had followed him through the door, but he'd expected that.

Between the tent and the fire was the body. As Reed edged his way around the fire, shuffling on the dirt, the bare legs, bright and orange in the light, came into clear view. The slender waist and upper body gleamed. But something was very different than before. The hair was wrong. There was no blood, no gaping slashes in the tender skin. The body was not that of his wife. The head lifted on its own, strands of dusky hair falling lightly to the sides of the face and over the supremely smooth, rounded shoulders. The woman sat halfway up, resting on her elbows, her nude body poised enticingly, the hint of a smile encouraging. Reed dropped to his knees between her legs, now aware of his own nakedness, and fully hardened erection. He was looking into the bright inviting eyes of Jessica Morraine. An invisible aura surrounding her seemed to draw him closer. Her skin shone, reflecting the fire in sensuous contours. The allure registered deep inside him, dredging up a hidden, shameful lust he'd never known he possessed. He wanted the body before him, so close it would be effortless to touch the moist, perfect flesh. He strained to resist, the urge growing, the need building to release a sexual tension that threatened to rob him of his sanity. Some instinctive, animal need to copulate, buried in the baser regions of his brain, had been excited, exaggerated out of control. The presence behind urged him on, silently, forcefully. One touch and Reed knew he'd lose the power to stop himself. He held back crazily, clenching his eyes against the intense stimulation. His guilt and thoughts of Devrie hammered at his conscience, tore his mind in two. He found himself wanting not just to enter the woman's body, but to possess it and destroy it, to drain it of life while he satisfied himself. That would be the supreme climax: to take the life, to feed upon it sexually. He craved the sensation, as if its continued denial would lead to complete madness—the only sure escape from which was nothing short of death itself.

The Indian's voice came, as if breathed directly into his ear, as if from God: *"You smell of fear."* A surge of strength, of control, returned to Reed's body and mind. He remained curled on his knees, blinding himself to the seduction that exuded from the woman, lying prone and naked only inches from him. He could still feel, smell, the power of her sex, the power of the force behind him, but he believed that if he could block his senses long enough, he could escape the mammoth desire.

The buzzing started, quietly at first, then crescendoing into a roar. He held his breath, squeezed his eyes tighter and bit down hard on his tongue until he tasted his own blood.

The alarm sounding, Reed opened his eyes to a dim blurry pattern of tiny squares, which he realized was the weave of his bed sheet. Dark smears stained the white cotton on the mattress and pillows. On his knees, legs curled tightly, he felt a cool stickiness on his lower lip and chin. His fingers came away red when he touched his mouth where pain glowed fiercely. He slammed a hand down on the alarm clock, silencing the clamor.

In the bathroom mirror he saw blood wiped over more of his face than he'd expected, the extent of the damage he'd done to his tongue more severe. He gazed in shock at the gnawed flap of pink skin he'd torn open with his teeth, fixating on the wound until the bleeding began to subside. Hoover's yelp broke his paralysis. The dog needed a walk and some breakfast. It was nine o'clock. Reed was only too happy to occupy himself with any task that took his mind off the dream and its implications, both known and those possibly unknown.

It was Saturday, August first, only five days from . . . who knew what? Completing the second pass around the motel's parking lot with Hoover, Reed arrived at a decision. The dream had prodded, charged his intuition—he felt certain again. That certainty compelled him to make one more effort. The alternative was to do nothing but wait and watch—another murder. He wouldn't do that, couldn't allow it to happen as long as he had any hope of preventing it.

Reed hurried Hoover along, fed and watered her, and then sat down at the small table in his motel room. He started on a fresh phone message pad:

Jessica,
    I know that Gart has told the police I've been bothering you and Lucy. To bother you is the last thing I

intend, and to harm Lucy is an intolerable notion. That's why I'm sending you this note instead of trying to speak with you again directly. Everything that I've told you about myself and my wife is true, and I only wish to protect you from the same fate she suffered. I understand that it's difficult for you, perhaps impossible, to believe that I have this knowledge of the future. While I may not be able to prove this to you, I will ask that you please allow me the benefit of the doubt, and take the precautions I've suggested: next week leave town, go far away and stay away until after August sixth—longer if you can. I know that someone or something intends to harm you, very possibly kill you. I sincerely believe that you are the next of life's soldiers as my wife's journal specifies, and that you are the next intended victim of whatever evil force is at work. I beg you to do what I've asked, if not for yourself, then for Lucy. You're doing a wonderful service for the good of humanity, and that is why you are in such great danger. Please don't disregard this letter.

—Reed

He folded the note and taped it closed, printing Jessica's name on the outside. He then led Hoover out the door and into the car.

The street was quiet and still except for a few yard sprinklers. Reed perceived no human forms disturbing the odd tranquillity of the suburban desert afternoon. The sun seemed to bake any noise right out of the air. Reed pulled to a stop well down the street from the Morraine household. He noted the CR-V parked in the driveway. The mailbox was mounted on a post set back about a foot from the curb. All he had to do was drop the note inside the box and leave. With only a little luck, she'd never know he'd been there until she found the letter. He looked over at Hoover to see if she would convey any canine instincts. She was noncommittal, so he elected to take the chance, and rolled the 4Runner toward the house, stopping like a mailman. He'd have to step out of the car to get to the box, and did so as quickly and inconspicuously as he could.

The box, he discovered, already contained a current issue of the *Journal of the American Medical Association* and several bills and letters. Reed propped the note up on top of the mail, leaning it against the wall of the box.

Gently he closed the mailbox door, and slipped back into his car. The windows of the house betrayed no sign of any inhabitants.

Feeling confident of some measure of success, Reed drove away. He'd at least tried. Whatever happened now, he thought, was beyond his control.

Among the chores for which Lucy was responsible on Saturdays was bringing in the mail. She ran out the door and down the grass yard to the box. Behind her Gart followed, having offered to keep her company on her little errand. She stopped and waited for him to catch up.

His offer had made her happy for a moment, but always the fact that he was her gymnastics coach raced up and spoiled the idea that she could just be friends with the man her mother was sleeping with. It just felt wrong for the same person to occupy both roles. Lately Gart had been spending more and more time at their house. Instead of just coming by to pick her mother up for a Saturday night date, he'd arrived at eleven o'clock that morning, arms full of brunch materials. He'd stayed all day, and would probably stay all night. Although Lucy had never really known her father, she knew that Gart could never fill that void. But her opinion on the subject didn't seem to carry a lot of weight. It was what her mother wanted, so that's the way it was.

Lucy stood on the curb next to the mailbox and waited, unable to maintain the temporary smile.

"Open up," he said. "Let's see what you got. Maybe you won a million dollars or something," Gart said with an exaggerated tone of expectation.

"I don't think so," she said despondently, as she popped the door and reached in. She was too short to see inside the box, and located the day's post by feel. In a single stack she withdrew the mail. On top there was an especially light piece, a single sheet of folded paper. When it looked as though the little girl might lose control of the envelopes and magazine, Gart came to her aid. He immediately noticed the folded piece of paper on top, "Jessica," hand-printed on the front. The lack of any postage or mark told him that a visitor had made a personal delivery.

"Okay, you take this half, and I'll take this half," he said, handing the magazine and several letters to Lucy, while he held on to the other envelopes and the note.

"See, we're a team, sport," he said with a smile that was just a little too big for the occasion.

"Yeah," Lucy acknowledged reluctantly. "What else did we get?"

"Bills," he answered, glancing through the stack. "Something you will learn to hate very quickly . . . when you're grown up."

Lucy was old enough, and quite aware enough, to understand why grown-ups hated bills; she was also old enough to know that the small piece of paper on top of the stack Gart carried a little too protectively was not a bill.

The single folded page held a mystery, so Lucy made a point of keeping track of it when they were inside the house again. It wasn't difficult. Standing over the kitchen table, where the mail always made its first landing, Gart made a pretense of studying the less important items, while he casually slipped the enigmatic paper into his pocket. Lucy was quite sure that he believed he'd succeeded in concealing it. That only confirmed her suspicions that it contained a secret—which further goaded her curiosity.

During the remainder of the afternoon she found opportunity to be always at least within earshot of Gart, keeping his pocket under surveillance. She listened closely to what was said when Gart and her mother spoke to each other. The subject matter was trivial for the most part; it was clear that he hadn't revealed the paper to her right away. Lucy wondered if it had something to do with her mother's hospital project, since everything that seemed important to her was somehow related to that one thing. But that didn't explain Gart's behavior. Why would he be secretive about the piece of paper? Something about this was different, sinister.

There was still enough natural light bleeding through the windows for Lucy to see from where she sat on the gold living room carpet that her mother had changed into her date clothes. Gart was on the couch reading some thick paperback novel with a setting sun on the cover. Or was it a rising sun? Lucy had been attempting to duplicate the image in crayon in her drawing pad. To the image of the sun peeking over the horizon, she added two cars and three people in the foreground. Two of the people were together, a man and a woman. The third, a man, was standing away from them, holding something like a short stick, but she colored the stick silver. Behind the people she drew a big yellow mountain, and in one of the cars she added the tan-colored dog.

The smaller picture of the orange hemisphere set against a burning sky came to rest when Gart tossed the paperback onto the coffee table, and shuffled up the stairs. Lucy took close notice when he and her mother disappeared inside her mother's bedroom. Lucy crept to the top of the stairs and listened closely at the door. She could only hear a quiet mumbling. The sound of compressing floorboards a minute later forced her to retreat back down the stairs to her drawing pad. The mood that emanated from the bedroom when the two adults again emerged was unmistakable. The paper had to contain some kind of bad news to warrant such secrecy and ill-ease, Lucy concluded. Suddenly the doorbell sounded. It was Jill Ann, her baby-sitter.

The fact that Gart and her mother made a special effort to appear as if nothing were out of the ordinary as they left for their date only reinforced Lucy's impressions to the contrary.

They had been gone for about an hour when Lucy found the occasion she'd been waiting for. Jill Ann was safely on the phone talking about her summer romance, and the ear-wash from the TV more than covered the sound of the bedroom door opening.

Her mother's room was a sort of magical place. There was so much history there, tucked into drawers, displayed on dressers and tables, hanging on the walls. It was an archive of her family, dating back too many years to count. But Lucy wasn't there this time to learn about her past. The present and the future were of greater immediate concern. She latched the door behind her and switched on the light.

She began the search on her mother's desk, which was a small municipality of stacked folders, letters, and books. The drawers were locked, but Lucy knew that her mother kept the key inside a small ceramic bowl on her dressing table.

She unlocked the main drawer first, and there was the piece of paper, just where she'd hoped to find it, on top of a disarrayed layer of cards and letters. The paper itself was small, folded in half only once, her mother's name printed in a precise hand. The tape no longer held the edges together. Lucy opened the note and read the clearly written words, not once but three times, before she returned it to the exact position in which she'd found it. After carefully relocking the drawer, she replaced the key in the bottom of the bowl.

J essica hesitated to open the door of the car after Gart had parked in front of the small Italian restaurant, one of the places they went fairly often for dinner on Saturday nights.

"You're worried," Gart said, turning off the engine. "You're worried he's going to be here, aren't you?"

She'd tried to be inconspicuous about it, but obviously Gart had noticed her scrutiny of the parking lot, of the restaurant, her apprehension about even getting out of the car.

"You've been on the lookout for that Toyota ever since we left your house."

"Well, so would you," she defended.

"And I have been. I've been watching as carefully as you have. But why are you so reluctant to admit the fact that he's got you scared?"

"Because I'm not so sure he's really dangerous."

"Not sure! He's followed you, followed Lucy, found out where you work and live, and now he's leaving threatening notes in your mailbox."

"He hasn't threatened me, Gart."

"What would you call it?"

"He's warned me."

"Oh, about what? Some mystery murderer who's got you targeted? Come on. The guy's wacko! Probably living some dual personality. He warns his victims that they're in danger, then attacks them exactly as he told them it would happen. I've seen documentaries about things like that. These guys actually want to get caught, so they tempt fate, confess their crimes in indirect ways. They leave trails, deliberate clues. They return to the scenes, and keep news items about what they've done. He told you himself that he was interested in Alana Kieran's murder. He may even have warned her the same way he's warning you."

"Are you suggesting that he killed Alana?"

"We may never know for sure."

Jessica shifted in her seat, her eyes once more scanning a wide radius. "He's never been here before in his life."

"Not that you know of."

"But when I met him he wasn't at all like that. He's an eminent geneticist. His own wife was murdered."

"Oh, so he killed his wife too."

"I didn't say that. The police obviously didn't think he did it. Besides, Lucy really likes him. She's incredibly intuitive. I'm just having trouble believing that he means to harm us."

"So. Are you going to let these 'warnings' go on until he makes good on them? I mean, what's next? Is he going to break into your house some night to warn you that someone's going to break into your house? Or that someone is going to kidnap Lucy? Come on, Jess. Wake up. He's not normal, and things like this escalate. You know it as well as I do. He's not going to just go away."

"I don't know." The problem tumbled in her head. "I just can't shake the possibility that he might be telling the truth."

Gart beat the heel of his hand against the steering wheel. "The truth! He's conning you, Jess. You don't know anything about him. And why take a chance, in any case?"

"How can doing what he's asking me to do put me or Lucy into any danger? It doesn't make sense, Gart."

"It has to be some kind of trick. That's all I can figure."

"Unless . . ."

"What?"

Jessica pondered a new thought intensely. ". . . unless, not doing what he's telling me to do is exactly what he really wants."

"Get the restraining order, Jess. It doesn't matter what he really wants. He's dangerous and you need to protect yourself."

Jessica thought for another moment, looked around the parking lot again, and then smiled at Gart. "Come on, let's go eat. I'm starving." Jessica boldly unlatched the door this time in an effort to shrug off the tension, but Gart grabbed her arm before she could step out.

"Promise me you'll file for the order. You've got grounds now. Hard evidence. It couldn't do any harm, and he might just get the message. And the police will have an official record of the complaint. Promise me."

She leaned over and kissed him on the cheek. "I'll be all right," she whispered in his ear. When his grip loosened, she lifted herself out of the car.

Reed had learned to sneak naps during the day, since the recurrent nightmare only seemed to come during the dark hours. But the fatigue of fearing sleep, dreading it, and getting it only in sporadic blocks was draining his energy like nothing had since med school.

Every evening he'd returned to the Ox Cart bar and grill. He knew full well that it was probably way off Jessica's list of places to go, at least until she was sure that he was long gone. Still he went there, ate, and afterwards would drive around looking for anything that might provide additional clues as to what he ought to do next.

He'd found nothing new to dissuade him from his present course, and nothing that compelled any specific action. So, with five days to go, he once again finished his dinner and coffee, and drove past the New Moon Saloon and up to his perch in the hills. From there he watched the sun set and the night settle in.

He let Hoover run around the wide turnout until she tired and curled up next to the front wheels. Reed sat on the hood, reclining on the windshield as he asked the stars who his enemy was. They only twinkled back their indifference, silent as the dry waves that lay beneath them to the north.

It was after midnight when Reed brought the 4Runner to a stop in front of his motel room. He unlatched the passenger door for Hoover, but strangely, she didn't hop out as she usually did.

"Come on, lazy. You're not that tired." Patting Hoover encouragingly on the rump, he opened his own door, and began to step out. Suddenly he saw stars again, then a burst of light, which seemed to bring the pavement up to the side of his face. A sharp impact jabbed dazzling pain into his side, robbing him of the ability to breathe. He fought the ache, drawing air as hard as he could, but his lungs only wanted to expel. Another impact in his other side made respiration nearly impossible. The whirl of violence was all too familiar. He was distantly aware of the bark of a dog and the sense of suffocation. The night—that night—came back to him in all its horror. His one thought, irrational as it might have been, was to save his wife—not fail her again. He twisted and turned in a desperate effort to glimpse his attacker this time. Then came another dull shove; he could scarcely tell where it landed, his body had become so numbed. He saw only speckled lights in front of him, and heard more muffled barking. He wondered with surprising calm whether that was the last sound he would ever hear. The thought brought with it a great sense of relief. Suddenly he felt no pain. Some time later the silence of the night returned, as did the air he needed to live.

TWENTY-THREE

Reed was breathing in the smell of asphalt and warm steam. He opened his eyes to see an extreme close-up of a shiny black knob with two exhaust holes at the end of a light tan snout. The brown eyes filtered into focus, staring back at him.

Reed tried to move, immediately aware of the epicenters of the surprise attack on his body. The pavement was still warm from the day, so he reasoned that he must not have been unconscious for very long. Not long enough for anyone to find him, apparently. Hoover nuzzled his face, drawing a wet tongue up his cheek. Reed pushed the dog's nose away, and managed to roll himself onto his side. His ribs roared, and the back of his head radiated a glowing pain through his cranium and down his neck to his shoulders and back. He couldn't seem to remember what had happened.

Gradually his strength returned, but as it did, so too did the discomfort intensify. He saw that the door of the 4Runner was still open, but there was no sign of any attacker. Working his way on hands and knees he was able to push the door of the car closed and reach the entrance to his room. Inside, it took all his power to turn on the light and climb onto the bed. All he knew for sure was that he'd been beaten seriously.

After several minutes of thumping agony, bright flashes accompanying every surge of his pulse, Reed finally rallied his strength, and dragged the phone onto his lap. In the process he noticed the big red LED's of the digital clock. It was one twenty-five A.M.

He dialed 911 and reported the incident. Five minutes later he was in an ambulance and on his way to the hospital.

Sheriff Clark Denton arrived at the hospital at nine o'clock the following morning. Reed had been treated and kept overnight for observation. He had a minor concussion, nine badly bruised ribs, and a slight sprain of the neck, but nothing was broken. Still, he'd been kept awake all night because of the injury to his head and for that he was both very thankful and very tired.

"Somebody sure has taken a liking to you," was Sheriff Denton's appraisal when he saw Reed in the bed.

"Yeah," Reed concurred.

"Any idea who?"

"Where's my dog?" Reed came back.

"She's fine. Holding kennel at the pound. You can go claim her when you're released. Now I'll ask again: Any idea who would want to lay you out?"

"No, not really . . . well . . . I don't know . . . maybe."

"I'm not much in the mood for twenty questions this morning, Dr. Haler."

"Fine, fine. The only person I can think of around here who might have an interest in beating the crap out of me is Jessica Morraine's boyfriend . . . at least he thinks he's her boyfriend."

"You're talking about Gart Hanta?"

"Mmm."

"And you think he might be feeling just a tad jealous, or worried 'cause you been nosing around where your nose ain't wanted?"

"Something like that."

"I see. Well, I'll try to have a word with him. Get his side. In the meantime, I've taken another look into your wife's case, and the Kieran case."

Reed tried to sit up with a great wince. "Yeah?"

"Compared the shoe impressions taken at each location. They weren't a match, but they were the same size foot. Same size guy at both scenes. That's what the experts say. Got me thinking, on the chance that you're right . . . maybe I do need more than one guy on this."

"And so . . . ?"

"So, here's my deal. I'll stake out the New Moon Saloon with two units outside and two inside over the twenty-four hours you think this 'murder' is supposed to happen. If nothing happens over that twenty-four hours, I want your ass out of town—that day. If anything does happen, a lot of people, including myself, are gonna want to know how you knew about it. And I don't think many of 'em are gonna buy this psychic message shit. I know I don't. So, that sound fair enough to you?"

"Fair enough."

"Okay, Dr. Haler," the sheriff said, walking away. "I'll let you know what I find out from this Gart fella. And . . . get well soon."

Reed just closed his eyes.

By three o'clock that day, with a pocket full of painkillers, Reed walked out of the hospital. On the way he noticed Jessica's colleague in pediatrics, Dr. Canidey, walking through the reception area. That made him wonder if Jessica was there too. It being Sunday, he figured that she probably wasn't. Dr. Canidey swept by without recognizing him, or simply choosing not to make the effort. Reed kept on walking, not bothering to say "Hi" either. At the loading area outside the front door, a cab waited. Four days, Reed thought, as he rode through town toward his motel. He started planning those four days in his mind. He would get himself cleaned up, a change of clothes, and then pick up Hoover. Then he remembered Devrie's journal in the glove compartment of his car. A wave of terrible fear that something had happened to it came over him. He remembered that he'd left the door of the car un-locked, the journal vulnerable, where it could have been taken after the attack. He knew that there was nothing he could do if it were gone, so he settled into an anxious hope, and continued making his plans. He'd have a few things to do—but first he needed a bit more rest . . . if he could get it.

A s Sheriff Denton had promised, Hoover was fine, and very happy to see Reed. When they got back to the motel she seemed to understand that Reed needed some sleep, and waited patiently at the foot of the bed. To Reed's great relief, the journal had still been inside the glove box as he'd left it.

He rested against the pillows. Every time he felt his eyelids slip-ping closed a wave of dread popped them back open. He knew he couldn't remain awake forever, and in his present drugged state he was afraid that the electronic alarm clock might not be sufficient to rouse him if the nightmare returned. He took the precaution of setting it for a two-hour interval anyway and finally let himself go, praying for peace, but preparing for hell.

H e had been right about the alarm not waking him, but thankfully wrong about the dream returning—at least for the time being. For some unknowable reason the vile torment had remained at bay, and he'd slept completely, but for how long he wasn't sure. The clock said one P.M. Hoover stirred by the door, quietly whimper-ing. Slowly Reed lifted himself from the bed, his chest thumping swells of a deep ache beneath the wide brace that was wrapped around him. The pounding in his head had settled to a mild reminder of the trauma he'd suffered. He'd been looking for a sign, and realized that one had been delivered . . . a little more forcefully than he'd wanted. Still he wasn't sure what to make of it. Without actually having seen who did it, he could only make educated guesses, and that process was becoming extremely tiresome.

"Okay, girl, just a second."

It didn't sound as if Hoover could wait another second, but she did. She was two feet out the door when she lost control.

"Who's the best girl?" Reed praised the Lab, with ample pats on the head. She seemed to know the answer. After a special bonus lap around the parking lot for being "such a good dog," Reed treated his companion to a fresh can of Alpo.

In the mirror he assessed the marbled darkness that covered his chest and back. The discoloration of the bruising was an intense contrast to the tanless white of his thinly haired skin. The tissue was swollen and tender. He was amazed that nothing was broken, and wondered if the doctors had made a mistake in their assessment. He decided that it didn't much matter, and replaced the brace.

Then it was time for another ride. A quick check in the yellow pages had provided the needed information. It didn't take long to find the store. Reed parked the 4Runner and let Hoover out on a leash.

The street was sparsely crowded for a Monday afternoon. At least he thought it was Monday. He checked the front page of the local paper in a curbside vending machine. It was Monday—the second of August . . . three days until the middle of summer.

The sporting goods store was not far from the library. By now he had learned his way around quite well.

As he'd expected, instead of objecting to Hoover's presence in the store, the young, heavy-set clerk praised the healthy-looking canine. Reed thought it would add to his credibility to have the friendly dog at his side on this particular errand.

It didn't take long for Reed to spot the item he wanted, as he hovered over the glass display case.

"May I see the Smith and Wesson forty-five?" Reed pointed out the weapon to the clerk, who wore a plaid flannel shirt in spite of the fact that it was ninety-five degrees outside.

"Nice choice," the clerk commented, scratching his blond-stubbled chin. The man reached into the case, and clutched the thick barrel of the weighty, smoke satin pistol. Reed took it handily. He pulled back the hammer slide, cocking the gun, then eased it back to the relaxed position. The exquisitely machined parts moved with remarkable smoothness, locking into place with mellow clicks. He remembered the rudiments of firearms operation from his father, who had taught him years ago how to shoot. This was the first time Reed had even touched a gun since he was twelve years old. But he remembered. "What are you asking for this?"

"Five fifty plus."

It was a little more than Reed had planned to spend, but he agreed and pulled out his MasterCard.

"I can only take a deposit for the weapon," the clerk informed Reed, "keep it for five days, then put it through."

"What?"

"You know, mandatory waiting period. Background check. Federal law, you know—five days."

"Shit!" Reed let slip. "I don't have five days." He set the pistol down on top of the case and scanned the store for alternatives. "Okay. Okay, let me see the Buck on the left there?" The clerk replaced the .45 and moved to a different part of the case. He grasped the carved walnut handle of the eight-inch hunting knife, and passed it to Reed. The heavy, mirror-polished stainless blade impressed; the sharpness of its edge inspired. The needle point could sink into flesh under the knife's own weight, Reed imagined.

"Any waiting period on knives?" he asked with a touch of sarcasm.

"Not yet anyway," the clerk said, smiling.

"Good. I'll take it."

He handed the knife back to the clerk, who slipped it into a leather carrying case.

"Be doing some hunting, fishing?" the clerk asked as he rang up the sale.

"Oh, maybe," Reed answered.

"You know," the clerk said, "deer season isn't for a month or so yet, but you could go out for fowl, small game."

"Oh, I know," Reed lied.

"Need a fishing license?" the clerk asked.

"No thanks."

"Okay. Comes to one thirteen thirty-five with the tax." Reed dropped the MasterCard on the glass surface, and gave Hoover a gentle pat on the nose.

H e'd seen it done but had never tried it himself. Hoover sat by, watching without criticism as Reed experimented with various techniques.

The old train station provided ideal cover from view, and the burned-out cottonwood made for an excellent target. He'd spent the afternoon throwing the knife at the blackened trunk, only succeeding occasionally, but gradually gaining a sense of the physical dynamics of the knife as it flew through the air. The necessary exertion was torture on his bruised bones and muscles, even with the brace wrapped tightly around his chest. He continued anyway.

There was a satisfying quality to the hollow *thunk* of the point sinking firmly into the soft, toasted bark of the cottonwood. After three hours of practice, Reed had become fairly adept at landing strikes from inside twenty feet. He wanted to do better, and left with the plan to return early the next morning.

R eed went through his routine of dinner at the Ox Cart and roadside contemplation of the universe, but his nagging injuries brought him back to the El Halcón early. The painkillers were only mildly effective, and lying flat on his back was the only true relief. As Reed took in the ten o'clock news there was a knock on the door. It was the sheriff.

"Evening, Dr. Haler," the lawman said when Reed answered.

"Evening, Sheriff."

"Sorry to bother you so late, but I saw your lights on and—"

"No, that's fine. What can I do for you?"

"I wanted to see how your recovery was going and to let you know that I spoke with Gart Hanta today, and he claims he was with Jessica Saturday night at the time you say you were attacked, which she's confirmed. So, unless you can give me something else to go on, I don't have much reason to suspect that he's the guy who assaulted you."

"Well, I guess that's that then. Thanks for checking into it."

"Yeah, sure. There is one other thing." The sheriff shifted his weight, and placed his hands on his hips. "Ms. Morraine has filed for a restraining order against you. Judge will rule tomorrow, and I'll tell you now she'll probably get it. She's very well liked around here, and there's a few people willing to testify that you've been hanging around her house, and where she works. Well, you get the picture."

"Jesus H . . ." Reed mumbled to himself. "Sheriff . . ."

"Yeah?"

"All I've done is try to protect her."

"I guess she doesn't appreciate your concern, Dr. Haler."

"I know, Sheriff, but if she's around—you know, in town—over the fifth and sixth . . . can you make sure someone keeps an eye on her? One of your men?"

Reed's request clearly surprised and confused Denton.

"Just for those days. Just until the stakeout at the New Moon is over."

Denton noticed the Labrador staring, almost grinning at him from behind Reed. He thought about it, wondering about Reed's sincerity, his motivation. How could keeping an eye on Jessica Morraine hurt in any case? he wondered. "Well," he said finally, "I guess that might be a good idea at that. But don't think for a second that by asking for this you've deflected any suspicion away from yourself."

Reed smiled at the idea.

"There's something I don't like about this whole business," Denton added.

"Sheriff, you can think whatever you want about me. Just keep an eye on her, okay?"

"Okay. And I'm gonna keep an eye on you too."

"I hope you do."

"Right. Well, good night, Dr. Haler. I'll be in touch."

"Good night, Sheriff, and thanks for stopping by."

Reed closed the door and turned the volume on the TV back up. How, he wondered, was he going to stay awake for nine more hours?

When he awoke at eight the next morning, Reed realized that he must have lost the fight to stay awake sometime around midnight or one. The television was still on, a morning news show greeting him with the latest on another growing crisis in the Middle East. For whatever reason, the dream had again stayed away. He wondered if the blow to the back of his head was somehow responsible, or maybe it was the painkillers. All that mattered was that he'd gotten some rest, and he'd made it through another night without the walk through damnation. Two more days, he thought, and maybe it would all be over . . . maybe.

He picked up the phone and dialed. He knew that Wally would be in the lab.

"Bohrs," Wally answered. The voice came as a glorious reminder that the world Reed had known was still there, that it wasn't just a figment of some imagined idealistic memory.

"Hey, Wal, it's Reed."

"Reed! My God! That's you. Good. Don't go anywhere! Listen, you've got to get your ass back here, now!"

"Slow down, Wal. That's why I'm calling. I'll be back very soon."

"No, Reed. Now. We've finished the preliminary assays on the site you came up with, and we got one hundred percent across the board on two hundred more random samples. We've got the grant money in the bank, and we've got approval to go ahead with some transfer tests. I can't believe you're not even here. Tim Hon resigned! Whitaker's about to soil himself . . . and hang you! This whole place is going nutty, man!"

"That's great, Wal. I'll be there in a few days. There's just one more thing I need to do. Great news about Hon. Tell Whitaker I'm sorry. I'll make it up to him, and to you. Remember—*Chez Panisse* . . . dinner . . . my treat, price no object."

"I wish you'd tell me what's so damn important. History is about to happen here, but not without you, dammit!"

"Keep it together. Just a few more days, Wal. I'll see ya."

"Wait, Ree—"

Reed hung up, and called Dale and Bettyanne, reassuring them that he was fine, and that he'd be home in a few days. He felt a pang of guilt about saying it with such assurance, not really knowing at all whether he'd be going home ever, or winding up a headline in the paper. Bettyanne made no secret of the fact that she was extremely worried about him.

Whatever the case, Reed had no choice but to remain, and to face whatever was to come. He sat on the bed for more minutes than he knew, as he realized for the first time since he'd left the Bay Area how much he missed his home, his friends, and his family.

H e stepped outside to find Sheriff Denton leaning against his patrol car, waiting.

"Sleep here in the parking lot?" Reed asked facetiously as he opened the door to the 4Runner, and let Hoover in.

"No, Dr. Haler, I didn't," the sheriff said.

Reed turned to Denton, who held out a single sheet of paper. Reed grabbed the sheet and looked at it.

"You're not to come within a hundred feet of Jessica Morraine, or her daughter."

"Guess the judge made his decision," Reed said, while he read the terms of the court order. Reed folded the paper, and stuffed it into his pocket.

"Any questions?"

"None. If you'll excuse me now, Sheriff." Reed pulled himself up into the big car.

"Dr. Haler."

Reed turned his head toward the sheriff.

"I will enforce this order . . . very strictly."

"I should hope so." Reed started the car and rolled up the window.

The pain was getting more bearable; he was recovering quickly, but still he needed the chest brace and an occasional pair of Motrin tablets.

It was another perfect day. There was no wind and only a few nicks of white interrupted the absolute blue hemisphere overhead.

Hoover happily chased flying things, while Reed continued to practice with the knife. Deep gouges in the cottonwood indicated signs of his improvement. By the middle of the afternoon, he was landing about seventy-five percent from over thirty feet. He stopped to rest when he sensed his ribs had had as much as they could take. But he was gaining fast in confidence that if he had to use the knife for self-defense, it would improve his odds of survival at least a little. The pistol would have been far preferable, he thought.

He found a mossy rock to sit on at the edge of the forest, where he rested, and filled his lungs with hot dry air. The old station building's rear side gloomed at him minaciously, as if in judgment of his skill with the weapon. But it also seemed to bestow a grudging approval, that he was doing what was right.

A mild but distinct fragrance floated on the soft breeze from the direction of the building. With it came a stillness, a silence that felt as deep as the black windows in the flagstone walls that faced him. He couldn't immediately identify the smell . . . or was it almost . . . a flavor? It was sweet like fruit. Hoover suddenly appeared from the weeds, head up, ears alert. She eyed the building as if she'd just spotted a large cluster of game hen. She gave a squelched snarl, and beat a quick path back toward Reed. She huddled by his feet, eyes still keenly set . . . on what, Reed couldn't tell.

"Girl, what is it?" he asked, encouragingly patting her collar fur. Her distraction continued, the scent still hanging in invisible clouds.

Peach! No, it wasn't peach. It was . . . apricot! Why would he be smelling apricot? he wondered. He grasped the knife by the handle, taking in the three hundred and sixty degrees around him. The forest offered no indication of the source of the odor. Hoover's attention was still on the building, so Reed turned back to the structure. There on the platform stood the woman with the green blouse and black skirt, neither smiling, nor frowning, only watching silently as before.

Reed's lungs contracted and seized; the hairs on his entire body pricked; his bruises cried out. He gulped involuntarily several times. He could feel his eyes water up and his heart surge into his throat. If he'd still harbored any doubt that the image was that of Alana Kieran, that doubt was now forever crushed into oblivion.

She didn't move and neither did Reed. His grip around the knife handle turned his knuckles to bone. He knew he wasn't imagining it, because Hoover saw it too. That much reassured him on one level, while hurtling him into an inexplicable terror on another. If it wasn't his imagination, then what was it? How could a dead woman be standing less than fifty feet from him? He reluctantly accepted the answer, but when he tried to move he found his muscles locked. He wanted to call out to her, but his larynx clenched shut. What did she want? The question repeated again and again in his mind. Why was she appearing to him? He wanted to ask these and so many more questions, but he was powerless even to utter a sound. He could only watch as she took a step back, effortlessly, through the tall grass, until she was at the corner of the building. Then, before Reed could collect his strength, she was slipping beyond the corner, and out of sight. Suddenly he was on his feet, running toward the platform, down and across the rail bed and up the other side, onto the platform. He rushed to the corner, around which the spectral vision of Alana Kieran had just passed.

"Wait!" he called out. Only blond grass and the pink stone side of the station greeted him. "Wait!" he cried again, his voice lost in the hot wind that bowed the weeds. He hurried to the front of the building and found exactly what he'd expected—more weeds and his car, still parked and empty. Then he noticed a flash of light flit across the back doors of the 4Runner. He turned around with a jump.

Nothing.

Back at the car, the glint dashed the other way. He looked around himself frantically, only to realize that he still held the knife, the blade's mirror finish reflecting the sun, its handle well lubricated in sweat. He twitched the knife several more times, playing with the fleck of light.

"Oh, shit!" he said with a heavy exhale. "Oh, shit!" He walked cautiously back around the station, terrified of what he might see around each corner. He found Hoover still crouched by the rock, panting.

Standing on the platform where the apparition had just been, Reed transferred his hold on the knife from the wet handle to the shiny blade. He examined the ground, the grass, and the wall of the station. Nothing indicated that anyone had just occupied the space. But he had no doubt that she had been there, in a form he could see. A new feeling of quiet confidence had suddenly taken root somewhere within him. So he aimed, closed his eyes, and hurled the knife at the cottonwood, a good forty feet away. The knife landed short, but it did stick into the tree at the base. He hugged his chest, trying to soothe the bruised bones. Had he been at full strength, he thought, there was little doubt that the knife would have found its mark.

Calling Hoover to his side, he tromped his way from the platform, through the grass, and over to the tree where the blade was planted in the root. It was time to get back, he thought, pulling the knife from the wood. He would set the alarm clock for his self-appointed two-hour nap. At least a little sleep was better than none . . . if sleeping would even be possible.

TWENTY-FOUR

The fire lowered; the legs came into view. Reed didn't see the Indian this time, didn't sense that presence any longer. It worried him.

He stepped closer. The upper body, the shoulders, and the head became visible as Reed advanced. He heard steps behind him. The silent laugher fully blocked the doorway as he—as it—returned from the hallway. It moved up behind Reed as it had before, its face shrouded, its breath hot and rank, foul with decay. Reed looked down again at the body, Jessica Morraine's body, moving with life, in the same place he'd last seen Devrie, mutilated, defiled beyond comprehension. He kneeled down; the fire roared with new life. The face was beautiful. He felt hot pressure from behind, forcing him to action. He was again aware of his lack of clothing, the fire's heat searing his skin. He crawled, the overwhelming force pushing him down. The earth hard on his knees, he was between Jessica's legs, half an inch from touching the slicked skin of her inner thighs. The heat on his back drove him forward, the impulse swelling, greater even than it had been before. The Indian's voice didn't come. He was losing. Fierce desire roiled inside him . . . savage lust prodding him ceaselessly. He lowered himself, down, on top of her body. Her breasts gleamed in the angrily fluxing orange bursts of fire. His pelvis thrust against hers, his free will obliterated. He felt himself enter her body. He fought insanely to hold his chest above hers, to prevent more contact, his arms spread to either side, pressing with futility. Her arms and legs wrapped around him, trapping his body against her responsive flesh. His skin clung to the sticky sheen that bathed the female torso. His lower body moved, seemingly of its own accord, but Reed knew that it was the dark figure, its power, forcing him into this vile performance. Her body moved with his, equally enraptured. He couldn't help the warm swell that rose up in his loins, the powerful surge of grotesque eroticism. He writhed faster, intending to finish the unholy act as quickly as possible, but the ultimate moment stayed away, just beyond reach. The next urge entered his mind through an unearthly hole in his sanity. His hands found the object that would give him his greatest satisfaction. Her neck was soft, smooth, and pulsing with blood. It was deliciously easy to squeeze, and as he did, he felt the powerful sweetness flood his body. She began to resist, to struggle, no longer in tune with his undulations. With each spasm he drew closer to the explosion of pleasure that awaited. The wave of sensation was mighty and monstrously glorious. He felt her strength flow from her genitals to his. The intensity of feeling was like no sex he'd ever had. His consciousness fell under the absolute domination of his physical climax, as he squeezed the life from her body. The throbbing between his hands now matched the rhythm of his stroke. Rather than the normal abatement after the initial peak of excitation, the sweet pain only heightened as the woman beneath him weakened, but time did not exist, as her body became an inanimate object. The pulse in her flesh ceased. Finally the brutal magnificence evanesced and Reed's awareness returned. The thought, the horror, of taking pleasure in anything so supremely repugnant brought instant nausea. He suddenly discovered that his right hand now gripped a hunting knife—not his own hunting knife, but a larger, heavier one—one which possessed a ghostly familiarity. The blade was bathed red to the hilt. A new, expulsive contraction seized his body in a great rush from his belly, when he saw that the body was no longer that of Jessica Morraine, but the disemboweled corpse that was once his wife.

The acidic burn flared in his throat as the vomitus gushed from his mouth and nostrils, quenching a scream. His strength left his body with the contents of his stomach, until he lost all control. He laid his head down in the bilious mixture of clotted blood on his wife's hard, cold breast, his eyes locked tightly closed—the only defense against the unimaginable scene of which he was somehow a participant. Breathing came only with tremendous effort—his body was frozen again. At last the voice came: *You smell of fear.*

Control of his limbs returned an instant later. He shot up, away from the death . . . no . . . it was his pillow. The motel room surrounded him once again as his eyes cleared and focused in the infirm light which scratched its way around the drawn curtains. His glance darted in a panicky circle. He was alone. The sound of the voice lingered in his head. It had brought him back to consciousness—had he truly been unconscious? He felt a coldness on the side of his face and under his body. He'd vomited on his pillows, and ejaculated in his "sleep." The memory of the nightmare possessed him. That there were actual, physical vestiges of the nocturnal terror brought the entire experience of the progressive nightmare to a new and beastly reality. Whether or not the act was real, Reed felt that he'd desecrated the most sacred and precious part of his life. He damned himself for not being strong enough to resist the power that had controlled him. The satisfaction, the extreme pleasure and duration of the orgasm, haunted him. Had he truly been unable to resist? Or had he simply been driven by his own perverse lust? He couldn't tell, and his self-loathing consumed him.

He looked at the clock. It was seven fifteen A.M. Why hadn't the alarm awakened him the evening before? he wondered, furiously. When he'd gone to bed at five thirty in the evening, he'd set the clock for seven thirty. Two hours. He would have had plenty of daylight left. When he examined the clock, he saw that it was set to go off at seven thirty exactly. So why hadn't it? he demanded of the silent room. Then he noticed the darkened LED indicator next to the letters "PM" on the face of the clock. He checked the alarm setting again.

"Goddammit!" he wailed. He'd set the clock for seven thirty A.M. not P.M. Tearing himself from the sheets, he flung himself into a pounding shower. His skin became raw under the scrubbing. Then he scrubbed more, remaining under the cleansing streams, until only shockingly cold water poured over him.

I mages and sensations from the dream crowded Reed's mind as he forced himself to eat. The diner was uncomfortably crowded. He felt that his fellow breakfasters were eyeing him suspiciously, as if he wore his guilt plainly, like a bull's horns on his head. The deepening circles under his eyes didn't help, he was sure.

It was no longer the dream itself that horrified him the most, it was the fact that he had enjoyed it, and even craved more. He now realized that he desired the dream again as much as he dreaded it. The prurient memory of overwhelming satisfaction, the sublime release, tortured him. It was all so clear and immediate, his memory almost eidetic, as if the dream had actually happened. But was he, himself, capable of such extraordinary depravity? Certainly the answer was "no." Or had a part of his mind been pried open somehow—the part in which sadistic, sexual psychoses lie dormant and buried in the sane? Was he slipping over to the other side, becoming part of nature's inevitable balance, as Maysie Fabrioso had described? Again he told himself "no!" Maysie was wrong. Nature was often ruthless in its corrections, true enough, but there was nothing normal about what was happening to him. No natural balance. It was an abomination, a perversion of nature in every sense. Or had humanity truly brought such horrors on itself? Had his own work really precipitated this demonic backlash? He wouldn't believe it, refused to accept it, and resolved to defeat it at any price.

After leaving the diner, he drove to the one place he felt a modicum of solace. The remainder of the day Reed spent alone, behind the old station building. He held the knife exactly as he had in the dream, but recalled that it had been different in the dream, bigger, deadlier. He slashed the blade through the air in daggering motions, as if rediscovering a long suppressed memory. Terrified, he examined the wide blade, almost expecting to find traces of blood. His own face stared back at him in the clean stainless surface.

He shook off the ill feelings, and continued practicing with the knife, steadily improving, and watched for Alana Kieran. There was no sign of her.

Hoover wasn't her usual active self either, as if she sensed Reed's mounting anguish. He decided that he would simply have to stay awake. He couldn't endure, couldn't risk slipping again into the sickening world of the nightmare. He had to consciously keep the temptation in check—a psychotic dichotomy of desire and revulsion. He felt that he'd somehow glimpsed the unconscionable realm from which serial rapists and murderers drew impetus to carry out their horrific acts. How could anyone do such things? It was a question as old as history. Now Reed feared that he knew at least part of the answer. He wanted to excise that realm from his brain, from the universe. But it was bigger than he was; that much he knew. It had touched him, infected him. He had to stay awake, at least until after the sixth. That was three days without sleep. He doubted he could do it, but perhaps freedom lay at the other side of those three days. For the first time he considered what might happen if, even then, the dreams didn't stop. He stepped to the cottonwood and worked the knife free. Staring again at the gleaming blade, he started to carve a two-inch-tall "D" into the side of the trunk. Under the cyanic sky, at that moment, he made a pact with himself. Should the dreams continue, he vowed, he would indeed excise the evil from his mind, and he held in his hand the instrument with which he would do it.

As Jessica spooned rice onto Lucy's plate, the little girl turned her head away.

"Come on now. You're going to eat your dinner," Jessica ordered, returning the pot to the stove. "Before Gart gets here."

"I don't want any," she protested.

"Lucy, please. I'll only be gone for a few hours. This is really important. Can you try to understand? I need to go to these meetings." At the opposite end of the table Jessica began selecting folders she intended to take with her.

"Why can't Reed come over instead?" the little girl asked.

Jessica stopped loading her briefcase. "Reed?"

"Yeah. Why can't we see him anymore?"

"Sweetie. Reed is . . . well, he's not really our friend. He's strange and we don't know him, and you know what we do when we meet strangers, right?"

"Yeah. But, Mommy?"

"Yes?" Jessica said as she resumed sorting papers, aware that Lucy didn't really buy the oversimplified explanation.

"I like Reed."

Jessica stopped again. "Luce, I liked him too. At first. But we just have to be a little bit careful about the people we decide to like."

"Mommy?"

"Yes?"

"I don't like Gart."

Jessica put her files down and sat in a chair next to Lucy. "Honey. Listen to me. Gart is a generous, kind man, and he loves you. Doesn't he always take really good care of you? He always tries to, you know?"

"Reed's trying to help us."

Jessica realized that Lucy had picked up on that notion. "Listen to me. Reed is going to be gone pretty soon, anyway. Far away." Jessica didn't want to admit that she was trying to convince herself, as much as her daughter, that she was doing the right thing. "So, why don't you eat your dinner, and when Gart gets here, you'll forget all about Reed. And I will too. Okay?" Jessica pressed to her feet, giving Lucy a kiss on the head. "I promise I won't be late."

The doorbell rang.

"Why don't you go answer the door," Jessica instructed. "You can eat your dinner when you're hungry, okay?"

Lucy shook her head and started shoveling rice into her mouth as though she hadn't eaten in days.

Jessica sighed, and went to open the front door. Gart stepped in, placing a light kiss on Jessica's cheek.

"So," he asked quietly, noticing that Lucy was in the kitchen. "Any more visits?"

Jessica shook her head, but that encouraging response didn't match the trouble in her eyes.

"What?" he asked, concerned.

"I . . . I've just been wondering, Gart. He . . . he got beaten up pretty badly. Do you have any idea why?"

"How the hell should I know?" he said, shifting back defensively. "Maybe he's been pissing off somebody else too."

"Shh!" Jessica gestured toward the kitchen. "She hears everything. I just can't help wondering . . ."

"What? Not that I . . . ? He's been back, hasn't he?"

"No, Gart. He hasn't. But you did go out for beer after we came back here on Saturday."

"Yeah, and I bought beer. You can ask the guy at SaveMart."

"I'm sorry, Gart. I'm not accusing you. I just don't understand who else would want to do that. And you did have the opportunity, in spite of what I told the sheriff. Talking to him made me feel like I was abetting a felon or something."

"You told him the truth."

"Not the whole truth and you know it."

"I really don't believe that you think I could do something like that. As much as I'd like to. God knows I've got reason." Gart regretted his last remark when he saw the sharp disapproval flash across Jessica's face. "He probably did it to himself just to get sympathy or something. Who knows what lengths he might go to? I told you he's crazy."

"I talked to the ER attending, Gart. It would have been nearly impossible for him to have given himself those injuries."

"So, what do you want, Jess? You want me to go and admit to something I didn't do?"

"Forget it. Forget I said anything." Jessica changed the mood when she heard footsteps in the kitchen.

Gart put a hand on her shoulder, stopping her from turning. "Hey," he said softly, "I love you. I'm just looking out for my girls."

She squeezed his hand. "I know. Thanks. I appreciate it." She lifted his fingers, and moved back toward the kitchen where Lucy was at the stove, scooping more rice onto her plate.

That evening Reed stopped at the sheriff's office to finalize the plan for the stakeout. He sat again in front of Denton's desk. This time several deputies were also there, listening as the sheriff outlined the plan:

"We'll have four undercover units in position at the New Moon Saloon at five tomorrow morning. We'll take twelve hour shifts. Two men inside and two outside. We'll secure the location from five A.M. on the fifth to first light on the sixth. I can't ask my force for any more than that, Dr. Haler."

Reed sat quietly and listened. Then he raised a finger. "Uh, what about putting somebody on to watch Jessica?"

Sheriff Denton indicated one of the men sitting on the couch. "Deputy Wright will take care of that. He'll keep close tabs on her throughout the day and night."

"Okay."

"So. What else?" the sheriff asked in general.

"Uh, I'd like to be there," Reed said, "at the saloon for the stake-out."

"Yeah. I thought you might," Denton acknowledged. "I don't recommend it, but I can't force you to stay away. But remember, Dr. Haler, we'll be there undercover, in unmarked vehicles. Being a stranger around here, you might stick out."

"I'll stay outside in the car."

"Just stay out of the way if something happens. Now, if nothing does happen, I want you gone by noon the sixth."

"That's the deal," Reed acknowledged.

"Okay, then," the sheriff said. "Let's get some sleep, and I'll see you all here in the morning before we head over to the location."

Reed left feeling deathly envious of the others who were going home to their wives and families for a good night's rest. He drove to the diner, picked up two large coffees, and headed out Route 160, past the New Moon Saloon and into the hills. He stopped at his favored turnout, and sipped at one of the steaming cups, holding Devrie's journal in his hand, close to his heart. Hoover curled herself up in the passenger seat.

When he'd finished the first cup of coffee, he began reading the journal again, from the very beginning to the very end, redigesting every word. When he had finished, he started over.

He was on the second cup of coffee by one thirty, and finished it an hour later. By three he'd completed reading the journal a third time. In spite of the aggressive caffeine tremors throughout his body, sleep beckoned him. He debated what to do to keep himself awake: the radio, more driving, a walk. The thoughts began to tumble in his mind incoherently. His eyelids sank; he wrestled against the pull that was dragging him into a swirling doze. He lost.

The sky was starless and black, but the fire erupted with new intensity, sparks spiraling up into the vacuum of space. The heat was on him and on the body below, sprawled, drawing him to it. Suddenly someone, some*thing* grabbed at his neck, moved between him and the writhing woman who lay on the ground. Black eyes burned at him; heavy breath steamed in his face. It was the Indian. Yet it wasn't. Something was different. The powerful arms stretched from below a mask, seizing him by the neck. The Indian was wearing some kind of animal headdress. But it was more than just a mask, it was the actual living head of a dog mounted on the broad shoulders of a man. The snarling struck terror through Reed. He shrieked, flailing his feet in a panicked attempt at escape, groping furiously at the beast that snapped at his throat. Reed lunged back, hitting his head into the car window with a solid *blonk*. He felt the lump swell under his fingers. As the interior of the 4Runner came into view, a sorrowful whimper emanated from between the front seats. Hoover grinned back at him apologetically, bobbing her head submissively, as if to ask forgiveness.

"Hoover," Reed said, holding a hand out, realizing that he'd just come terrifyingly close to losing himself in the nightmare again. "Oh my God." He leaned over, patting the fur under her ears. She looked into his eyes, evaluating his level of consciousness—at least that was how it seemed. "Good girl. Good, good girl! Thank you," Reed praised the animal in amazement. She crawled over to his seat, pawing him affectionately, and trying to lick his face.

"Okay. That's good. That's a good, good dog." He pushed her away playfully, continuing to praise and thank her. Her whimpering didn't stop after she was again on her side of the car. It took a minute, but then it occurred to him that Hoover simply needed to go for a walk, as he himself did, badly. Then he saw that the journal had fallen from his lap to the floor. He leaned down to pick it up, and as he lifted it by the back cover, he realized that the Polaroid was no longer there. It wasn't on the floor of the car either, or in the glove box. Then he saw something written on the last page, something he was certain hadn't been there before. It took his breath, and flooded him with a drowning, molten surge. The letters were printed in tall, clean, block capitals, in dark ink, and oriented sideways on the page:

ALANA

The letters held him captive, for how long Reed didn't know, before he squelched the tears with the back of his hand, and finally shoved the journal back in the glove compartment. He needed to get out, get some air, and empty his bladder. Spilling out of the car in a panic, he landed on his side, Hoover bounding over him. Lying on the gravel, he feverishly tried to gather control of his emotions, and subdue the pain. On the verge of losing it completely, he battled the fierce temptation to succumb. He fought, strained, and suppressed, and little by little brought the rampant fire in his heart and head back under his command. After the tumult abated and he got to his feet, Reed led the galumphing Lab up the road for about half a mile. The air was still and cold, but it was exactly what he needed.

The sense of violation was fresh, as immediate and present as it had been the morning he'd awoken next to Devrie's lifeless body. He felt certain that it had been the predator who had attacked him in the parking lot. That same person had broken into his house, and left the bassinet on his bed. The same person had stolen the Polaroid, and written the name in the back of the journal. Why then, Reed wondered, had the fiend not killed him yet? He filled his chest to capacity multiple times. The effects of the dream, the coffee, and the name at the end of the journal had not worn off completely, but the walk helped him settle down.

When less than half an hour remained before the *rendezvous*, he climbed back into the 4Runner, and coasted back down to the valley, focusing all his senses and thoughts on the purpose that lay ahead. A single car was in the lot when Reed pulled off the road in front of the New Moon Saloon. In the driver's seat he recognized the sheriff; in the eastern sky he saw the first warning of another broiling day.

The sound of the doorbell was unexpected. Jessica had been up for almost an hour, and was only minutes from leaving for work. So, instead of walking out the door, she answered it. Standing on the front stoop was Deputy Sheriff Aaron Wright. The tall, skinny deputy stood with a cocky stance, his weight mostly on one leg, dark glasses hiding his eyes.

" 'Morning, Dr. Morraine. Deputy Wright." He reached out to shake hands.

"Good morning, Deputy. What can I do for you?"

"Actually, I'm going to be doing something for you."

"Oh, really?"

"Yeah. Seems a guy named Reed Haler's got the idea that you might be in some kind of danger over the next twenty-four hours, so, I'm on protection duty till about this time tomorrow."

"Oh," Jessica said, glancing down in surprise. "I see. So, what does that mean exactly . . . protection duty?"

"It means that I'll be driving behind you on your way to work, and again on the way home, or wherever you go. Overnight I'll be in the car parked right out front here. I might check on you from time to time, and basically just keep an eye on things. You know . . . protection. I'll also be enforcing the restraining order against Dr. Haler . . . if I have to."

"Ah. Okay, well, thank you . . . I guess."

"If you need anything at all, or you notice anything suspicious, I'll never be more than a shout away, okay?"

"I really don't think this is quite necessary."

"Sheriff's orders."

"Sheriff's orders, huh? Okay. Whatever."

"Fine. I'll be in the car. Just pretend I'm not there."

"Sure, Deputy . . . uh . . ."

"Wright. Aaron Wright."

Jessica nodded with a forced smile, and closed the door. Lucy was in the kitchen wondering who it had been.

"We've got police protection," Jessica announced.

"Mom?" Lucy then said, with uncharacteristic hesitation.

"Yeah?" Jessica answered, clearing the breakfast things away.

"I'm scared."

Jessica looked at her daughter, who'd barely touched her bowl of Frosted Flakes. "Sweetie, you don't have to be scared. Nobody's going to hurt us. We've got the whole police department keeping an eye on us."

Lucy stared down at her cereal. "I want to go away."

"What?"

"Like Reed told us to."

Jessica stopped her gathering, and sat down next to Lucy, taking the child's hands in hers. "Lucy, listen to me. We can't trust a total stranger, which is what Reed is. I understand that you're scared. He scares me too. That's why we have a policeman right outside to protect us if he tries to come anywhere near. Okay?"

Her mother's reassurances didn't calm Lucy at all. "Mom?"

"Yeah, sweetheart?"

"What if there's somebody else besides Reed who wants to hurt us?"

Jessica studied her daughter's face; the lines of strain matched her own. Her daughter seemed just as aware of the situation as she was, perhaps more so. "Lucy . . . who in the world would want to hurt us?"

"I don't know."

"Well . . . I don't think we have anything to worry about. Now come on, finish your breakfast. I need to get to work." Jessica went back to picking up items from the table.

When Lucy had gone to brush her teeth, Jessica grabbed the phone and dialed. "Hi, Gart, it's Jess," she said when the line picked up. "Yeah, we're on our way over in just a minute, and I was wondering if tonight after Lucy's gymnastics class you might feel like coming over again. She's feeling a little nervous about things and now they've got a deputy guarding the house. Frankly it's making me pretty nervous too . . . and maybe . . . you wouldn't mind staying over tonight . . ."

The sheriff had Reed park the 4Runner a mile down the road from the New Moon Saloon, then drove him and Hoover back to the stakeout location—the reasoning being that Reed's vehicle might be known to the perpetrator, tipping him off to the surveillance. The sheriff and his deputies had driven their own private cars for the same reason.

They parked as inconspicuously as possible, the sheriff well off to the side of the saloon so he'd have some view of the front, the others in the rear, normally reserved for employees.

Reed kept Hoover on a leash, which ran through the back window of the sheriff's Mercury Tracer, and looped around the inside door handle. This way she could remain outside the car, yet under control. Reed was careful to keep her positioned in close so that the car concealed her from view. From where he crouched in the backseat, Reed could see and talk to her through the window if she got restless. On the ground next to her, Reed had placed her food and water bowls. The only problem was the intense sun. The dog constantly sought the car's shadow.

"This is the first undercover operation I think we've ever had around here," Sheriff Denton observed after several uneventful hours.

"Mmm," Reed acknowledged, preoccupied. He studied the front and side of the building that were visible from his vantage point. A double wooden door, twin crescent moons facing each other on each, marked the center of the structure. Wide but short windows with drawn venetian blinds and neon beer signs flanked the doors, one on each side.

Reed knew there was an exit in the back which served as an employee entrance. The buxom redhead who worked behind the bar had pulled in around eleven-thirty in a primer-gray twenty-year-old Datsun 280-Z, parking in back. Several hours later a battered Lincoln Town Car rolled behind the building, a slick-haired, round-bellied man at the wheel—the owner, whose name, Reed learned from the sheriff, was Mort.

The sides of the small building were solid brick. The front door was the only other apparent way in or out, unless one used a window, of course.

It was about three in the afternoon, and three cars had arrived in the front lot, each carrying just one person. All three had been men from about age thirty-five to fifty; all getting an early start it seemed.

The two deputies inside the saloon wore concealed microphones, which transmitted to the sheriff's car. So far there had been very little to report, the conversation consisting of a little local gossip and sports. It remained that way until the sun went down.

Dinner for Reed and the sheriff was pizza and Coke. After they had finished, a large pickup truck pulled into the lot. A heavy, bearded man whom the sheriff didn't recognize, wearing a black leather vest, got out with a young woman. Both seemed about twenty-eight or twenty-nine. As the couple went inside, the sheriff noticed that the truck had Kansas tags. Two hours later the couple hadn't left, but the word from inside was that they were drinking each other into oblivion, and playing a lot of pool.

"Well, Dr. Haler," the sheriff commented from the front seat, "at the very least we'll get a few more DWIs than usual tonight."

"Mmm," Reed acknowledged. The doors to the small building kept Reed's full attention. People continued to come and go at intervals. None of them sparked particular suspicion. It had been a relatively slow night with a total of about fifteen customers by eleven-thirty.

Deputy Wright had been doing his duty well all day. It was a simple job, and he liked the fact that it was so easy, yet seemed so important. He'd stayed a respectful distance behind Jessica Morraine's car as she dropped her daughter off with her gymnastics coach in the morning, and then continued on to the hospital. Around mid morning he tailed her to her office where she saw her patients. It had been dull, but that was better than the alternative, he thought.

Jessica had introduced the deputy to Gart when she stopped to pick up her daughter at the elementary school after her gymnastics class. Wright had agreed, when Jessica had mentioned it, that it might be a good idea for Gart to stay with her and Lucy overnight—just in case.

From the school, Wright followed the Honda back to the residential outskirts, and parked on the street in front of the house.

Two hours later a blue Ford Escort pulled over a few spots ahead of Wright's cruiser, and Gart Hanta got out. The strong-looking man gave Wright a friendly wave of recognition as he walked up to the front door and pressed the bell. Wright watched as Jessica admitted Gart to the house.

At around ten-thirty P.M., noticing that quite a few lights were still on, Wright rang the doorbell. Jessica answered, Gart standing a few inches behind her.

"Yes?" Jessica asked, noticing that the deputy had finally removed the sunglasses.

"Hey. Just checking in on you folks."

"Oh. Well, nothing to report," Gart said, over Jessica's shoulder.

"Okay, then. Have a good night. I'll uh, check in one more time in the morning to make sure everything's okay." Wright's slightly sarcastic smile was intended to belittle the necessity for his presence outside.

"Thanks, officer. I think we'll be just fine," Jessica said, picking up on the deputy's attitude.

"Yeah, I'm sure you will."

"Good night."

Jessica closed the door, and Wright strolled back down the front lawn to his squad car. With a mild chuckle, he scanned up and down the dark, deserted street, before settling into the driver's seat. It was a long time before sunrise, he thought, and then poured himself a fresh cup of coffee from his plaid Thermos.

PART IV

She'll try to twist away, but that will only goad him, strengthen his hold, and sour his voice further. "Hold still, damn you, little bitch!" His free hand will pass over her a final time, then a black mouth will gape wide beneath her. Against her skin she'll feel the rough inside wall of the ebony throat into which he will force her, feet first. She'll struggle, pushing against the wall of the strange vertical tunnel with her toes. Amazingly she'll feel his hands loosen their hold as she writhes her way free. She'll curl and bend with elation. She'll fall away from his terrible clutches, but her feet won't reach any bottom. She'll stop inside the throat, its sides pressing in on her from every direction as it swallows her. The momentary euphoria will disintegrate almost instantly into horror. The more she will struggle, the tighter it will squeeze. The smell will be strong of smoke, something burned. She'll see only a jagged circle of stars above her when she cranes her head back. Around her she'll see only a pure darkness, feel nothing but the tightening of the tunnel, squeezing the air from her, holding her even more tightly than the man's arms had. She'll stop struggling, knowing that if she doesn't, she'll only wedge herself deeper, and eventually suffocate. The pressure on her body will be unbearable, until she starts to lose sensation in her extremities. The last thing she will hear, before the tears burst from her eyes, will be an engine starting, then steadily fading until no sound exists save her own helplessly restricted breath. Her prayers will remain unanswered.

TWENTY-FIVE

There had been no alarm, no indication of any emergency what-soever by the time the New Moon Saloon closed for the night at two A.M. The last customer wandered out to his car and drove off just before the owner, with his domed abdomen, emerged from the front doors, and stepped over to the sheriff.

"Your boys are in the back playing cards," Mort said. "I'll have somebody here by six to get the keys back." The man's great round belly drooped heavily as he leaned down on the open window of the car.

"We'll be here," Denton responded.

Mort gave the top of the Tracer a slap, then lumbered around to the back of the establishment, where his Lincoln was parked. After Mort had left the premises, the night fell into full silence apart from the chirp of insects and the occasional howl of coyotes. Reed fought the tiredness in his eyes; on the ground just outside the car he could hear Hoover twitching in a dream. The New Moon Saloon sat in empty, deserted solitude. Nothing stirred but a gentle summer wind from the west. The sky was fogged with stars, the nail-clipping moon but a momentary snag in the thick fabric of the Milky Way. Tomorrow night there would, of course, be no moon at all.

Reed maintained full concentration on the little building and its immediate surroundings. Each time a chance motorist raced past on the highway, Reed's heart accelerated, only to settle again as the vehicle moved harmlessly into the distance. This occurred only several times during the four hours between two and six, but each time it did Reed fully anticipated the confrontation that would either set him free, or end his life, or perhaps both.

At about five-thirty Reed had to take a bathroom break. He quietly unlatched the back door of the Tracer, and pulled himself out of the car. Hoover, once again awake, looked up at him as if to ask when they were going home. He leaned down and patted her head. She settled her chin back between her front paws, not liking, but accepting the answer.

Reed relieved himself at the edge of the parking lot. The air was dry and cold, and smelled profoundly clean. He drew in as much of it as he could, gaining energy with each breath. As he relaxed his bladder, he scanned the terrain. The barren hills and mountains told of neither good nor ill, only quiet anticipation of the coming heat. The darkness began to loosen its hold on the sky as the emerging eastward glow dimmed the millions of white sparks overhead. For the first time, Reed began to consider the real possibility that nothing would happen there in front of the New Moon Saloon, on that morning . . . or the next . . . or the next. Perhaps it had all been a misguided adventure fueled by insufferable grief and some desperate need to exact justice—no, vengeance. As the sky lightened, and only the call of waking thrushes and barn swallows violated the desert hush, his confidence was slipping badly.

Reluctantly, he ambled back to the car, gave Hoover another pat, and slipped inside the Tracer.

"I make it another half-hour," Denton said as Reed settled into his semireclined position in the backseat.

"Yeah, about a half-hour," Reed concurred.

The sheriff's walkie-talkie crackled, followed by the electronic voice of one of the deputies inside the bar.

"Bill's ahead four games to three, otherwise all quiet as of 'O-five thirty,'" the voice said.

"Roger that, Jay. I've got money on you, you know. Now kick his ass. Will advise, over," Denton responded.

"Roger. Do my best, over and out."

The policemen's light banter annoyed Reed, partly because it stripped the mission of its seriousness, but mostly because it was becoming increasingly appropriate. With each minute Reed was appearing more and more a paranoid fool. Still nothing happened. No one approached. There hadn't even been a passing car in over an hour.

Reed heard Hoover stand up outside the car door and shake her coat, as if sloughing off the night air. The eastern sky was now an even glowing violet, warming to a light peach at the horizon. Through clouded eyes Reed saw a pair of feeble headlights, which were unable to compete with the bold, orange prelude of sunlight that rocketed across the valley floor and through the windshield of Sheriff Denton's car. Reed realized that he'd been close to dozing off. Now he was upright in the seat, senses honed, observing the activity in the parking lot. A car pulled in and stopped right next to the Tracer. Reed wiped his vision clear, and leaned forward. The man in the other car was speaking to the sheriff across rolled-down windows. The clock on the dashboard said six-o-five. It was only the bar employee sent to collect the keys, and relieve the deputies inside.

Daylight was only minutes away. Reed saw his search coming to a premature end. The other car rumbled back behind the building.

Sheriff Denton picked up the walkie-talkie. "Time to call it a night, boys. Fella's coming around back for the keys. Over."

"Roger that, Sheriff. Over."

"Roger. Denton out." The sheriff turned back to Reed. "I don't know about you, but I'm about ready to git the shit out-a-here."

"Wait. Just a little longer, Sheriff. Please."

"Dr. Haler. When my deputies come out of that bar, we're leaving. And you're going to get your ass out of town before noon. And if I hear that you've been snooping around anybody, or hanging around this bar, I'll take you in. I swear to God."

Two cars emerged from behind the bar. The two deputies acknowledged over the walkie-talkie that they were okay and that all was well inside.

"See you guys back at the station," Denton communicated back. The two deputies rolled out of the parking lot and down the highway back toward town.

"Get your dog there, Dr. Haler. I'll take you back to your car."

Reed opened the back door, taking up Hoover's leash. "Has to be," he whispered to himself. "This has to be it. Has to be, dammit!" He scanned in all directions. In the orange dawn, the desert hills looked as barren and lifeless as Mars.

He pounded the top of the sheriff's car. "Shit!" he wailed.

"Hey!" the sheriff barked from inside. "It's not my car's fault!"

Reed urged Hoover into the backseat. "Yeah, I know. I'm sorry, Sheriff." He gave one more look around. Desert. "I'm sorry." He dropped into the backseat next to the dog, and pulled the door closed.

Denton started the engine, and drove slowly onto the highway. Reed kept his eye on the saloon as it shrank away behind him. "It fucking has to be," he whispered one last time, the furrows between his eyes cutting very deep.

Noon," Denton had said as his parting word to Reed, when the sheriff dropped him and Hoover off where the 4Runner waited in a wide turnout at the side of the road. He had until noon to be out of town, and out of luck.

Hoover, at least, seemed happy to be climbing back into the Toyota. She gave Reed a joyful grin as he turned the key in the ignition. It was then that he realized how hungry he was, and thought of the diner located on the same piece of road at the edge of town.

Reed sat at the counter. The eggs and toast had tasted better in his mind than they did in his mouth, but the coffee was good. He didn't have the energy or the inclination to read the paper as he would have done under ordinary circumstances. What happened outside his own world mattered very little to him that morning. What happened in his own life was mattering less to him by the minute as he contemplated returning to Marin County, and starting his life over again, his wife and daughter's killer still unknown and still a threat. He began to schedule the remainder of the day, trying to figure out how he was going to work some sleep in before his noon departure.

Behind the cash register at the end of the counter hung a cheap picture calendar, the photo for August featuring a fly fisherman, waist-deep in a mountain stream, set against a stupendous snowy peak. Reed's focus went to the current date. Summer was only half over, but it seemed like the end . . . the end of every season, of every year, of everything good. He took another bite of his cooling eggs when something in the little box on the calendar, indicating the sixth of August, apprehended his eye. It troubled him, but he couldn't quite get hold of why. Then he saw, at the bottom of the box, the indication "new moon." He hadn't noticed it on his own personal planning calendar, but that was because his calendar didn't bother to include "trivial" things like the lunar cycles.

He looked around the room. There were half a dozen people in the diner at six-thirty that morning. None paid him any attention; none looked unusual or suspicious. He couldn't bring himself to let go of his cause. It had been his constant companion for two weeks, and would probably remain so for the rest of his life, he realized. Outside the window of the diner he looked for any clue to guide him. Nothing stood out. It was quiet, and the roadway was deserted.

He turned back to the counter, the cash register, and the calendar. "Stupid," he whispered, and finished his coffee. Still trying to salvage this stupid idiot chase, he thought. He would have ordered a refill, but knew he needed sleep. He paid the bill and left the little eatery. Hoover was dozing on the passenger seat when Reed climbed up into the car.

He pulled out of the parking lot slowly, feeling in no hurry to return to the El Halcón. He was almost glad when he was stopped by a red light. His mind was as numb as his body felt. In spite of his vague plans to return home, he'd resigned himself to the inevitability of the nightmare, and made the decision to stop resisting it. If it came again, he had the knife. He'd made a pact with himself, and he was prepared to carry it out. As he drove, he considered the possibility that he was witnessing his last sunrise. It warmed his heart to think of the torment coming to an end, of perhaps being reunited with Devrie. But he had to confront the entity in the nightmare one more time, to be sure that there was no escape, no hope.

He only saw one other car on the road, but Reed kept his speed a little under the limit. The other car was moving only slightly faster, but in the opposite direction. He wouldn't have given the vehicle a second thought except that Hoover was suddenly wide awake. She needed a walk, he thought.

"Soon, girl," he said, extending a hand to the Labrador. When he touched the soft coat, he felt the tremendous eruption of her bark in his fingers. She was on her feet, pawing at the seat, staring out the back window.

Reed had swerved into the oncoming lane accidentally, startled by Hoover's sudden outburst. He corrected his position on the road, and looked over to the dog, who was growling and continuing to bark at the rear window.

"What the hell's the matter now?" He knew her well enough by then to know that she wasn't going to stop until she found the source of her agitation. Looking back, he saw the other car receding, heading out of town. Reed hadn't taken any notice of the driver, but he had seen that the car was a green sedan. Pulling over did nothing to quell the dog, so he tried to talk calmly to her, which only seemed to make matters worse.

"Hoover, I'm too tired for this today," he told the dog. Inside he knew that she wasn't upset for a frivolous reason, and he doubted that she needed a walk.

The vociferous animal seemed almost on the verge of panic, and began nudging Reed's shoulder. He took another look back. The green sedan was now completely out of sight. Still Hoover carried on, scratching at the seat, and yelping at ever increasing volume.

The fly fisherman came back to Reed's mind. The calendar from the diner. August sixth, the middle of summer and the "new moon." Devrie's journal entries were flashing across his brain. It all jelled in his mind for an instant, then melted away again, like a chance glimpse of a reflection in a car window as it races past. But it left him with a thunderous doubt, a torturous new thought. Perhaps he'd simply been wrong about the New Moon Saloon. Perhaps the "no moon" reference in Devrie's journal had to do with the day . . . today . . . the sixth of August and the New Moon itself, and not the Saloon at all! If that were true, it would mean that he'd been a day early in his planning. It made all too much sense—too much terrible sense.

"Okay. Okay. We'll go see, girl."

The 4Runner was again the only car on the road, so Reed pulled a U-turn, and drove back toward the town limits, in the direction from which he'd just come.

Deputy Wright was proud of the fact that he had lasted the night without falling asleep. He had about four cups of coffee in him, and felt the jitter to his knees. When the call came from Sheriff

Denton that he could wrap up the protection detail and return to the station, he gave himself a pat on the back.

"Yes, sir. Looks like everything's okay here. I'll let 'em know inside that I'm heading out, over."

"Fine, Denton out."

Deputy Wright got out of the squad car, and staggered up to the door. The caffeine had robbed him of a little coordination, on top of the fact that his feet were asleep. He shook off the creaks, and pressed the doorbell, feeling a little reluctant to wake the house at that hour. But it was part of the job. After a minute he pressed again, then again after another minute, before he resorted to pounding on the locked front door. When that failed to produce a response, he peered in through the living room window. Noticing that the light was still on, he rapped several times on the glass. Either the people inside were mighty heavy sleepers, Wright thought, or the house was empty. The deputy quickly moved around to the back, his neck muscles tightening under his shirt collar as his heart shifted into a higher gear. A low, chain-link fence enclosed the dirt backyard, necessitating a small climb. What he saw next threw him into a run.

The sliding glass door was standing open; Wright pulled his .38 service revolver as he neared the rear entrance. Stepping clumsily from nervousness, he crept along the back wall until he was next to the opening. He choked on the air itself, listening as keenly as he could. His imagination ran wild with scenes of butchery inside, the perpetrator standing proudly in the middle of the carnage, eyes wild and hungry for more killing. Cocked sidearm leading the way, Wright gulped down what he prayed wouldn't be his last breath, and swung around, prepared to fire. The vacuum of an empty kitchen met him. His palms grew sweaty on the weapon's knurled wood handle. He feared he might accidentally discharge the gun, he found himself squeezing it so tightly.

"Good morning," he called out. "Anybody home?" Only the silent house answered.

Wright assessed everything as he moved through the kitchen.

Nothing seemed to be out of the ordinary; there was no sign of any forced entry, or of a struggle. An empty glass sat on the dining room table; below it, a powder blue bathrobe was neatly folded on one of the dining room chairs. The living room appeared in order as well. "Anybody here?" he called out again. Nothing.

He made a quick pass through the family room, then moved quietly up the stairs. The first bedroom was the smallest of the three. The door was open, and a single unmade bed with daffodil sheets informed him that it was the little girl's room. But it lacked a little girl. The other three doors on the second level were closed. His heart thumping violently in his ears, Wright readied the .38, and tested the knob of the next door. It turned, and in a single, rapid move he threw the door open, prepared to fire. No one was inside that bedroom either. Again the bed was unmade, as if someone had gotten up in a hurry. Wright checked behind the door and in the closets, but found nothing.

He tried the knob on the next room. It, too, was unlocked, and turned out to be a home office, the floor and desktop layered in files and document storage boxes. One wall was dedicated entirely to books. But no one was there.

The bathroom remained. This time he found the knob locked. Wright brought his foot to bear on the door, pistol aimed at whatever lay on the other side. The casement around the latch gave way, but not completely. He had to repeat the procedure several times before making a successful breach of the opening. But something kept the door from completing its full inward swing.

He brought the revolver to eye level, trying feverishly to arrest the shaking in his arms. Immediately he saw what was stopping the door—a pair of hairy legs. No sound came from the small room. Wright stepped closer, elbows locked, his finger one spasm from pulling the trigger. As he approached the doorjamb, he saw more of the body, which was lying face up on the floor. He saw the tan boxer shorts hiked up the thighs and circling a narrow waist, a dingy white T-shirt covering a well-built upper torso. A muscular right arm lay across the chest, and a neck that needed a shave emerged from the crewneck collar. Wright shoved his way into the bathroom, and found himself standing over the body of Gart Hanta . . . and that body was quite dead.

R eed gunned the 4Runner back down the highway in the direction of the New Moon Saloon. After a mile and a half, he saw that he was gaining on the green car, which he could now see was a Chevrolet Cavalier. He eased back to the speed limit. Hoover had settled down again too, which somehow didn't make him feel any better.

The car ahead didn't stop when it passed the saloon, so Reed didn't stop either. It did, however, make the turn north toward the Sand Dunes, toward the dry waves. Reed followed; the Chevrolet accelerated. Now he knew.

By degrees Reed increased his speed along the straight smooth highway. Soon he was doing over ninety, but still he wasn't catching up with the Chevy. At that rate it wouldn't take long to reach the entrance to the Dunes monument grounds. There, Reed thought, a gate might stop the Chevrolet. Perhaps there was even a guard on duty who would radio for the police. Then Reed saw that the driver of the Chevrolet cared little about official entrances. The green Cavalier had angled off the road and was jetting a cloud of dust across the flat leading to the mountains of sand.

Ahead, the great dunes loomed in swirls of dusty beige and gray, their peaks sparking orange-pink against the lavender sky in the dawn light.

"Hold on, girl," Reed said to Hoover, who crouched down on the floor in front of the passenger seat, wedging herself in.

Reed could see the tire tracks at the point where the Chevrolet had left the road. He laid a new pair right on top of them.

The ditch at the side of the road was mercifully shallow, but at the speed Reed was traveling, it brutally hammered the 4Runner's suspension. Then it was a matter of dodging boulders, stumps, and thickets of scrub brush which appeared randomly from the thickening dust wall in front of him. Visibility in the Cavalier's wake was only about thirty feet, which gave Reed only an instant to react to oncoming obstacles. He knew that if he stayed right on the other car's tire tracks, he'd have a relatively clear path, and yet he had to do it practically blind. The need for a sudden turn could send him right into a huge rock or a tree, or into a shallow gully, all of which held potentially fatal consequences. He drove on in spite of the danger, in spite of the pounding, jarring ride and beastlike roar of the powerful engine. Sand was coating the windshield, further blocking visibility. Reed hit the wipers but they quickly jammed with grit.

With a burst of light, the way ahead was suddenly clear; the 4Runner had emerged from that blinding cloud, the reason immediately apparent. The Chevrolet had veered sharply, as Reed had feared. He saw the other car angling to the right for only a moment before he realized that he was seconds from impacting a wall of sagebrush and low junipers. He wrestled the wheel, piling over rocks and scrub. A fury of stones and sand blasted the vehicle from below, creating a continuous impregnable din. The Toyota bucked and groaned as it scarred a path across the virgin desert floor. Hoover stayed low, her head braced against the underside of the dashboard.

The Chevrolet still commanded a sizable lead over its pursuer, but would soon hit the soft powder at the base of the first colossal rise. The front bumper of the Toyota caught the spindly arm of a small juniper, uprooting the bush and dragging it along for the ride. Rifts in the silica layer bounced the vehicle fiercely as Reed followed a path parallel to that of the Chevrolet. It became impossible for him to negotiate the uneven surface with its many obstructions and maintain a speed sufficient to overtake the Cavalier—which enjoyed a comparatively smooth piece of land on its approach.

But it was only a matter of minutes before the sand would become too deep, too soft, and the Chevrolet would bog down. Reed hadn't even thought that far ahead. What would he do when this became a foot race? He popped open the glove compartment and gripped the fat, wooden handle of the knife. Using his teeth to undo the snap of the leather case, Reed unsheathed the broad hunting blade. He hadn't considered what weapons might be onboard the Chevy, what the driver might have at the ready. At that point he didn't care. Turning around and giving up was more terrifying than facing death. His life had become a form of death anyway, a death in which he was stripped of his purpose, of his reason to care about others or himself. At least true death held the chance that he'd be with Devrie again in some eternal, spiritual realm beyond the evils and pain of the living world. As long as that chance existed, he had more fear of continuing life as he knew it, than of the unknown that awaited beyond his last breath.

Still, there was a life worth fighting for, a life that, if saved, might then offer hope of redemption for his own. For now Reed had no doubt that the driver of the Chevrolet either had already killed, or was intending to kill, Jessica Morraine on this day, the new moon, in the middle of summer.

Reed could see that the car ahead was slowing. The 4Runner handled the thickening sand better than the smaller car, and as the Chevy lost traction, the Toyota gained ground.

The accelerator was on the floor, but the 4×4 was now losing speed as well. But now the sand coming from the Chevy's back wheels shot into the air like twin geysers. Only about fifty yards separated the two vehicles, and that was shrinking fast. Reed tightened his hand around the knife. A clear path opened between himself and the Chevrolet. Although with the deepening sand the Toyota would fare only slightly better, Reed kept the pedal firmly pressed as he drew closer.

Then the spray of sand from beneath the Cavalier's wheels stopped. Reed bore down on the arrested car, watching for any movement. The driver's door opened; Reed hit the brakes, instantly stopping the 4Runner some thirty feet behind. A large man stepped from the car, dressed in physician's scrubs, a black woolen cap, dark dungarees, and tan cowboy boots. He appeared to be empty-handed.

The man moved with an unnerving nonchalance to the rear of the car, and inserted the key, opening the trunk. He seemed oblivious to the fact that a big four-wheeler had just chased him across the desert to the base of a massive pile of sand at ten to seven in the morning.

As the lid of the Cavalier's trunk lifted, Reed saw the man pull something from his back pocket with one hand, while leaning into the trunk. The hair was the first thing that registered next in Reed's mind. It draped in matted bundles over the man's arm as he lifted a woman, dressed only in her underwear and a long T-shirt. In a single movement, using only one arm, the man had her out of the trunk, on her feet and facing the point of a very long knife. It was only then that the man looked in Reed's direction. Reed knew the blade, and he recognized Jessica, her face a sculpture of terror behind the wraps of tape that covered her mouth. More tape bound her arms behind her, and her ankles. Dark bruises and fresh wounds mottled and streaked her body. It took another second for Reed to recognize the man. Jessica's associate from the hospital, Dr. Louis Canidey, now stood poised to take her life.

Reed adjusted his own knife, grasping the blade. Hoover passed him an encouraging look from beneath the dashboard as he opened his door, and stepped out onto the swirling sand.

"Dr. Haler, I wasn't sure you were going to get to see this," Canidey said with an expectant smile. "But I'm glad you're here. I think you'll like it." With the knife's point, Canidey touched Jessica's midriff behind her cotton shirt. Reed could see her body trembling, her breath coming in sporadic bursts.

Reed tightened his hold on his own weapon, remembering the feeling of throwing it into the cottonwood, repeating the action in his head again and again, wondering if he'd have any chance to repeat it one more time in reality.

Canidey pushed the tip against Jessica's belly . . . harder . . . her own convulsive breathing placing her in danger of forcing penetration.

"She's gonna be a good one, I can tell," Canidey opined, glancing down for any sign of blood from Jessica's abdomen. . . . The fabric remained white.

Reed imagined that once Canidey saw the crimson stream, he would move quickly into his free killing mode.

"You killed my wife, didn't you," Reed said, looking for what reaction he didn't know.

"Did I?" Was Canidey's answer. "Perhaps." He nodded as if searching his memory. "Yeah. Probably."

"Who else have you killed, and raped? How many?"

"Who's keeping track?" Came the reply.

"I am." Reed said.

"Really. Well, that's thoughtful of you. I didn't know anyone cared that much." Canidey was now every bit the dominating figure Reed recalled from the night in the Sierras. Reed realized that the man had worn the black cap pulled down over his face on that occasion. Now it seemed Canidey didn't care that his identity was plain to see. In fact, as he toyed with the knife, circling Jessica's navel with the point, he began to giggle . . . the baleful, silent giggle Reed knew so well from his memory and his nightmares.

"By the way, Reed," Canidey continued. "I never did get a chance to tell you how much I enjoyed your presentation."

Reed frowned. Another jab struck his memory. Presentation! Something was rushing back to him.

"Come now," Canidey pushed. "I hope you remember mine. The symposium in May? San Francisco? It was a delightful evening, and a quite successful one for you at least, if I'm not mistaken. You must have really charmed the hell out of those serpents from the NIH."

Canidey had been there. It was now as fresh as yesterday. The big man's presentation for Jessica's hospital had immediately followed his own. Reed recalled that he hadn't paid any attention to it, hadn't even remembered the man's name. But now it was clear, a wall of smoke blown away as if a picture had appeared before him in minute detail.

Then Reed perceived a slight movement in Jessica's head. She was staring at him through eyes that told of more than the horror of the moment. It was as if she were trying to beam a message to him, telepathically. The movement of her head was side to side. Reed took that to mean "no." "No" to what? He wondered.

Canidey picked up on the effort at subtle communication and

drew the knife back, ready for a grand strike at Jessica's middle. She kept her eyes locked on Reed.

It had to be then. She relaxed her legs in an effort to drop from the clamp of Canidey's arm. It was just enough. Just enough room, just enough time for Reed to aim and think for an instant of the man in front of him as a burned out old cottonwood tree. He let the knife fly, and watched. Jessica wasn't able to free herself on her own. Only when Reed's knife found its mark in Canidey's neck did the big man release his hold. His effort at impaling her plunged instead into his own forearm as she slipped free. He dropped his knife in confusion, clutching with both hands at the blade in his neck, not quite able to believe what he felt. The rush of blood was instantaneous.

Jessica squirmed away in a frantic scramble, sand flying into her face, and her eyes. She couldn't see, she only fled, as fast as her bound limbs would allow.

Reed bolted toward his target, fully overwhelmed by the moment of revenge. He picked up Canidey's dropped knife and, without pause, drove it into the broad sternum. From behind Reed came a muffled, panicked groan. It was Jessica. But Reed's attention could not be wrested from his purpose. He pulled the long instrument from Canidey's chest. Twin rivers of blood poured down the man's front; the sand at his boots turned dark as wine as he sank to his knees. Reed waited until the man rocked back, on the verge of toppling to the ground. Canidey touched the knife handle still protruding from his neck almost curiously, as if it were a strangely pleasant, if unusual, phenomenon. Reed glared his rage into the eyes of the murderer.

Another contained squeal came from behind, but Reed couldn't hear anything except the thrumming of his heart—the fuel of this justice. Canidey's lack of any indication of fear or pain only enraged Reed further. The man almost seemed to be smiling. Then he truly was smiling as he looked back into Reed's fevered eyes. A voice gurgled from Canidey's lips. The words were scarcely audible, but Reed heard them: "God bless you." The smile widened, and the whole body began to tremble with its mute, pathological laughter.

Reed sank the knife into a fresh spot until it would go no further. As Canidey fell away, Reed maintained tight hold on the knife, not yet prepared to relinquish control. Suddenly Jessica rolled herself into the back of Reed's knees, knocking him to the ground. She was crying in a horrible fit. Using the knife still in his hand, Reed worked to cut Jessica free from the tape, but that did nothing to settle her. Hands loose, she pulled the remaining tape from her face and crawled over to the bleeding, dying man on the ground, sputtering words at him: "Where is she, you son-of-a-bitch?" Her tears fell and mingled with the blood still pumping liberally from the opened neck. She grabbed at his head, pulling the black cap off, and shook him by the hair. "Where is she? You tell me where she is, you fucker! Don't you die!" Canidey only offered the self-satisfied grin, his body going into a final, jiggling spasm. The blood stopped pumping; the chest stopped rising. Jessica shook him harder. There was nothing left behind the gray vacuums of his eyes, yet traces of the grin remained.

Jessica turned, her arms and chest splattered red. She looked at Reed with a ghastly rancor. "Why did you have to kill him? Why?"

Reed stared back at her, unsure whether he'd heard her correctly. "What did you say?" he asked, spitting sand and wiping it from his face.

"Why did you have to kill him?" Jessica repeated through a mask of anguish.

"Are you out of your fucking mind? He was about to kill you, and me!" Reed stormed back.

"He took Lucy . . ." she continued.

The flush drained from Reed's face.

". . . and hid her away. He hid her away someplace. He was the only person on earth who knows where she is, you stupid bastard!" She finished her statement screaming, charging him with clenched fists.

He covered his head with his hands until he found a chance to wrestle her under control. Forcing his arms around her, he hoped to quell the raging desperation and grief that surged through her convulsing, punished body.

"Now we'll never find her, goddamn you! You just killed my baby! Goddamn you! *GODDAMN YOU!*" Her energy would not abate. If anything, her strength continued to grow, until Reed was finally able to roll her under his weight. He managed to lock his legs around hers and work his forearm under her chin, the knife, sharp with the scent of blood, only inches from her neck. The feel of Jessica's body under his struck a malignant, horrifying familiarity in Reed's mind. He was no longer certain whether or not he was living the moment, or whether this was the nightmare, continuing to its conclusion. But now control—or more exactly, the illusion of control—was his. He held the killer's knife exactly as he had in the dream. An amazing sense of power surged into his body and mind, the power to realize, to express the alien savagery that possessed him.

Finish the dream, a voice said, as if coming from behind him.

Jessica's eyes drilled their frenzied terror into Reed's, exciting the primitive fury that threatened to burst his veins. It seemed as though Canidey weren't dead at all, but again standing, hovering over Reed's shoulder, stoking this perverse lust. Reed saw visions of himself, bright flashes in his mind, imagined himself inside her while he drew the life from her body. The prospect swelled into a maniacal thrill, a blast of heat, pumping him full of uncontainable energy. He desired it without bound. Yet a shrinking particle within him sought to turn the knife on himself, to kill the invader. There was no other way to spare Jessica's life. But he could finish the dream.

Finish the dream! A fresh wave of fire, a vicious yearning flooded his thoughts. *Finish the dream!... Finish the dream!* It rang like a command. He could live the dream!

The knife's razor edge gleamed through a dark coating of thick blood. The part of himself, nothing more than an invisible grain in a universe of evil, rose, like that glint of light on the finely honed blade, to the edge of his soul. He clung to it with every twisting molecule that he could still call his.

Jessica had stopped resisting as Reed, using all his strength, brought the knife's point toward his own throat. She stared up at him, the shock and horror contorting her face, as his intention became apparent.

"No," she scarcely whispered.

The temptation to pull the knife into his neck was acute, but Jessica's soft command paralyzed him.

Finish the dream. Reed was frozen in space, on the verge of splitting in half. *Finish the dream.* He had to end it. The shaking steel point teased the stout whiskers on his Adam's apple.

He anticipated the pain, but embraced his waiting liberation, when the barking interceded. Reed wasn't sure what it was at first. It came again, louder, closer. A dog was growling in his face. A show of teeth.

Hoover. The dog's name jumped into Reed's mind, and then came recognition. Hoover barked again, but this time without hostility. Reed saw the knife, poised to stab, as if not in his own hand, but in that of a desperate thief holding him hostage. Then the other familiar words echoed from somewhere deep in his mind: *You smell of fear.*

Another bark.

Beneath him, Jessica's lips formed the word "no" over and over, her head shaking side to side.

You smell of fear, came again, now overriding all other voices in his head.

Hoover whined in his ear. Like a bubble bursting at the surface of a bottomless sea, Reed's head cleared. In an instant his free will was restored, and he tossed the lethal shank of steel to the side, nearly insane with the horror of his thoughts, his impulse. He rolled off the woman, letting his head come to rest on the sand. Jessica could only lie where she was, her eyes tightly closed. Hoover padded around uneasily at Reed's side, still at the ready to fend off her master's enemies, both within him and without.

A hundred feet above their heads, wind drew sand off the pointed tops of the highest dunes in gentle blond curls like those of a young girl's hair. Sheets of the tiny moving particles skittered across the rib-patterned surface surrounding the unnaturally still group. The sound was as powdery light as ice crystals drifting across a frozen lake.

Reed could not look at Jessica, his shame so overpowering that he could only weep, the realization of his actions erupting inside him. "I'm sorry. I'm so, so sorry," he repeated again and again. His moment of revenge—the guiding purpose that had directed his every movement and thought during the past month—might now lead to still another murder. The grin on Canidey's face the moment before his death, had conveyed the baleful exultation of some pernicious victory. It wasn't sane, but it was logical. The image of that smile, the stifled giggle, and Canidey's last words held Reed's mind in a terrible comprehension. It was as if Canidey had expected to die, had known it would happen, as if it had actually been part of a grotesque plan. The possibility that he had played right into it drowned Reed in unmerciful self-abomination. He was faced with the fact that his own desperate act had perhaps eliminated any chance there might have been to find the child. Perhaps it was already too late. But what if it weren't, and the helpless little girl was, even at that moment, slipping closer and closer toward a horrifying end? Reed tortured himself with the question a million times over every second.

Thus a minute of eternity passed in the desert morning. Then the drone of police sirens found its way between the tufts of sage brush and mesquite boughs to the foot of the great dunes. Reed hadn't noticed her there before, but as the police and emergency vehicles neared, her image stole his attention, and gripped him at the core. Just over a low rise in the sand some fifty yards away, Alana Kieran stood . . . watching . . . wearing the same expressionless countenance. Perhaps she'd come to acknowledge the death of her assailant after five years of waiting. From the sight before him, Reed somehow drew the strength to cope with, if not understand, his own tortured mind. He thought for a moment that he'd lost hold of reason altogether, that the trauma of the bloody encounter was producing hallucinations. Yet Alana Kieran's gaze was firmly on him, her presence as real and visible as his own. Perhaps she'd somehow helped pull him back from the wicked vortex into which he'd been spiraling. It was impossible to know, yet somehow he did know that the demon in his head was now gone.

TWENTY-SIX

Reed was aware that by the time the emergency vehicles arrived, the manifestation of Alana Kieran would be gone—and it was. He offered no resistance when Sheriff Denton placed the handcuffs on his wrists. A paramedic wrapped Jessica in a blanket, and loaded her into the back of an ambulance, unleashing a rambling plea for someone to find her daughter. She wasn't making a lot of sense, but the urgency of the situation quickly became apparent.

Reed was first examined at the scene, then taken to the Alamosa

County Hospital, where he was examined a second time more thoroughly. Samples of blood, sweat, and soil were taken from every part of his body for evidence. He was cleaned up, given fresh clothes, and transferred to the jailhouse at the police station where he was held for questioning.

Denton sat on a straight-back chair and talked to Reed through the bars of a holding cell.

"So you don't deny that you stabbed and killed Dr. Louis Canidey?"

"I don't deny it, but it was self-defense, Dr. Morraine can tell you that. But you should really be concentrating on finding her daughter." Reed fought the exhaustion. He hadn't really slept in almost three days, and his eyelids weighed a ton.

"Ms. Morraine doesn't have to tell me anything. And believe me, we're looking for the little girl right now, and I think you might be able to help us narrow the search . . . a lot."

"I think I have a right to have an attorney present . . ."

"You certainly do. Call whomever you wish."

"Don't you guys have to appoint one?"

"You're not under arrest . . . yet."

"Sheriff, you know I said something like this was going to happen. You know it."

"I know that's what you told me. But as I figure it . . . sounds like kind of a back-assward way of trying to get away with killing somebody . . . trying to make yourself look innocent ahead of time."

"Have you talked to Jessica? Has she told you that I had nothing to do with this Canidey guy? That I saved her life?"

"Actually, she seems to think that if you hadn't shown up around here in the first place, none of this would have happened."

"Oh, Jesus! Sheriff, I told her to leave town. I warned her but she didn't listen. I've told you the honest-to-God truth. I was trying to stop Canidey from killing again, and thank the Lord I succeeded, so far."

"Did you, really?" The sheriff dropped his notepad on the floor next to his chair and leaned forward, resting his elbows on his knees. He lowered his voice, as if exchanging confidences with an old friend. "How 'bout the little girl? Are you gonna keep your trap shut until the stink of her maggot-lined corpse tells us for you?"

Reed held his head, unable to fully process the situation. His mind was blanker than the concrete floor between his feet when it came to good ideas. "If I knew where she was I'd take you there myself."

"I can tell you one thing for sure, Doctor Reed Haler. If she does turn up dead, you're gonna be looking at three possible murder charges."

"Three?"

"Okay, I'll make like you don't already know. Gart Hanta was found dead this morning in Jessica Morraine's bathroom."

This brought Reed's head up. "Dead?"

"Poisoned. A lethal dose of cyanide."

"Cyanide?"

"You wouldn't happen to be keeping any of that particular compound around would you?"

"Have you found any?"

"Maybe."

"Was he alive yesterday?" Reed questioned.

"Last seen by Deputy Wright last night. Alive and well. He was staying over at Dr. Morraine's house. Wright found the body early this morning."

"And you think that I killed him too, even though I was in the backseat of your car all night?"

"It's known as conspiracy, Dr. Haler."

"If Canidey were my coconspirator, why in hell would I stab him to death?"

"My next question."

"I met Canidey once when I visited Jessica at the hospital."

"Yeah. So it seems."

A female deputy whom Reed didn't recognize entered the holding area carrying a sheet of paper. She walked across the tiled floor in a hurry, a gentle bounce in her short brown hair. The young deputy handed the paper to Denton, her eyes on Reed as if he were one of America's Most Wanted.

Sheriff Denton lifted himself upright, a big sigh escaping as he took the page. "Well, Dr. Haler, looks like you're entitled to that lawyer after all. Judge thinks there's probable cause to arrest you. Conspiracy to commit homicide. I'd have to agree."

Reed watched as the deputy, hair bouncing, strode back out of the room.

"You've got to be kidding," Reed muttered.

The sheriff proceeded to administer the Miranda warnings. As Reed listened, it was as if a cyclone whirled around him, spinning him in crazy circles that tore at his senses. But instead of twirling upward in a column of air, he was spiraling down into a ghoulish hole.

"Dr. Haler, I know I can't make you, but why don't you start by telling me where Lucy Morraine is hidden? Or do you want to wait for your legal counsel?"

"Sheriff," Reed said in a voice that was not his own, a voice born from experience in the vilest realms of human existence, "I lost my wife and my own unborn child to the man I killed today, and I'd kill him a million times over if I had the chance. But if I knew how to save the life of the little girl he's hidden, don't you think I'd do it for my own sake? For my daughter's sake?"

Denton looked Reed hard in the face. He saw eyes like steel rivets against a leaden pallor. He could think of nothing he felt comfortable saying in response.

"What's happened to my car?" Reed then asked.

"What?" the sheriff said, a little startled.

"My car. What's happened to it? I'd like to get my wife's journal from the glove compartment, if I might."

"Your car is in the police impound. We're going to have to hold it and everything inside it as evidence for the time being."

"And my dog?"

"She's fine."

Reed's gaze again fell upon the floor.

"You want me to call the PD's office now?" Denton asked.

Reed said without looking up, "Yeah. Why not?" As the sheriff stepped out of the holding area, Reed leaned over on the cot. Before he was even fully reclined, he was asleep.

Teams had been immediately dispatched to search for the missing girl. Upon release from the hospital, Jessica had demanded to be taken to the police station, where radio contact was established with the search parties. They had started from the point where Lucy had last been seen: her bedroom. The house, it had been quickly determined, was empty. From there the search had fanned out in all directions. By one o'clock in the afternoon, there was still no sign of her.

Sheriff Denton asked Jessica to tell him everything she knew about Canidey. Sitting in Denton's office at the station house, she dissected her mind for any detail that might offer hope, but there was nothing she could say about the doctor that seemed to narrow the search possibilities.

"I didn't know him all that well," she said, her voice timorous and laden with compounding dread. "He was a fairly competent doctor as far as I could tell. We worked together for almost five years. But we never became friends, and he never went out of his way to make my job any easier. He spent a lot of time on the road. Did a lot of fund-raising and attended conferences around the country. He was fanatically religious, but when he was here, he did the minimum and went home, basically. I really could have used somebody more dedicated in my department."

"Tell me again about last night," Denton asked.

"Gart and I were in my room. He was asleep but I was watching television. It was really late, about four. I was awake because I was still nervous, you know. I'd left all the lights in the house on. Otherwise, I acted like everything was all right, but I couldn't fall asleep. Then I heard knocking from downstairs, like someone at the door. I figured it was the deputy, checking in again or needing to tell us something. I woke Gart up and we went downstairs. We saw Dr. Canidey standing at the back door. He looked like he was in trouble, or needed some help, so I asked him through the glass what the problem was. He said there had been an emergency and that he needed to use the phone right away. Knowing him well enough, I said sure, and opened the door. He came in and sat down at the dining room table. It seemed like something was wrong with him, the way he kept looking around, and shifting. He asked if he could have a glass of water, so I got him one and asked him what had happened. But he didn't answer. He took a sip and set the glass down on the table. Then I brought the phone over to him. He was digging though his coat pocket mumbling that he didn't remember where he'd put the number. First he pulled a roll of tape from his pocket and set it on the table. Then he pulled out a small glass vial and emptied some granular powder into the water. He put the vial back in his pocket and dug around some more. I asked him what he was doing . . . what the powder was. He didn't say anything, but he pulled . . ." Jessica wrestled with the words, ". . . from the other pocket, he pulled out a knife . . . a huge knife."

"Was Gart there while this happened?" Denton asked.

"He was sitting at the opposite end of the table. Before Gart could do anything, Canidey had his arm around my head with his hand over my mouth and the blade pressed against my neck. He ordered us to keep quiet or . . . he'd . . . slice my head off. He told Gart to drink the glass of water or he'd show him the inside of my neck."

"And Gart drank the water."

"Yeah. He drank the whole glass. Less than a minute later Gart was on the floor, barely breathing."

"Then what happened?"

"Then Dr. Canidey took his hand away from my mouth and told me to wrap the tape around my head so that my mouth was covered. The whole time he kept the knife pointed at my throat. I did what he told me. Then he told me to take my robe off. I did, then he tied my arms behind my back and my ankles together with the tape. He put another piece around my head after that. I could barely breathe. He wrapped it really tightly. After that he dragged me out the back door, across the yard, and to his car that was parked in the vacant lot behind the house. He opened the trunk and forced me inside. I tried to scream but it was impossible. He closed me inside. After that I don't know what happened. It sounded like he went back into the house. He was gone for only about five minutes, maybe longer, I don't know exactly. I heard his footsteps on the gravel when he returned, and then the back door of the car opened and closed like . . . like he'd put something in the backseat." Jessica had battled fresh tears to that point. But now they were winning again. "Then I heard the front door of the car open and close and the engine started. He drove for . . . I don't know . . . it seemed like hours."

"Could you tell what kind of roads he was on?"

"All kinds of roads. Some were smooth, others really bumpy like he'd gone off the road completely at times."

"I see. What do you remember then?"

"I remember that we stopped several times. Once though, he opened the back door again. I could feel . . . that he lifted something from the backseat. Then I . . . I heard her cry, Sheriff. I heard Lucy cry. I tried to make a noise that she could hear. I don't know if she heard me or not, but I heard him . . . I heard him say: 'You did this on purpose, didn't you? You little whore!' I don't know what he meant by it. But then he walked off with her. About ten minutes later he came back. This time, though, he didn't put anything in the backseat. He'd left her somewhere. Somewhere, Sheriff, and I don't know where she is . . . she's my little girl, Sheriff . . . she's the only thing in the world I've got left." Jessica's voice had broken into a helpless sob as grief and terror swarmed all around her.

Denton let the moment settle while he brought Jessica a cup of tea. "I know it's hard, but can you tell me what happened after that?"

Somehow Jessica found a hole in the misery just large enough for her to continue. "Well, it seemed like I'd been in the trunk for hours when suddenly he started driving really fast, at least it seemed really fast. I didn't know where he was taking me, or how far we'd driven. I just knew he'd taken my daughter somewhere and left her. Then it was like he'd gone off the road again. I was getting beaten up pretty bad in there. There were a lot of bumps and I couldn't hang on to anything. I thought I could hear another car behind us, so I imagined we were being chased. I didn't hear any sirens though, so I didn't think it was the police. Finally we slowed down and stopped, like we were stuck in a ditch or a swamp or something. Then the trunk opened and he yanked me out. It took my eyes a second to adjust to the light. It was blinding at first. But I saw Reed Haler, facing us. Dr. Canidey held the knife to my stomach. Reed had a knife in his hand too, holding it by the blade, you know, like he was getting ready to throw it. And then he did throw it when I tried to pull away . . ." Jessica paused, filtering the images through her memory, ". . . and he got him. Right in the neck. I tried to stop Reed from killing him, but I couldn't talk through the tape, and I don't think anyone could have stopped him anyway. He was sort of, crazy. He kept stabbing Dr. Canidey in the chest. After he was pretty near dead, Reed cut the tape off me. I guess I was a little crazy by then too. All I knew was that my daughter was missing, and the one person who knew where she was . . . was . . . well after a few more seconds Dr. Canidey was dead."

"Do you think this Reed guy knows where she is and is just keeping quiet about it?"

"I don't know. I really don't know. But I do know that he killed Dr. Canidey . . . and now . . . no one knows anything for sure . . ."

"Is there anything else about Reed that might help us? Something he might have said to you? Anything at all about him that you can remember, even something that doesn't seem important?"

Denton could see that Jessica was searching her memory almost violently, demanding it yield the answer.

"Take your time. Think back to the first time you spoke to him. Where was that?"

"It was at the Ox Cart."

"What did he say? How did he start the conversation?"

"He was looking at Lucy. Flirting with her a little bit. But in a nice way. It was friendly . . . I mean it was fine, he wasn't . . . threatening or anything. Still, it made me uneasy at first."

"Tell me what he said."

"He . . . complimented Lucy, and then . . ." Jessica took a moment to piece together the moments of the evening, which suddenly seemed like a lifetime ago. "Then he asked me . . . if I knew anything about . . . the old train station building." Jessica bit her lip in thought, remembering how interested Reed had been in the abandoned building.

"Okay, okay. That's good, Jessica." Denton let the story rest there. He wanted to put in some search time personally.

The tall grasses bowed in submission under the wheels of Denton's police cruiser as the sheriff pulled the car to a stop in front of the destitute, flagstone building. He switched off the engine and at first just listened to the quiet wind sift through the spruce and ponderosa pine. Methodically he opened the door and stepped out, going through the mental process and checklists of criminal investigation. The building looked as he'd always remembered it. He moved slowly as he walked, taking in everything he could, remaining open to any possibility. At the central archway he peered inside the dark, cavernous hollow, cocked his head slightly, and listened to the vacant interior. He could almost hear the sound of bustling passengers, luggage-laden porters, and the chuff of a waiting steam locomotive, primed and loaded for a long, steep haul through the frosted Rockies of late summer. "BY LAW, LAND AND RAIL SHALL WE SURVIVE AND PROSPER." He remembered the words etched into the archway above his head, had first seen them at the age of eight growing up in Alamosa. He'd decided that the word "law" came first for a reason. Now he was the law. He'd fulfilled his self-appointed mission in life, and wasn't about to fail anyone, least of all a helpless child, whose life he'd sworn to protect. Calling the little girl's name into the cavity, his voice filled the stone shell, but echoed back unaccompanied. He stepped gingerly over the fallen wooden barricade and into the gutted edifice, looking for any detail which would betray a hiding place suitably sized for a seven-year-old girl. A single set of footprints trailed conspicuously into the middle of the dark hall, but looped around and returned to the archway. Denton called Lucy's name again, but was once more denied the sounds of life. His careful search soon became a hunt. Feverishly he darted his flashlight from corner to corner, shouting the girl's name in futility as he shed light on crevices, alcoves, and nooks, which hadn't felt the glow of illumination in nearly a century. The daunting vacancy seemed to be nothing more than that. Reluctant to abandon the interior, he finally turned his search to the exterior, examining every conceivable location which might secret the child. The barren walls provided few such opportunities, and the sheriff completed a full circuit of the grounds little wiser than when he'd arrived.

He stood again in front of the main archway, staring into the perpetual night inside the building. His frustration and anger were only superseded by his sense that the old station possessed greater significance than was visually apparent. But there was no sign of the girl, alive or dead, visual or otherwise.

Denton turned in the archway to survey the land around him. Down the gentle slope and across the grassy fields where Alana Kieran's body had been found, Denton observed the rust-brown strata of rails passing through the yard of the new station below. Among the stagnant train cars, sprinkles of movement caught his eye, but there was nothing out of the ordinary, no suspicious activities.

The strained caw of a magpie jarred the quietude without warning as the large bird took flight from the top of a nearby spruce. Denton could hear, almost feel, the powerful stroke of the black and white wings as the bird swept over his head, alighting high on the crest of the central gable above him. A second sharp caw from the magpie's hooked beak announced its arrival atop the castlelike structure. The bird's polished obsidian eyes regarded the horizon from its perch, an emperor evaluating the soundness of his domain. Denton felt a cool rush under his skin. The sudden flutter had startled him and he sensed now that valuable time was evaporating. He began the short walk back to the parking area and his police cruiser. The tracks only caught his attention because his own car was parked parallel to them. He immediately stopped, midstep, and kneeled on the dirt surface of the parking area. The tire impressions were distinct. It had been a large vehicle, Denton knew from his long police experience and familiarity with four-wheel drives. Then Denton noticed a second set of tracks crossing the first some feet away. This second set was laid on top of the first, though both sets appeared fresh and bore little sign of erosion. The second set, Denton could tell, were from a smaller car, probably a passenger vehicle.

Being careful not to disturb the tire markings, Denton circled around to the cruiser and opened the passenger door. Inside the glove compartment was a Polaroid instant camera, which he always kept loaded with film. He proceeded to photograph the two sets of tracks until he had spent all ten shots. From those pictures it wouldn't be too hard to tell if a tire type matched the tracks. Having established that much, molds could be made from the actual impressions, and castings created which could be used for exact comparison with an actual tire. Denton knew that a certain 4Runner and a Chevy Cavalier, already in police custody, would make two excellent starting points.

TWENTY-SEVEN

It seemed to Reed that only an instant had passed since he'd fallen asleep until he awoke to the sound of the door opening. He cleared his eyes, not sure if he was really awake or not. Someone leaned partially into the room.

"Wake up! You've got a visitor," the sheriff imparted coldly.

Reed wasn't sure at first who the visitor was, but as he sat upright and focused, he saw a swirl of red hair atop a round cheeky face.

"You can have a seat right there," the sheriff indicated, pointing to a wooden chair which faced the cage. "Don't get within five feet of the bars. There's a button on the wall right next to you if you need any assistance. We'll be right outside. You've got fifteen minutes."

Maysie Fabrioso thanked the sheriff, and waited for him to step out before she faced the prisoner.

Reed cleared his eyes in a hurry and stood up. "Ms. Fabrioso! My God! What are you doing here?"

When the door clicked shut, she sat down, pulling the chair up close to the bars and extending a hand to Reed, which he shook vigorously.

"You got my message?" Reed asked.

"I arrived home yesterday," she informed him. "I knew something had happened. Then it came like a flood." She sighed and began speaking a hundred miles an hour. "Good Lord, Dr. Haler! You certainly have gotten yourself into some serious shit. I'm actually on my way to Las Vegas. Vacation. But I had to stop here on my way through. I've got some things to tell you, Dr. Haler, some difficult things, but first I need you to tell me everything you've done since you left my house."

Reed recounted to Maysie his journey up until the moment of her sudden arrival. "Can you tell if Lucy's still alive? Can you help find her?" he finished the lengthy narrative.

Maysie didn't answer right away. Reed could tell that she was concentrating, letting her eyes drift from side to side, her head tilt ever so slightly. "Dammit!" she uttered just above a whisper. The lines in her forehead deepened, but to no apparent benefit. "No . . . I'm afraid I can't see it. I can't . . . I can't get anything," she said finally. "It's still blocked."

"How can that be? I killed the son of a bitch!" Reed protested.

"Yes, but that didn't clear the channel. In fact, that sealed it closed. I think that he actually meant for you to kill him."

Maysie's confirmation of Reed's worst fear suffocated him. "So," his voice trembled as he tried to form the words, "it was a trick? I did exactly what he wanted me to do?"

"It's possible. But I think the little girl's mother was a secondary target as well, so you didn't fail, Dr. Haler. You did save her life."

"But in killing Canidey, you're saying that I may have indirectly killed her daughter?"

"I think that's exactly what he wanted, and for you to blame yourself."

"Well, I do blame myself, and I know that everybody around here blames me too."

"The little girl was the true target. The same way your daughter was. *She* was the next of life's soldiers, not her mother."

"What?"

"I know this sounds confusing, but Lucy Morraine is going to be a doctor."

"She told me that's what she wanted to be," Reed recalled.

"She's going to carry on your work now that your daughter can't."

"Oh, God. My work?"

"Yes. That's what I discovered immediately after I heard your message on my answering machine. You see, you can't finish what you've started with the years you have left to live. You just can't do it. You'll get far, you'll lay the groundwork, but the breakthrough that you're pursuing will lead to things you never intended, and will only come in the next generation—your daughter's generation, or now Lucy's generation. That's the real reason your daughter was killed."

"Because she would have discovered a means to prolong the human lifespan indefinitely . . ."

"I believe so. Your wife too would have learned that reason eventually from her own precognitive abilities. That's why she was killed as well, so she would never be able to prevent your daughter's death. She was already beginning to send a warning, though she didn't realize it."

"The journal."

"Yes. Your daughter would have carried on your work had she lived. When that possibility was eliminated, another one came along in the form of Lucy Morraine. And that possibility, according to the nature of things, had to be eliminated as well."

"Maysie, you're telling me that I'm ultimately responsible for all this senseless killing."

"Try to understand—"

"I've only tried to save lives in my work, that's what I understand. Now you're saying for that I deserve to lose the lives that mean the most to me in the world? Well, bullshit!"

"You're not being punished. This has nothing to do with restitution. It's simply the way the universe works. It's the way life preserves itself."

"They're innocent, Goddammit!" Reed wailed at the ceiling.

"I know how ironic it sounds."

He lowered himself to the cot and held his head in his hands. He realized that Maysie wasn't speaking from mere speculation . . . she really knew what could actually happen.

"I sincerely doubt that Canidey even knew the underlying reason he chose the victims he chose," Maysie continued. "He thought that he picked people at random, or according to his own criteria of divine justice. The true forces directing him were probably beyond his own awareness."

"And how the hell do you know all this?"

"When you've seen as much of this kind of thing as I have, Dr. Haler, you start to recognize some patterns to it all. Things will always be kept in balance. Sometimes it's ugly—uglier than we can stand—but it's always in proportion. And sometimes life has to be ended in order for it to continue. We're talking about a power that's far beyond our comprehension."

"So, I've killed my family."

Maysie could see that Reed was on the verge of collapse into terminal self-loathing.

"No, you didn't, Dr. Haler. You only did what seemed right, and in spite of what I just said, I also think that you have a chance now to find this little girl. Somehow you managed to overcome Canidey's hold on you. You weren't supposed to survive, and neither was Jessica, but so far you both have. I must say, I'm truly impressed. But even though you're free of Canidey, you're still not out of danger. Still, you've altered the course of things, and I think you might be able to figure out where the little girl is."

"Me? I'm locked in a cage on murder charges, and I don't think she's under the cot!"

"But maybe you know something that I can help interpret. I'm trying to help you, Dr. Haler. Now think!"

"Of what?"

"That's up to you to figure out."

"You're the psychic, for Chrissake!"

"Just think of anything you may have seen or done since you arrived here that stands out. Anything at all."

"Alana," was out of Reed's mouth almost before Maysie had stopped speaking. This drew him back, just enough, from the brink of emotional dissolution.

Reed had filled Maysie in on the history of Alana Kieran's murder, but he had left out the part about seeing spectral visions of her.

"Alana. Yes, what about her?"

"Well," he began tenuously, "you may not believe this, but . . . I saw her, or her ghost or something."

"When and where?" Maysie came back, completely unshaken by the revelation.

Encouraged by her reaction, Reed continued, as if new purpose had been stoked within his soul. "I first saw her at the old train station, near where she was killed. She appeared there a second time, and then I saw her this morning at the Sand Dunes. Just after I killed Canidey."

"Why do you think you saw her there today?"

"Why? I thought I was hallucinating. Maybe it was because she wanted to acknowledge her murderer's death. I don't fucking know. I'm still not sure I really believe it myself."

"You must believe it, Dr. Haler. It's the truth, and there's more to her appearance today than you think. There's a connection some-where."

"The only connection is to that train station, and I'm sure the whole area has been well searched by now."

"Think, Dr. Haler. There's something more. She had to appear to you for a reason. I think that reason was to help you."

"How could it help? If I even told anyone about it they'd ship me right off to some mental hospital."

"You don't have to tell anyone but me. Open your mind and think of everything you know as a whole picture. You'll begin to see the answer as if you're standing right in front of it."

"I can't do that like you do."

"You're going to have to try. If Lucy's still alive, you're her only hope."

All the details twirled in Reed's head, a jumble of incongruous, fantastic pieces of some incomprehensible whole, which he now had to make sense of. But none of it made sense, and he was panicking.

"I can't!" he bellowed.

"Yes," Maysie said calmly, ". . . you can. I know it."

There was a knock on the door. It opened a crack, and Denton leaned in. "Time's up," he barked.

The soothing tone of Maysie's voice had been enough to calm Reed down. "I'll try," he finally resolved. "I don't have a clue how to do it, but I'll try."

"Good."

"Thanks for coming."

"I hope I've helped."

"You've really been . . . a miracle. Thank you."

"Good luck, Dr. Haler."

They both stood and shook hands between the bars again before Maysie turned and walked to the door.

"Ms. Fabrioso," Reed said. She paused and turned back. "If Lucy does somehow manage to survive this, won't she still be in danger . . . for the rest of her life?"

Maysie gave Reed an uncertain shrug. "If she decides to pursue the research, she will never be safe. But that's where you might be able to change things." One last, confident smile came over her face. Reed returned that gesture, and sat down on the cot trying to make himself comfortable, so that he could concentrate on the impossible task before him. Thoughts of the little girl, hungry, scared, and possibly in terrible pain, perhaps coming closer to death every minute that he failed, fogged his mind. That somehow his life's work had started the whole tragic mess ate away his heart. In the face of these treacheries, he forced himself to sort through all the memories that plagued him, looking for the tail of thread that would lead to the solution. It seemed completely hopeless.

T he reports coming in had all been negative since Denton had left the police station on his own search mission. Jessica had remained there, listening, waiting, and praying. A pulse of restrained hope ran through her heart when Denton had returned, a look of scant optimism on his face, and a stack of snapshots in his hand.

"Well?" Jessica said, springing to her feet, unable to endure another second without some information, good or ill.

"Please," Denton urged, "sit down. I didn't find her. Okay. I'm sorry." He eased her back into the chair. "I didn't find her."

The pulse Jessica had felt a moment before turned to a hard frost. It wasn't the miracle. "Then what's . . . ?" she asked, frantically pointing at the pictures.

"Hey, Rick," Denton summoned one of the deputies, "come over here and take a look at these." Denton laid the Polaroids out on his desk.

A young, clean-shaven man with a light sparkle in his eyes stepped eagerly over to Denton's desk.

"I found something," Denton continued, both to the deputy and to Jessica, "that might place Reed's car at the old train station. It could implicate him further. Maybe provoke him to talk. I don't know. We'll have to check to see if these tire tracks are even from his car. Then we'll check this second set." Denton pointed out the two patterns he'd found in the fine soil. "See whose car they belong to. Rick, take these pictures with you to the lot and do a visual analysis of the tires on the Cavalier and the 4Runner."

Jessica stared at the sheriff, incredulous. "My daughter is out there somewhere, possibly dying, and all you do is take pictures of some tire tracks!"

In her mind Jessica knew that the sheriff was doing all he could, but that didn't quell her inflamed emotion, her stinging temper. "Why aren't you out there looking for her? You go find her, all of you!" she shouted. "Find my baby!"

"Jessica, listen to me," Denton said, offering her the encouragement of his open hand. "I'm going to talk to Reed again. With this in his face, he might just crack."

Jessica took Denton's hand and held on. Then she raised her head and addressed him firmly, with new strength. "Sheriff," she said, her voice now steady and confident. "Before you do that, if it's all right with you, I'd like to talk to Reed myself."

Denton's eyebrows lifted. "Really?"

Jessica nodded. "I need to ask him why . . . to his face."

The clock above the door told Reed that darkness was only minutes away. There had been no word concerning the search for Lucy. If anything had been discovered, Denton was in no hurry to report it to him. The deputy on duty guarding Reed stood up when the door to the holding area opened. Reed's hopes for good news were instantly erased when he saw Jessica's face.

Denton led Jessica into the room. She asked if she could talk to Reed alone. Reluctantly the sheriff agreed and instructed the guard to step out.

"Don't go closer than five feet from the bars. We'll be right outside the door if you need anything," Denton assured.

She nodded and sat down.

Reed wiped the yellow gunk from his eyes, and stared at her through the bars. Tears landing at her feet, she didn't look at him as she spoke.

"Why did you come here?" she began. "To this town? I just want to know why."

Reed waited until she lifted her head before he said anything. "I've told you why."

"Do you really think anyone believes you had some psychic vision that sent you here to protect me and my daughter from a mad killer?"

Reed had no adequate response. "No. I suppose not," he confessed.

"Then why did you come here? And tell me the truth, or so help me I'll kill you myself."

"I've told you the truth, Jessica. The sheriff can verify my wife's murder if you want. What else can I offer you?"

"Just give me my little girl back. That's all I want."

Reed pressed the heels of his hands against his head. He sifted through the entries of the journal over and over in his mind, searching for some missed clue, some hidden meaning he'd overlooked. He had been certain that all nine entries had been realized. The final one: *Forbidden, forever hidden inside the trunk,* Reed had interpreted as indicating Jessica's being trapped in Canidey's car trunk. He thought its meaning was clear; he'd been through it a hundred times. The journal was mute beyond that. But Jessica hadn't been in the trunk forever. She had escaped that fate. But had that just been because of his own intervention? It didn't seem to fit.

He'd made mistakes before, he recalled. He had to be making one now. He played back the day's events in his mind countless times, analyzing, searching. His brain was stuck in a useless circle. How could he know where Lucy was? How could he know? With each hour that passed, the sickness in his heart grew. He seethed at the idea that somehow this man had actually implicated him in the possible death of another innocent victim. His head ached; his stomach roiled; his whole spirit had nearly collapsed. As if by sheer instinct to survive, he tried to stay focused on those thoughts which brought some degree of peace: Hoover, who had kept him on track more than once; Devrie, whose love had been his ultimate source of strength; and Alana, the daughter that he should have had. He relished the idea that she would have undertaken the continuation of his work. He tried to draw the elements together. Then: "I saw Alana Kieran today," he said, unable to think of anything else to talk about. "That was going to be my own daughter's name . . . Alana."

Jessica looked at him, mystified, hurt, as if he were making a sadistic mockery of the situation at the time of her greatest suffering.

"I'm very serious," he went on. "At the Dunes. She was there, or some vestige of her was there. It's not the first time I saw her either."

"You're out of your fucking mind." Jessica started to get up.

"Wait," Reed almost shouted. Now he was on his feet too. "Wait a second," he repeated several times. "And at the old train station. Maybe . . . hidden in the trunk. Maybe . . ."

Jessica was heading for the door as Reed seemed to slip into a delirium she didn't want to witness.

"Tell them to look at the old train station, and to take Hoover with them. Take my dog to the old station building." Reed did shout this time.

The door to the holding area flew open. The sheriff caught Jessica who was nearly running toward him.

"Please, Sheriff!" Reed yelled, "I think I know where Lucy is! Take my dog to the old train station as fast as you can!"

Denton led the procession of cars up the hill to the parking area in front of the dilapidated station. He did his best to avoid destroying the delicate tire impressions, but time was of far greater importance. Jessica rode with Denton, wanting to be as close as she could to the leading edge of the search. Hoover was in the back, her head between the two front seats, excitedly watching through the windshield. As other cars came to a stop, the sheriff instructed teams of two to gradually work their way to the rear of the building. All were to look for a large, burned out cottonwood tree at the edge of the forest.

"You'll know it by a 'D' carved in its side," Denton specified.

There were easily fifty people there and more arriving by the minute. Some were official search party members, and others just concerned citizens, or those beset with morbid curiosity. The darting beams of multiple flashlights preceded the clusters of men and women through the tall grass. The sky still had a cool glow in the west, but on the ground, the woods were as dark as a mine shaft.

Hoover leapt from Denton's cruiser, barking loudly as she cut a path to the station. She waited for the sheriff and Jessica to catch up before she bolted again, around the side of the building and to the rear. The tree wasn't immediately apparent in the frothy blackness behind the station. As the teams all directed their flashlights into the forest, however, it became plain which one Hoover was interested in. Jessica ran, stumbling on rocks, through the grass, down into the rail bed and up the other side to the tree. Denton stayed right behind, directing the beam from his flashlight on the ground in front of her. Hoover barked and scratched at the black cylindrical tower. Jessica's hands found the "D" on the trunk almost, it seemed, before her eyes did.

As Denton circled the tree, a tiny noise came from inside it, nothing more than a squeak.

"She's in there!" Jessica shouted. "Hurry, she's in there!"

Instantly a group of about ten surrounded Denton and hoisted him up. He pointed the flashlight down into the narrow opening at the top. About five feet below he saw a head of light auburn curls. The faint squeal came again, which told him she was alive. It appeared that she was wedged in so tightly that she couldn't even raise her head to look up at him. She simply made the only noise she could. Denton holstered the big flashlight, unclipped his utility belt and dove blindly into the hollow trunk. The top of her head was just beyond his reach. "Hold my legs, I need another fifteen inches," he yelled up to those who had him at the knees. Still more people joined the effort, forming a type of human pyramid, which came to a point at Denton's inverted feet. Bright lights suddenly illuminated the scene from a news crew that had just arrived. The pyramid slowly lowered Denton deeper into the tree until his hands found Lucy's shoulders, pressed in snugly. He tried to work his fingers between the sides of the hollow trunk and her arms and back, but there was simply no room, nothing for him to hold on to but her head and the collar of her pajama top. "Lucy," he said, as calmly as he could. "Can you feel anything under your feet to push against?"

She squealed and shook her head.

"Okay. That's okay. We're going to get you out of here. I promise you. I'll be back." Denton gave the order to be lifted back out of the tree. When he emerged empty-handed, there was an audible mumble of dismay. "We're going to have to cut a hole below her feet," Denton shouted above the drone of activity. He directed his orders to the several paramedics in the group. "We need a chain saw and an ax and anything else that will help us make a hole below this line." He used a key to mark the trunk, indicating his best estimate of where her feet ended. "Somebody go get them. NOW!"

Instructions shot back and forth among the emergency medical technicians and two of them sprinted off in the direction of a fire truck that was parked in the lot of the station.

"Lucy, it's Mommy," Jessica shouted into the side of the tree, pressing against it as closely as she could. "Hang on, baby. We're going to get you out right now! I love you, sweetie. Don't give up."

Denton had to pull Jessica away when the wood cutting tools arrived. One of the men yanked the starter cord on the chain saw and revved the motor.

"Start at the bottom," Denton advised. The man worked the loud, buzzing tool through the thick tree wall until he'd made a deep slice to the trunk's hollow core. Denton was again hoisted up to the tree's open top. "How you doing in there, kid? Nod if you're okay." He could see her head moving the right way. "Okay. Good. Everything's going to be all right." He lifted his head out of the trunk and was lowered back to the ground. "Let's keep going."

Little by little, checking their progress frequently with flashlights and by Denton getting nods from Lucy, the EMT's carved an opening in the base of the tree until they could see the bottoms of the child's feet. When the hole was large enough, one of the men slid his head and arms inside. He placed one hand under each of her soles, wrapping his fingers tightly, and told her that he was going to push her up. Denton, again at the top, and held at the knees, reached down. "Okay, Lucy, are you ready?" With his hands he felt her head nodding. "All right. Here we go. Ready? Push," he called down to the paramedic below. Lucy let out a muffled scream as the man beneath her applied upward force. Denton could feel her rise slightly, but her shriek halted progress instantly. She had moved enough, however, to enable Denton to work his fingers ever so slightly down the sides of her shoulders. "We're going to try again, Lucy. Okay? Can you hang in there for me?" He felt the reassuring nod. "Great. Here we go. Push!"

She cried out again, but this time Denton managed to get his fingers down to her underarms. "Keep pushing!" he ordered. Her body shuddered in his hands, and he knew she was in great pain, but now he had a good grip under her shoulders. "Pull me up," he called out to those who had him by the legs. Together, Denton and Lucy rose from the vertical tunnel into the fresh air.

This time when the sheriff emerged, he was carrying a very dirty, very scared, and very tired little girl. He gently passed Lucy to the paramedics, who waited with a stretcher. Jessica stayed at her daughter's side as the emergency medical personnel clipped the tape from her head and body. They performed first aid and a rapid field examination before they proclaimed her safe to be moved. Hoover sat by at the edge of the crowd, simply watching the rescue unfold.

Jessica gave her daughter a big smile and a teary kiss on the cheek. Lucy wrapped her arms weakly around Jessica's neck and remained that way until mother and daughter were both inside the ambulance.

Apart from some severe bruises, skin abrasions, and lost circulation, the doctors agreed that Lucy was going to be fine. Sheriff Denton stayed at the hospital until he was satisfied that Lucy and her mother were going to be all right. The little girl, they said, would probably need to stay for a couple of days until she was completely stable.

Walking out of the ER to his squad car, Denton wondered what he was going to do about Reed. He would have to take the dog back to the pound, but it wouldn't be without a mountain of regret. In spite of everything, the dog had just helped him save Lucy Morraine's life. That somehow softened his thoughts about Hoover's owner. Now the sheriff truly didn't know what to think.

R eed had been sitting on the edge of his cot in the holding cell for what felt like an infinity of minutes when the door again opened. The deputy with the dark bouncy hair leaned into the room, not exactly smiling, but at least not with the look that made Reed feel as if he belonged on a Wanted poster.

"They found her. And she's okay," was all the deputy said, and then she was gone.

Reed realized that he was on his feet, and that his hands were on the bars of the cell door. The ache suddenly lifted, as if by some magical cure. He didn't care at that moment if they locked him up for the rest of his life. No matter what happened to him now, he thought, in his heart he found all the freedom he needed.

R eed remained in custody for another day, until he was brought before a judge and formally charged with manslaughter and conspiracy to commit kidnapping and murder. He pleaded "not guilty" to all the charges and was taken back to jail. He didn't want to call anybody he knew, didn't want any of his friends or family to know what was happening. His court-appointed attorney was a warm, friendly-faced man of Native American descent by the name of George Campache, who looked from his demeanor and dress as if he'd be more at home on the range than in the courtroom. Campache wanted to get as many of Reed's associates and friends as he could, for character witness testimony, but to the attorney's complete dismay, Reed refused to provide information about anyone.

"They're going to kill us without somebody to back you up, Dr. Haler," Campache had said. "It's as simple as that. You knew where the kid was, you knew something like this was going to happen, and you killed Canidey. Dr. Morraine is ready to testify against you, the police are ready to testify against you, the hospital staff is ready to testify against you. This whole town is ready to testify against you, and you don't want one witness in your defense?"

Reed regarded the lawyer with a look of confidence. "Let them testify," he said. "I have nothing to hide. I've told the entire truth and that's what I'll tell in court."

"Your case . . . your trial," Campache conceded as he stood up to leave. Before the attorney opened the door, he said, "Your life."

Jessica entered her daughter's bedroom with a warm cup of tea and a big smile. Lucy had been home since that morning, but had slept most of the day. Now she was awake in her bed, coloring in her drawing pad. Jessica had replaced the daffodil bed sheets with ones bearing Sesame Street characters.

"You look like you're feeling a lot better," she encouraged, stroking a light finger across Lucy's forehead.

"Yeah," the seven year old responded, a heaviness in her voice.

"What's wrong?" Jessica asked, knowing that keeping their mutual trauma an okay subject for discussion was essential to healing.

Lucy looked up from her drawing. "What's going to happen to Reed?"

Jessica wasn't quite prepared for that question. "Well, sweetheart, he's going to stay in jail, for a long, long time."

"Why?" Lucy asked, almost crying. The news seemed to greatly upset and puzzle the girl.

"Because he tried to hurt us."

"He didn't hurt us, Mommy. Dr. Canidey did."

"Lucy. I know it's hard to understand. But Reed helped Dr. Canidey do the things that he did. So, that's just as bad as if Reed had done them himself. Do you see what I mean?"

"But he didn't, Mommy. I know he didn't. Reed tried to help us."

"Shh!" Jessica leaned over and gave Lucy a long kiss on the head. "I know none of this makes sense right now. All you have to do is remember that everything is going to be all right, that we're all safe now."

"Don't let them keep Reed in jail, Mommy."

Jessica frowned, not sure what to say. She decided to change the subject. "Why don't you have some tea and let me see what you've been drawing?"

Lucy turned her coloring book around for her mother, and then picked up the cup of tea from her nightstand.

On the page was the picture of the rising sun Lucy had copied from the cover of Gart's paperback. Lucy didn't know why her mother suddenly looked strange and wasn't saying anything.

Jessica only stared at the drawing, childlike in every way, except that it was exactly correct in impossible detail. The yellow mountains, the colors of the cars, the open trunk, the sunrise, the clothes the people were wearing . . . the knives they held . . . even the tan dog in the bigger car. The scene was precise and unmistakable.

"Uh . . ." Jessica tried to say. "Luce. What is this a picture of?" She couldn't disguise the tremors in her voice. She'd told Lucy nothing of the details of what had happened or where, and she'd been with her daughter every minute since Lucy had been rescued.

"That's you and Reed and Dr. Canidey. And that's Hoover."

Jessica looked at her daughter, then back to the drawing, her mouth stuck in the middle of her next word, but the word wouldn't come. Then Jessica noticed something else in the drawing. In the background, behind the other people and off to the side, was the faint rendering of a woman's head and shoulders, as if she were standing just beyond the ridge of a gentle hill. She had dark hair, pulled back, and a green top.

"Who is this?" Jessica asked, pointing at the figure, afraid to hear the answer. When it came, Jessica's mouth went completely dry.

Very calmly, between sips of tea, Lucy said, "That's Dr. Kieran."

"Oh my God!" Jessica mumbled, her hand covering her mouth.

Lucy didn't understand why the drawing was making her mother cry.

TWENTY-EIGHT

He's telling the truth," Jessica said to Sheriff Denton after showing him Lucy's drawing, and explaining what her daughter knew of the incident.

Denton couldn't remove his eyes from the drawing, comparing what he saw on the page with his own memory. His lower jaw hung down. "Uh huh. And she hasn't been out of your sight since the rescue? There's no possibility she might have heard something mentioned, seen a news story?"

Jessica shook her head. "No chance. I've been making a point of keeping the details from her until the initial shock has a chance to settle."

Denton kept studying the drawing, as if something in it would explain its existence. His frustration only grew, the harder he looked. "Why did you draw this picture?" he finally asked Lucy, who sat by her mother in front of his desk.

"Because that's what I saw," the little girl said, her bruises still a terrible reminder of recent events. Denton was amazed at how she seemed to be handling the aftermath with such courage and maturity.

"Where did you see it?"

"It was like TV. Except in here," she answered plainly, pointing to her head.

"Like TV. In your head?"

Lucy nodded.

"Uh huh. When did you see this picture . . . in there?" Denton asked, pointing at the same spot above her ear.

This made Lucy crunch her nose up in thought. "Um, it was when my mom and Gart went on a date."

Jessica thought back. "The last date we went on was the Saturday before last."

"Oh. Okay," Denton said, then stopped in thought. "That would be . . . five days . . . before it happened," he said softly, as if the information might be too shocking to anyone within earshot.

This came as news to Jessica as well. She looked at her daughter again, the scared amazement renewed in her eyes.

"Yeah." Jessica finally confirmed. "Five days before it happened . . ."

"So," Denton directed to Lucy, working hard to keep his composure. "Do you think Dr. Haler is telling us the truth?"

"I know he is," she said, with the same matter-of-factness that informed all of her speech.

"Well, okay. I guess . . ." The sheriff wasn't sure what Lucy's answer meant in terms of Reed's case, but he knew for sure that he had to schedule a meeting as soon as possible with the county prosecutor, and an expert in child psychology. As perplexed and confused as Denton was, he was also suddenly a lot more inclined to think that the little girl in front of him might be right about Reed Haler after all.

The nights had been gloriously restful, even though Reed was living in the county lockup. The horrid dream had stayed away, and his fears of its return were diminishing. He'd caught up on a lot of sleep, even if it was on a two-by-five-foot cot with his liberty still very much in doubt.

The splinter of sunshine sneaking through the small window in the door was his only indicator that another beautiful day had blossomed outside. The guard on duty, who Reed had learned was named Sandra Caliz, was a petite and startlingly attractive young woman with short black hair and skin as smooth as coffee ice cream. Sandra seemed a most unlikely candidate for a prison guard, but she was the one who brought Reed his breakfast every morning.

On the fourth morning of his incarceration, Sandra brought a surprise along with Reed's breakfast. As she slipped the tray of rolls, coffee, and orange juice through the meal slot, she mentioned that he was to go to a special hearing at eleven o'clock.

Reed sat up on the edge of the cot. "What do you mean by special?"

"I don't know. That's the message from Mr. Campache's office. They called just a few minutes ago. So, you're supposed to be ready to go by ten thirty." She smiled at him as though she were his camp counselor preparing him for the day's hiking trip.

"Ten-thirty," Reed confirmed, returning the pleasant expression. Reed almost perceived a blush in her warm complexion as she walked away. For an instant he let himself feel the desire to walk again a free man. The mood, the fleeting sensation of joy, of hope in a salvageable future, instantly melted away when thoughts of his perdition, his incomprehensible loss, stormed his mind with fresh vigor. That he'd let his heart feel anything but pain, even for a moment, gave him a rush of guilt. He wasn't ready for life yet. He couldn't imagine its continuation with anything resembling pleasure, wouldn't allow it. But maybe someday . . . maybe.

Reed sat at the back of the prison transport van, shackled and flanked by two armed guards as he rode to the courthouse. He was led to a secure waiting room just off the courtroom. George Campache was there waiting inside, wearing his usual kindly smile.

"What's this all about?" Reed asked, as he sat down next to his attorney. "They going to try to pin a few more unsolved crimes on me?"

Campache checked his watch and stood up. "See you out there," he said, giving Reed a pat on the shoulder. Then he stepped through the door to the courtroom.

Fifteen minutes later, at precisely eleven o'clock, Reed was led to the defense table. He saw Jessica and Lucy seated next to Sheriff Denton in the front row of the spectators' gallery.

"All rise," the bailiff ordered.

The room moved to its feet.

Judge Peter Riglio twirled a pen in his fingers as he spoke. Thick black hair ringed his otherwise bald head, giving him the appearance of a skinny Friar Tuck. "Will the defendant please state his name." The judge's voice was soft and unthreatening.

"Reed Terrence Haler."

"Dr. Haler. This hearing has been convened this morning because of new developments in your case. I've listened to accounts from law enforcement and the county prosecutor. I've examined a report from a state-appointed child psychologist. And I've heard witness testimony. As to the death of Dr. Louis Canidey, the government is satisfied that you acted in self-defense and the defense of Dr. Jessica Morraine. As for the death of Gart Hanta, the government is satisfied that Dr. Canidey acted alone. As for your own knowledge of Lucy Morraine's whereabouts as of August sixth of this year, well . . . we're all very grateful, if more than a little mystified.

Anyway—to make a long story short—based on new information provided by the above-mentioned, a decision to drop criminal charges against you was reached. This hearing is to inform you of that decision. The people of the State of Colorado apologize for any inconvenience. You're free to go, Dr. Haler." Judge Riglio concluded with a quick nod.

He couldn't help it. This time Reed let the rush of euphoria have its way. As the court officer removed the shackles, and Campache shook his hand, Reed could almost feel the gleeful look coming from Lucy's eyes. Instantly he realized that he owed his freedom to the little seven-year-old with the rusty curls. Jessica, holding her daughter's hand, offered Reed a tenuous and uncertain smile, still not fully able to grasp the complex of impossible circumstances which had led to that moment. He knew that would take some time.

A pocketful of loose change, his hunting knife, and Devrie's journal had been returned to Reed in due course, along with a change of clothes. After signing for the items, he made his way out to the impound lot where the 4Runner had been parked for nearly a week.

"I won't be needing this anymore," Reed said, holding out the knife to the lot officer, who was little more than a kid. "You can keep it if you want."

The young recruit said a polite "thank you," as he handed Reed his car keys. Hesitantly the officer accepted the weapon as though it might jump out of his hand by itself.

"I wouldn't blame you if you got rid of it as soon as I drove out of here," Reed said with an understanding smile.

That seemed to ease the officer's mind a little about holding the object, which had recently been central to so much infamy.

"Thank you," Reed acknowledged, before walking through the garage to his car. As he opened the door and pulled himself up behind the wheel, he held the journal tightly in his hands, not opening it, just holding on to it like a life ring tossed to him from a sinking ship. Eventually he tucked the journal into the glove box and started the engine.

He collected Hoover at the city pound and wheeled the Toyota away, his companion once again in her rightful place next to him.

All that was left was to retrieve the rest of his belongings and check out of the motel. While he was in his room he placed a phone call to Wally Bohrs; he got Wally's voice mail. "Hey Wal, it's Reed. Hope things are still together, there. I'll see you tomorrow. We've got some . . . some important things to talk about." He hung up and dialed again.

"Reed, is that you?" Bettyanne said when the line picked up.

Reed cleared his throat. "Hi, yeah it's me."

"I knew it. I just knew it. Dale," Reed heard her call into the background, "I told you he'd call today. Reed, we've been so worried. What's going on? Are you coming back soon? Tell me what's been going on."

"I'm coming back. I'll be there tomorrow. Everything's fine. We'll talk when I see you."

"But you're okay?"

"Yeah, I'm just fine."

"Oh, thank God! You see," Bettyanne said, talking to Dale again, "I told you he was all right."

"Listen, I've gotta go. I'll call when I get in."

"Okay, Reed. Be safe and get home as soon as you can. We love you."

"I love you too."

"Oh, Reed, one other thing."

"Yeah?"

"Your father and mother have both called us, wondering where you've been."

"Oh yeah?"

"Yeah. Your father said he was planning on coming out again to see you, but hasn't been able to reach you on the phone. Your mom is terribly worried. Please call them back as soon as you can."

"Yeah. I will. Thanks. Thanks a lot, Betty."

"Sure. And drive safe."

"I will."

" 'Bye."

Lastly Reed placed two more calls to his parents just to let them know that he was all right. It was too soon to tell them of the extraordinary things that had happened. For that he decided to wait until he was home. Everything still seemed a little too unreal. He wanted to make sure that he was still really alive himself before recounting his experience, before making any plans. But, he resolved, when he did get home, he was going to make a lot more time for all of his family.

He turned off the light next to the bed, and walked out of the room. After throwing his bag into the backseat, he dropped the key off at the front desk. A gaggle of reporters from the local press was waiting in the lobby wanting an interview. Reed only said that he was glad to be going home.

The Ox Cart was crowded and lively. Reed sat in a booth with Jessica and Lucy eating strawberry ice cream.

"I know this doesn't really make up for much," Jessica said, her battle scars still glowing, but showing signs of repair. Lucy too seemed almost back to normal.

"There's nothing to be made up for," Reed answered. "I don't blame you for a second, for anything."

"Then why do I feel guilty as hell?"

"None of this stuff is easy to believe. I'm not sure I believe it even now. How could I expect you to have believed it on my word alone?"

"Hmm." Jessica smiled to herself, contemplating the unbelievable. "What is it, Reed? What is it for?"

"Your daughter's gift?"

"Yeah."

"Haven't got a clue. But I know it's a good thing."

"Yeah. I guess. Well, I think Lucy has something for you."

"Oh, really?"

"Yeah," Lucy said, reaching under the table. She pulled up a thin, flat package the size of a record jacket, and handed the present, wrapped in gold foil paper, across the table to Reed. He took the gift carefully, pretending to listen to the contents as he lightly shook it.

"What could this be?" he asked.

"Open it," she instructed.

"Okay." Reed peeled back the foil to reveal a crayon drawing. At the top were the words: "FOR REED. I'LL NEVER FORGET YOU. LOVE, LUCY." The picture was of a tall brick building with lots of windows. Over the front door was a sign that said: "ALAMOSA CHILDREN'S HOSPITAL." The sun was a big, yellow ball in a clear, blue sky. All around were mountains and trees. On the roof of the building there were four figures, two of them taller than the others, all of them holding hands except the one that was clearly a tan-colored dog.

"And who are these people?" Reed asked, even though it was obvious.

"That's me and Mommy and you, and Hoover."

"Oh. I see. Well, this is the prettiest picture I've ever seen. Thank you. I'll keep this with me forever." He leaned over the table and gave Lucy a kiss on the cheek. Her face suddenly lost its smile, its joy.

"Well, what's the matter?" Reed asked with exaggerated compassion.

Lucy looked down at her ice cream without responding.

"She doesn't want you to leave," Jessica filled in.

"Well," Reed said to Lucy. "I have a feeling that I might be back."

Lucy ventured a glance up, not smiling, but not on the verge of tears anymore either. "Really?"

Reed looked at Jessica. There was what Reed hoped was approval in her beautiful eyes. "Really," he said.

"Good, 'cause Mommy needs help with the hospital."

"Is that right?"

Jessica sighed in agreement. "Well, a group of bible-thumping businessmen from Texas just came through with an offer of a pretty sizable donation."

"That's great news. Congratulations."

"Thanks. It's a start. Truth is, I sure could use some support from a place like San Francisco University or someone like . . . yourself."

Reed could tell that Jessica had debated momentarily before adding her last comment.

"Uh, well." He found it hard to resist looking at Jessica's soft face, the sensuous fall of her coppery hair, the way she brushed the ends back off her neck with the flick of her finger. "Yeah. There may be something I could do. If I still have a job, that is."

"Well, if you don't, I hear there's an opening at Alamosa County. Pediatrics ever interest you?"

"I'll keep it in mind," he answered, taking the suggestion seriously, and intentionally allowing his true feelings to color his words, aware that the gesture was not lost on either of the two women. "Oh, I almost forgot," he then said, bringing the moment back from a potentially dangerous edge. This time it was Reed who reached under the table. "I've got something for you too, Miss Lucy." He handed her a package, smaller but not as thin as the one she'd given him. It was wrapped in paper printed with a bright pattern of violet morning glories.

"Wow," she said. "Thanks." She shook the package as Reed had done, and listened to it. "What is it?"

"Open it."

She peeled back the paper and held in her hands a soft, cloth-bound book full of blank pages.

Jessica threw him a concerned look, but Lucy nearly crawled over the table to give him a kiss. "Thank you," she said, not in the high squeal of a euphoric child, but with a calm seriousness, which told Reed that she knew exactly what the blank book was meant for. Inside the front cover was written: FOR THE NEXT OF LIFE'S SOLDIERS. LOVE, REED.

"Always keep it near," he said, returning the kiss.

"I will . . . forever," she promised.

Reed checked his watch. He wanted to get on the road while there was still some light left.

Hoover was waiting patiently in the car when Reed, Jessica, and Lucy walked out to the parking lot. The evening sun was warm and a light breeze brought the scent of the hills across the valley.

Reed picked up Lucy, giving her a long hug and a final kiss. "Have a great year in school, and give your mom all the help she needs."

"I will."

Reed set the girl down, and found himself staring into Jessica's eyes. He didn't know what to do next. There were so many things to express, so many feelings for which words were useless. When he sensed her leaning closer, but after some hesitation, he encircled her in his arms. "I'm so sorry," he whispered softly. "I didn't mean for any of this to happen."

"I know that now. I'm sorry I doubted you."

"You have nothing to apologize for. You did everything right. I just wish to God I could undo it all."

"Everything's going to be okay . . . someday," she said, letting a little sarcasm ring through.

They let the embrace linger just a little longer than either had initially intended.

"Thank you," Reed said into her ear, a flood of emotion threatening to crumble the brave facade he'd so diligently maintained all afternoon.

"We owe you our lives," Jessica uttered, as if the fact seemed to defy reality.

"I'd say it's mutual."

Finally they released their hold on each other, and let the inches between them turn into feet. Reed opened the door and climbed into the Toyota. He saw that his weren't the only moist eyes.

"I'll call you when I get home," he promised.

"You'd better," Jessica said.

"Yeah, you'd better," Lucy reinforced.

"I will."

Reed started the engine and backed the 4Runner out of the parking lot. He pointed the nose of the Toyota west, and with a final wave, eased the car into motion.

Working his way through town for the final time, he drove no faster than ten miles an hour. He felt as though he'd been there for years, it all looked so familiar. Yet the whole world looked to him like a place into which he'd just been born. Nothing meant what it had. Somehow what was good was bad, what was bad was good: nothing was truly as it appeared, and nothing would ever seem the same again. Reed had once and forever accepted that.

As he accelerated onto Route 17, heading toward the interstate, he felt nothing but the awe of nature as he passed by the dry waves of the Great Dunes lying ten miles to the east in the Blood of Christ. What had happened there seemed like something he'd only read about in the paper, as if someone else had entered his body and lived the terrible journey for him. Perhaps, he thought, it was better that way. It somehow made it easier to get on with the future, whatever that future held.

Nothing could ever replace Devrie and the daughter he should have had. Those scars would never heal completely. But with the setting sun leading him home, he opened his mind and his heart, and he began to see a picture as though he were standing right in front of it. There was still work to be done, lives to be saved, and enemies to be confronted on this strange little planet. Deep down he knew that he had to put an end to his current research . . . if he still could. But even more importantly, it was now his moral duty to divert Lucy's attention from it. That fact was enough to ensure that their paths would cross again. As difficult as it was to believe, Reed realized that Maysie was right. He wondered what would have happened if Tim Hon's line of research had been approved five years ago instead of his own. He elected not to speculate.

He glanced over at Hoover, who was busy watching the world go by. Then Reed again looked down at Lucy's drawing, where he'd propped it between the seats. He smiled at the picture; they looked for all the world like a happy family. Maybe, he thought, the years ahead full of uncertainty . . . just maybe.